EDITH WHARTON

(1862–1937) was born in New York, the daughter of Lucretia Rhinelander and George Frederic Jones. In 1885 she married a Boston socialite, Edward Robbins Wharton and lived with him in Newport, Rhode Island, frequently travelling to Europe where she became friendly with Henry James. But her marriage was an unhappy one and Edith turned to writing. Her first novel, *The Valley of Decision*, appeared in 1902. She went on to publish an average of more than a book a year for the rest of her life. Her first critical and popular success came with *The House of Mirth* (1905). Then followed her richest period of literary activity which included *The Fruit of the Tree* (1907), *Madame de Treymes* (1907) and *The Reef* (1912). Her husband's mental health steadily declined and in 1910, when they had moved permanently to France, the marriage finally broke up, ending in divorce in 1913.

Edith Wharton's writing was largely abandoned during the First World War. She threw herself into war work for which she was awarded the Cross of the Légion d'Honneur and the Order of Leopold. After the war she moved to an eighteenth-century villa north of Paris, and spent her winters in a converted monastery on the Riviera. *The Age of Innocence* was published in 1920, winning the Pulitzer Prize. She was the first woman to receive a Doctorate of Letters from Yale University and in 1930 she became a member of the American Academy of Arts and Letters. One of America's greatest novelists, Edith Wharton died in France at the age of seventy-five. Virago publishes *The Reef, Roman Fever* (1964), *The Fruit of the Tree, Madame de Treymes, Old New York* (1924), *The Children* (1928), *The Mother's Recompense* (1925), *Hudson River Bracketed* (1929) and *The Gods Arrive* (1932).

D1581623

VIRAGO
MODERN
CLASSIC

NUMBER
253

EDITH WHARTON

THE
GODS ARRIVE

With a New Afterword by
MARILYN FRENCH

*The gods approve
The depth and not the tumult of the soul.*

Virago

Published by VIRAGO PRESS Limited 1987
41 William IV Street, London WC2N 4DB

First published in New York by D. Appleton & Co. 1932
Copyright 1932 by D. Appleton & Co.
Renewal Copyright © 1960 William R. Tyler

Afterword Copyright © Belles-Lettres Inc. 1987

British Library Cataloguing in Publication Data

Wharton, Edith
    The Gods arrive.—(Virago modern classics)
    I. Title
    813'.4   [F]   PS3545.H16
    ISBN 0-86068-622-1

Printed in Finland by
Werner Söderström, a member of Finnprint

For

W. V. R. B.

Sunt aliquid manes.

Propertius

BOOK I

ONE OF the stewards of the big Atlantic liner pushed his way among the passengers to a young lady who was leaning alone against the taffrail. "Mrs. Vance Weston?"

The lady had been lost in the effort to absorb, with drawn-up unseeing eyes, a final pyramidal vision of the New York she was leaving—a place already so unreal to her that her short-sighted gaze was unable to register even vaguely its towering signals of farewell. She turned back.

"Mrs. Vance Weston?"

"No—" she began; then, correcting herself with a half-embarrassed smile: "Yes."

Stupid—incredibly! But it was the first time the name had been given to her. And it was not true; she was not yet Mrs. Vance Weston, but Halo Tarrant, the still undivorced wife of Lewis Tarrant. She did not know when she would be free, and some absurd old leaven of Lorburn Puritanism (on her mother's side she was a Lorburn of Paul's Landing) made her dislike to masquerade under a name to which she had no right. Yet before her own conscience and her lover's she was already irrevocably what she called herself: his wife; supposing one could apply the term irrevocable to any tie in modern life without provoking Olympian laughter. She herself would once have been the first to share in that laughter; but she had to think of her own situation as binding her irrevocably, or else to assume that life, in its deepest essence, was as brittle as the glass globe which the monkeys shatter in the bitter scene of

Faust's visit to the witch. If she were not Vance Weston's for always the future was already a handful of splinters.

The steward, handing her a telegram, and a letter inscribed "urgent," had hurried away on his distribution of correspondence. On the envelope of the letter she read the name of her lawyer; and as he was not given to superfluous writing, and as telegrams were too frequent to be of consequence, she opened the letter first. "Dear Mrs. Tarrant," she read, "I am sending this by hand to the steamer in the hope of reaching you in time to persuade you not to sail. I have just heard, from a safe source, that your husband knows of your plans, and is not disposed to consent to your divorcing him if you persist in leaving the country in the circumstances of which you have advised me." (She smiled at this draping of the facts.) "Indeed, I suspect he may refuse to take divorce proceedings himself, simply in order to prevent your re-marrying. I should have tried to see you at once if I were not leaving for Albany on professional business; but I earnestly beg you, if my messenger reaches you before you are actually off . . ."

Halo Tarrant lifted her eyes from the letter. No; she was not actually off. The decks were still in the final confusion of goodbyes; friends and relatives were lingering among the passengers till the landing gong should hurry them ashore. There was time to dash down to her cabin, collect her possessions, and descend the gangplank with the other visitors, leaving a note of explanation for the companion she was abandoning. For his sake as well as her own, ought she not to do it? What she knew of her husband made her ready enough to believe that a headlong impulse of reprisals might make him sacrifice his fixed purpose, his hope of happiness, a future deliberately willed and designed by himself, to the satisfaction of hurting and humiliating her. He was almost capable of wishing that she *would* go away with Vance Weston; the mere pleasure of thwarting her would be keen enough to repay him. He was a man who grew fat on resentment as others did on happiness . . . For an instant her old life rose before her. This was the man she had lived with for ten years; he had always been what he was now, and she had always known it. The thought frightened her even now—she had to admit that he could still frighten her. But the admission stiffened her will. Did he really imagine that any threat of his could still affect her? That she would give up a year, perhaps two years, of happiness, of life—life at last!—and sit in conventual solitude till the divorce, conducted with old-fashioned discretion and deliberation, permitted him to posture before his little world as the husband who has chivalrously "allowed" an unworthy but unblamed wife to gain her liberty? How quaint and out-of-date it all sounded! What did she care if she divorced him or he divorced her—what, even, if he chose to wreak his malice on her by preventing any recourse to divorce? Her life had struck root in the soul-depths, while his uneasily fluttered on the surface; and that put her beyond all reach of malice. She read the letter twice over, slowly; then with a smiling deliberation she tore it up, and sent the fragments over the taffrail.

As she did so, she felt a faint vibration through the immense bulk to which her fate was committed. It was too late now—really too late. The gong had sounded; the steamer was moving. For better or worse, she had chosen; and she was glad she had done so deliberately.

"We're off!" she heard at her side, in a voice of passionate excitement. She turned and laid her hand on Vance Weston's; their eyes met, laughing. "Now at last you'll have your fill of the sea," she said.

He shook his head. "Only a week . . ."

"Ten days to Gibraltar."

"What's that you've got?"

With a little start she looked down at her hand. "Oh, only a telegram. The steward brought it. I forgot . . ."

"Forgot what?"

"Everything that has to do with that dead world." She made a gesture of dismissal toward the dwindling cliffs of masonry. "The steward called me Mrs. Vance Weston," she added, smiling.

He responded to her smile. "Well, you'll have to get used to that."

They both laughed again, for the mere joy of sipping their laughter out of the one cup; then she said: "I suppose I ought to open it . . ."

"Oh, why? Now we're off, why not drop it into the sea as a tribute to old Liberty over there? We owe her a tribute, don't we?" he said; and she thought, with a little thrill of feminine submission: "How strong and decided he seems! He tells me what to do—he takes everything for granted. I'm the weak inexperienced one, after all." She ran her finger carelessly under the flap of the telegram.

Now that they were off, as he said, it did not much matter whether she opened her telegrams or threw them to the waves. What possibility was there in her adventure that she had not already foreseen, agonized over and finally put out of mind as inevitable or irrelevant? With that last letter she had tossed her past overboard. Smiling, brooding, still thinking only of himself and her, enclosed in the impenetrable world of their love, she opened the telegram under their joint gaze.

They read: "Happiness is a work of art. Handle with care." The message was unsigned, but no signature was necessary. "Poor old Frenny!" Her first impulse was to smile at the idea that any one, and most of all an embittered old bachelor like her friend George Frenside, should think it possible to advise her as to the nature or management of happiness. Her eyes met Vance's, and she saw that they were grave.

"I suppose he remembered something in his own life," Vance said.

"I suppose so." It made her shiver a little to think that some day she too might be remembering—*this*. At the moment, happiness seemed to have nothing to do with memory, to be an isolating medium dividing her from the past as completely, as arbitrarily, as this huge ship had detached her little world of passengers from the shores of earth. Suddenly Halo recalled having said to Frenside, in the course of one of their endless speculative talks: "Being contented is so jolly that I sometimes think I couldn't have stood being happy"; and his grim answer: "It's a destructive experience."

Poor Frenside! Poor herself! For she had not known then what happiness was, any more (she supposed) than he did. Destructive? When the mounting flood of life was rumouring in her ears like the sea? As well call spring destructive, or birth, or any of the processes of renewal that forever mantle the ancient earth with promise.

"I wonder what it feels like to remember," she said obscurely. Vance's smile met hers. "How extraordinary!" she thought. "Nothing that I say to him will need explaining . . ." It gave her a miraculous winged sense, as though she were free of the bonds of gravitation. "Oh, Vance, this—it's like flying!" He nodded, and they stood silent, watching the silvery agitation of the waters as the flank of the steamer divided them. Up and down the deck people were scattering, disappearing.

Rows of empty deck-chairs stood behind the lovers. The passengers had gone to look up their cabins, hunt for missing luggage, claim letters, parcels, seats in the dining-saloon. Vance Weston and Halo Tarrant seemed to have the ship to themselves.

It was a day of early September. Wind-clouds, shifting about in the upper sky, tinged the unsteady glittering water with tones of silver, lead and rust-colour, hollowed to depths of sullen green as the steamer pressed forward to the open. The lovers were no longer gazing back on the fading pinnacles of New York; hand clasped over hand, they looked out to where the sea spread before them in limitless freedom.

They had chosen a slow steamer, on an unfashionable line, partly from economy, partly because of Halo's wish to avoid acquaintances; and their choice had been rewarded. They knew no one on board. Halo Tarrant, in the disturbed and crowded days before her departure, had looked forward with impatience to the quiet of a long sea-voyage. Her life, of late, had been so full of unprofitable agitation that she yearned to set her soul's house in order. Before entering on a new existence she wanted to find herself again, to situate herself in the new environment into which she had been so strangely flung. A few months ago she had been living under the roof of Lewis Tarrant, bound to him by ties the more unbreakable because they did not concern her private feelings. She had regarded it as her fate to be a good wife and a devoted companion to her husband for the rest of their joint lives; it had never occurred to her that he would wish a change. But she had left out of account the uneasy vanity which exacted more, always more, which would not be put off with anything less than her whole self, her complete belief, the uncritical surrender of her will and judgment. When her husband found she was not giving him this (or only feigning to give it) he sought satisfaction elsewhere. If his wife did not believe in him, his attitude implied, other women did—women whom this act of faith endued with all the qualities he had hoped to find in Halo. To be "understood", for Lewis Tarrant, was an active, a perpetually functioning state. The persons nearest him must devote all their days and nights, thoughts, impulses, inclinations, to the arduous business of understanding him. Halo began to see that as her powers of self-dedication decreased her importance to her husband decreased with them. She became first less necessary, then (in consequence) less interesting, finally almost an incumbrance. The discovery surprised her. She had once thought that Tarrant, even if he ceased to love her, would continue to need her. She saw now that this belief was inspired by the resolve to make the best of their association, to keep it going at all costs. When she found she had been replaced by more ardent incense-burners the discovery frightened her. She felt a great emptiness about her, saw herself freezing into old age unsustained by self-imposed duties. For she could not leave her husband—she regarded herself as bound by the old debt on which their marriage had been based. Tarrant had rescued her parents from bankruptcy, had secured their improvident old age against material cares. That deed once done would never be undone; she knew he would go on supporting them; his very vanity compelled him to persist in being generous when he had once decreed that he ought to be. He never gave up an attitude once adopted as a part of his picture of himself.

But then—what of her? She tried not to think of her loneliness; but there it was, perpetually confronting her. She was unwanted, yet she could not go. She had to patch together the fragments of the wrecked situation, and try to use them as a shelter.

And then, what would have seemed likely enough had it not been the key to her difficulty, had after all come to pass. An infirm old cousin died, and her will made Halo Tarrant a free woman. At first she did not measure the extent of her freedom. She thought only: "Now I can provide for my people; they need not depend on Lewis—" but it had not yet dawned on her that her liberation might come too. She still believed that Tarrant's determination to keep whatever had once belonged to him would be stronger than any other feeling. "He'll take the other woman—but he'll want to keep me," she reasoned; and began to wonder how she could avoid making her plea for freedom seem to coincide with her material release. To appear to think that her debt could be thus cancelled was to turn their whole past into a matter of business—and it had begun by being something else. She could not have married anybody who happened to have paid her parents' debts; that Tarrant had done so seemed at the time merely an added cause for admiration, a justification of her faith in him. She knew now that from the beginning her faith had needed such support . . . And then, before she could ask for her freedom, he had anticipated her by asking for his; and, so abruptly that she was still bewildered by the suddenness of the change, she found herself a new woman in a new world . . .

All this she had meant to think over, setting her past in order before she put it away from her and took up the threads of the future. But suddenly she found herself confronted by a new fact which reduced past and future to shadows. For the first time in her life she

was living in the present. Hitherto, as she now saw, her
real existence, her whole inner life, had been either
plunged in the wonders that art, poetry, history, had
built into her dreams, or else reaching forward to a future she longed for yet dreaded. She had thought she
could perhaps not bear to be happy; and now she was
happy, and all the rest was nothing. She was like someone stepping into hot sunlight from a darkened room;
she blinked, and saw no details. And to look at the future was like staring into the sun. She was blinded, and
her eyes turned to the steady golden noon about her.
Ah, perhaps it was true—perhaps she did not know how
to bear happiness. It took her by the inmost fibres,
burned through her like a fever, was going to give her
no rest, no peace, no time to steady and tame it in her
dancing soul.

ৠ II ৡ

HALO HAD said: "Now you'll have your fill of the sea—" and Vance Weston had smiled at the idea that ten days could be enough of infinitude. Hitherto his horizon had been bounded by the prairies of the Middle West or walled in between the cliffs of the Hudson or the skyscrapers of New York. Twice only had he drunk of that magic, in two brief glimpses which had seemed to pour the ocean through his veins. If a lover can separate the joys of love from its setting, he felt a separate delight in knowing that his first days and nights with Halo were to be spent at sea.

When his wife's death, and Halo Tarrant's decision to leave her husband, had brought the two together a few months previously, Vance had seen no reason for not seizing at once on their predestined happiness. But Halo felt differently. When she went to him with the news of her freedom she supposed him to be separated from his wife, and thought that he and she might resume their fraternal intimacy without offense to Laura Lou. Then, when she had run him to earth in a shabby outskirt of New York, she had discovered that he also was free, freed not by the law but by the fact that his young wife had just died in the tumble-down bungalow where Halo had found him. There she learned that there had been no lasting quarrel between Vance and Laura Lou, and that they had never separated. Expecting to find a deserted husband she had encountered a mourning widower, and had been paralyzed by the thought of declaring her love under the roof where

Vance's vigil by his wife's death-bed was barely ended. Vance had hardly perceived the barrier that she felt between them. He lived in a simpler moral atmosphere, and was quicker at distinguishing the transient from the fundamental in human relations; but he would have felt less tenderly toward Halo if she had not been aware of that silent presence.

"But she's there, dearest—can't you feel it? Don't you see her little face, so pleading and puzzled . . . as it was that day when she was angry with me for going to see her, and turned me out of her room—do you remember? Oh, Vance, it was all for love of you—don't I *know?* I understood it even then; I loved her for it. I used to envy her for having somebody to worship. And now I see her, I feel her near us, and I know we must give her time, time to understand, time to consent, to learn not to hate me, as she would hate me at this minute if you and I were to forget her."

Vance had never before thought of the past in that way; but as he listened Halo's way became his, and her evocation of Laura Lou, instead of paining or irritating him, seemed like saying a prayer on a lonely grave. Such feelings, instinctive in Halo, were familiar to Vance through the pity for failure, pity for incomprehension, which glowed in his grandmother's warm blood. New York and Euphoria called things by different names, and feelings which in the older society had become conventionalized seemed to require formulating and ticketing in the younger; but the same fibres stirred to the same touch.

Vance and Halo, that spring evening, had parted after a long talk. Halo had gone to join her parents at Eaglewood, their country place above Paul's Landing; Vance had returned to his family at Euphoria, with the idea of settling down there for a year of writing, away from all the disturbances, material and moral, which had so long hampered his work. By the end of the year Halo would have obtained her divorce, his book (he was sure) would be finished, and a new life could begin for both. Vance meant to go on with the unfinished novel, "Magic," which had been so strangely stimulated by his wife's illness, so violently interrupted by her death. That sad fragment of his life was over, his heart was free to feed on its new hopes, and he felt that it would be easy, after a few weeks of rest, to return to his work.

They had all been very kind at Euphoria. His father's business was recovering, though his spirits were not. A younger and more unscrupulous school of realtors had robbed Mr. Weston of his former prominence. Though he retained its faint reflection among his contemporaries he was a back number to the younger men, and he knew it, and brooded over the thought that if things had gone differently Vance might have been one of his successful supplanters. Lorin Weston would have liked to be outwitted in business by his own son. "I used to think you'd be a smarter fellow than I ever was," he said wistfully. "And anyway, if you'd come back and taken that job they offered you on the 'Free Speaker' you could have given me enough backing to prevent the Crampton deal going through without me. I was a pioneer of Crampton, and everybody in Euphoria knows it. But those fellows squared the 'Free Speaker' and so their deal with the Shunts motor people went through without me. And it's not much more'n three years ago that I sold that house your grandmother used to live in for less than what Harrison Delaney got the year after by the square yard for that rookery of his down the lane—you remember?" Vance remembered.

"Oh, well," interrupted Mrs. Weston, in the nervous tone of one who knows what is coming, and has heard it too often, "there's no use your going over that old Delaney deal again. I guess everybody has a chance once in their lives—and anyhow, Harrison Delaney's waited long enough for his."

"Well, he *did* wait, and I couldn't afford to. He smelt out somehow that Shunts Amalgamated were buying up everything they could lay their hands on down Crampton way; and he pocketed his million—yes, sir, one million—and sent for that girl of his, who was on some job over at Dakin, and the story is they've gone over to Europe to blow it in—gay Paree!" Mr. Weston jeered a little mournfully. "Well, son, I always kinder hoped when you'd worked the literature out of your system you'd come back and carry on the old job with me; and if you had I guess we'd be running Crampton today instead of the Shuntses."

However, the Euphoria boom was not confined to Crampton, and Mr. Weston's improved situation enabled him to pay Vance's debts (though the total startled him), and even to promise his son a small allowance till the latter could get on his feet and produce that surest evidence of achievement, a best-seller. "And he will too, Vanny will; just you folks reserve your seats and wait," his grandmother Scrimser exulted, her old blue eyes sparkling like flowers through her tears.

"Well, I guess father'll be prouder of that than what he would of a real-estate deal," Mae, the cultured daughter, remarked sententiously.

"I will, the day he gets up to Harrison Delaney's figure," Mr. Weston grumbled; but he circulated Mrs. Scrimser's prophecy among his cronies, and Vance's fame spread about through Euphoria. The women of the family (his grandmother not excepted) took even more pride in the prospect of his marrying into one of the "regular Fifth Avenue families." "Well, if they wouldn't listen to me I guess they'll all be listening to *you* some day soon," Mrs. Scrimser said, humorously alluding to an unsuccessful attempt she had once made to evangelize fashionable New York. They all gloated over a snap-shot of Halo which Vance had brought with him, and his mother longed to give it to the "Free Speaker" for publication, and to see Vance, on both literary and social grounds, interviewed, head-lined and banqueted. But they were impressed, if disappointed, by his resolve to defend his privacy. He had come back home to work, they explained for him; one of the big New York publishers was waiting for his new book, and showing signs of impatience; and the house in Mapledale Avenue was converted into a sanctuary where the family seer might vaticinate undisturbed.

Never before in Vance's troubled life had he worked with an easy mind. He had written the first chapters of "Magic" in an agony of anxiety. Fears for his wife's health, despair of his own future, regrets for his past mistakes, had made his mind a battle-ground during the months before Laura Lou's death. Yet through that choking anguish the fount of inspiration had forced its way; and now that he sat secure under the Mapledale Avenue roof, heart and mind at peace, the past at rest, the future radiant, the fount was dry. Before he had been at home a week he was starving for Halo, and stifling in the unchanged atmosphere of Euphoria. He saw now that the stimulus he needed was not rest but happiness. He had meant to send Halo what he wrote, chapter by chapter; but he could not write. What he needed was not her critical aid but her nearness. His apprentice days were over; he knew what he was trying to do better than any one could tell him, even Halo; what he craved was the one medium in which his imagination could expand, and that was Halo herself.

For two or three months he struggled on without result; then, after a last night spent in desperate contemplation of the blank sheets on his desk, he threw his manuscript into his suit-case and went down to announce his departure to the family. He travelled from Euphoria to Paul's Landing as quickly as changes of train permitted; and two days later rang the door-bell of Eaglewood, and said to the Spears' old chauffeur, Jacob, who appeared at the door in the guise of the family butler: "Hullo, Jake; remember me—Vance Weston? Yes; I've just arrived from out west; and I've got to see Mrs. Tarrant right off . . ."

That had happened in August; now, barely three weeks later, Halo sat at his side in a corner of the liner's deck, and the night-sea encircled them, boundless and inscrutable as their vision of the future. There was no moon, but the diffused starlight gave a faint uniform lustre to the moving obscurity. The sea, throbbing and hissing in phosphorescent whirls about the steamer's keel, subsided to vast ebony undulations as it stretched away to the sky. The breeze blew against the lovers' faces purified of all earthly scents, as if it had circled forever over that dematerialized waste. Vance sat with his arm about Halo, brooding over the mystery of the waters and his own curious inability to feel their vastness as he had once felt it from a lonely beach on Long Island. It was as if the sea shrank when no land was visible—as if the absence of the familiar shore made it too remote, too abstract, to reach his imagination. He had a feeling that perhaps he would never be able to assimilate perfection or completeness.

"It's funny," he said; and when Halo wanted to know what was, he rejoined: "Well, when people tell me a story, and say: 'Here's something you ought to make a good thing out of', if what they tell me is too perfect, too finished—if they don't break off before the end—I can't do anything with it. Snatches, glimpses—the seeds of things—that's what story-tellers want. I suppose that's why the Atlantic's too big for me. A creek's got more of the sea in it, for people who want to turn it into poetry."

She pressed closer to him. "That's exactly the theme of 'Magic', isn't it?"

"Yes," he assented; and sat silent. "Do you know, there's another thing that's funny—"

"What else is?"

"Well, I used to think your eyes were gray."

"Aren't they?"

"They're all mixed with brown, like autumn leaves on a gray stream."

"Vance, wouldn't it be awful if you found out that everything about me was different from what you used to think?"

"Well, everything is—I mean, there are all sorts of lights and shades and contradictions and complications."

"Perhaps I shall be like your subjects. If you get to know me too well you won't be able to do anything with me. I suppose that's why artists often feel they oughtn't to marry."

"What they generally feel is that they oughtn't to stay married," he corrected.

"Well—it's not too late!" she challenged him.

"Oh, but they've got to marry first; artists have. Or some sort of equivalent."

"You acknowledge that you're all carnivora?"

He turned and drew her head to his cheek in the dimness. "I said perfection was what I hadn't any use for." Their laughter mixed with their long kiss; then she loosed herself from his arms and stood up.

"Come, Vance, let's go and look at the past for a minute."

"What's the past?"

She drew him along the deck, from which the last of the passengers were descending to the light and sociability below; they retraced the ship's length till they reached a point at the stern from which they could see the receding miles of star-strown ocean. "Look how we're leaving it behind and how it's racing after us," Halo said. "I suppose there's a symbol in that. All the things we've done and thought and struggled for, or tried to escape from, leagued together and tearing after us. Doesn't it make you feel a little breathless? I wonder what we should do if they caught up with us."

Vance leaned on the rail, his arm through hers. The immensity of the night was rushing after them. On those pursuing waves he saw the outstretched arms of his youth, his parents, his grandmother, Floss Delaney, Mrs. Pulsifer, the girls who had flitted across his path, and the little white vision of Laura Lou springing like spray from wave to wave. He pictured a man suddenly falling over the ship's side, and seized and torn to pieces by the pack of his memories—then he felt the current of Halo's blood beating in his, and thought: "For a little while longer we shall outrace them."

❦ III ❧

THE MONUMENTAL Spanish sky was full of cloud-architecture. Long azure perspectives between colonnades and towers stretched away majestically above an empty earth. The real Spain seemed to be overhead, heavy with history; as if all the pictures, statues, ecclesiastical splendours that Vance and Halo had come to see were stored in the air-palaces along those radiant avenues. The clouds peopled even the earth with their shadow-masses, creating here a spectral lake in the dry landscape, there a flock of cattle, or a hamlet on a hill which paled and vanished as the travellers approached. All that Vance had ever read about mirages and desert semblances rose in his mind as the motor-coach rolled and swayed across the barren land.

The names of the few villages that they passed meant nothing to him. The famous towns and cities of Spain already sang in his imagination; but there were none on this road, and the clusters of humble houses on bare slopes could not distract his attention from that celestial architecture. At first he had been oppressed by the emptiness of the landscape, its lack of any relation to the labours and joys of men. Stretching away on all sides to the horizon, the *tierras despobladas* seemed to lie under a mysterious blight. But gradually he ceased to feel their gloom. Under a sky so packed with prodigies it began to seem natural that people should turn their minds and their interests away from the earth. On the steamer he had read a little about the Spanish mystics, in one of the books that Halo had brought; and now he thought:

"No wonder everything on earth seemed irrelevant, with all those New Jerusalems building and re-building themselves overhead."

As the sun declined, cloud ramparts and towers grew more massive, nearer the earth, till their lowest degrees rested like marble stairways on the hills. "Those are the ladders that Jacob's angels went up and down," Vance mused; then the gold paled to ashes, and the sky-palaces were absorbed into the dusk. The motor-coach crossed a bridge and drove into a brown city, through narrow streets already full of lights. At a corner Halo asked the conductor to stop, and entrusted their bags to him. "Come," she said; and Vance followed her across a wide court where daylight still lingered faintly under old twisted trees. She pushed open a door in a cliff-like wall, and they entered into what seemed total darkness to eyes still blinking with Spanish sunshine. Vance stood still, waiting for his sight to return. It came little by little, helped by the twinkle of two or three specks of flame, immeasurably far off, like ships' lights in mid-ocean; till gradually he discerned through the obscurity forms of columns and arches linked with one another in long radiating perspectives. "The place is as big as that sky out there," he murmured.

He and Halo moved forward. First one colonnade, low-vaulted and endless, drew them on; then another. They were caught in a dim network of architectural forms, perpetually repeated abstractions of the relation between arch and shaft. The similarity of what surrounded them was so confusing that they could not be sure if they had passed from one colonnade to another, or if the whole system were revolving with them around some planetary centre still invisible. Vance felt as if he had dropped over the brim of things into the mysterious world where straight lines loop themselves into curves.

He thought: "It's like the feel of poetry, just as it's beginning to be born in you"—that fugitive moment before words restrict the vision. But he gave up the struggle for definitions.

The obscure central bulk about which those perpetual aisles revolved gradually took shape as sculptured
walls rising high overhead. In the walls were arched
openings; lights reflected in polished marble glimmered
through the foliation of wrought-iron gates. Vance was
as excited and exhausted as if he had raced for miles
over the uneven flagging. Suddenly he felt the desire to
lift his arms and push back the overwhelming spectacle
till he had the strength to receive it. He caught Halo's
arm. "Come away," he said hoarsely. Through the dimness he saw her look of surprise and disappointment.
She was used to these things, could bear them. He
couldn't—and he didn't know how to tell her. He
slipped his arm through hers, pulling her after him.

"But wait, dearest, do wait. This is the choir, the
high-altar, the Christian cathedral built inside . . . It's
so beautiful at this hour. . . Don't you want . . . ?"

He repeated irritably: "Come away. I'm tired,"
knowing all the while how he was disappointing her. He
felt her arm nervously pressed against his.

"Of course, dear. But what could have tired you?
The hot sun, perhaps . . . Oh, where's the door?" She
took a few uncertain steps. "There's only one left open.
The sacristan saw us come in, and is waiting outside. All
the doors are locked at sunset; but he's watching for us
at the one we came in by. The thing is to find it."

They began to walk down one of the aisles. Farther
and farther away in the heart of the shadows they left
the great choir and altar; yet they seemed to get no
nearer to the door. Halo stood still again. "No—this
way," she said, with the abruptness of doubt. "We're

going in the wrong direction." Vance remembered a
passage in the Second Faust which had always haunted
him: the scene where Faust descends to the Mothers.
"He must have wound round and round like this," he
thought. They had turned and were walking down another low-vaulted vista toward a glow-worm light at its
end. This led them to a door bolted and barred on the
inner side, and evidently long unopened. "It's not that."
They turned again and walked in the deepening darkness down another colonnade. Vance thought of the
Cretan labyrinth, of Odysseus evoking the mighty dead,
of all the subterranean mysteries on whose outer crust
man loves and fights and dies. The blood was beating in
his ears. He began to wish that they might never find the
right door, but go on turning about forever at the dark
heart of things. They walked and walked. After a while
Halo asked: "Are you really tired?" like Eurydice timidly guiding Orpheus back to daylight.

"No; I'm not tired any longer."

"We'll soon be out," she cheered him; and he
thought: "How funny that she doesn't know what I'm
feeling!" He longed to sit down at the foot of one of the
glimmering shafts and let the immensity and the mystery sweep over him like the sea. "If only she doesn't tell
me any more about it," he thought, dreading architectural and historical explanations. But she slipped her
hand in his, and the touch melted into his mood.

At last they found the right door, and a key ground
in response to Halo's knock. Vance felt like a disem-
bodied spirit coming back to earth. "I'd like to go and
haunt somebody," he murmured. It was night outside,
but a transparent southern night, not like the thick
darkness in the cathedral. The court with the old
twisted orange-trees was dim; but in the streets beyond
there were lights and shrill human noises, the smell of

frying food and the scent of jasmine. When they got back to the hotel and were shown to their room, Vance said abruptly: "You go down to dinner alone. I don't want anything to eat. I'd rather stay here . . ."

"You don't feel ill?" she asked; but he reassured her. "I'm only overfed with the day . . ." She tidied her hair and dress, and went down. It was exquisite to be with a woman who didn't persist and nag. He flung himself on the bed, his nerves tranquillized, and watched the stars come out through a tree under the window. Those branches recalled others, crooked and half-bare, outside of the window of the suburban bungalow where he had nursed his wife in her last illness. They were apple-branches; and he remembered how one day—a day of moral misery but acute spiritual excitement—he had seen the subject of his new book hanging on that tree like fruit. "Magic"—the story he had meant to write as soon as he was free. And he had been free for nearly a year, and had not added a line to it. But now everything would be different. With Halo at his side, and the world opening about him like the multiple vistas of that strange cathedral, his imagination would have room to range in. He shut his eyes and fell asleep.

The opening of the door made him start up, and he tumbled off the bed as Halo entered. "It took forever to get anything to eat. Did you wonder what had become of me?"

"No. I must have been asleep. But I'm as hungry as a cannibal. Can't we go out somewhere and get supper?" He felt happy, renewed, and as famished as a boy who has been sent to bed dinnerless.

The streets hummed with nocturnal chatter. Gusts of scent blew over secret garden-walls; and in the narrower thoroughfares of the old town they caught, through open arch-ways, glimpses of white courts with hanging lanterns, and plants about fountains, and gossiping people grouped in willow armchairs. Halo's Spanish was fluent enough to make her at ease in the scene, and she found a little restaurant smelling of olive-oil and garlic, where diners still lingered, and a saffron mound of rice and fish was set before Vance. He revelled in the high-seasoned diet, the thick sunny wine, the familiarity and noise of the friendly place, the contrast between the solitude of the cathedral and the crowded common life at its doors. He longed to wander from street to street, listening to the overlapping gramophones, the snatches of hoarse song, excited talk from door-step to door-step, the wail of muleteers driving their beasts to the stable, the whine of beggars on the steps of churches. It was strange and delicious to be sitting there at ease with this young woman who knew what everybody was saying, could talk to them, laugh with them, ask the way, bandy jokes, and give him the sense of being at home in it all.

After a while they got up and walked on. "Do you want to see some dancing? I daresay we could find a place," Halo suggested, as they caught a rattle of castanets from a packed *café*. But Vance wanted to stay in the streets. He liked to wander under the night-blue sky, and to speculate on what was going on behind the white walls of the houses, and the gates that were beginning to be shut on the darkened patios. They strayed down one street after another, through little squares shadowed with trees, to the market quarter around the cathedral, where, at the base of those mute walls, the shrieking of gramophones contended with the smell of fish and garlic. Then they turned the flank of the cathedral, and followed an unfrequented lane descending between convent-like buildings to the river. All was hushed and dim. They went out to the middle of the fortified bridge, and leaning on the parapet looked from the sluggish waters below to the mountain-like mass of the great church.

Vance gave a chuckle of satiety. "I don't believe I could bear it if there was a moon!"

Halo had not spoken for a long while. "That's what I used to feel about happiness," she said.

"That you couldn't bear it?"

"Yes."

"Well—and now?"

"Oh, now . . . you'll have to teach me . . ."

"Me? I never knew what it was, either . . . not this kind . . ."

"Is there any other?"

He pressed her close. "If there is, I've got no use for it."

They stood listening to the sound of the lazy river. The darkness drooped over them, low and burning as the curtains of an Olympian couch; and Vance, holding his love, thought how little meaning the scene would have had without her. He had seen it all before, after all —in inklings, in scattered visions; at the movies, at the opera, in the histories and travels he'd read; in "Gil Blas" and Gautier and "The Bible in Spain"; in sham Spanish cafés and cabarets; who was going to tell him anything new about Spain? The newness, the marvel, was in his arms, under his lips—this girl who was his other brain, his soul and his flesh. He longed to tell her so, in words such as no other woman had heard; but the poverty of all words came over him. "See here, let's go home to bed." They linked arms, and went back up the hill to the hotel. It was so late that even a Spanish porter was hard to rouse—but at length they climbed the stairs and stole into their room. Through the window the smell of frying oil and jasmine flowers blew in on them; and Vance wondered if in all his life any other smell would be so mingled for him with the taste of Halo's lips and eyelids.

⚝ IV ⚝

THE NEXT morning Vance announced that he meant to spend at least a month at Cordova. He said "*I* mean," as naturally as if the decision concerned only himself, and he would not for the world have restricted his companion's liberty. But this was not a surprise to Halo. She knew the irresistible force which drove him in pursuit of the food his imagination required. It was not that he was forgetful of her, but that, now they were together, his heart was satisfied, while the hunger of his mind was perpetual and insatiable.

In spite of herself she was slightly disconcerted by his taking their plan of travel into his own hands. She, who had worked it out so carefully, considering the season, the probable weather, the number of days to be given to each place, saw that all this meant nothing to him and reflected with a pang that she had outgrown the age of impulse. It was seldom nowadays that she remembered this difference between them. At first she had been continually conscious that he was the younger, and this had kept her from acknowledging to herself that she was in love with him. Even afterward there were times when he had seemed a boy to her; but now that they were lovers she felt in him a man's authority. But in practical matters she was conscious of her greater experience, and half-vexed at his not perceiving it.

"But, darling, you haven't seen Seville yet—or Murcia or Granada. And we ought to go up to Ronda before the weather turns cold. You've no conception of the wonders . . ."

He looked at her with a whimsical smile. "That's why . . ."

"Why?"

"It takes me such a darned long time to deal with wonders. I'm slow, I suppose. I don't care for more than one course at a meal."

She shrugged a little impatiently. "Oh, don't use your gastronomic preferences as an argument, dearest!"

"You mean they're too crude?"

"No; but they contradict your other theory. The theory that artists need only a mouthful of each dish."

"Oh, damn artists! I just want to please Vance Weston," he rejoined imperturbably, his arm about her shoulder. She laughed, and kissed him; but inwardly she thought: "I must just adapt myself; I must learn to keep step."

After all, wasn't it what she had wanted to marry him for? The absorbing interest of seeing his gift unfold under her care had been so interwoven with her love that she could not separate them. But she liked to think that she loved him because she believed in his genius, not that (as a simpler woman might) she believed in his genius because she loved him. Yet here she was, on the point of letting her petty habits of routine and order interfere with his inspiration! What did it matter if they spent the rest of the autumn at Cordova—or the rest of the year? "You feel as if you could write here?" she suggested, remembering how once before his art had flowered under her influence; and he smiled back at her: "Just at this minute I feel as if I couldn't write anywhere else." But they agreed that work would be impossible in their one noisy room at the hotel, and Halo set out to find quieter and roomier quarters. In her young days, before her marriage to Tarrant had immersed the family in luxury, Mr. and Mrs. Spear had taught their children that to combine picturesqueness with economy was one of the pleasures of travel. Scornful of the tourist who rated plumbing above local colour, and had to content himself with what could be asked for in English, the Spears, polylingual and ingratiating, gloried in the art of securing "amusing" lodgings at famine prices. The gifts developed in those nomad years came to Halo's aid, and before night she had driven a masterly bargain with the owner of the very quarters she wanted. The rooms were bare but clean, and so high above the town that they commanded the jumble of roofs and towers descending to the bridge, and a glimpse of the brown hills beyond. Vance was enchanted, and the unpacking and settling down turned the lovers into happy children. Though Vance lacked Halo's skill in driving nails and mending broken furniture he shared her love of order, and his good will and stronger muscles lightened her task. Before long his room was ready, and at a carefully consolidated table on which Halo had laid a fresh sheet of blotting paper and a stack of "author's pads" of a blue that was supposed to be good for the eyes, he sat down to his novel.

"Nobody ever fixed me up like this before," he said with a contented laugh. She remembered the comfortless house in which she had found him after Laura Lou's death, and wondered what happiness could equal that of a woman permitted to serve the genius while she adored the man.

"Do you think it's going to be as good a place for work as the Willows?" She coloured at her allusion to the old house on the Hudson, where she had spent so many hours with Vance while he was writing "Instead"—the novel the critics had acclaimed, and his publishers had resented his not consenting to repeat. All through one fervid summer the two had met there, unknown to

Vance's wife and to Halo's husband. At that time she had imagined that she and Vance were only friends; yet, though she had ceased to meet him when his sudden outburst of passion broke down the feint, she could not recall their stolen hours without compunction. But there was none in Vance's eyes.

"I'm going to work a thousand per cent better here, because at the Willows I was always in a fever for you, and you kept getting in between me and my book."

"What a nuisance I must have been!" she murmured hypocritically; and added, half laughing, half in earnest: "And now—I suppose you already take me for granted?"

Their eyes met, and she saw in his the inward look which sometimes made him appear so much older than his age. "Oh, my soul—mayn't I?" he said; and: "Vance," she cried out, "what I want is just to be like the air you breathe . . ."

He lit a cigarette, and leaned back, comfortably surveying the blue pages. "That's only the beginning of all the things you're going to be," he declared. He held out the bundle of cigarettes, and she bent to light one from his, and stole to the door, pausing to say: "Now I'm going to leave you to your work."

She went to her own room to finish her unpacking; then she sat down in the window, and let the waves of bliss flow over her. More than once since she had left New York she had tried to look into the future and picture her probable destiny; but while her life held this burning core of passion she could fix her thoughts on nothing else. She had been too starved and cold before; now she could only steep herself in the glow.

No one would understand, she knew; least of all her own family. Mr. and Mrs. Spear had always regarded themselves as free spirits, and were certainly burdened with fewer social prejudices than most of their friends and relations. Mrs. Spear had specialized in receiving "odd" people at a time when New York was still shy of them. She had welcomed at her house foreign celebrities travelling with ladies unprovided with a marriage certificate, and had been equally hospitable to certain compatriots who had broken their marriage tie when such breaks were a cause of scandal. But though she sympathized with "self-expression", and the mystical duty to "live one's life", and had championed the first adventurers in the new morality, she had never expected any one belonging to her to join that band of heroes. She was a Lorburn of Paul's Landing, and people of pre-Revolutionary stock, however emancipated their sympathies, conformed to tradition in their conduct. Mrs. Spear had herself conformed. Her marriage had been a defiance, since she had married out of her own set, or her own class, as her family would have put it; but it was a defiance sanctioned by church and law, and she had never dreamed of her daughter's taking liberties with those institutions. Grieved as she was at Halo's leaving her husband, Mrs. Spear had accepted it as inevitable, and had bowed, after another struggle, to the further inevitability of her daughter's re-marriage; but she had been genuinely shocked, and deeply hurt, by Halo's decision to go away with her lover before her divorce. Mrs. Spear had not been violent and denunciatory, like her husband, whose resentment was doubled by the fact that he could not air it in the newspapers. Mrs. Spear knew that the day was past when parents, especially parents who have coquetted with Bohemia, can call down curses on a dishonoured daughter. But she did feel that Halo was dishonouring herself, and that every influence should be used to save her. If the break with Tarrant was unavoidable, why could not her daughter wait until he had taken the necessary steps? "Lewis is always a gentleman. You must admit that. You can count on his assuming all the blame," Mrs. Spear had pleaded, her beautiful eyes full of persuasion and perplexity.

"But, mother, supposing I'd rather share the blame —why shouldn't I take the necessary steps for *that?*" Halo rejoined, trying to evade her mother's entreaties. Mrs. Spear merely replied: "Don't talk like your brother, please"—for Lorry Spear was noted for his habit of dealing with serious questions flippantly; and Halo, conscious of the ineffectualness of any argument, could only repeat: "Mother, I must go with him—I must. He needs me"—though she knew that to her mother such a plea was worse than flippancy.

"If he really needs you, dear, he'll have the strength of character to wait for you for a year. If he hasn't—" Mrs. Spear left the ominous conclusion unspoken.

"Oh, but, mother darling, it's not that . . . I suppose you're thinking of other women . . ." Halo felt herself burning inwardly at the suggestion.

"It's not an unusual weakness—with artists especially," Mrs. Spear drily interposed.

"No," Halo conceded; "I suppose we shouldn't have much art without it . . . But what I mean is so different . . . He needs me for his work . . . I can help him, I know I can . . ."

"Of course he'll make you think so—oh, it's all so unlike you, darling!" cried poor Mrs. Spear, feeling herself as short of arguments as her daughter.

"No, it's like me," Halo exclaimed passionately, "only I've never really been myself before. Don't grudge me the chance." She bent over, trying to kiss away her mother's tears; and on this unsatisfactory conclusion they had parted.

At first Halo's view had differed little from Mrs. Spear's. To wait till she was divorced, and go to Vance Weston as his wife, had seemed the natural, the obvious arrangement. But when Vance came back from Euphoria, ill-looking, unsettled, unable to work, and pleading not to have his happiness postponed, she had given way at once. She herself hardly knew whether passion or pity had prevailed; but she felt, as she had said to her mother, that this was her first chance to be her real self, and that no argument, no appeal to social expediency or to loftier motives, should deprive her of it. Words like dignity and self-respect seemed to belong to an obsolete language. Her dignity, her self-respect! What had become of them when she had endured to live with a husband she despised? Yet she had remained with him for reasons much less potent than those which called her to her lover. Was she really the same woman who, on the steamer a few weeks earlier, had hesitated over her lawyer's warning letter, and asked herself whether she ought not to turn back? Now it was her past that she was ashamed of, not her present; there were lyric moments when her flight with Vance seemed like an expiation.

These phases of the struggle were over; she regarded them as indifferently as if they had belonged to some other woman's story. It was sweet to her now to know that she had gone to Vance without hesitating. "In such a heaven as ours there's no marrying or giving in marriage," she thought, as she sat there nursing her happiness; and awed by the perfectness of her well-being she hid her face in her hands.

"What quiet there is in deep happiness," she mused. "How little I ever imagined this lull in the middle of the whirlpool!" But the stars still danced about her, and when she tried to disentangle her mind from their golden whirl she felt a lassitude, a reluctance she could not explain. "All that matters is that he's sitting there next door, tranquil, happy, at work again—and that it's my doing," she thought. She longed to open his door and steal in, as she used to at the Willows, when he would break off every now and then to read aloud what he had written. But she remembered what he had said of her "getting in between him and his book," and she went back to her seat, reflecting that their moments together were no longer numbered, and that her present task was to defend his privacy, not to invade it.

The room was very still. The afternoon light, slowly veering, left in shadow first one group of roofs and towers, then another; the cloud-masses faded into twilight. At length Halo got up. Their lodging was without electric light, and she was sure Vance would not know how to light the oil-lamp she had put on his table. She was glad of the excuse for joining him . . .

"Vance," she said, opening the door. No one answered, and she saw that the room was empty. The door which led to the landing was ajar—he had evidently gone out. Probably he had felt tired after his hours of writing, and had wandered away without thinking of telling her. She lit the lamp and looked about her. Cigarette ends strewed the floor, and the blue writing pad on the desk, immaculate, untouched, looked up at her ironically. He had not written a line . . .

She stood struggling with a sense of disappointment. He had seemed so sure that he wanted to go on with his work—that this was the very place where it would come to him without an effort! Well, what of that? Did she still imagine that an artist, a creator, could always know in advance exactly in what conditions and at what hour the sacred impulse would come?

She went back for her hat and coat, and descended the dark narrow stairs. Slowly she sauntered through the streets that led to the cathedral, peering with short-sighted eyes to right and left in the hope of meeting him. Lamps had begun to twinkle in the houses. Before long the sacristan would pass on his rounds and close the cathedral doors. Halo thought: "He's surely in there; I must find him before the place is locked up." She pushed back the leather curtain and went in.

At first the darkness confused her. Each figure straying among the shadows seemed to have Vance's outline; but as she drew nearer she found herself mistaken. From aisle to aisle, from Christian altar to Moorish *mihrab,* she explored the baffling distances; but Vance was not there. She returned to the outer world, and began to walk back through the modern quarter; and suddenly, in front of a glittering café, she found him installed at a table. He greeted her with a smile, and said: "What will you have? I had to take a vermouth because it was all I knew how to ask for."

"I've been hunting all over for you—" she began; then broke off, annoyed by the maternal note in her voice. "I thought you might want a Spanish drink, and an interpreter to order it," she added laughing.

"No. I got on all right. I've been all up and down the place; then I sat down here to watch the crowd." He waited while she ordered a cup of coffee, and went on: "I couldn't write a line after all."

"What you need is to take a good holiday first, and not bother about your book."

His remote and happy smile enveloped her. "I'm not bothering about anything on God's earth." He was looking at her curiously. "Do you know, you've got just the shape of the head of one of those statues of the Virgin they carry in the processions—you remember: the one they showed us yesterday in that chapel? A little face, long, and narrowing down softly to the chin—like a fruit or a violin; the way yours does . . . God, I wish I could draw! I believe I might have . . ." He leaned across and twisted his fingers through hers. "What's the use of sight-seeing, anyhow, when I've got you to look at?"

The blood rose to Halo's face. She felt a sudden shyness when he looked at her with those eyes full of secret visions. How long would it be before he had gone her round, and needed new food for his dream? She thought: "Shall I have to content myself with being a peg to hang a book on?" and found an anxious joy in the idea.

When she had finished her coffee Vance pushed back the table. "Come—let's go down to the bridge and listen to the river in the dark . . . I don't believe I'll ever write a line again; not in this place anyway," he declared serenely.

ℰ V ℱ

HALO WONDERED at her own folly in imagining that
Vance, with a whole new world pressing on his imagination, would be able to take up the thread of his work
with the composure of a seasoned writer. Life with him
was teaching her more about the creative processes. She
saw that Vance himself had not yet taken his own measure, or calculated the pressure of new sensations and
emotions on his inventive faculty. His impulse was either to try to incorporate every fresh suggestion, visual
or imaginative, into the fabric of his work, or to build a
new story with it; but when the impressions were too
abundant and powerful they benumbed him.

For the moment he appeared to have lost even the
desire to store up his sensations. What he wanted was to
study Spanish history and art, to learn the language, to
let the fiery panorama roll past his idle imagination. If he
had known how to paint, he told Halo, that might have
been an outlet. It was a pity, he thought, he hadn't gone
in for painting instead of writing—painting, or perhaps
sculpture. Some palpable flesh-and-blood rendering of
life, rather than the gray disintegration of words. He
recalled the hours he had spent in New York, on the
broken-hinged divan in the studio of the young woman
sculptor, Rebecca Stram, watching her mauling her
clay. . . "I tell you what it is: words are the last refuge
of the impotent. Writing is inexcusable in anybody who
isn't blind or paralyzed. It's an infirmity, a palsy—that's
what it is. The fellows who 'grab' life, as Goethe called
it, are the conquerors who turn it into form and colour

38

. . . Damn words; they're just the pots and pans of life, the pails and scrubbing-brushes. I wish I didn't have to think in words . . . I sometimes feel as if I had them in my veins instead of blood. Sometimes I even wish I didn't have you to talk to, so that I could get away from words forever . . . Why don't you tell me just to hold my tongue, and live?"

This was one mood; but in others he declared that in yielding to it he had blasphemed against the Holy Ghost. "The tongue of fire descends on a man in one form or another, no knowing which; all a fellow can do is to catch the flame and nurse it, whatever it happens to produce . . . The other day I was haranguing you about the difference between plastic expression and interpreting things in words. Utter rubbish, of course. Why the deuce didn't you tell me so? The difference is in the mind, not in the material or the tool. If words are a man's tools he's got to paint or model with *them* . . . or compose symphonies with *them* . . . that's all. Look here, Halo—any idea what I've done with vol. three of Prescott? No—? I had it with me yesterday when we went out to Medina Zahara, didn't I? And my Spanish grammar too! Lord, did I go and leave them both out there, do you suppose?"

Halo sighed, and thought that as for the Prescott it didn't really matter. She had brought with her all the latest and most erudite works on Christians and Moors in the peninsula; but after a glance at Dozy, and a little half-hearted plodding in Hume, he had disappointed her by rejecting all her authors for Prescott and Washington Irving. "But, Vance, dear, they were so undocumented. Prescott was wonderful for his day, of course; but so much that we know now was not available then. And as for Washington Irving . . ." Vance laughed, and turned over on his face in the grass where he and Halo were sitting, on the sunburnt downs above Cordova. "Well, they just roll over me like waves," he said, leaning his chin on his locked hands and gazing down at the ancient city. He lay there in silence, his brows wrinkled against the glare, with now and then a faint tremor of the nostrils, like the twitching of a sensitive animal's. Once he stretched out a hand, stroking the short grass and plucking at a clump of dwarf herbs that he crushed against his face. "Smells like sun and incense—as if it was the breath of the old place." He held out the tuft to Halo. It was hot and aromatic, full of the flame of a parched earth and the vibration of bees. "It's like my happiness," she thought. She lay there in an idle ecstasy. Overhead a great bird of prey circled against the blue; and Halo remembered how she had once thought of happiness as something bright-winged, untameable, with radiant alien eyes. Now the wings were folded and the strange guest lay asleep in her heart. She was no more afraid of it than a young mother is of her child; only perpetually conscious of it, watching it with wakeful eyes, as the mother watches while her child sleeps. And she thought: "If I could get quite used to it perhaps it would get used to me too, and never stir. If only I could learn to stop watching it."

Vance raised himself on his elbow. "See here," he broke out, "what I really want is to write poetry. From the very first I've always felt inside of myself that for me it was that or nothing. All the rest is just pot-boiling. Using words to tell stories with is like paving the kitchen-floor with diamonds. God! Words are too beautiful to be walked over in that way, with muddy feet, like the hall oil-cloth. Supposing Keats had used *his* words to write best-sellers with? Don't it strike you like turning a Knights of Pythias picnic loose down there in the cathedral? Words ought to be received at the door of

the mind with lighted torches and incense and things—
like one of the big church ceremonies you described to
me. See here, Halo—when did you say they danced before the altar of the cathedral at Seville? I wish I could
get that into poetry. . ."

The bright confusion of his mind sometimes
charmed and sometimes frightened her. She was so
much afraid of laying clumsy hands on his capricious
impulses that she felt herself sinking into the character
of the blindly admiring wife. Yet that had not been her
dream, or his. She remembered how her frank criticism
had guided and stimulated him while he was writing
"Instead", and she did not quite know why she had become so uncertain and shy in talking with him of his
literary plans, so fearful of discouraging or misdirecting
him. Sometimes she asked herself if it would not have
been better if they had stayed in America, in some out-
of-the-way place where this tremendous vision of a new
world would not have thrust itself between him and his
work. Yet she felt it must be a weak talent that could
not bear the shock of wonder and the hardening processes of experience. Presently the mass of new impressions would be sorted out and dominated by his indefatigable mind, and become a part of its material—and
meanwhile, what mattered but that he and she were together, with these waves of beauty breaking over them?
All she had to do was to hold her breath and wait. She
slipped her hand in his. "Do you remember when you
read me your first poetry, that morning up on Thundertop?"

A few days later Vance came in from one of his
dreaming rambles about Cordova, and said, with illuminated eyes: "I've met a man who says we're fools not to
go straight off to Granada."

Halo could not repress a faint movement of impatience. It was a little exasperating to have this information imparted as a novelty. Vance seemed to have no recollection of her having told him repeatedly that they ought to get to Granada before the rainy weather began.

"A man? What sort of a man?"

"He said his name was Alders," said Vance, as if that settled everything.

Halo made a hasty mental calculation of the probable cost of cancelling the lease of their lodgings, which they had had to take for the rest of the season. The landlady would certainly be nasty; but Halo had fought such battles before, and instantly began sharpening her mental weapons. "Well, all right. Do you want me to get ready?"

"He says we ought to," Vance repeated serenely.

For the next two or three days he vanished frequently to rejoin his new friend. Halo gathered that Alders was a wandering American who wrote—at least he was planning a book on Saint Theresa. "For the present he's just letting Spain soak into him," Vance explained. He did not offer to produce Alders for Halo's inspection, and she did not suggest that he should. She was beginning to realize that in throwing in her lot with Vance's she had entered into an unknown country—as unknown to her as Spain was to him, and with far fewer landmarks to guide her. When Lewis Tarrant made a new acquaintance, and imparted the fact to his wife, his words at once situated the person in question, socially and intellectually. But Vance could not situate anybody. He could only say that he liked a fellow, or didn't like him. He seemed to think that in some mysterious way the impressions he could not sum up in words would be telepathically communicated to Halo; but this was impossible, for they had no common ground of reference.

Halo tried to bridge the gulf by declaring cheerfully: "Well, I'm sure I'll like him if you do," but Vance answered, with a sort of school-boy vagueness: "Oh, I dunno that I like him as much as all that," making no allusion to Halo's possible opinion of Alders. He seemed to regard Alders as exclusively his own, as a child might a new toy.

A few more days passed; then Vance suddenly announced that he thought it would be fun to go over to Granada in the touring car that was starting the next morning. Could Halo be ready, did she think? After another mental readjustment she said, yes, of course, if he'd be home in the afternoon in time to pack his things; to which he cheerfully agreed.

At the tourist agency Vance surprised her by engaging three seats. Alders, he said, was going to Granada too, and had asked to have his ticket taken for him. An exclamation of annoyance was on Halo's tongue; but she repressed it, and bought the ticket.

The next morning, when they arrived at the square from which the car started, Vance said: "Here's Alders," and a nondescript young man in a shabby gray suit came forward. He greeted Halo with an awkward bow, and started to climb to Vance's side; but at the last moment he bent over to say something to the conductor, as the result of which he was transferred to a seat several rows behind them, and a girl with large horn spectacles and a portable gramophone was pushed into his place. Vance laughed. "You scared him—he's as shy as a hawk." He seemed content to know that his new friend was making the journey with them, and bound for the same destination.

At Granada they went for a night to an hotel in the town, and the next morning Vance proposed that they should look for rooms in one of the English *pensions* on the Alhambra hill. Alders, who knew the place well, had given him several addresses; and though Halo was beginning to resent Alders's occult participation in their affairs, she agreed to the suggestion. But half way up the hill Vance deserted her, captivated by the carolling of fountains under the elms, and the shadowy invitation of the great Moorish archway. "See here, Halo—this beats everything. Do you mind if I wait for you here while you look for rooms? I shouldn't be any good anyway," he said persuasively; and Halo, admitting the fact, went on alone.

On the hillside below the hotels she wandered about, consulting Alders's list, till a dusty stony lane ended unexpectedly at a gate inscribed: "English Pension. View. Afternoon Tea"; and in a tumble-down house among oranges and pomegranates she was shown two rooms high up on a roof-terrace. The rooms were comfortless, and not too clean; but the terrace overhung the fairest landscape on earth. Halo concluded her bargain and hurried back rejoicing to the Alhambra. She was impatient to lead Vance up to this magical proscenium, and hear his cry at first sight of the snow peaks and green plain. She found him curled up in a coign of the wall above the city. He seemed to have forgotten the errand on which she had left him, and protested at being obliged to leave his warm corner. "What's the use of finding such a place if you come and root me out of it?" "I've found something even better—come and see!" she exulted; and reluctantly he let her lead him out of the Alhambra and up the hill. But when she introduced him to the terrace he cried out: "Say, are we really going to live here? Why the devil did you let me waste all that time at Cordova? Alders *told me*—"

Halo laughed ironically. "I told you long before

Alders. Only you're so used to the sound of my voice that I don't believe you hear it any longer."

He was looking at her with beauty-drunk eyes. "Maybe I don't," he agreed contentedly, turning back to lean over the parapet. Halo could not help being a little vexed that they should owe the discovery of this vantage-ground to Alders. She might easily have found it herself—but it was in pursuance of his indications that she had turned down that uninviting lane. She wished she were able to feel more grateful.

Alders came up to see if they were satisfied. He himself lodged, mysteriously, somewhere below in the town; but he was always on the Alhambra hill. That first day they asked him to tea, in one of the little tea-rooms near the Alhambra, and afterward he walked up with them to the Generalife. His shyness in Halo's presence persisted—or at any rate, his reserve. For she was never, then or afterward, sure if he were shy or merely indifferent, any more than she could decide if he were young or old. She could barely remember, when he was out of sight, what he looked like. There was something shadowy and indefinite about his whole person. His dullish sandy hair merged into the colour of his skin, his thin lips were of the same tint as his small unkempt moustache. She had seen straw-coloured and sand-coloured people, but never any whom protective mimicry had provided with so complete a neutrality. His manner was neutral too, if anything could be called a manner which seemed rather a resigned endurance of human intercourse. Judging from Mr. Alders's attitude one would have supposed that his one aim was to avoid his fellow beings; but Halo presently discovered that this shrinking exterior concealed a ravenous sociability.

She recognized in him the roving American with a

thin glaze of culture over an unlettered origin, and a taste for developing in conversation theories picked up in random reading, or evolved from an imperfect understanding of art and history. He told them that among his friends (he implied that they were few but illustrious) he was known as "The Scholar Gypsy"—adding that the name (taken, he smilingly explained, from a poem by Matthew Arnold) had been conferred on him because of his nomadic habits; perhaps also, he concluded, of his scholarly tastes. He made these boasts with such disarming modesty that Halo could not resent them, though she failed to understand the impression they produced on Vance. But gradually she discovered that under his literary veneer Alders possessed a miscellaneous accumulation of facts and anecdotes about places and people. His mind was like the inside of one of the humble curiosity-shops on the way up to the Alhambra, where nothing was worth more than a few pesetas; but these odds and ends of cosmopolitan experience amused Vance, and excited his imagination, though Halo noticed that he was less impressed by them than by Alders's views on Croce or Spengler, or the origin of religious mysticism in Western Europe. Vance's ravenous desire to learn more and more—to learn, all at once, everything that could be known on every subject—was stimulated by his new friend's allusions and references, and Halo saw that he ascribed her own lukewarm share in their talks to feminine inferiority. "Of course general ideas always bore women to death," he said in a tone of apology, as they climbed to their pension after a long afternoon with Alders at the Alcobazar. "But you see I was pretty well starved for talk out at Euphoria—and in New York too. God! When I think of the raw lumps of ignorance those fellows used to feed me, at the Cocoanut Tree and at Rebecca Stram's . . . I tell you what,

Halo, going round with a man like Alders, who's got art
and philosophy at his fingers' ends—"

She was on the point of interrupting: "Yes, but
only there—" but she saw Vance's glowing face, and understood that he was getting from his new friend something which a scholar like George Frenside might not
have been able to give him. There was excitement in
the very confusion of Alders's references, and reassurance in their audacity. Vance seemed to feel that he too
might become a scholar after a few more talks with
Alders, and that the wisdom of the ages might emerge
from a breathless perusal of Samuel Butler and Have-
lock Ellis.

It was hard on Halo to have it thought that such
flights were beyond her; but she told herself again that
at this stage her business was to hold her breath and
watch. Though she resented Alders's incursion into
their lives she was relieved that Vance did not expect
her to share in his confabulations with his new friend;
and she came to see how natural it was that to a youth
who had lacked all artistic and intellectual training the
other's shallow culture should seem so deep. The clever
young writers he had known in New York had read only
each other and "Ulysses"; here was a man full of the
curious lore of the past, who could at any rate put the
Cocoanut Tree clan in their true perspective.

This hunger and thirst of Vance's was all the more
touching to Halo because she knew that his eagerness to
learn everything at once was due not to superficiality
but to the sense of time lost and of precious secrets kept
from him. "If only I'd had Alders's advantages!" he
burst out one evening, in passionate retrospection; and
she could not help answering: "It was funny, though,
his thinking you'd never heard of Matthew Arnold."

"Well, I don't believe those Cocoanut Tree fellows

have; or if they have, they've thrown him overboard without reading him. They haven't got time to embalm dead bodies, they say—leave that to the morticians. And there they sit and talk endlessly all day long about nothing! Look here, Halo—I sometimes think I was meant to be a student and not a writer; a 'grammarian', like the fellow in the Browning poem. Alders was telling me last night how many years the Jesuit novitiate lasts—he thought at one time of being a Jesuit. Well, I tell you what, it gave me a big idea of those old fellows who weren't afraid of being left behind . . . weren't always trying to catch up . . . catch up with *what?* Why; just with other fellows who were trying to catch up. Did you ever think of the beauty of not giving a damn if you were left behind?"

Yes; in those ways Alders was good for him. His talk was a blurred window; but through it the boy caught glimpses of the summits. Halo could have given him a clearer sight of them; but she recognized that the distance was yet too great between her traditional culture and Vance's untutored curiosities. This dawdling Autolycus, with his bag of bright-coloured scraps, might serve as a guide where she was useless.

Luckily there were days when Alders was off on his own mysterious affairs, and Halo had her lover to herself. Then life burned with beauty, and every hour was full of magic. Vance's successive declarations that he meant to write poetry, to take up painting, to immure himself in a scholar's cell, no longer frightened her. It was enchanting to watch the tumult of his mind, sun-flecked, storm-shadowed, subsiding in moonlit calm or leaping sky-ward in sun and gale. This journey was a time of preparation from which his imagination would come forth richer and more vigorous. Occasionally she wished his idleness were not so total, for she was afraid the lost habit of work might be hard to recover; but when she hinted this, he rejoined that she didn't understand the way the creative mind was made. "There's Alders, now—I suppose you might think he was loafing. . . Well, he's *amassing*. A very different thing. He told me he might very likely lie fallow another year before he wrote the first line of his book about the influence of Byzantine art on El Greco."

"On *what?* I thought he was collecting material for a life of St. Theresa."

Vance frowned impatiently. "Yes; he was. But he's put that aside, because he felt he ought to go into sixteenth century art in Spain before he tackles mysticism. He says you can approach spiritual phenomena only from the outside; the way they manifest themselves in art and architecture and the whole social structure. . . If you don't get that into your system first . . ."

Halo made no answer, and Vance continued, still in a slightly irritated tone: "I don't suppose you want me to be like those fellows that are sent to Europe for a year on a college scholarship, and are expected by the Faculty to come back with a masterpiece? I've heard you on the subject of those masterpieces. And a novel isn't a thesis anyhow—it's a live thing that's got to be carried inside of you before it can be born. I suppose I'm a trial to you sometimes," he concluded.

"Only when you imagine that I don't understand." But he protested that he never did; and side by side on their high-hung terrace they watched the full moon push up above the Sierra.

❧ VI ❧

THEIR ROOMS were not easy to warm, and the October winds began to rattle the windows; but Halo and Vance were loth to leave, and they always managed to find a warm corner in the courts of the Alhambra, or sheltered by the ilexes of the Generalife, where Vance could "lizard" in the sun, and turn over his dreams like bright-coloured shells and pebbles. He had begun again to discuss his literary plans with Halo; but he only toyed with them as distant possibilities. He still seemed to regard his genius as a beautiful capricious animal, to be fed and exercised when it chose, and by him alone; and she forbore to remind him of the days when her nearness had seemed necessary to inspire his work, and her advice to shape it. She told herself that in becoming his mistress she had chosen another field of influence, that to be loved by him, to feel his passionate need of her, was a rapture above the joys of comradeship; but in her heart she had dreamed of uniting the two. She was learning now that the ways of nature were slower and more devious than her sentimental logic had foreseen; and she tried to lose herself in the rich reality of her love.

Now and then they spoke of leaving Granada; but the talk did not reach any practical conclusion. Their plans offered to Vance as many alluring alternatives as his literary future, and what he liked best was to lie stretched out on the warm red wall of the Alhambra and dream of being elsewhere.

Alders, by his own account, had many friends in

Granada—he talked especially of an old Marquesa who lived in a palace behind the cathedral, with a statue of a captive Moor over the door. The old Marquesa, Alders said, was an authentic descendant of Bobadilla's, a wonderful woman in whose veins flowed the purest blood of Castilian and Moorish chivalry. One met at her house the oddest and most interesting specimens of the old Andalusian aristocracy. Regular palæoliths, they were; it would be a wonderful chance for Weston to document himself in such a prehistoric *milieu*, especially as he was thinking of laying the scene of his next novel in Spain . . . "Oh, are you?" Halo interrupted, glancing eagerly at Vance, who said, well, he'd had an idea lately that something amusing might be done with a young American in the wine business, sent to study the trade at a Spanish port in the eighteen thirties, say. . .

Alders declared that the possibilities of such a subject were immense, and he proposed that he and Vance should go to the Marquesa's that very evening; the lady, it appeared, still kept up the picturesque custom of the nightly *tertulia*, an informal reception at which people came and went as they pleased till daylight. Alders explained this to Halo in his shy halting way, and though she doubted the antiquity of the Marquesa's lineage, and even its authenticity, she assumed that Alders naïvely believed in them, and wondered how, without offending him, she could decline to be of the party. But he continued, more and more hesitatingly: "You don't mind, do you, Mrs. Weston, if I carry off Weston this once? It's all in the interest of his work . . . an exceptional opportunity. . ." Halo disliked being asked by a man like Alders if she "minded" anything that Vance chose to do; and her laugh perhaps betrayed her irritation. "I'm sure it will amuse you—you'd better go," she said to Vance, as if it were he who had made the sugges-

tion. There were times when she could not help treat-
ing Alders as if she had not noticed that he was there.

The next morning she gathered from Vance that
the Marquesa was in fact a rather splendid figure, in a
vast mouldy palace with "huge things hanging on the
walls—you know—," and a lot of people coming and
going, men and women, eating ices and talking a great
deal. His vague description gave Halo the impression
that he had been among people of the world, and she
was annoyed, in spite of herself, that Vance should have
figured as the hanger-on of Alders.

"I'm glad you've had a glimpse of Spanish society;
but it's rather odd that your friend didn't think of asking me to go with you." The words really reflected her
dislike of Alders rather than any resentment at not
being included in the party; but when they were spoken
she felt how petty they sounded. "Of course," she added
quickly, "I didn't want to go—that sort of thing bores
me to tears; I merely meant that if Alders had known a
little more about the ordinary social rules he would
have felt he ought at least . . ." She stopped, silenced
by the colour that rose to Vance's forehead.

"Vance—" she exclaimed, in sudden anger, "do
you mean it was because . . . Does Alders know that
we're not married?"

Vance looked at her in surprise. "Why, of course he
knows. I told him the very first thing how splendid
you'd been . . . coming to me straight off, like that
. . . he thought it was great of you. . ."

"Oh, don't please! I mean, I don't need Alders's
approval—." She could hardly tell why she was so indignant; had she been asked point-blank if she were Vance
Weston's wife she would certainly have denied it, and
have said that she called herself so only for the con-
venience of travel. But this concerned only herself and

Vance, and the discovery that he had been talking her over with a stranger picked up at a café was intolerable to her. Alders, of course, had cross-questioned Vance to satisfy his insatiable craving for gossip; but how could Vance have fallen into such a trap?

"Why, you don't mind, do you? I thought you'd have despised me for pretending," Vance began; but without heeding him she interrupted: "That was the reason, then! He proposed to you to go with him alone because he knew you were travelling with your mistress, and he couldn't have asked his Marquesa to receive me? Was that it?"

Vance reddened again. "He said how funny and fossilized that kind of people were . . . but I never thought you'd care; you always seem to hate seeing new people."

"Of course I don't care; and of course I hate seeing people I don't know anything about. . ."

"Well, then that's all right," said Vance.

"I don't know what you call all right. Most men would resent such a slight—"

"What slight?"

She saw that his perplexity was genuine, but that made it none the less irritating. There were moments when Vance's moral simplicity was more trying than the conventionalities she had fled from.

"Can't you see—?" she began; and then broke off. "I sometimes think you keep all your psychology for your books!" she exclaimed impatiently.

"You mean there are times when you think I don't understand you?"

"You certainly don't at this moment. I won't speak of the good taste of discussing our private affairs with a stranger—but that you shouldn't see that any slight to a woman in my situation. . ."

"What about your situation?" he interrupted. "I thought you chose it—freely."

"When I did, I imagined you would know how to spare me its disadvantages!"

He stood silent, looking down at the rough tiles of their bedroom floor. Halo was trembling with the echo of her own words. The consciousness that their meaning was not the same to him made her feel angry and helpless. An impenetrable wall seemed to have risen between them.

"You mean that you hate our not being married?" he brought out, as if the idea were new to him.

"Certainly I do, when you put me in a position that makes it hateful."

"Like that old woman last night not wanting to receive you? It never occurred to me you'd want her to."

"Or that you ought not to have gone yourself, if she didn't want me?" His eyes were again full of surprise. Halo laughed nervously.

"I don't understand," he went on. "I thought you didn't care a straw about that sort of thing."

"I shouldn't if I felt you knew how to protect me."

She saw from his expression that her meaning was still unintelligible to him, and that he was struggling to piece her words together.

"What is there to protect you from?"

"Vance—if you can't understand!" She paused, her heart in a tumult. "How does your mother feel about the way we're living together?" she broke out abruptly.

A shade of embarrassment stole over his face. "How on earth do I know?"

"Of course you know! She hates it—and me, probably. I daresay she wouldn't receive me if I went to Euphoria with you. And my mother hates it quite as much. My going away with you like this made her terribly unhappy. And yet you say you don't understand—!"

"Oh, see here, Halo—if that's what you mean! Of course I know how my mother feels about marriage in general. It's all nonsense about her not receiving you; but I daresay she's unhappy about our being together in this way. The marriage ceremony is a kind of fetish to her. And I suppose your mother feels the same. But I never thought you would. I thought that for you our being together like this—so close and yet so free—was more than any marriage. I never dreamed you didn't look at it as I do. I thought you'd always felt differently from the people around you about the big things of life."

Halo was silent. She was bewildered by his incomprehension, yet moved by his evident sincerity. "You're terribly logical—and I suppose life isn't," she said at length, forcing a smile.

Vance stood before her, his gaze again bent on the floor. She saw that he felt the distance between them, and was wondering how to bridge it over. "I guess you worry about a lot of things that I haven't yet learned to take into account. What do you think we ought to do?" he asked abruptly.

The blood seemed to stop in her veins. She looked at him helplessly. "To do—to do?"

"I suppose," he interrupted, "the real trouble is that you don't like Alders."

This flash of insight startled her. She was beginning to see that though the conventional rules of life still perplexed him, and perhaps always would, he was disconcertingly close to its realities.

"If you don't want me to go around with Alders, I won't, of course. He said the other day he thought maybe you didn't want me to."

The mention of Alders renewed her irritation.

"How can you think I want to interfere with you in any way? What I can't understand is your lowering yourself to talk me over with a stranger."

There was another silence, and she began to tremble inwardly. To discuss things with him was like arguing with some one who did not use the same speech.

"I guess I'm the stranger here, Halo. I can't understand your supposing that I'd speak of you to anybody in a way that could lower either you or me. I don't yet know what's made you angry."

"Angry? I'm not angry! I can't bear to have you speak of me as if I were a silly woman with a grievance."

"I suppose everything I say is bound to sound to you like that, as long as I don't understand what the grievance is."

"When a man says he doesn't understand a woman it's because he won't take the trouble."

"Or feels it's useless."

"Is that what you feel?"

"Well—maybe I will, soon."

"No. Don't be afraid! I shan't be here then—"

She heard the echo of her own words, and broke off dismayed. A longing overcame her to be taken into his arms and soothed like a foolish child. Of course that would come in a moment. She felt her whole body drawing her to him; but though she waited he did not move or speak. He seemed remote, out of hearing, behind the barrier that divided them. She thought: "He's been through scenes like this with Laura Lou, and he's sick of them. . . He thought that with me everything was going to be different. . ."

At length Vance said slowly: "You must do whatever you want." She did not speak, and he added: "I guess I'll go out for a walk." His voice sounded cold, almost indifferent. How could she have imagined he was

waiting to snatch her to his breast? He was simply counting the minutes till their senseless discussion was over,
and he could make his escape. His inflexible honesty was
deadly—she felt herself powerless against it, and could
think of nothing to say. He took up his hat and went
out, carrying her happiness with him.

❧ VII ❧

Halo sat alone among the ruins. It was one of the moments when life seems to turn and mock one's magnanimity. When she had torn up her lawyer's letter, and cast in her lot with Vance's, she fancied she was tearing up all the petty restrictions of her past. In her new existence the meaner prejudices would no longer reach her. All the qualities in her which could serve the man she loved—her greater experience, her knowledge of the world, her familiarity with Vance's character, her faith in his genius—seemed to justify her decision. It was to be her privilege to give him what he had always lacked: intellectual companionship and spiritual sympathy. And now, for a whim, for nothing, she had risked her hardwon happiness and dropped to the level of any nagging woman—all because he had unwittingly offended the very prejudices from which she imagined he had delivered her!

The worst of it was that she was no untaught girl among the first pitfalls of passion. Psyche turning her lamp on the secret face of love was a novice; Halo Tarrant knew the ways of men, yet at the first occasion she had repeated Psyche's blunder. She had found out now how little importance Vance attached to the idea of marriage—and she had shown him the social value it had for her. Everything that she had meant to leave undefined and fluid in their relation her own act had forced him to define and crystallize, and thereby she had turned the lamp on her own face. Yet she could not help feeling as she had felt. Her relations with the men she had grown up among had been regulated by a code of which Vance did not know the first word, and she now saw how such tacit observances may be inwoven with the closest human intimacies.

"Laura Lou couldn't understand a word of what he wrote or thought; but in my place she would have known at once that in discussing her situation with a stranger he was only proving his admiration for her." And she recalled a whimsical axiom of George Frenside's: "No passion can survive a woman's seeing her lover hold his fork in the wrong way."

The absurdity of it shook her out of her depression. Yes, a real passion could; she meant to prove it! She would show Vance that she understood his heart as well as his brain. She would propose to him to have Alders to dine that very evening, she would even suggest Vance's going off on a trip with his new friend if he wanted to. She would prove to him that her only happiness was in knowing that he was happy. Already she marvelled that anything else had seemed of the least moment. . .

The hours went by, and she sat alone in the dreary pension room. Rain-clouds hung low on the Sierra; summer seemed to have passed with the passing of her unclouded hours. She recalled Vance's impulsiveness, his moody fits. What if he had taken the train and gone off, heaven knew where, away from her tears and her reproaches? He would come back, of course; in her heart she was sure of him; but meanwhile what irreparable thoughts might he not be thinking?

She went down alone to lunch; then she rambled out aimlessly, hoping to run across him in some corner of the Alhambra hill. But a bleak wind blew over the ramparts, shaking the leaves from the elms, and she returned, chilled and discouraged, without having found him. She thought to herself: "I ought to have gone with him when he went out. I ought not to have let him carry away that distorted image of me. . . I ought to have done something, said something, that would have blotted it out before his eyes had grown used to it. . . And I stood there, and couldn't think of anything!"

She recalled her differences with Lewis Tarrant, the low-pitched quiet conflicts from which she always emerged more worn than after a noisy quarrel. No doubt Vance was feeling at this moment as she used to feel after those arid arguments. He would never say of her again that she was like the air he breathed! She sat down and rested her tired head on her arms.

She was still sitting there when the door opened and he came in. At the turn of the door-handle she knew he was there, and sprang up. "Vance—!" She stood looking at him, filling her eyes with his face as if he had come back from the dead.

He gave a shy laugh, and one hand fumbled in his pocket. "You liked this the other day—." He pulled out a little packet. "Here." He pushed it into her hand. She was touched by the boyishness of the gesture; but instantly she thought: "He used to make up his quarrels with Laura Lou by bringing her presents . . ." and his impulse seemed to lose its spontaneity.

"But, Vance, I didn't want a present—." Seeing his look of disappointment she regretted the words. "Oh, but this is lovely," she hurried on, slipping through her fingers an old peasant necklace of garnets and enamelled gold. She remembered having admired it one day in an antiquary's shop. "I didn't even know you knew I'd seen it," she said, her voice shaken by the returning rush of happiness.

"I didn't. Alders told me; he notices those things more than I do," said Vance with simplicity.

Halo's heart dropped. She looked at the necklace

with disenchanted eyes. Then she thought: "If he tells me the truth it's because he still loves me, and doesn't feel that he has to pretend"; and she slipped the trinket about her neck. Vance looked at her earnestly. "You really like it?"

"I love it—but you've been very extravagant, haven't you?"

He laughed and shook his head. "Call it a wedding present."

Halo echoed the laugh. "A wedding present? Oh, please not, darling; because I want to wear it at once!"

"Well, you won't have to wait long, will you? Can't we get married pretty soon now?" Vance looked at her shyly, as though making the offer to a young girl he secretly worshipped, but was afraid of frightening by a too impulsive word.

Halo saw that he was trying to reassure her, to convince her of his love; he had trembled for their future as she had. For a moment she found no words; then they came, quick and passionate. "No, no! Don't let's talk of that now. It won't be soon, at any rate; my divorce, I mean; probably not for a long time—I don't care if I never get it. Nothing can be as perfect as this. If there's any way of being happier, I don't want to know it—it would frighten me! In heaven there's no marrying or giving in marriage. Let's stay in heaven as long as we can." She went up to him and found the safety of his arms.

Their second honeymoon had the factitious fervour which marks such reconstructions. Halo had grown afraid to take her happiness for granted, and afraid lest Vance should detect her fears. The simplest words they exchanged seemed to connote a background of artifice. There were times when the effort to be careless and buoyant made her feel old and wary; others when the perfection of the present filled her with a new dread of the future. There was hardly an hour when she could yield without afterthought to the natural joy she had known during her first weeks with her lover.

She had hesitated for a long time before answering the letter her lawyer had sent to the steamer; now she wrote briefly, thanking him for his advice, but saying that the affair must take its course. For her part she would not attempt to interfere. She was travelling abroad with Vance Weston, as her husband could easily assure himself, and he was at liberty to divorce her if he preferred a scandal, and was unwilling to let her have her liberty without it. To her mother, from whom she had received several letters full of distressful entreaties, she wrote in the same strain. "Dearest, dearest, do try to understand me, and be patient with me if you can't. I love Vance, I believe in his genius, I went to him because he was lonely and unhappy and needed me, and I mean to stay with him as long as he wants me. If Lewis won't let me have my divorce on the terms we had agreed on he can easily get all the evidence he needs and take proceedings against me. But if he would rather forego his freedom than give me mine, even on those conditions, his decision can make no difference to me, for I shall be proud to live with Vance as his mistress. Nothing that Lewis does can really hurt me, and it seems a pity he should sacrifice his own happiness when he is so powerless to interfere with mine."

The words, as she re-read them, sounded rather theatrical, and she would have preferred to avoid such a declaration of independence; but it had the advantage of defining her situation, and cutting off her retreat. She would have liked to show the two letters to Vance, but she refrained lest he should think she was trying to re-

mind him of what she had given up for him. Such a
reminder might seem like a claim, and in her heart she
was afraid to make it; yet an instant later she thought:
"Whatever happens, I must keep him now," and seeing
in a flash the desert distances of life without him she forgot her magnanimous resolve to respect his freedom.

To Vance, it was obvious, the whole episode had
been less important. He had never even asked her how
she knew she would not be able to obtain her freedom
immediately; the question of divorce and marriage
seemed to have dropped out of his mind. "He takes what
I say so literally," she reflected, "that I daresay he thinks
I really don't care about it"; yet the possibility that he
might think so was a surprise to her. But no doubt he
had had many lovers' quarrels with Laura Lou, perhaps
with other women of her type, and was used to pacifying
them with a kiss and a present. Probably he regarded
such incidents as inevitable interruptions to his work,
and had learned to dismiss them from his mind as soon
as they were over. . . Ah, if only he were working now!
If she could have seen any returning impulse of activity,
any trace of that impatience to express himself which
had been his torment and rapture when she had first
known him, how eagerly she would have banished her
anxieties, how jealously she would have defended his
privacy! The hours he spent away from her were not
spent in solitary toil, but in dreaming and dawdling, or
in long discursive sessions with Alders at restaurants and
cafés. She made a fresh effort to conceal her dislike of
Alders, and he sometimes came up to the pension to
dine, and went with them afterward to the tawdry
dances in the gypsy quarter, or to concerts of local
music in the cafés. But Alders was never wholly at his
ease with her, and was therefore less entertaining to
Vance than when the two were alone. "He gets all

wooden when you're around. I guess he's woman-shy. I can see he doesn't amuse you," Vance commented unconcernedly. Halo understood the reason; she saw that Alders knew she had taken his measure, and that he ascribed her lack of cordiality to his not being exactly in her class. To Alders, the victim of unsatisfied social cravings, she was the fashionable woman in whose company he was not at ease; whereas Vance, for whom social distinctions did not exist, felt no constraint in her presence because to him she was as different from every one else as a nymph or an angel. And after two or three evenings of heat and noise and bad tobacco in the sham underworld of gypsies and guitarists she let Vance rejoin his friend without her.

There was no physical jealousy in the irritation which his absences caused her. As a woman she was still sure of her hold; as a comrade and guide she felt herself superseded. When he began to work again he might still need her as audience and critic; but meanwhile his restless mind was always straying from her. He had begun to learn Spanish, and this was the only task he had persisted in. His insatiable intellectual curiosity made him chafe at the obstacle of a strange language; and tramping the streets with Alders was a quicker method of learning than reciting conjugations to a snuffy professor. Meanwhile, with the beginning of the autumn rains, their rooms had become too cold and damp, and they began to look about for others. But one morning Vance abruptly announced that he wanted to go for a couple of months to some sea-port in the south—say Malaga or Cadiz—where he could settle down to his new book in the proper environment.

"Your new book?" Halo echoed, eagerly.

Yes, he said; he was beginning to want to get to

work again. And he ought to know something about life in a Spanish trading port if he was to situate his story there, oughtn't he—the story of the young American sent over from Boston or Salem in the eighteen thirties, to learn the wine business in Spain: the subject Alders had first suggested. He'd been thinking it over a good deal lately, and gradually it had taken hold of him. He liked the idea of a heroine who could be called *Pilar*— she was to look like that little Virgin with the pear-shaped face that they'd seen at Cordova. Well—hadn't Halo anything to say to the idea? he broke off, as she continued to listen in silence.

"I thought you meant to go on with 'Magic'," she said at length.

"Well, so I did—but now I don't. I don't suppose it's any use trying to make you see. . ."

"I think I see. It's perfectly natural that new scenes should suggest new subjects."

He looked at her with a smile of relief. "I'm glad you feel that—"

"Only you said you'd never do another story like 'Instead'—a 'costume piece', I mean. I thought you were determined not to go back to that, but always to do contemporary subjects."

"Oh, these 'neverses' and 'alwayses'! Who was the gent who talked about some word or other not being in the lexicon of youth? I'm sure the lexicon of art has no hard-and-fast words in it like always and never. I do what I'm moved to do; any artist, even the greatest of 'em, will tell you it's all he *can* do. It's the eternal limitation. . . See here, Halo, I didn't mean to bother you again with this kind of talk. Nobody but a writer can understand—but you must trust me to know what I'm after; what I'm driven after, as it were."

She recognized the Alders vocabulary, and said with a slight shrug: "What I do understand is that it will do you good to get to work again."

Instantly his eyes darkened. "Ah, that's it! You're disappointed in me—you think I've just been losing my time all these months?"

"We shall be able to judge of that better when you begin to write again," she answered, smiling.

"All right, then. What do you say to Cadiz? The climate's better there, isn't it? Or I might call her Concepcion, perhaps—that's even funnier, if she's to be married to a Puritan from Salem. Don't you think so?"

Halo hesitated. She had meant, when they left Granada, to propose that they should go to Florence or Rome for the winter. She felt that Vance needed the stimulus of a cultivated society; she would have suggested Paris if their situation had not made it embarrassing for her to settle down in a city where, at every turn, she was sure to run across friends and acquaintances. Until the matter of the divorce was settled in one way or another she preferred to avoid such encounters. But now she decided that she must let him have his way, lest he should feel that, at the very moment when his writing mood returned, she had needlessly interfered with it. "By all means, let's try Cadiz," she agreed.

"But you don't believe in my idea for the new novel?"

"I believe in your trying it out, at any rate."

"You're a great girl, Halo," he said joyously. "I love the way you look when you hate a thing, and think you can persuade people that you like it."

It was on the tip of her tongue to answer: "I suppose you mean the way I look at Alders—" but she refrained, and merely said with a laugh: "It's the first

principle of every woman's job." Inwardly, she was
wondering what had made Vance suddenly decide to go
to Cadiz. She felt sure that Alders had suggested the
change, and that he had his own reasons for wishing to
exchange Granada for the south. But the next day
Vance asked her if she would mind if Alders came up to
say goodbye. She minded so little that she had to bear in
mind Vance's remark on her inability to conceal her
feelings. "Goodbye? Oh, Alders is off too, is he? Yes, of
course I'll see him." But she still felt that, unless Alders
had found some one else to prey on conversationally,
this leave-taking was probably only a feint.

Alders appeared punctually, and overcame his shyness sufficiently to thank her for her kindness, and
mumble something about its being a privilege he would
never forget. She was on the point of asking him if he
would not be turning up later at Cadiz; but she refrained lest he should act on the suggestion, and merely
remarked that she supposed he thought the time for
leaving Spain had come.

"No, not leaving Spain; I don't expect to do that
for some time. Only leaving Granada." With increased
timidity he explained that he was joining a big shooting
party in Estremadura—rather a romantic sort of affair,
as they were to stay in a fortified castle among the
mountains, a place belonging to the old Marquesa. Her
sons had organized the party in honour of a young
cousin from Palermo who had come to Spain for the first
time, to visit the Marquesa; and as he didn't know a
word of Spanish, and as Alders spoke Italian, the latter
had been invited to join the expedition—"in the character of interpreter," Alders added, with a fresh access of
modesty which manifestly invited contradiction.

"The poor young man—what a blessing for him to

find somebody he can talk to!" Halo said cordially; and Vance added: "And somebody who knows the country inside out, like Alders."

"Oh, he's very much on the spot; he'll make his own discoveries. But it will be amusing to do what I can. As a collector of human antiquities, these great heraldic names always appeal to me." Alders addressed himself to Halo: "I once planned out a book on the relation between heraldry and religious symbolism. Take the Babylonian Fish God, for instance, who figures in the Zodiac, and then in the Roman catacombs as the sacred emblem of the Christ . . . and finally as the *armes parlantes* of some great mediæval family. I am sure you will recall which, Mrs. Weston? The idea is not without interest. . . But you've so many friends in European society," Alders broke off. "Very likely you know the Marquesa's cousin. It's a great name in Calabria . . . there's a cousinship with the Spanish Bourbons." He waited long enough to enjoy the taste of his own words, and to let Halo enquire the name. "The Duke of Spartivento," he replied devoutly.

After Alders had taken his leave, Vance sat indolently swinging his legs in the window-seat, while Halo returned to the task of sorting their books and gathering up the odds and ends which had accumulated in their little sitting-room. They had engaged places in the motor-coach for Cadiz, and both were full of the happy excitement of departure.

"What was that he called his new friend?" Vance mused. "It sounded like a thunderclap."

"Spartivento."

"Well, that's some name. What does it mean? Windjammer, I suppose?"

"More like wind-divider, I should say. It's the name of a big promontory off the coast of Southern Italy or

Sicily. Calabria, probably, as the family come from there."

"Why, are there real people called that? I had an idea Alders had made it all up. He gets word-drunk, sometimes."

"Oh, no. Not this time. It's really one of the titles of an old Italian family. I've often heard of them."

Vance lapsed into a marvelling silence until Halo, looking up from her work, abruptly accused him of having spirited away Ford's "Gatherings in Spain". But he merely declared that he knew where the book was, and stood staring at her with visionary eyes. "What a name! What a name! It sounds like that poem of Christopher Smart's, with every line beginning 'Glorious'. I should hate to have to live up to it, though, wouldn't you?"

Halo, absorbed in her task, replied absently that very likely the owner didn't; and Vance continued to murmur: "Spartivento—Spartivento: the wind-divider. Dividing the winds. Why, that's what genius ought to do, isn't it?"

"Genius," Halo replied gaily, "ought first of all to find me 'Gatherings in Spain'."

BOOK II

❦ VIII ❦

On a day of the following September Vance Weston was walking down the Boulevard Montparnasse.

He seemed to himself a totally different being from the young ignoramus who had left New York with Halo Tarrant a year previously. To begin with, he was the author of a second successful novel. "The Puritan in Spain", dashed off in a rush of inspiration during the previous autumn and winter, had come out in the spring, and attained immediate popularity. It was a vivid tale, sultry and savage as the Spanish landscape—so one reviewer said. Another compared it with "Carmen", to Mérimée's disadvantage; and a third declared that it combined the psychological insight of Tchekov with the sombre fatalism of Emily Brontë.

Vance did not wholly share these views. The thing had come too easily; he knew it had not been fetched up out of the depths. When he was among friends and admirers, with the warm breeze of adulation blowing through him, he remembered that greater geniuses had suffered from the same dissatisfaction, and his disbelief in his book grew more intermittent. But when he was alone he recalled the passionate groping conviction with which he had written "Instead", and the beginning of the unfinished novel, "Magic", and the feeling returned that those two books had been made out of his inmost substance, while the new one sprang from its surface. "The Puritan in Spain" was better written and more adroitly composed than its predecessors; there were scenes—little Pilar's death, or young Ralston's return to

73

Salem—that Vance could not re-read without a certain pleasure. These scenes had assuredly been written with the same conviction as those in the earlier books; yet now he felt only their superior craft. One half of him was proud of the book, and believed all that his readers said in praise of it; but the other half winced at their praise. "What's the use of doing anything really big? If ever I do, nobody'll read it. . . Well, and what if they don't? Who am I writing for, anyhow? Only the Mothers!" he thought savagely.

He swung along down the Boulevard Montparnasse and the Boulevard Raspail to the Seine. The sight of moving waters always arrested him, and he leaned on the parapet and watched the breeze crisp the river. The sun-flecks on the water mimicked the yellowing leaves of the trees along the banks, and streets and river were dappled with the same gold. Vance felt young and happy, and full of power. "Wait till I get my teeth into the next—" he thought, his joyous eyes on the river, the boats, the bridges, the gray palaces seen through fading trees. He would have liked to spend the rest of his life in that setting of foliage and buildings; yet he was beginning to feel that he would never get to work while he remained in Paris. "The Puritan in Spain" had been written in three months at Cadiz, in solitude and monotony—for the life there, alone with Halo, had been desperately monotonous. They knew no one; his friend Alders had vanished, and Vance had made no new acquaintances. He had imagined that once he was at work Halo's presence would be the only stimulus he needed; and no doubt it was, since the book had been written. But he had not felt her imagination flaming through him as it had when they used to meet at the Willows. The dampening effect of habit seemed to have extinguished that flame. She listened intelligently, but she no longer collaborated; and now that the book was done he knew she did not care for it. Perhaps that was the real source of his dissatisfaction; he told himself irritably that he was still too subject to her judgments.

During their first months together he and she had lived in a deep spiritual isolation; at times they seemed too close to each other, seemed to be pressing on each other, pinning down each other's souls. With the first intrusion from the outside, with the appearance of his queer friend Alders, from being too near they had suddenly become too far apart, at times almost out of sight; and since Alders had left them, and they had gone to Cadiz, there had been something strained and self-conscious in their relation, delicious though certain moments were.

His book finished, Vance was in a fever to get away, not only from Cadiz but from Spain; and Halo, after suggesting that they should end the winter in Italy, agreed that Paris might be best. She seemed to understand that after their months of solitude he needed the stimulus of a great city, the contact with conflicting views and ideas. He did not have to tell her—one never had to explain things to her. At first she had hesitated when he mentioned Paris, and he remembered her outbreak of resentment at not being invited to the old Marquesa's, and was reminded that she was sensitive about meeting strangers to whom her situation had to be explained; but when he asked her if she would rather go to some quiet place where they needn't bother with people she said she didn't see why they should have to do with people who bothered them. Now that the book was done, she added, he ought to go about again, and see something of the literary world; and so they decided on Paris.

Halo, almost at once, found a little flat with a studio, in a shabby friendly house near the Luxembourg; and her brother Lorry Spear, who had been living for some years in Paris, helped the pair to settle down, and introduced them to his friends. Vance had last seen Lorry Spear on the day when the latter had borrowed ten dollars of him. Lorry had never returned the ten dollars, and had figured mysteriously in a far more painful episode. Some valuable books had disappeared from the library of the Willows, which then belonged to old Mr. Tom Lorburn, Mrs. Spear's cousin, and Mr. Lorburn had suspected Vance of stealing and selling them. They had eventually been found at a second-hand bookseller's, and brought back (it was whispered) by Lewis Tarrant; and no more was said, or suggested, as to Vance's connection with the incident. But Vance knew, and so did Halo, that Lorry Spear had been the last person in the library of the Willows before the books vanished, and that he had been there alone.

This had left an unpleasant taste in Vance's mouth; but he had travelled too far from the raw boy of those days to be much affected by what concerned him; and like everything which did not strike to the quick, the affair had faded from his mind. Moreover he knew that Halo was fond of her brother, though aware of his weaknesses, and that she was glad to be near him again.

Life in Paris had roused in Vance a thousand new curiosities and activities. So far he had chiefly frequented the young men and women who met at the literary cafés of Montparnasse, and at the studios of the painters and decorators of the same group. In this world Lorry Spear was an important figure. He had made a successful start as a theatrical designer (also, it was rumoured, with Tarrant's aid) and his big studio in the painters' quarter off the Boulevard Raspail was the centre of an advanced group of artists and writers. A young woman with violently red hair and sharp cheek-bones presided over it when she could spare the time from a mysterious bookshop in the Latin Quarter, which she and a girl friend managed. The red-haired young lady, whose real name was Violet Southernwood, had been re-christened Jane Meggs when she threw in her lot with Lorry, who declared himself unable to endure the sound of so nauseatingly pretty a name. "A flower and a tree—southernwood's a shrub, isn't it? Well, anyway, I don't want anybody around here who smells of nature to that extent. And I should have had to call myself Mossy Stone, which would—what? Oh, well, Jane don't mind a joke, do you, my own?"

Miss Meggs said what nauseated *her* was having to associate with anybody who got his jokes out of Words-worth; but Lorry replied that Wordsworth was the au-thor of some of the most virulently hideous lines in En-glish poetry, and would soon be recognized as the Laureate of the new school of the Ugly-for-the-Ugly—"which is all ye need to know," he ended, while Miss Meggs groaned: "Lord—and he's read Keats too!"

Such pleasantries were too reminiscent of the Co-coanut Tree, and Rebecca Stram's studio, where Vance had picked up his first smattering of the new culture, and he preferred Alders's second-rate learning to this wholesale rejection of the past. But the group contained other elements. Among the young men, would-be writ-ers and painters, who laughed at Lorry's oracles, and idled away the hours capping each other's paradoxes, there were a few, French or English, who had joined the circle out of curiosity, and the exuberance of youth, but had already taken its measure. With two or three of them Vance and Halo had at once made friends, and founded a little circle of their own. These young men all professed the philosophic nihilism which was the creed of their group; but they were scholarly, analytical, intellectually curious and the cheap fireworks of Lorry's followers no longer satisfied them. What interested Vance, however, was less the nature of their views than the temper of their minds. He felt in all of them the fine edge of a trained intelligence—the quality he had always groped for without knowing what to call it or how to acquire it. Now, wherever he went, he seemed to meet it; as though it were as much a part of Paris as the stately architecture, the beauty of streets and river, and the sense of that other accumulated beauty stored behind museum walls. All through this great visual symphony he felt the fine vibrations of intelligence, the activity of high-strung minds. The young men who sat the night through talking with him were but obscure participants in this vast orchestration; but its rumour was always behind their talk. At first the life satisfied all Vance's needs. To look and listen and question was as stimulating as creation. Then, as always happened, he began to feel the need of setting his mind to work on the new material he had amassed, away from the excitement of discussion. This rhythmic recurrence of moods seemed to be a law of his nature, but he did not know how to formulate it to himself, still less to make it clear to Halo. It seemed hopeless to try to explain his sudden impulses of flight from everything that was delighting his imagination and expanding his mind. As he leaned on the parapet in the September sunshine he was thinking of this, not irritably or even impatiently, but with a sort of philosophic detachment. Communion with Halo had once been the completion of his dreams; now, when his thoughts took flight, she was the obstacle that arrested them. When he thought of her he felt almost as hopeless of explaining himself as he had with Laura Lou. She, who was alive and vibrating at so many

points, failed to feel the rhythm of his inner life. Everything on the surface of his intelligence she instantly
caught up and flashed back; he could laugh and talk
with her by the hour in the freedom of perfect understanding. But of the forces stored in him during his solitary wanderings, and his talks with this group of young
men, she guessed nothing, perceived nothing; and to this
he had made up his mind without any feeling of loneliness or resentment. He was beginning to discover that
he no longer needed a companion in these explorations
of the depths; what he most wanted then was to be alone.

Now and then he and Halo went off for a week-
end, to see some of the wonderful places she had told him
about. The first time Vance was alight with fervour and
curiosity. They had chosen Senlis, and loitered all day
around its ramparts, in its ancient streets, and on the
wall overlooking the mossy golden flanks of the cathedral tower. Then they went down into the square before
the west front of the cathedral, and stood gazing at the
death of the Virgin over the west portal, and at the
saints and prophets poised among the delicate grasses
and lichens of the cornice. Vance was in the state of re-
ceptiveness into which great impressions steal like angels. If he had been alone, and had not had to tell Halo
how beautiful he thought it, his well-being would have
been complete.

The experiment was so successful that Halo was
eager to repeat it; and soon afterward they went to
Chartres. She had decided that they must spend the
night there, so that Vance should see the cathedral in all
its aspects, at dusk, at sunrise, under the stars, and when
noonday jewelled its windows; she gave him the impression that they were going on a kind of spiritual honeymoon. It was unlucky that the day before he had been
seized by the desire to plan a new book, and was in that

state of inward brooding when the visible world becomes a blank; but Chartres was Chartres, the treasury of visions and emotions, the fountain of poetry and dreams. . . He only wished he hadn't read and heard so much about it. . .

And then, when at last he was face to face with the cathedral, he couldn't see it. He stood there, a little lump of humanity, confronting a great lump of masonry; that was as far as he could get. All the overwhelmingness left him standing in front of it, open-eyed and utterly insensible. Halo led him from one façade to the other, and at each halt he felt her watching him in tender expectancy. At last they went in, and walked slowly about that vast luminous world—and still he felt nothing, saw nothing. A band of trippers dragged by, deaf and vacant-eyed, a guide buzzing about them with dates and statistics. Halo gave them a contemptuous glance; but Vance thought: "They feel the way I do." Halo was elaborately tactful; she waited; she kept silent; she left him to his emotions; but no emotions came. He almost wished she would scream out: "Well, aren't you going to say *something?*"—and he thought despairingly: "When will it be over?"

They went to a little tea-shop and had tea (thank God!), and came back and saw twilight fall on towers and buttresses, and dusk deepen to night under the sculpture of the porches. They dined, and came back to see the blueish-gray mass shimmering gigantic under the stars. Then they wandered through the streets and stopped at a café for a glass of vermouth. Vance felt that he would soon have to say something, and he would have given the world to slip away before Halo spoke. "Well, dearest—?"

He emptied his glass, and stared sullenly into it. "Well, I just don't see it."

"Don't *see* it?"

"Not a glimmer; not of what you expect me to. . . It's not my size, I suppose."

"Not your size?" Halo echoed, in the tone of one who has fitted Chartres into her cosmogony without an effort.

Vance felt the inadequacy of words. "I don't *see* it, I tell you. I don't care for it. There's too much of it; yet there isn't anything in it—not for me."

Halo stood up and slipped her arm in his. "You're simply overwhelmed by it—as you were that first evening at Cordova. I was like that when I came here the first time; but tomorrow . . ."

"Oh, no; I don't want to wait till tomorrow. I want to go home now. Can't we—isn't there a night train? There's sure to be one. . ."

He would have liked to tell her that his mind was full of his new book, passionately grappling with its subject. If he had, she would have been full of sympathy and understanding; but he did not want sympathy and understanding. He felt sulky and baffled, and wanted to remain so. The masculine longing to be left alone was upper most; he wanted to hate Chatres without having to give any reason.

"It's not my size," he repeated obstinately.

He saw the immensity of her disappointment. "I know—I'm a Yahoo. But let's go home," he pleaded. They caught a train, and got back to Paris, tired and heavy-eyed, at daylight; and for some time Halo proposed no more week-ends.

But one afternoon, a month later, he went off with two of the young men he had met at Lorry Spear's—a young English painter named Arthur Tolby, and Savignac, a French literary critic. They were not in pursuit of sights; both his companions knew the environs of Paris well enough to take them for granted. But they knew of an inn, fifty miles away, where the food was good enough to satisfy the Frenchman, and there was a chance of trout-fishing for Vance and Tolby. They started in Tolby's rattling motor, hours later than the time appointed, and toward sunset came to a town of which Vance was too lazy to ask the name. As they reached it, a sudden thunderstorm rolled up and burst above them. The sky was black, the roads became river-beds. They decided to wait till the worst of the deluge was over, and Tolby took his car to a garage for a little tinkering. The young men dropped Vance under the porch of a church, and he went in to get shelter. His thoughts were all tangled up in his new novel—a big unwieldy subject full of difficulty and fascination. When he entered the church in this unknown town his eyes were closed to the outer world; he simply wanted to take refuge from the weather. The church was empty, immense, and dark as night. There was a cluster of candles before a distant shrine, but the nave and aisles were unlit, and the thunder-cloud hung its pall before the windows. Vance sat down, and was listening absently to the roar of the storm when a flash illuminated the walls of glass, and celestial fields of azure and rose suddenly embowered him. In another instant all was dark, as if obliterated by the thunder following the flash; then the incandescence began again—a flowering of magical sky-gardens in which every heavenly hue blossomed against a blue as dazzling as sunlight; and after each flowering came extinction.

Vance sat among these bursts of glory and passages of darkness as if alternate cantos of the Paradiso and the Inferno were whirling through him. At length his friends came, they scrambled into the motor, and he left the vision behind. To his companions he said no word of it; he did not even ask the name of the town. They reached their destination late, and sat half the night in the inn garden, watching the moon on a placid river, and talking about the new experiments in painting and literature, about Eddington and Whitehead, Pure Poetry and Thomism, and the best trout-flies for the stream they were to fish. . .

These memories flowed through Vance's mind as he sat on the parapet looking across the Seine. His months in Paris had been rich in experience; if his receptivity sometimes failed him when Halo had most counted on it, he had secreted treasures unsuspected by her, such as the sights and sounds of the river, or that fragment of heaven torn from the storm in the unknown church. Surcharged and happy, he got up and strolled on.

❦ IX ❧

HALO TARRANT, when she and Vance decided to come to Paris, had looked forward to the adventure with dread. Free love, she found, was not the simple experiment she had imagined. The coast of Bohemia might be pleasant to land on for a picnic, yet the interior of the country prove disappointing. She had fancied that in the tolerant air of her brother's studio she would shake off this feeling. She knew it was not based on moral scruples (morally speaking the business was still a labyrinth to her) but on a sort of inherited dislike of being unclassified, and out of the social picture. The social picture, as understood in the Lorburn tradition, had never existed for Lorry; or so he had led his sister to suppose. It had probably never occurred to him to marry Miss Jane Meggs, or to Miss Meggs to expect or wish that he should. Almost all the young men of the group stood in the same unfettered relation to one or more young women; and the few married couples among them tried to excuse their inferior state by the show of a larger liberty.

Among such people, Halo told herself, she would certainly lose the last of her old prejudices. After the cramping hypocrisy of her life with Lewis Tarrant it would be refreshing to be among people who laughed at the idea that there could be any valid tie between young men and women except that of a passing attraction. But from the first she had felt herself an outsider in this world which was to set her free. She liked some of the people she met at her brother's, she was amused and interested by nearly all of them, and she tried to cultivate a friendly tolerance toward the few she found least sympathetic. But she had dropped out of her own picture without yet fitting into this one. Just as she imagined herself to be growing happy and at home among those harum-scarum people with their hysterical good-nature and their verbal enormities, she became suddenly aware that her real self was still ruled by other ideas, and that her new companions all knew it. Beauty, order and reasonableness grew more and more dear to her in the noisy anarchy of Lorry's circle, and the audacities she risked, instead of making her new friends feel that she was one of them, only caused them a vague embarrassment. She had wanted Bohemianism on her own terms, as a momentary contrast to convention; and finding its laws no less irksome that the others, she bore them less philosophically because she did not believe in them.

The delay about her divorce did not trouble her greatly. In that easy-going world such matters seemed irrelevant, and she smiled to think how bitterly she had resented Vance's going without her to the party at Granada. Since then she had put away childish things, and whether she and Vance married, or remained as they were, seemed of no consequence compared to the one vital point: would he weary of her, or would she be able to hold him? Sometimes she thought that if they could be married before he grew tired, their marriage might consolidate the bond. But in Lorry's world it would have occurred to no one that marriage was in itself more permanent than a casual love-affair; the new generation argued that it was easier to separate if you were married, since divorce formalities were easier than a sentimental break.

Nevertheless she clung to the thought of marriage; and soon after their arrival in Paris she wrote to ask her

lawyer the reason of the delay, and to repeat that, if
Tarrant would not let her divorce him, she hoped he
would take proceedings against her at once. The answer
was not what she had expected. The lawyer wrote that
Tarrant no longer wished for a divorce. He not only refused to take proceedings, but declined on any terms to
set Halo free. No reasons were given; but the lawyer was
satisfied that, for the present, any appeal against this decision would only harden Tarrant's resolve. He advised
Halo to wait, in the hope that her husband's mood
might change; and her knowledge of Tarrant made her
accept the advice.

From Frenside and her mother she learned soon afterward that Tarrant's projected marriage with Mrs.
Pulsifer was off, and she suspected that this wound to his
vanity had been the cause of his sudden opposition.

This new obstacle was a blow to her; but she did
not speak of it to Vance. She had resolved not to make
any allusion to their marriage unless he raised the question; and since their talk at Granada, when he had asked
her about the delay in her divorce, he seemed to have
dismissed the matter from his mind. Probably it made
no difference to him if they were married or not; perhaps, even, it was a relief to feel that the tie between
them depended only on their pleasure. Whatever happened, she could not tell Vance about that letter. . .

There were moments when such questions weighed
little in the balance of her daily joys; but these joys became more necessary because of what they had to replace. She had to love Vance more passionately, and to
believe in his genius more fervently and continuously,
because she had staked so much on her love and her
faith. Vance as a lover still filled her life with radiance,
and her tenderness grew with the sense of his eager longing to make her happy; but it was in the region of

thought and imagination that she had dreamed of a lasting hold over him, and it was in this region that she found herself least wanted.

She did not begrudge the hours he spent with his new friends. Men with quick discerning minds, like Arthur Tolby and young Savignac, interested her as much as they did Vance, and she was proud of their appreciation of her lover. They would never have encouraged him, as Alders had, to repeat himself by writing another novel like "Instead"—a "costume piece" which drew its chief effects from a tricky use of local colour. Savignac had told her privately what he thought of the book; it was ever so pretty—ever so clever—but what business had a man of Weston's quality to be doing novels like ladies' fancy-work, or an expensive perfume? He ought to be tackling new difficulties, not warming up old successes. Yes; Halo knew it all; she did not need to have it pointed out, and there was a sting in the fact that this clever young man thought that her affections blinded her, or that her literary standards were less exacting than his. She had always known that Alders's cheap enthusiasms were misleading Vance; but her hints had been wasted. And now, after an evening with his new friends, he could come back and say, quite unconsciously: "Of course I know 'The Puritan' is just pretty wall-paper—something pasted over the rough stuff of reality. Tolby called it that yesterday. Not an ounce of flesh-and-blood in it, not a breath of real air. Don't I know? Why didn't you have the nerve to tell me so? A fellow gets balled up in his subject, and doesn't see which way he's going. You might have told me that I was just re-writing 'Instead' in a new setting."

A year ago she could hardly have refrained from saying: "But, darling, I did tell you, and you wouldn't listen!" She was too wise for that now, and she merely replied: "I'm so glad you've had these talks with Savignac and Tolby. A fresh eye is always such a help—"

"Oh, I oughtn't to need any eye but my own," Vance grumbled jealously: and she went away smiling to put on her newest hat for an out-of-door dinner in the Bois. "The next book—the next book," she thought, "will show them all what he really is." There were times when she caught herself praying for that next book as lonely wives pray for a child. . .

All this passed through her mind as she sat one afternoon in her brother's studio, encumbered with half-finished stage-settings and models of famous theatres, and waited for him to come in. She envied Lorry the place he had made for himself in the busy experimental world of the arts. From an idle and troublesome youth he had turned into a hard-working man, absorbed in his task, confident of his powers, and preoccupied only by the eternal problem of getting money enough to execute his costly schemes. The last of these, she knew, was a great musical spectacle, to be expressed entirely in terms of modern industrialism, with racing motors, aeroplanes and sub-marines as the protagonists, prodigies of electric lighting, and stage effects of unprecedented complication. For the present there was little hope of carrying out this apocalyptic plan, and only the providential appearance of a rich American with a craving to be æsthetically up-to-date could make the dream come true. Lorry, deserting his impecunious friends of Montparnasse, had taken to haunting fashionable hotels and millionaire nightclubs; but hitherto his possible patrons had shied away from his scheme, and as Halo sat waiting she noticed that the stage-settings and models for "Factories," which filled the working-table in the middle of the room, were already gray with dust.

Waiting for Lorry was always an uncertain affair, but Halo seldom had any engagements, and her unoccupied hours weighed on her less heavily away from home. If any one had told her, a year ago, that a young woman living with her lover in Paris could be lonely, and find the time long, she would have smiled at the idea as Vance did at her hints about his work; but now she had given up trying to conceal the truth from herself. Before long, perhaps, Vance would want to begin to write again, and then she would be happy; but meanwhile even love and Paris were not enough.

At last the door opened, and she heard Lorry's step. Luckily he was alone, and they would be able to have a talk before the afternoon crowd turned up. He came in whistling a negro spiritual, said: "Hullo, child—you there?" and walked with an absent eye toward the model of the last scene of "Factories". He stood before it for a long time, passing from spirituals to the latest *Revue* catch, and screwing up his eyes in meditation. As his sister watched him she thought how changed he was since he had found the job he was meant for. He would always be unreliable about money, careless as to other people's feelings, sweetly frivolous, gaily unfeeling; but where his work was concerned he was a rock. He had found the right ballast for his flighty nature, and would no doubt have said that the rest didn't matter. Halo looked at him with envy.

"Lorry," she said, "can't you find me a job?"

He swung around and scrutinized her with those handsome ironic eyes which were a shade too near together for security.

"A job? Why, I thought you had one! I thought you'd chucked everything else for it."

She was on the point of answering, with a touch of bitterness: "I thought so too—" but she checked herself.

"Don't be a goose! What I want is some sort of occupation while Vance is working. I've never learnt to be
lazy, and I feel at a loose end, with all the rest of you
absorbed in your village industries. Why can't I have
one too? Won't Jane take me on as an apprentice in her
book-shop?"

Lorry Spear pulled his hands out of his pockets and
ceased his whistling. "It's you who are the goose, my
dear," he said. "When are you going to get married?"

She looked at him in surprise. It was the last question she had expected; but she rejoined with a laugh:
"Is that your idea of an occupation?"

"For you, yes. A good deal more in your line than
selling censored books in Jane's back shop."

Halo coloured a little. "I didn't know you were so
particular about either literature or morals."

Lorry's face took on an expression of irritated se-
verity. "Hang it, I'm particular about everything—from
my own point of view. I like things to be in the pattern.
Old Jane's in my pattern—so are her books. Naturally a
man feels differently about his sister."

Halo was silent, and he continued, in his light
sharp voice: "I should have thought that as a mere matter of taste a woman like you wouldn't want to be mixed
up with the rabble that come here. It's all right for a
fugue—I'm all for a night off now and then; but I don't
suppose you're going to settle down among them, as one
of them, are you? Has it never occurred to you that it
leaves a bad taste in a man's mouth to have to introduce
his sister to the kind of women who come here? 'His sister? Who is she? Oh, just one of us'. You can't hear them
snicker; but I can. If I haven't spoken till now it's because I expected, any day, to hear that you and Weston
were to be married."

Halo sat looking at her brother with growing astonishment. He was aflame with one of the brief fits of self-righteousness which used to seize him when he tried to borrow money, or to justify some kind of doubtful transaction; but she wondered why he had chosen her as a pretext.

"Oh, no; of course not," he pursued indignantly. "My feelings are the last thing you ever think of—how a man likes it when he knows the fellows he sees are saying behind his back: 'His sister? Oh, anybody can have her the day her novelist chucks her.' Look here, Halo, I've made myself a situation I'm proud of, and here you come along and behave as if you wanted to do me all the harm you can—as if you'd gone out of your way to offend our family pride and ridicule our traditions! Of course if Weston had any sense of what he owes you—"

Halo interrupted him with a laugh. "Really, Lorry, I suppose I oughtn't to let you go on. But all those obsolete words sound so funny in this atmosphere that I can't take them seriously; and I don't believe you expect me to. I don't know that it's any of your business to ask why I don't marry Vance—it's not a question I expected to hear under this roof. As a matter of fact, I suppose we shall marry when Lewis makes up his mind to let me have my divorce; but such matters seem so secondary to any one as blissfully happy as I am—"

Her brother gave an ironic shrug. "*You* blissfully happy? Bless your heart—just go over and look at yourself in the glass! You're better looking than ever, but your cheek-bones are coming through your skin and your eyes look as if you'd tried to rub out the circles under them with a dirty India rubber. And then you talk to me about being happy!"

Halo shrank at the challenge, but met it with a laugh. "I thought you liked ravaged beauties—I've been living on lemon juice and raw carrots on purpose. But if you want to see me led to the altar by my seducer you'd better persuade Lewis to let me divorce him, or to get a divorce from me, if he prefers. When he does, I daresay Vance and I will marry."

Lorry stood before her in an attitude of contemplation; at last he said: "Look here, Halo—I hold no brief for Lewis, though he did me a good turn once. But if a man agrees to let his wife divorce him, I can understand his feeling that she might wait to join her lover till she's got her decree."

"No doubt the principle is a good one. But in my case only one thing counted. Vance wanted me; I had to go to him."

Lorry gave an impatient shrug. "That's so Ibsenish. Talk of obsolete words! Your whole vocabulary is made up of them. What was there to prevent your seeing your young friend on the quiet?" He laid a half-friendly, half-rebuking hand on her shoulder. "My poor old girl, when a lady's such a lady, all the night-life and the adultery won't wipe out the damned spot. . . I'm sorry; but you offend me æsthetically; you really do; and that's the worst sin in my decalogue."

"What a picture, Lorry! It would be funny if you turned out to be the most conventional member of our family."

"I'm the most everything of our family, my dear; haven't you found that out? I push things to their logical conclusions, while the rest of you live in a perpetual blur. That, I may add, is why I don't marry and found a family."

"And why you enjoin me to?"

"Certainly. It's the safest way, for people who can't see around the next corner. And you're one of them."

Halo sat staring down at the rough cement of the

studio floor. She felt suddenly weary of the effort of bandying chaff with her brother. Weary of that, and of everything else. What he said had taken the strength out of her. It was not the first time that she had been struck by Lorry's penetration. No one could see more clearly into human motives, or drive his argument home more forcibly when it was worth his while. For some reason which escaped her, it was worth his while now; but that did not arrest her attention, for her mind was riveted on the image of herself which his words evoked. She had no need to look in the glass; in his description her secret anxieties were revealed to her, feature by feature. It was true that she would never be at home among these people whose way of living was not the result of passion but of the mere quest for novelty. Contact with the clever mocking young women who, like herself, were living with their lovers, seemed to belittle her relation to Vance. When everything which was sacred to her in that relation would have appeared to them incomprehensible or ridiculous, how could she ever imagine herself one of them? She had always felt a latent repulsion for them: for the capable free-spoken Jane, with her thriving trade in forbidden books and obscene drawings, for her friend and business partner, Kate Brennan, whose conversation echoed and parodied Jane's, and for all the other women of the group, with their artistic and literary jargon, picked up from the brilliant young men whose lives they shared, and their noisy ostentation of emotions they seldom felt, and sins they probably did not always commit. Halo stood up and looked about her, at the stacked-up stage-settings, the dusty electrical and photographic apparatuses, the hideous sub-human faces grimacing from futurist canvases, the huge plaster group of two women evilly contorting themselves against a background of theatrical posters. It had all seemed so free and jolly and clever—and Lorry's words had crumbled the whole show to dust.

"Well, I'm off," she said. "If Vance comes, tell him not to wait for me."

Lorry seemed to feel a touch of compunction. "Oh, look here, old girl—" he glanced at his watch a little nervously—"don't go till I've built you up with a cocktail."

She shook her head with a smile. "I'm beyond cocktails. It's this stuffy weather—I feel so lifeless. I'm going home to lie down."

She detected a tinge of relief in his eyes as he followed her toward the door. "So long, then, my dear. If Weston turns up I'll send him back to smooth your pillow." He laid his hand on hers. "See here, Halo; why don't you go home—really?" His eyes looked into hers simply and kindly, as they used to when he and she were children. She pressed his hand and went out without answering.

The studio was at the back of an untidy walled enclosure, encumbered with the materials of an adjoining carpenter's shop. As Halo emerged into the street a glittering motor drove up and stopped. The chauffeur, after a glance of doubt and disapproval, jumped down to open the door, and there descended a heavily built lady dressed with sober opulence. It was clearly unusual for her to set foot to the ground in such a quarter, for she looked as dubious and disapproving as the chauffeur. As she surveyed with lifted nose and eye-glass the unpromising front of the carpenter's shop, the rifts in the pavement, and the general untidiness of the half built-up street, Halo thought: "New York—and Park Avenue!" An instant later she identified the lady. "Mrs. Glaisher! How fat she's grown. They all do, when they own opera boxes and Rollses." She remembered Mrs. Glaisher as one of the chief ornaments of the old expensive New York group which her parents had belonged to and broken away from. Mrs. Glaisher was a necessary evil. Once in the winter one had to hear Tristan or the Rosenkavalier from her opera box, and once to dine off gold plate in her Gothic refectory. But for the rest of the year she was the object of proverbial pleasantry among the clever people who met at Mrs. Spear's. What on earth could she be doing here now? Why, probably looking for Lorry! The thought interested Halo, but did not surprise her; she knew that Mrs. Glaisher was always panting and puffing after what she called "the latest thing". Perhaps she had just discovered Lorry; perhaps —very possibly—it was she on whom he was counting to finance the costly stage-setting of "Factories". The idea was so amusing that Halo forgot her own troubles, and decided that she would guide Mrs. Glaisher to the studio for the pleasure of hearing what she and Lorry had to say to each other. Halo had a high idea of Lorry's verbal arts, and he would need them all to bridge the distance between Mrs. Glaisher's extremest mental effort and the most elementary explanation of "Factories".

Mrs. Glaisher still wavered, as if seeking guidance. Simultaneously, the two women moved a few steps toward each other; then Mrs. Glaisher, pausing, appeared to absorb Halo's presence into her eye-glasses, to turn it over and reject it. After one deadly glance of recognition she averted her gaze, and walked on as if there were no one in her path, and Halo, from the street, was left to contemplate her broad and disapproving back. She had been cut, distinctly and definitely cut, by Mrs. Glaisher.

The idea was so new that she burst into a laugh. She caught an expression of surprise on the chauffeur's disdainful face, and then—could it be?—a fleeting but unconcealable grin. Mrs. Glaisher's chauffeur was joining her in her laugh at Mrs. Glaisher.

"But it's all New York that has cut me!" she chuckled to herself; for she knew that every act and attitude of Mrs. Glaisher's was the outcome of a prolonged and conscientious study of what her particular world approved and disapproved of. The idea of being excluded, ruled out, literally thought out of existence, by all those towering sky-scrapers to whose shelter the statue of Liberty so falsely invites the proscribed and the persecuted, filled Halo with uncontrollable mirth, and she sped homeward cheerfully humming: "I've been cut by Mrs. Glaisher—Mrs. Glaisher—Mrs. Glaisher. . ."

As SHE unlocked her door Halo heard animated talk in the studio. The voices were Savignac's and Tolby's; they were speaking with great vivacity, as if the subject under discussion provoked curiosity and amusement. Still humming to herself: "I've been cut by Mrs. Glaisher—Mrs. Glaisher—" Halo thought: "How I shall make Vance laugh over it!" and she tried to catch his voice among the others. But if he were there he was doubtless listening in silence, stretched out on the brown Bokhara of the divan, his arms folded under his head, and watching between half-shut lids his cigarette smoke spiral upward. "Shall I tell him before the others?" she thought, with an impulse of bravado.

"Well—!" she cried out gaily from the threshold. Only Tolby and Savignac were there; as she turned the door-handle they ceased talking and her "Well!" rang out in the silence. Savignac rose, and Tolby, who was bending over the fire, continued to poke it. "They were talking of me!" she thought, and Lorry's phrase flashed through her mind: "The fellows are saying to themselves: 'His sister? Oh, anybody can have her the day her novelist chucks her'."

That was what these young men, whom she liked, and who were sitting over her fire waiting for her to come in, were probably saying. If not, why should they stop talking so suddenly, and lift such embarrassed faces? It had been very comic to be cut by Mrs. Glaisher; it seemed to put things in their right perspective, and rid Halo of her last scruples. But the idea that her lover's friends had fallen silent on her entrance because they had been caught discussing her situation did not strike her as comic, and she felt a sudden childish ache to be back in the accustomed frame-work of her life.

She came in and shook hands with the young men. "What have you done with Vance?" she asked lightly.

Tolby gave a laugh. "Why, we were talking about him—if that's what you mean."

"Oh—about *Vance?*" In her relief she could not help stressing the name. "Is that why you both look so guilty?"

Tolby laughed again, and Savignac rejoined: "Yes, it is. But for my part I'm going to confess. I don't like his book—at least not as much as I want to."

"Oh, I know you don't. And Tolby doesn't either. But he had the courage to tell me so." Inwardly Halo was thinking: "What an idiot I am! As if these young fellows cared whether Vance and I are married or not! They know we love each other, and for them that's all that counts. These are the kind of people I want to live among." She sat down by the fire, and said: "One of you might find the cocktail shaker. I'm too lazy."

Tolby made the necessary effort, and while they sipped, and lit their cigarettes, Halo continued gaily: "But, you know, Vance doesn't really care for the Spanish novel himself. Has he shown you 'Magic', the one he began two years ago?"

"No," Tolby rejoined. "He said it was no use showing it because it was definitely discarded; but last night at Savignac's he read us an outline of this big new thing he's planning. Derek Fane, of the 'Amplifier', was there, and Weston wanted his opinion. That's the book we were talking about."

"Oh—" Halo murmured. There was a big new book, then; and Vance hadn't yet seen fit to speak to her about it, much less to read her the outline with which the young English critic had been favoured. Why did he no longer talk to her about his work? The idea that it must be her fault made her spirits droop again; but she thought: "I mustn't let them see that I haven't heard of it." She leaned back and puffed at her cigarette. "Well —how does it strike you?"

Tolby gave a shrug. "Not my job—I'm no critic."

Halo laughed. "Savignac can't get out of it on that pretext."

"No," Savignac admitted. "But I can say that I'm a critic only within certain limits."

"Is this out of your limits?"

"It's out of my scale. Too big—"

"For human nature's daily food," Tolby interpolated. "That's my trouble. I think the proper measure of mankind is man."

"Well—?"

"Well—did you ever read Maeterlinck on the Bee —or, rather, I should say, on THE BEE? Rather before your day, but—you have? Well, then you'll understand. When I began to read that book I had imagined the bee was a small animal—insect, in fact; something to be spoken of in a whisper, written of in airy monosyllables —an idea justified by the dimensions of the hives in which, I'm assured by competent authorities, a whole swarm can be comfortably lodged, and carry on their complicated civic and domestic affairs. . . Well, as I read Maeterlinck, the bee grew and grew—like Alice after eating the cake. With each adjective—and they rained like hailstones—that bee grew bigger. Maeterlinck, in his admiration for the creature's mental capacity, had endowed it with a giant's physical proportions. The least epithet he applied to it would have fitted a Roman emperor—or an elephant. That's what the creature became: a winged elephant. That bee was afflicted with giantism, as they say in French. You didn't know that giantism was a glandular disease? Certainly! And Maeterlinck didn't give his thyroid *piqûres* in time —he let the creature swell and swell till it turned into an earth-shaking megatherium among whose legs rogue elephants could have romped. . ." Tolby laughed, refilled his pipe, and stretched his contented ankles to the fire. "That's what I told Weston, in my untutored language."

Halo echoed his laugh; then she said tentatively: "But I don't quite see how I'm to apply your analogy." She was trying to conceal from them that Vance had never breathed a word to her of the new book.

Tolby raised himself on an elbow. "Savignac's the man to give you the reasons; it's his trade. But he won't; he's too polite. I'm just a blundering brute of a painter, who can't explain himself in anything but pigments. And I don't know why I don't like Goliaths, except that they've always proved so much less paintable than the Davids."

"But is it the subject you think too big? Or the characters?"

Savignac plunged in. "It's the scale of the pattern. It's all part of a pattern, subject and characters. It's to be an attempt to deal microscopically, with the infinitely little of human experience, incalculably magnified, like those horrid close-ups of fever microbes, when you don't know whether you're looking at a streptococcus or the villain of a Chinese drama. Till I can find a reason why the meanest physical reflexes should have an aesthetic value equal to the windows of Chartres, or the final scenes of Faust, I shall refuse to believe that they may be legitimately treated as if they had."

"I should refuse even if I found the reason—but

then I'm a mere empirical Briton," Tolby rejoined.

Halo sat silent, trying to piece together these comments. She began to guess why Vance had not talked to her of the book. He had evidently caught the literary infection of Jane Meggs's back shop, and was trying to do a masterpiece according to the new recipe; and he had guessed that Halo would warn him against the danger of sacrificing his individuality to a fashion or a school. Vance was curiously wary about guarding the secrets of his work from premature exposure; but hitherto he had seemed to feel that with her they ran no risk. Now, instinctively, he had anticipated her disapproval; and in a certain way it proved her power over him.

For a while she reflected; then she said: "But if Vance's elephants are winged, like Maeterlinck's, and use their wings, won't that justify his subject and his scale?"

Savignac nodded. "Perfectly."

"Then I suppose all we can do is to wait and see."

"Manifestly. And in the meantime all we can do is to wait for Vance," Tolby interrupted. "He told us to be here by six—we were to hear the first chapters. And it's nearly eight now. Have you any idea where he is?"

"Not the least." Halo got up, lit a lamp, drew the heavy linen curtains. The studio, as she shut out the dusk, grew smaller and more intimate. Tolby threw another log on the hearth, and the rising flame reminded her of the New York winter evenings when she and Vance had sat over the library fire, wandering from book to book, from vision to vision. "We were nearer to each other then," she thought.

Half-past eight struck, and the two young men said they would go off to dine, and drop in afterward to see if Vance had turned up. They tried to persuade Halo to accompany them to the restaurant which the group frequented; but she said she would wait, and join them later with Vance. She drew a breath of relief when they left; she wanted to sit down quietly and think over what they had said of this new book.

The first chapters were finished, apparently, since Vance had convoked his friends to hear them read. She knew where he kept his papers when he was working; it would have been easy to open a drawer in the old cabinet against the wall and rummage for the manuscript. She longed to see it, to assure herself that Vance's treatment of his subject would justify itself—that she would discover in it a promise which Savignac and Tolby had missed. Their literary judgment, to which she had attached so much importance, suddenly seemed open to question. After all, they were both very young, they belonged to a little clan like the others, a number of indirect causes might unconsciously affect their opinion. "Perhaps he's doing something that's beyond their measure," she thought, fastening on the idea with immediate conviction. But much as she desired to confirm it by reading the manuscript she could not bring herself to open the drawer where she was sure it lay. It was the first time that Vance had not taken her into his confidence; and whatever his reasons were, she meant to respect them. If there had been a letter from a woman in that drawer, she reflected, it would have been almost easier to resist looking at it. The relation between herself and Vance had hitherto been so complete that her imagination was lazy about picturing its disturbance. She could not think of him as desiring another woman; but she suffered acutely from the fact that, for the first time, he had not sought her intellectual collaboration.

It was the maid's evening out, and there was no food in the house; but Halo did not feel hungry. She thought: "When he turns up, we'll go out and have supper, as we did that first night at Cordova, when he couldn't eat for the beauty of it." That was only a few months ago; but she was beginning to discover the arbitrariness of time-measures in the sentimental world. The memory seemed to come out of another life.

She stretched herself on the divan, and took up a book to which she gave only the surface of her thoughts. Nine struck, then half-past; almost immediately afterward, it was ten o'clock. She was beginning to think of street accidents and other disquieting possibilities when, toward eleven, the bell rang, and she jumped to her feet. Vance always carried his latchkey; but he might have mislaid or lost it. She ran to the door and opened it on a messenger with a telegram. She fumbled for a franc, and tore open the message under the faint gaslight of the landing. It was dated Paris, and ran: "Off for a day or two to think over book all right love Vance."

Nothing more; no explanation; no excuses; no specifying of place or date. The baldest and vaguest statement of fact—and no more. . .

Familiar voices rose from below, and she caught sight of Tolby's faded Homburg hat at the turn of the stair. "No," she called down to it, "he's not here, he's not come back; but it's all right. I've just had a wire. He had to dash off to see somebody . . . a publisher, yes, a publisher—in London. . . Oh, no, thanks; really not; I'm too sleepy for supper. When I'm alone I don't keep Montmartre hours. . . Thank you, my dears, thank you. . . No—don't come up!"

Halo carried the telegram back into the studio and sat down to re-read it. The words stared at her with secretive faces that yielded no hint of the truth. But why had she so spontaneously fibbed about the message to those young men? In the easy world of Montparnasse everybody came and went without making excuses or giving reasons; only the old instinct of order and propriety, reasserting itself in her, had made her invent that silly story about a London publisher. Lorry was right; she evidently was not cut out to be a poet's love! She smiled defiantly, whispered to herself: "We'll see—" and immediately felt it incumbent, in her new character, to develop a healthy hunger and thirst. In the pantry she found cheese and stale biscuits, which she consumed with the help of a cocktail; then she said: "Now I'll go to bed, like a sensible woman—" and, instead, lit a cigarette and threw herself again on the divan.

The room had grown very still. The friendly fire burned itself out, and she was too lazy to get up and light it. Suddenly it occurred to her that everything she had done for the last year—from choosing her hats and dresses to replenishing the fire, getting the right lamp shades, the right *menu* for dinner, the right flowers for the brown jar on Vance's table—everything had been done not for herself but for Vance. She had no longer cared to make her life comely for its own sake; she thought of it only in relation to her love for Vance. She understood how a young woman full of the pride of self-adornment might turn into a slattern if her lover left her. . . She must suggest that to Vance for a story. . .

But now she saw what must have happened. Alders, she was sure, had turned up again and persuaded Vance to go on a trip with him. Poor Alders knew well enough that he bored her, that she secretly disliked him; he would prefer to pour his second-rate eloquence into Vance's uncritical ear. No doubt he and Vance had gone to stay with some of Alders's pseudo-fashionable friends; and Vance, aware of the faint smile with which Halo would greet such a project, had preferred to go without telling her. . . Well, probably she deserved it; she had always been too critical, had made her likes and dislikes too evident. As if they mattered, or anything did, except that she should go on serving and inspiring this child of genius with whom a whim of the gods had entrusted her. . .

Yet was it likely that Vance would have gone off on a trip with Alders? The friends he had made in Paris, the comrades of these last stimulating months, had relegated Alders to an obscure corner of the background. Vance hardly ever spoke of Alders nowadays—the only time Halo could remember his mentioning the name, he had said: "Poor old Alders," with a shrug of comprehension. "I wonder what's become of Alders's duke—you remember, the one with the name like the clanging of shields?" No; it was not likely that he had gone away with Alders.

If Tolby and Savignac had not been spending that very evening with her at Vance's invitation, and in the expectation of hearing the first pages of his new novel, Halo would have concluded that the three friends had improvised another trip together. Tolby and Savignac were Vance's closest friends nowadays; their companionship had become such an intellectual necessity to him that Halo would have been neither surprised nor resentful if he had gone with them without including her in the party. But Vance had invited his friends to his house, and had obviously meant to be there to receive them; it was after he had made the arrangement that something had occurred, something mysterious, inexplicable, which had caused him to change his plans too hurriedly to give Halo any clearer explanation than this cryptic telegram. It was not Alders who had worked that change.

Halo started up in sudden alarm. Supposing it were not Vance who had sent the telegram? Memories of mysterious abductions, of forged messages from victims already dead, rushed through her agitated mind. There was no telephone in the flat, or even in the *concierge's* lodge below; the old-fashioned building, like most of its kind, was without such conveniences. She would have to go to the nearest police-station, and say—say what? That her husband had not come home for dinner, but that she had had a telegram from him telling her that he was all right, and would be back in two or three days. No— that was scarcely worth carrying to the police. She decided to wait.

Her glance, wandering about the studio, fell again on the old walnut cabinet in which she was sure that Vance had put the manuscript; and suddenly she decided to get it out and read it. She felt that she had the right to do so. If he had withdrawn his confidence from her she must find out about him in other ways. . . She took up the lamp and carried it across to the cabinet. She noticed that her hand was trembling. "One would think I was a jealous woman expecting to find a love-letter," she smiled to herself—and felt the smile harden on her lips.

What a fool she had been! Why shouldn't there be love-letters in that drawer? How was it that never, till that moment, the most probable reason for Vance's gradual detachment had occurred to her? Intellectual companionship? Spiritual union? Rubbish! A young man with a fiery imagination wanted a new woman—a succession of new women—for his flame to feed on. The lives of the poets and artists all proved it—showed how the flame devoured one lovely victim after another, how many had to be heaped on the pyre of genius! If Vance had ceased to talk to her about his work it was because he was talking about it to some other woman. Since the beginning of the world there had been no other clue to the withdrawal of one lover from another. All Halo's intellectual subtleties shrivelled up in the glare of this truth.

She set the lamp down and stood studying the carved doors behind which the answer to the riddle perhaps lay. She no longer thought of the novel—what she saw, through those worm-eaten panels, was a packet of letters in a woman's writing. Was the writing known or unknown to her? Even that she could not guess. Her imagination, racing backward over the last weeks and months, scrutinized one after another the feminine faces in their group, trying to recall some significant glance or word of Vance's. But though these young women obviously interested and amused him, he seemed to treat them all with an odd detachment, and she could not remember his having shown a preference for one above the others. But how did she know that in the course of his Parisian wanderings he had not come across some one she had never seen or even heard of? The chance propinquity of a café or a cinema might have sufficed to undo her life, and put this burning anguish in her heart —this pain so new that she pressed her hands to her breast and whispered: "Oh, God, dear God—only not *that!* Oh, God, don't let it be that!"

It seemed too cruel for endurance that all the treasures of her love for Vance, and the passionate year which had been its flowering, should be at the mercy of some unknown woman's laugh, of the way her eyelashes grew, or her shoulder sloped as the dress drooped from it. . .

"But how do I know it's an unknown woman?" She remembered how long she and Vance had loved each other without its being suspected; she recalled all the divices and prevarications that had shielded their growing passion, and had seemed so natural and necessary. He might have been carrying on an intrigue for weeks with some woman they were meeting constantly at cafés, at dances, at Lorry's. . . She broke off, as if her brother's name had brought enlightenment. At Lorry's—but of course! What else was the meaning of Lorry's unaccountable diatribe against the women who came to his studio? He had told Halo they were not fit to associate with her; and she had laughed, and wondered what could be the cause of this new prudery. Now she saw how the bits of the puzzle fitted into each other, and smiled at her own dulness. What he had obviously been trying to do was to warn her of Vance's peril. Perhaps he was jealous of Vance; perhaps Jane Meggs had been too kind to him. The power of such women was so insidious that though Lorry despised Jane, and laughed at her, he could not do without her, and he had probably meant Halo to take the warning and pass it on to Vance.

Then again—what was it that Tolby and Savignac had hinted about the new book? Why, that it belonged to the type of literature in which Jane Meggs specialized. Not the kind she kept in her back shop; they could hardly have meant that; but that Vance had been too much influenced by the stream-of-consciousness school which Jane's group proclaimed to a bewildered public to be the one model for modern fiction.

Jane Meggs! How a woman of that sort would know how to flatter Vance, astonish his inexperience, amuse him by her literary jargon, fascinate him by her moral perversity. Even the ugliness which Jane flaunted as though it were *her* kind of beauty, the kind she wanted and had deliberately chosen, might have a coarse fascination for him. Perhaps at this very minute he was with

her, in the little flat to which she boasted that even
Lorry had never been admitted. . .

Halo turned from the cabinet. She no longer
wanted to open its hidden drawers. How should she bear
the sight of the truth, when the imaging of it was so intolerable?

VANCE, WHEN he left the quay, had meant to turn home-ward. He liked strolling at twilight through the Luxembourg quarter, where great doorways opened on court-yards with mouldering plaster statues, where the tall garden walls were looped with bunches of blueish ivy, and every yard of the way, behind those secretive walls, a story hung like fruit for him to gather. But he found it harder than ever to leave the Seine. Each moment, as night fell, and the lights came out, the face of the river grew more changing and mysterious. Where the current turned under the slopes of Passy a prodigal sunset flooded the brown waves with crimson and mulberry; at the point where he stood the dusky waters were already sprinkled with fluctuating lights from barges and steam-boats; but toward the Louvre and Notre-Dame all was in the uncertainty of night.

Tolby and Savignac were to come that afternoon to hear him read the first chapters of his new novel: "Co-lossus". After pouring out to them, the night before, his large confused vision of the book, Vance had suggested their hearing what he had already written; but he re-gretted it now, for in the discussion which had followed they had raised so many questions that he would have preferred not to show the first pages till he had worked over them a little longer. Besides, in the excitement of talking over his project, he had forgotten that if they came for the promised reading Halo would find out for the first time that he was at work on a new novel. Vance had not meant to keep his plan a secret from her; in such matters his action was always instinctive. His impulse was simply to talk over what he was doing with whichever listener was most likely to stimulate the dim creative process; and that listener was no longer Halo. Vance was sure that he loved her as much as ever, was as happy as ever in her company; it was not his fault or hers if the deep workings of his imagination were no longer roused by her presence.

This did not greatly trouble him; he took his stimulus where he found it, as a bee goes to the right flower. But since Halo's outburst at Granada, when he had gone to the old Marquesa's without her, he had felt in her a jealous vigilance which was perhaps what checked his confidences. She seemed to resent whatever excluded her from his pursuits; but though it troubled him to hurt her he could not give up the right to live his inner life in his own way, and the conflict disquieted and irritated him. Of late he had forgotten such minor problems. When he was planning a new book the turmoil of his mind was always enclosed in a great natural peace, and during those weeks of mysterious brooding he had not once thought of what Halo would think or say; but now he felt she would be hurt at his having told Tolby and Savignac of the new book before she knew of it.

His first idea was to get hold of his friends and put off the reading; but a glance at his watch showed that they must already be at the studio awaiting him. The worst of it was that they had probably told Halo what they had come for. . . . "Oh, hell," Vance groaned. He stood still on the crowded pavement, thinking impatiently: "If only I could cut it all——." Well, why shouldn't he? This book possessed him. What he wanted above everything was to be alone with it, and away from everybody for a day or two, till he could clear his mind and get the whole thing back into its right perspective——

just to lie somewhere on a grass-bank in the sun, and think and think.

He looked up and down the quays, and then turned and signed to a taxi. "Gare de Lyon!" he called out. He felt suddenly hungry, and remembered that somebody had said you could get a first-rate meal at the Gare de Lyon. Dining at a great terminus, in the rush of arrivals and departures, would give him the illusion of escape; and the quarter was so remote that by the time he got home his friends would probably have left, and Halo have gone to bed . . . and the explanation could be deferred till the next day.

In the station restaurant a crowd of people were eating automatically in a cold glare of light. He had meant to order a good dinner, and then wander aimlessly about the streets, as he liked to do at night when ideas were churning in him. But the sight of all those travellers with their hand-luggage stacked at their feet, and something fixed and distant in their eyes, increased his desire to escape, and again he thought: "Why not?" He snatched a sandwich from the buffet, and hurried to the telegraph office to send a message to Halo; then, his conscience eased, he began to stroll from one platform to another, consulting the signboards with the names of the places for which the trains were leaving . . . Dijon . . . Lyons . . . Avignon . . . Marseilles . . . Ventimiglia . . . every name woke in him a different sonority, the deeper in proportion to the mystery. Lyons, Marseilles—the great cities—called up miles of streets lined with closely packed houses, and in every house innumerable rooms full of people, all strange and remote from him, yet all moved by the common springs of hunger, lust, ambition. . . That vision of miles and miles of unknown humanity packed together in stifling propinquity, each nucleus revolving about its own tiny orbit, with passions as intractable as those that govern heroes and overthrow kingdoms, always seized him when he entered a new city. But other names— Avignon, Ventimiglia, Spezia—sang with sweeter cadences, made him yearn for their mysterious cliffs and inlets (he pictured them all as encircled by summer seas). His geography was as vague as that of a mediaeval mapmaker; but he was sure those places must be at least as far off as Cadiz or Cordova, and he turned reluctantly from the enchanted platform.

On a signboard farther on he saw a familiar name: Fontainebleau. Though it was so near he had never been there; but he knew there was a forest there, and he felt that nothing would so fit in with his mood as to wander endlessly and alone under trees. He saw that a train was starting in ten minutes; he bought his ticket and got in.

A man in the compartment, who said he was an American painter, told Vance of an inn on the edge of the forest where he would be away from everybody— especially from the painters, his adviser ironically added. He himself was going on to Sens, where they didn't bother you much as yet. . . Vance got out at Fontainebleau, woke up the keeper of the inn, and slept in a hard little bed the dreamless sleep of the runaway schoolboy.

The next morning he was up early, and as soon as he could coax a cup of coffee from the landlady he started off into the forest. He did not know till then that he had never before seen a forest. In America he had seen endless acres of trees; but they were saplings, the growth of yesterday. Here at last was an ancient forest, a forest with great isolated trees, their branches heavy with memory, gazing in meditative majesty down

glades through which legendary cavalcades came riding.
For miles he walked on under immense low-spreading
beeches; then a trail through the bracken led him out
on a white sandy clearing full of fantastic rocks, where
birch-trees quivered delicately above cushions of purplish heather. Still farther, in another region, he came
on hollows of turf brooded over by ancient oaks, on
pools from which waterbirds started up crying, and grass-
drives narrowing away to blue-brown distances like the
background of tapestries. The forest seemed endless; it
enclosed him on every side. He could not imagine anything beyond it. In its all-embracing calm his nervous
perturbations ceased. Face to face with this majesty of
nature, this great solitude which had stood there, never
expecting him yet always awaiting him, he felt the same
deep union with earth that once or twice in his life he
had known by the seashore.

After a while he grew tired of walking, and lay
down to ponder on his book. In that immemorial quiet
the voice of his thoughts came to him clear of the other
voices entangling it. He had tried to explain the book to
his two friends, and he knew he had failed, perhaps because he could not detach his own ideas from the dense
thicket of ideas which flourished in the air of Paris. Or
perhaps his friends' minds were too well-ordered and logical to tolerate the amorphous mass he had tried to force
into them. "Colossus"—he had pitched on the title as
expressing that unwieldy bulk.

The endless talks about the arts of expression
which went on in the circle presided over by Lorry and
Jane Meggs had roused in Vance a new tendency to self-
analysis. Especially when they discussed the writing of
fiction—one of their most frequent themes—he felt that
he had been practising blindly, almost automatically,
what these brilliant and intensely aware young people

regarded as the most self-conscious of arts. Their superior cultivation made it impossible to brush aside their theories and pronouncements as he had the outpourings of the young men in Rebecca Stram's studio; he felt compelled to listen and to examine their arguments, fallacious as some of them seemed.

When they said that fiction, as the art of narrative and the portrayal of social groups, had reached its climax, and could produce no more (citing Raphael and Ingres as analogous instances in painting) —that unless the arts were renewed they were doomed, and that in fiction the only hope of renewal was in the exploration of the subliminal, his robust instinct told him that the surface of life was rich enough to feed the creator's imagination. But though he resisted the new theories they lamed his creative impulse, and he began to look back with contempt on what he had already done. The very popularity of "The Puritan in Spain" confirmed his dissatisfaction. A book that pleased the public was pretty sure not to have been worth writing. He remembered Frenside's saying that "Instead" was a pretty fancy, but not to be repeated, and he knew that "The Puritan" was simply a skilful variation on "Instead". Evidently he was on the wrong tack, and his clever new friends must be right. . .

But what was the alternative they proposed? A microscopic analysis of the minute in man, as if the highest imaginative art consisted in decomposing him into his constituent atoms. And at that Vance instantly rebelled. The new technique might be right, but their application of it substituted pathology for invention. Man was man by virtue of the integration of his atoms, not of their dispersal. It was not when you had taken him apart that you could realize him, but when you had built him up. The fishers in the turbid stream-of-consciousness had reduced their fictitious characters to a bundle of loosely tied instincts and habits, borne along blindly on the current of existence. Why not reverse the process, reduce the universe to its component dust, and set man whole and dominant above the ruins? What landmarks were there in the wilderness of history but the great men rising here and there above the herd? And was not even the average man great, if you pictured him as pitted against a hostile universe, and surviving, and binding it to his uses? It was that average man whom Vance wanted to depict in his weakness and his power. "Colossus"—the name was not wholly ironic; it symbolized the new vision, the great firm outline, that he wanted to project against the petty chaos of Jane Meggs's world. Only, how was it to be done?

He tried to carry over his gray theory into the golden world of creation; but the scents and sounds of the forest made him drowsy, and he lay on a warm slope, gazing upward, and letting the long drifts of blue sky and snowy cumulus filter between his eyelids.

Presently he grew hungry, and remembered that before starting he had stuffed his pockets with sandwiches and a flask of wine. He made his meal, and continued to lie on the grass-bank, smoking and dozing, and murmuring over snatches of sylvan poetry, from Faust's Walpurgis ride to the branch-charmed oaks of Hyperion.

At last he got up, shook the tufts of grass from his coat, and wandered on. The afternoon was perfect. The sun poured down from a sky banked with still clouds, and the air smelt of fading bracken and beech-leaves, and the spice of heather bloom. Why couldn't he always live near a forest, have this populous solitude at his door? What were cities and societies for but to sterilize the imagination? People were of no use to him, even the

cleverest, when it came to his work—what he needed
was this tireless renewal of earth's functions, the way of
a forest with the soul. . .

He pulled off his coat and swung along in his shirt-
sleeves, glowing with the afternoon warmth of the
woods. It seemed impossible that outside of those enchanted bounds winds blew, rain fell, and the earth
plunged on toward a decaying year. He thought of purple grapes on hot trellises, of the amber fires of Poussin's
"Poet and the Muse", of Keats's mists and mellow fruitfulness, and the blue lightning-lit windows in the name-
less church. He had lost all sense of direction, and did
not know whether he was near the edge of the forest, or
far from it, when suddenly he came on an open space
flooded with sun, and a bank where a girl lay asleep. At
least he supposed she was asleep, from the relaxed lines of
her body; but he could not be sure, for she had opened
her sunshade and planted it slantwise in the ground, so
that its dome roofed her in, and hid her face.

Vance stood and looked at her. She was as sunlit
and mysterious as his mood. A dress of some thin stuff
modelled the long curves of her body; her ankles were
crossed, and the slim arched feet, in sandal-like shoes,
looked as if feathers might grow from them when she
stirred. But she lay still, apparently unaware of him and
of all the world.

He gazed at the picture in a mood of soft excitement. He wanted to lift the sunshade and surprise the
wonder in her eyes. But would she be surprised? No;
only a little amused, he thought. Dryads must be used to
such encounters, and she would simply fit him into her
dreams, and put her arms around his neck and her lips
to his.

Perhaps every man had his Endymion-hour—only
what if Diana, instead of vanishing in a silver mist,

should say: "Let's go off together," and give Endymion her address? No . . . she must remain a part of his dream, a flicker of light among the leaves. . .

He turned away, still in the nymph's toils. As he walked on he saw coming toward him a stoutish common-looking young man with a straw hat tilted back on his head, and a self-satisfied smile on a coarse lip. He wore a new suit of clothes and walked jauntily, swinging his stick and glancing ahead as if in pleasant expectation —an ordinary, not unkindly-looking youth, evidently satisfied with himself and what awaited him. Was he on his way to meet the roadside dryad? Had she fallen asleep as she lay in the sun and waited? Vance was annoyed by the thought; in looking at the man's face he seemed to have seen the girl's, and the world of earthly things re-entered the forest. He did not scorn those earthly things; a common good-natured man kissing a flushed girl under a tavern arbour was a pleasant enough sight. But he wanted something rarer in his memory of the forest, and he turned indifferently from the meeting of Diana and Endymion.

❦ XII ❧

HE GOT back late to the inn, and after dining went to bed, and to sleep—the sleep of a young body replete with exercise, and a mind heavy with visions. But in the middle of the night, he sat up suddenly awake. The moon streamed across his bed and fringed with a blueish halo the chair and table between himself and the window. "Diana after all!" he thought, his brain starting into throbbing activity. He seemed to be in the forest road again, watching the sleeping girl; and he asked himself how he could have left her and gone on. There she had lain, mysterious goddess of the cross-roads, one of the wandering divinities a man meets when he is young, and never afterward; yet he had turned from her, afraid of disenchantment. What cowardice—what lack of imagination! Because he had seen a common-looking man coming toward her, and had concluded that she must be like him, he had run away from the magic of the unknown, the possibilities that lie in the folded hour. And now it was too late, and he would never see her again, or recapture his vanished mood. . .

It was not the fear of hurting Halo which had held him back. At the moment he had not even thought of her. But now he suddenly saw that, should he ever drift into a casual love-affair, she would probably suffer far more than poor Laura Lou with all her uncontrollable fits of suspicion and resentment. The idea was new to him; he had always pictured Halo as living above such turmoils, in the calm upper sphere of reason. But now he understood that her very calmness probably intensi-

119

fied her underlying emotions. There swept back upon him the physical and mental torture of his jealousy of Floss Delaney, the girl who had taught him the extremes of joy and pain, and he was oppressed by the thought that he might have made Halo suffer in the same way.

He wondered now how he, who vibrated to every pang of the beings he created, could have been so unperceiving and unfeeling. His imagination had matured, but in life he had remained a blundering boy. He had left Paris abruptly, without warning or excuse, he had not even followed up his vague telegram by a letter of explanation. But how explain, when the explanation would have been: "Darling, I love you, but I want to get away from you"?—After all, he mused, they were both free, and Halo knew that there are times when a man needs his liberty. . . But what if "liberty", in such cases, means the license to do what would cause suffering if found out? License to wound, and escape the consequences? He lay on his bed, and stared into the future. How did two people who had once filled each other's universe manage to hold together as the tide receded? Why, by the world-old compulsion of marriage, he supposed. Marriage was a trick, a sham, if you looked at it in one way; but it was the only means man had yet devised for defending himself from his own frivolity.

He was struck by something august and mysterious in the fact of poor humanity's building up this barrier against itself. To the Catholic church marriage was a divine institution; but it seemed to him infinitely more impressive as an emanation of the will of man. . . He fell asleep muttering: "That's it . . . we must be married . . . must be married at once . . ." and when he woke, Diana and the moon were gone, and the autumn rain clouded his window.

He woke in a mood of quiet. It was almost always

so: after a phase of agitation and uncertainty, in which he seemed to have frittered away his powers in the useless effort to reconcile life and art, at the moment when he felt his creative faculty slipping away from him forever, there it stood at his side, as though in mockery of his self-distrust. So it had been when Laura Lou was dying, so no doubt it would be whenever life and art fought out their battle in him. He dressed and called for his coffee; then he sat down to write.

That girl in the forest! He knew now why she had been put there. To make his first chapter out of— glorious destiny! He laughed, lit a cigarette, and wrote on. Oh, the freedom, the quiet, the blessed awayness from all things! One by one the pages fell from table to floor, noiseless and regular as the fall of leaves in the forest. His isolation seemed invulnerable. Even the rain on his window was in the conspiracy, and hung its veil between his too-eager eyes and the solicitations of the outer world, shutting him into a magic-making solitude. . .

The day passed in that other-dimensional world of the imagination. His pen drove on and on. The very fact that Halo was not there to pick up the pages, and transfer them to the cool mould of her Remington, gave a glorious freedom to his periods. There they lay on the floor, untrammelled and unwatched as himself. He recalled the old days of his poverty and obscurity in New York, when he had sat alone in his fireless boardinghouse room, pouring out prose and poetry till his brain reeled with hunger and fatigue; and he knew now that those hours had been the needful prelude to whatever he had accomplished since. "You have to go plumb down to the Mothers to fish up the real thing," he thought exultantly.

Night came, and he turned on the weak electric

light and continued to write. To his strong young eyes the page was as clear as by day. But at last the pen slipped from his hand, and sleep overcame him.

When he woke he felt chilly and hungry, his wrist was stiff, his eyes and forehead ached. The scribbled-over sheets lay at his feet in a heap—dead leaves indeed! He had come back to reality, and the world where he had spent those fervid hours had vanished in mist. He thought of Halo, of Paris, of all the interwoven threads of his life; he felt weak and puzzled as a child. "I must get back," he said to himself; and he gathered up his papers.

It was late when he reached Paris; but he took his way home on foot through the drizzle, down the Boulevard Sebastopol to the Seine, and through the old streets of the left bank to the Luxembourg. He was trying to put off his home-coming; not because he was troubled by the excuses and explanations he might have to offer, but because he dreaded the moment when the last frail shreds of his dream should detach themselves. After one of these plunges into the depths he always rose to the surface sore and bewildered; it was a relief to know that at that hour Halo would probably be in bed and asleep, and explanations could be deferred till the morrow. "Unless," he reflected, "she's out—at the theatre, perhaps—or dancing." It was the first time since they had been together that he had pictured Halo as having a life of her own, a personality of her own, plans, arrangements, perhaps interests and sympathies unknown to him. "Funny . . ." he reflected . . . "when I go away anywhere I always shut up the idea of her in a box, as if she were a toy; or turn her to the wall, like an unfinished picture. . ." And he recalled the distant days in New York, when he saw her so seldom, and when, in their long hours of separation, his feverish imagination followed her through every moment of her life, stored up every allusion to her friends, her engagements, hunted out the addresses of the people she had said she was lunching or dining with, and tried to picture the houses in which she was being entertained, what she was saying to the persons about her, and how her voice sounded when it was not to him that she was speaking. . .

He found his latchkey, and entered the narrow hall. The door leading to the studio was half-open. Through it he saw the lamp on his desk, a cluster of red dahlias in the brown jar, and a table near the fire with wineglasses, chafing-dish and a bottle of white wine. Such an intimate welcome emanated from the scene that he drew back with the shyness of an intruder. She was out; he had been right; but before starting she had prepared this little supper for her return. Supper for two; probably for Tolby and herself. She had always liked Tolby —the young Englishman was more like the type of man she had been used to in her own circle of friends. He had Tarrant's social ease, the cool bantering manner which Vance had long since despaired of acquiring. Yes; she was probably with Tolby. . . The thought was curiously distasteful.

A door opened, and from the bedroom Halo came out. She had flung a crimson silk dressing-gown over her shoulders, and her dark hair fell about her temples in soft disordered curls. She looked sleepy, happy and unsurprised. "I thought you'd be back tonight." She put her arm about his neck, and he plunged with all his senses into the familiar atmosphere of her perfume, her powder, the mossy softness of her hair. "I knew you'd be as hungry as a wolf," she laughed, drawing him to the table by the fire. "Do you remember that night at Cordova? Come and see if I've provided the right things."

He looked about him with a low satisfied laugh. "It's good to get back," he said, laying a kiss on her bare nape as she stooped above the chafing-dish. She turned her face, and he saw that it was all his, from trembling lashes to parted lips. "Well, how did the work go?" she asked, putting him aside while she bent to break the eggs into the dish; and he answered: "Oh, great—but the best of going away is the coming back. . ."

"Look! Fresh mushrooms!" she cried, uncovering another dish; and as the warm savour of the cooking filled the air he threw himself back into his armchair, folding his arms luxuriously behind his head and said, half-laughing, half-seriously: "Do you know I could have sworn I saw you yesterday in the forest, asleep under a white umbrella? But your face was hidden, so I couldn't be sure."

"And you didn't look?"

"No, I didn't look."

She tossed him the corkscrew, scooped the smoking mess of eggs and mushrooms into their two plates, and said laughingly: "Come."

He uncorked the Chablis, drew his chair up, and fell joyfully upon the feast. How she knew how to take a man, to ease off difficult moments, what to take for granted, what to leave unsaid! What he had told her was true; a home-coming like this was even better than the going away. A bright hearth, good food, good wine; the sense of ease, of lifted burdens, and a great inner exhilaration at the thought of work to come—this was how love repaid him for his escapade. He looked at Halo, and surprised her eyes fixed on his; and suddenly he felt that at the very heart of their intimacy the old problem lurked, and that never, even in their moments of closest union, would they really understand each other. But the sensation barely brushed his soul. The next moment it was expanding in the glow of fire and wine, and Halo's eyes shone with the old confiding tenderness. He filled his glass and began to talk to her about the new book.

How easy it was now to pour out what he had so jealously guarded before! The fruit was ripe, and it was sweet to heap it at her feet as she sat listening in the old way, her lids lowered, her chin propped in her hand. Nothing escaped her—she listened with every faculty, as she used to in the long summer days at the Willows. She said little, put few questions; but when she spoke it was always to single out what he knew was good, or touch interrogatively on some point still doubtful. The night was nearly over when he gathered up his pages. "Lord— what an hour! I've tired you out; and I've never even asked what you've been up to while I was away." With sudden compunction he put his arm about her.

"What I've been up to? Accepting dinner invitations for you, for one thing! You won't mind? Lorry wants you to dine at the studio tomorrow: a big blowout for Mrs. Glaisher, who has developed a sudden interest in theatrical art and may possibly—he thinks probably—help him to produce his ballet. You know how hard he's been trying for it."

"Mrs. Glaisher? Who on earth's Mrs. Glaisher?"

"Why, don't you remember? One of the principal characters in your next-but-one-novel: 'Park Avenue'. She's waiting to sit to you: a Museum specimen of the old New York millionairess. If only she would subsidize 'Factories' Lorry's future would be assured—or so he thinks. And he implores you on his knees to come and help him out. Mrs. Glaisher's very particular; she's named her guests, and the author of 'The Puritan in Spain' was first on the list. I'm sorry for you, darling— but you've got to go."

"Oh, shucks," Vance growled. "I don't believe she ever heard of me."

"How little you know of the world you're trying to write about! Mrs. Glaisher has found out that it's the thing for the rich to patronize the arts, and she means to eclipse Mrs. Pulsifer. Suppose she should found a prize for the longest novel ever written—just at the moment when 'Colossus' appears?" She put her arms about Vance's neck and laughed up at him. "You'll go, dear— just for Lorry?"

"Oh, all right; but don't let's think of boring things now." He brushed her hair from her forehead, and looked deeply into her eyes; then, when she slipped away, he sank into his chair and abandoned himself to the joy of re-reading the words freshly illuminated by her praise.

When he pulled himself out of his brooding, and went to bed, Halo was asleep. He had carried in the lamp from the studio, and stood shading it with his hand while he looked down on her. Usually, when she slept, her features regained their girlish clearness; and she was once more the Halo Spear who had lit up the dark old library at the Willows; but now youth and laughter were gone, her face was worn and guarded. "This is the real Halo," he thought; and he knew it was the effort to hide her anxiety behind a laughing welcome which had left those furrows between her eyes.

"If only," he mused in a burst of contrition, "I could remember beforehand not to make her unhappy . . ."

❦ XIII ❧

From the moment of entering Lorry Spear's studio Mrs. Glaisher dominated it. Vance was not the only guest conscious of her prepotency. She was one of the powerful social engines he had caught a glimpse of in the brief months of his literary success in New York, three years earlier; but at that moment his life had been so packed with anxieties and emotions that he could hardly take separate note of the figures whirling past him.

The only woman he had known who vied in wealth and worldly importance with Mrs. Glaisher was the lady who had invited him to her huge museum-like house, shown him her pictures and tapestries, and failed, at the last moment, to give him the short-story prize on which all his hopes depended. But Mrs. Pulsifer was a shadowy figure compared with Mrs. Glaisher, a mere bundle of uncertainties and inhibitions. Mrs. Glaisher was of more robust material. She was as massive as her furniture and as inexhaustible as her bank-account. Mrs. Pulsifer's scruples and contradictions would have been unintelligible to a woman who, for forty years, had hewed her way toward a goal she had never even faintly made out.

After a long life devoted to the standardized entertaining of the wealthy, Mrs. Glaisher had suddenly discovered that Grand Opera, *pâté de foie gras*, terrapin and Rolls-Royces were no longer the crowning attributes of her class; and undismayed and unperplexed she had begun to buy Picassos and Modiglianis, to invite her friends to hear Stravinsky and Darius Milhaud, to patronize exotic dancers, and labour privately (it was the hardest part of her task) over the pages of "Ulysses".

As Vance watched her arrival he guessed in how many strange places that unblenching satin slipper had been set, and read, in the fixity of her smile, and the steady gaze of her small inquisitive eyes, her resolve to meet without wavering any shock that might await her. He thought of Halo's suggestion for his next novel, and was amused at the idea of depicting this determined woman who, during an indefatigable life-time, had seen almost everything and understood nothing.

Lorry's studio had been hastily tidied up, as Jane Meggs and her friend understood the job; but Vance saw Mrs. Glaisher's recoil from the dusty floor and blotched walls, and the intensity of her resolve to behave as if Mimi Pinson's garret were her normal dwelling. Electric lamps dangling in uncertain garlands lit up a dinner-table contrived out of drawing-boards and trestles, and the end of the room was masked by a tall clothes'-horse hung with a Cubist rug, from behind which peeped the competent face of the *restaurateur* charged with the material side of the entertainment; for Lorry had seen to it that, whatever else lacked, wine and food should be up to the Park Avenue standard.

With Mrs. Glaisher was a small sharp-elbowed lady, whose lavishly exposed anatomy showed the most expensive Lido glaze. Her quick movements and perpetual sidelong observance of her friend reminded Vance of a very intelligent little dog watching, without interfering with, the advance of a determined blind man. "Oh, don't you know? That's Lady Pevensey—the one they all call 'Imp'," Jane Meggs explained to Vance as Lorry led him toward Mrs. Glaisher. The others all seemed to know Lady Pevensey, and she distributed handshakes, "darlings", and "I haven't seen you in several ages", with such impartial intimateness that Vance was surprised when Savignac, to whom she had just cried out: *"Tiens, mon vieux, comme tu es en beauté ce soir!"* enquired in a whisper who she was.

The party consisted of Lorry's trump cards—the new composer, Andros Nevsky, who, as soon as he could be persuaded to buckle down to writing the music of "Factories", was to reduce Stravinsky and "The Six" to back numbers; the poet, Yves Tourment, who, after an adolescence of over twenty years, still hung on the verge of success; Sady Lenz, the Berlin ballerina, who was to create the chief part in Lorry's spectacle; Hedstrom, the new Norse novelist, and Brank Heff, the coming American sculptor, whom the knowing were selling their Mestrovics to collect; and, to put a little fluency and sparkle into this knot of international celebrities, such easy comrades and good talkers as Tolby, Savignac, and others of their group.

Vance was so much amused and interested that he had forgotten his own part in the show, and was surprised when Lorry called him up to be introduced to Mrs. Glaisher, and he heard that lady declare: "I told Mr. Spear I wouldn't dine with him unless he invited you, not even to meet all the other celebrities in Paris."

"Ah, no: Nosie's so headstrong we couldn't do anything with her," Lady Pevensey intervened, startling Vance by putting her arm through his, and almost as much by revealing that Mrs. Glaisher was known to her intimates as "Nosie". "Nosie's been simply screaming to everybody: 'I *must* have the man who wrote "The Puritan"', and when Lorry found you'd disappeared without leaving an address Nosie couldn't be pacified till she heard that you'd turned up. Lorry, darling, you've put Vance next to her at table, haven't you? Oh, Jane, love, tell him he *must!* I know she idolizes Nevsky, and she's been dying for years to meet darling Yves—but she won't be able to speak a word of French to them, much less Norwegian to Hedstrom," (this in a tragic whisper to Lorry) "so for God's sake pacify the Polar Lions somehow, and let Nosie have her Puritan."

But with foreigners as his guests Lorry protested that he could hardly seat his young compatriot next to the chief guest of the evening, and Vance was put opposite to Mrs. Glaisher, who sat between Lorry and the silent and bewildered Norse novelist. Vance was amused to see that Lorry had chosen the most inarticulate man in the room as Mrs. Glaisher's neighbour. In this way he kept her to himself, while Lady Pevensey, on his right, was fully engaged between Yves Tourment and Savignac's sallies from across the table.

Lorry had done his job well. The food was excellent, the champagne irreproachable; he had dressed up in the gay rags of Bohemia an entertainment based on the most solid gastronomic traditions, and Mrs. Glaisher, eating truffled *poularde* and *langouste à l'Américaine,* was convinced that she was sharing the daily fare of a band of impecunious artists.

Down the table, Nevsky, in fluent Russian French, was expounding to Jane Meggs his theory of the effect of the new music on glandular secretions in both sexes, and Brank Heff, the American sculptor, stimulated by numerous preliminary cocktails, broke his usual heavy silence to discuss with Fraülein Sady Lenz her merits as a possible subject for his chisel. "What I want is a woman with big biceps and limp breasts. I guess you'd do first rate. . . How about your calves, though? They as ugly as your arms? I guess you haven't danced enough yet to develop the particular deformity I'm after. . ."

When the conversation flagged Jane Meggs started

it up again with a bilingual scream; and above the poly-
glot confusion rose Lorry's masterful voice, proclaiming
to Mrs. Glaisher: "What we want is to break the old
moulds, to demolish the old landmarks. . . When Clé-
menceau pulled down the Colonne Vendôme the fools
thought he was doing it for political reasons . . . the
Commune, or some such drivel. Pure rot, of course! He
was merely obeying the old human instinct of destruction . . . the artist's instinct: destroying to renew.
Why, didn't Christ Himself say: 'I will make all things
new'? Quite so—and so would I, if I could afford to buy
an axe. Just picture to yourself the lack of imagination
there is in putting up with the old things—things made
to please somebody else, long before we were born, to
please people who would have bored us to death if we'd
known them. Who ever consulted you and me when the
Pyramids were built—or Versailles? Why should we be
saddled with all that old dead masonry? Ruins are what
we want—more ruins! Look what an asset ruins are to
the steamship companies and the tourist agencies. The
more ruins we provide them with the bigger their divi-
dends will be. And so with the other arts—isn't every
antiquary simply running a Cook's tour through the
dead débris of the past? The more old houses and furniture and pictures we scrap, the more valuable what's left
will be, and the happier we'll make the collectors. . . If
only the lucky people who have the means to pull down
and build up again had the imagination to do it. . ."

"Ah, that's it: we *must* have imagination," Mrs.
Glaisher announced in the same decisive tone in which,
thirty years ago, she might have declared: "We *must*
have central heating."

"If you say so, dear lady, we shall have it—we shall
have it already!" cried Lorry in an inspired tone, lifting

his champagne glass to Mrs. Glaisher's; while Yves Tourment shrilled in his piercing falsetto: *"Vive Saint Hérode, roi des iconoclastes!"*

Mrs. Glaisher, who had paled a little at her host's Scriptural allusion, recovered when she saw that the words were not meant to deride but to justify; and at Yves Tourment's apostrophe she exclaimed, with beaming incomprehension: "Who's that whose health they're drinking? I don't want to be left out of anything."

Presently the improvised dinner-table was cleared and demolished, and the guests scattered about the studio, at the farther end of which a stage had been prepared for Fraülein Lenz. Mrs. Glaisher, slightly flushed by her libations to the iconoclasts, and emboldened by her evident success with the lights of Montparnasse, stood smilingly expectant while Lorry and Lady Pevensey brought up the notabilities of the party; but linguistic obstacles on both sides restricted the exchange of remarks, and Vance, who had stood watching, and wishing Halo were there to share his amusement, soon found it his turn to be summoned.

"You're the person she's really come for, you know; do tell her everything you can think of," Lady Pevensey prompted him: "about how you write, I mean, and what the publishers pay you—she's particularly keen about that—and whether you're having an exciting love-affair with anybody; she adores a dash of heart-interest," she added, as she pushed Vance toward the divan on which Mrs. Glaisher throned.

Vance remembered a far-off party at the Tarrants', the first he had ever been to, and how Halo had dragged him from the book-shelf where he had run to earth his newly-discovered Russian novelists, and carried him off to be introduced to Mrs. Pulsifer. That evening had been a mere bright blur, to which he was astonished to find himself contributing part of the dazzle; whereas now he looked on without bewilderment or undue elation. But he did think it a pity that Halo, on the pretext of a headache (though really, she owned, because such occasions bored her) had obstinately refused to accompany him.

Mrs. Glaisher's greeting betrayed not only her satisfaction at capturing a rising novelist but the relief of being able to talk English, and of knowing his name and the title of one of his books. She began at once to tell him that on the whole her favourite among his novels was "Instead", because of its beautiful idealism. She owned, however, that "The Puritan in Spain" was a more powerful work, though there were some rather unpleasant passages in it; but she supposed that couldn't be avoided if the author wanted to describe life as it really was. She understood that novelists always had to experience personally the . . . the sensations they described, and she wanted to know if his heroine was somebody he'd really known, and if he'd been through all those love scenes with her. It was ever so much more exciting to know that the characters in a novel were taken from real people, and that the things described had actually happened; even, Mrs. Glaisher added, wrinkling up her innocent eyes, if they were such naughty things as Mr. Weston wrote about.

Vance's friends had accustomed him to subtler praise, and he only stared and laughed; but seeing Mrs. Glaisher's bewilderment he said: "Well, I suppose we do mix up experience and imagination without always knowing which is which."

Mrs. Glaisher gave him a coy glance. "You won't tell me, then? You mean to leave us all guessing? What's the use of making a mystery, as long as you're a free man? I know all about you; do you suppose I'd be half as interested in your books if I didn't? I know the kind of life you young men lead; and your ideas about love, and the rest of it. We society women are not quite such simpletons as you think. We go around and see—that's what makes it so exciting to meet you. I know all about your adventures in Spain . . . or at least just enough to make me want to hear more. . ."

Vance reddened uncomfortably. What did she know, what was she trying to insinuate? Her stupidity was so prodigious that it struck him that it might be feigned . . . but a second glance at her candid countenance reassured him. "I've had plenty of castles in Spain, but no adventures there," he said.

Mrs. Glaisher shook her head incredulously. "When anybody's as much in the lime-light as you it's no use thinking you can fool people. . . But I see the dancing's beginning. . . I'm coming!" she signalled to her host, advancing to the armchair he had pushed forward for her. Half-way she turned back to Vance. "I do delight in these Bohemian parties, don't you? Won't you give me one some day? Not a big affair, like this; but Imp and I would love it if you'd let us pop in to tea alone, and see how a famous novelist lives when he's at home."

Vance hesitated. Halo always gave him to understand that she was weary of the world she had grown up in, and particularly of the New York in which she had figured as Mrs. Lewis Tarrant; but he had promised her to help out Lorry's party, and he knew the success of "Factories" might depend on Mrs. Glaisher's enjoyment of her evening. No doubt Halo would be willing to offer a cup of tea in such a case; she might even reproach Vance if he made her miss the chance of doing her brother a good turn.

"I'm sure Mrs. Weston will be very glad . . .

she'll send you a note," he stammered, embarrassed by
the memory of his former blunders, and of the pain they
had caused her.

Mrs. Glaisher swept his face with an astonished eye-
glass. "Mrs. Weston? Really—? I'd no idea. . . I supposed you were living alone. . ."

"No," said Vance curtly.

"Do excuse me. I'm too sorry. I was told you were a
widower. . . But perhaps you've remarried lately?"

What was the answer to that, Vance wondered, tingling with the memory of Halo's reproaches. "I supposed of course Spear must have told you. . . I'm to be
married to his sister. . . She and I . . ." he stopped,
his ideas forsaking him under Mrs. Glaisher's frigid
gaze.

"His sister? But he has only one, and she's married
already. Her name is Mrs. Lewis Tarrant. Her husband
is in Paris. He's an old friend of mine; he came to see me
only yesterday. Poor fellow—in spite of all he's been
through I understand he has a horror of divorce . . .
and I don't suppose," Mrs. Glaisher concluded, rising
from the divan with a pinched smile, "that even in your
set a woman can be engaged to one man while she's still
married to another. . . But please forget my suggestion. . . *Such* a pity, young man, with your talent,"
Mrs. Glaisher sighed, as she turned to enthrone herself
in the armchair facing the stage.

Jane Meggs, Lady Pevensey and Kate Brennan
grouped themselves about her, and the rest of the guests
crouched on cushions or squatted cross-legged on the
floor. Nevsky, at the piano, preluded with a flourish of
discords, and Sady Lenz suddenly leapt from behind
parted curtains in apparel scant enough to enlighten the
American sculptor as to her plastic possibilities. Vance
heard Mrs. Glaisher give a little gasp; then he turned

and slipped toward the door. As he reached it Lorry Spear's hand fell on his shoulder.

"Vance. Not going? What's up? This dancing's rather worth while; and Mrs. Glaisher wanted me to arrange a little party with you somewhere next week—I could lend you this place, if you like."

"Thank you. Mrs. Glaisher has already invited herself to our quarters; but she backed out when she found she might meet Halo."

Lorry's brows darkened; then he gave a careless laugh. "Oh, well, what of that? You know the kind of fool she is. The sort that runs after *déclassée* women in foreign countries, and are scared blue when they meet somebody from home who doesn't fit into the conventions. Why did you tell her about Halo?"

Vance stood with his hands in his pockets, staring down at the dusty studio floor. He raised his head and looked into Lorry's handsome restless eyes. "You asked Halo to send me here tonight, didn't you—to help you to amuse Mrs. Glaisher?"

"Of course I did. You don't seem to realize that you're one of our biggest cards. I'm awfully grateful to you—"

"And you told Halo you'd rather she didn't come?"

"Lord, no; I didn't have to. Halo knows how women like Mrs. Glaisher behave. I'd have been sorry to expose her to it. Not that she cares—she wouldn't have chucked everything for you if she had. But see here, Vance, you can't go back on me like this. For the Lord's sake see me through. Halo promised you would. And Imp Pevensey wants to talk to you about going to London next spring and getting launched among the highbrows. You need a London boom for your books, my dear boy. Damn—what's wrong with the lights? That fool Heff swore to me he knew how to manage them. . ."

Lorry dashed back toward the stage, where Fraülein Lenz's posturing had been swallowed up in darkness. Vance continued to stand motionless, his mind a turmoil. At length the lights blazed up, and under cover of the applause at Fraülein Lenz's re-embodiment he made his way out.

IN THE courtyard he stood and looked about him. A cold drizzle was falling, but he hardly noticed it. His resentment had dropped. It was no use being angry with Lorry, who took his advantage where he found it, and thought no harm. What was really wrong was the situation between Vance and Halo—the ambiguity of a tie which, apparently, he could neither deny nor affirm without offending her. What else, for instance, could he have said to Mrs. Glaisher? How could he have pretended that he was living alone without seeming to deny his relation with Halo? Yet, by not doing so, he had subjected her—and himself—to a worse humiliation.

Such questions would not have arisen if she had obtained her divorce at once, as they had expected when they left America. But the months had passed, and Vance (as he now became aware) had hardly given the matter another thought, had in fact been reminded of it only at the moment of the scene provoked by his going alone to the old Marquesa's. He had asked Halo then if they could not marry soon; she had turned the question with a laugh, and he had carelessly dismissed it from his mind.

Since then he could not remember having thought of it again till the night before, in his midnight musings at Fontainebleau. He had always considered himself as much pledged to Halo as if the law had bound them, and would have had a short answer for any one who hinted the contrary; and the question of marriage or non-marriage had seemed subsidiary. In Lorry Spear's group, and that of the writers and artists who came to Vance's studio, such questions were seldom raised, since the social rules they implied hardly affected the lives of these young people. But now Vance saw, as he had for a brief instant at Granada, and again at Fontainebleau, that Halo would never really think and feel as these people did. She had sacrificed with a light heart her standing among her own kind; but something deeper than her prejudices or her convictions, something she could sacrifice to no one because it was closer to her than reason or passion, made it impossible for her to feel at ease in the new life she had chosen. Only yesterday Vance had imagined that jealousy might be the cause of her disquietude; now he saw it was something far harder to dispel. Whatever he might do to persuade her of his devotion, to convince her that no other woman had come between them, her loneliness would subsist; in their happiest and most confiding moments it would be there, she would be conscious, between herself and him, of a void the wider because she knew he could not measure it.

A word of Mrs. Glaisher's had enlightened him. She had said that Tarrant (whom she evidently knew well) had a horror of divorce; and she had doubtless heard this from him recently, since she had mentioned that he was in Paris, and had been with her the day before. Tarrant unwilling to divorce—this, then, must be one of the sources of Halo's preoccupation! Vance wondered why she had kept it from him; perhaps, poor child, because she had feared he might feel himself less bound to her if he knew there was no prospect of their marrying. But that was not like Halo. More probably she had kept her secret because she was resolved to let nothing cloud their happiness. It would be like her to want him to know only the joys of her love, without its burdens.

Vance had been astonished to hear from Mrs. Glaisher that Tarrant was in Paris. The situation was full of perplexity. Halo had often told him that she would never have asked her husband to set her free, that it was he who had begged her to divorce him, presumably that he might marry Mrs. Pulsifer. She had never alluded to any alteration in Tarrant's view; she had never once referred to the question. No doubt she knew of the change; her lawyers must surely have advised her of it; and if she had concealed the fact from Vance it was probably because she knew its cause, and was herself in some way connected with it. At the idea the blood rushed to Vance's forehead. Was it not likely that this man, who was still Halo's husband, had come to Paris purposely to see her, to try to persuade her to go back to him? Moody and unstable as he was, he might well have wearied of the idea of marrying another woman, and begun to pine for Halo, once he knew he had lost her.

For a moment Vance's heart sank; then he reflected that Mrs. Glaisher's statement might have been based on the merest hearsay. Why should Tarrant have confided his views to her? The delay in the divorce might have been caused by a mere legal technicality, some point in dispute between opposing lawyers. And to attach any particular significance to Tarrant's arrival in Paris was absurd. He belonged to the type of Europeanized American who is equally at home on both sides of the Atlantic and accustomed to come and go continually, for pleasure, for business, or simply from the force of habit.

Vance wandered down Lorry's street and turned into the Boulevard Raspail. The more he considered the question the less probable he thought it that Tarrant's presence in Paris had to do with his divorce. Tarrant never intervened personally when he could get any one to replace him; whatever his purpose was, he would probably not wish to meet Halo. . . . But what had he come for? Vance was seized with a sudden determination to find out. The time had come when Halo's situation and his own must be settled, and Tarrant held the key to it.

He walked on through the rain, musing on these problems, and wishing he could meet Tarrant at once—this very night, before going home and seeing Halo. If only he had asked Mrs. Glaisher where Tarrant was staying! It would be easy enough to find out the next day; but Vance's blood was beating too violently for delay. He wanted to bring Halo some definite word as to her divorce; and he determined to try to run Tarrant down at once and plead with him to release her, if it were really true that he was no longer disposed to.

As he walked on, wondering where he was likely to come across Tarrant, Vance recalled Halo's pointing out the hotel where she and her husband had always stayed in Paris. It was one of the quiet but discreetly fashionable houses patronized by people who hate the promiscuity of "Palaces" but cannot do without their comforts. The hotel, Vance remembered, was not far from the Boulevard Raspail, and he decided to go there and enquire. He knew Tarrant's tendency to slip into a rut and shrink from new contacts, and thought it likely that the hotel people might know of his whereabouts even if he were not under their roof.

The drizzle had turned to a heavy rain, and when he reached the street he was in search of the façade of the hotel was reflected from afar in the wet pavement. But within a few yards of the door Vance paused. Even if Tarrant were staying there, and were actually there at the moment (it was long past midnight), he would most probably refuse to receive a visitor. And should Vance leave a note asking for an appointment, if answered at all, it would certainly be answered by a refusal. He had worked long enough under Tarrant in the office of the

"New Hour" to be familiar with his chief's tactics. It was Tarrant's instinct to retreat from the unknown, the unexpected, to place the first available buffer between himself and any incident likely to unsettle his nerves or alter his plans; and if Vance should ask to be received, the obvious buffer would be his lawyers.

Vance stood irresolute. How on earth was he to get at the man? If he waited till chance brought them together he knew the other's adroitness would find a way out. He would cut the scene short and turn on his heel. . . . The uselessness of any attempt to reach him seemed so obvious that Vance turned and walked back toward the Boulevard. He had almost reached it when a taxi passed, approaching from the opposite direction. As it came abreast of him a lamp flashed into it, and he saw Tarrant inside. Vance turned and raced back toward the hotel. The taxi stopped at the door and Tarrant got out and opened his umbrella before he began to hunt for his fare. He was in evening dress, and as perfectly appointed as usual, but in the rainy light he looked paler and older. Vance hung back till the carefully counted fare was in the chauffeur's hand; then he went toward the door.

"Tarrant!" he said, "I—I want to speak to you . . . I must."

Tarrant turned under his umbrella, and surveyed him with astonishment. "I don't—" he began; then Vance saw the colour rush to his pale face. *"You?"* he said. "I've nothing to say to you." He started to enter the hotel.

Vance stepped in front of him. "You must let me see you—now, at once. Do you suppose I'd ask it if it wasn't necessary? Please listen to me, Tarrant—"

Tarrant paused a moment. Under the umbrella Vance could hardly see his face, but he caught a repressed tremor in his voice. "You can write. You can write to my lawyers," he said.

"No! Not to you, and not to your lawyers. You'd turn me down every time. I've only two words to say, but I'm going to say them now. I'll say them out here in the street if you don't want me to come in."

The rain by this time was falling heavily. Vance had no umbrella, and his thin overcoat was already drenched. Tarrant looked down nervously at his own glossy evening shoes. "It's impossible," he said.

"What's impossible? You can't refuse me—"

He saw Tarrant glance toward the illuminated doors of the hotel, and meet the eyes of the night porter, whose dingy face peered out at them with furtive curiosity.

"I don't know why you come here at this hour to make a scene in the street . . ." Tarrant grumbled over his shoulder.

"I won't make it in the street if you'll let me come in. I don't want to make a scene anyhow. I only want a few minutes' talk with you; I've got to have it, so we may as well get it over."

Tarrant looked again at his feet, which were splashed with mud. "I can't stay out here in this deluge," he began. "If you insist, you'd better come in; but your forcing yourself on me is useless . . . and intolerable. . ."

He walked up the steps, and Vance followed. The revolving doors swung open and the two men entered the warm brightly lit lounge. A few people, evidently just back from the theatre, sat at little tables, absorbing drinks from tall glasses. Tarrant turned to the porter. "Is there anybody in the reading-room?" The porter glanced in, and came back to say that there was a gentleman there writing letters.

Tarrant seemed to hesitate; then he turned and walked toward the lift. Vance followed. Tarrant did not look back at him or speak to him. They entered the lift and stood side by side in silence while it slowly ascended; when it stopped they got out, and, still in silence, walked down the dim corridor to a door which Tarrant unlocked. He turned an electric switch and lit up a small sitting-room with pale walls and brocaded curtains. Vance entered after him and shut the door.

Tarrant put down his umbrella. He stood for a moment with his back to Vance, staring down at the empty hearth. Then he turned and said: "Well?"

His thin high-nosed face with the sharply cut nostrils was drawn with distress, and the furrows in his forehead had deepened; but his gray eyes were now quiet and unwavering. Vance knew that he had gone through the inevitable struggle with his impulse of evasion and flight, and that, finding escape impossible, he had mastered his nerves, and was prepared to play his part fittingly. Vance felt a secret admiration for the man whose worldly training had given him this discipline; he knew what mental and physical distress Tarrant underwent after such an effort of the will. "Poor devil," he thought . . . "we're all poor devils. . ."

"Well?" Tarrant repeated.

"Well—I want to speak to you about Halo. I want you to tell me what you intend to do."

Tarrant's face darkened; but in a moment he recovered his expression of rather disdainful indifference. He took off his hat and overcoat, and laid them carefully on a table in the corner of the room; then he turned toward the fireplace and threw himself down in an armchair. "You'd better sit down," he said, glancing coldly toward the chair facing him.

Vance paid no heed; not that he resented the invitation, but because, in his state of acute inner tension, he was hardly aware that it was addressed to him. Tarrant waited for a moment; then, as his visitor did not move: "I supposed," he said, "it was for something of this sort that you'd come, and I can only say again that it's no use. I should have thought you'd have understood that what you have to say had better be said to my lawyers."

Vance flushed. "I suppose you think you're bound to answer in this way; but what use is that either? I've got nothing to say to your lawyers—or to hear from them. I'm not here to make a row or a scene. I only want to put you a straight question. I've heard you've changed your mind about letting Halo divorce you, and I want to know if it's true. Is it?"

Tarrant sat with his long delicately-jointed fingers twisted about the arms of his chair. After a moment he turned slightly, reached out toward a table near by, and took up a packet of cigarettes. He drew out a gold-mounted lighter, lit a cigarette, puffed at it once or twice, and rested his head thoughtfully against the back of the chair. Vance stood leaning against the wall, watching every movement of Tarrant's with a sort of fascinated admiration. He knew that each of those quiet and seemingly careless gestures was the mask of an inner agitation, and envied the schooling which had put Tarrant in command of such a perfectly disciplined set of motions.

At length Tarrant spoke. "When my wife left my house to join you she must have known that her doing so would make me change my mind about letting her divorce me."

Vance gave an impatient shrug. It was the tone he had heard so often at the office, when Tarrant was trying to shake off an importunate visitor. But he reflected that it was only a protective disguise assumed to hide the moral disarray of the real man—as his lighting a cigarette had been done to occupy his hands, lest Vance should notice their nervous twining about the chairarms. And again Vance was filled with a queer pity for his antagonist.

"You mean to say that, as she's put herself in what's called the wrong, you're going to refuse to let her get a divorce against you? Well, it's your technical right, of course. But there's nothing to prevent your getting a divorce against *her;* there'll be no difficulty—" Vance broke off, but Tarrant made no answer. He sat in the same attitude of resigned attention, his gaze engrossed with the cigarette-smoke curling up from his lips. "That's what I came here to ask you; do you mean to divorce her?" Vance continued.

Tarrant bent forward to shake the ashes of his cigarette onto the hearth. "Is this—" he began, and then broke off. "Are you here at—at her request?"

"No. She had no idea I was coming."

"But you think she wished you to?"

"On the contrary—she would probably have done all she could to stop me. That's why I didn't tell her."

During this interrogatory Tarrant's profile was turned toward Vance, and the latter noticed that the edge of his thinly cut nostril was white and drawn up, like that of a man in pain. "After all, I suppose he did love her once," Vance thought.

Tarrant straightened himself, and moved about so that he faced Vance. "You might have spared me this intrusion. I can't see what good you thought it would do. My wife knows I've given up all idea of divorcing her."

"Or letting her divorce you?"

Tarrant gave a barely audible laugh.

Vance stood silent, still leaning against the wall. The wetness of his overcoat began to penetrate to his skin, and he shivered slightly, and pulled the overcoat off. As he did so he saw Tarrant's colour rise.

"I really don't see," Tarrant said, as though answering Vance's unconscious gesture in removing his coat, "what can be gained by any more talk. I've told you what you wanted to know."

Vance shook his head. "No; it's not enough. You say you don't want to get a divorce. But I don't suppose you've forgotten that not much more than a year ago it was you who asked your wife to set you free? It was then that she left you; not till then."

Tarrant stood up, and took a few steps across the room and back. His eyes fell on Vance's wet overcoat, and on the shoulder-blades to which his dress-coat damply clung. "You're wet through," he remarked.

"Never mind that. I want to talk this thing out with you. You admit that when Halo left you it was because you asked her to; because you wanted to be free. And now you turn round and say you don't want to be free any longer, and therefore won't let her be either. Isn't that it?"

Tarrant went to a small upright cabinet between the windows. He took from it a bottle of brandy and a glass, and pouring water into the glass added some brandy and drank it down. "I'm subject to chills; my feet are very wet." He turned to Vance with a cold smile. "I'm not as young as you are. . ." The restless colour rose to his face again and he added, with a hesitating gesture toward the bottle: "Will you—?"

Vance made a sign of refusal, and Tarrant, as though regretting his suggestion, drew his lips together, and stood upright, his hands thrust into his pockets.

"And now you say you don't want to be free, and won't let her be," Vance persisted. "Is that so, or isn't it?"

Tarrant cleared his throat. "It is so—as far as the

external facts go. As to my private motives . . . you'll excuse my keeping them to myself. . ."

Vance uttered a despairing sigh. Again and again in his short life he had come upon this curious human inability, in moments of the deepest stress, to shake off the conventional attitude and the accepted phrase. The man opposite him, whose distress he recognized and could not help pitying, seemed to be struggling in vain to express his real self, in its helpless vanity, humiliation and self-deception. The studied attitude of composure which gave him a superficial advantage over an untutored antagonist was really only another bondage. When a man had disciplined himself out of all impulsiveness he stood powerless on the brink of the deeper feelings. If only, Vance thought, he could help Tarrant to break through those bonds! There must be a word that would work this miracle, if he could find it. Above all, he reminded himself, he must try not to be angry or impatient.

"I suppose," he began, "you feel you've got a right to talk like that. From the point of view of society, or civilized behavior, or whatever you call it, you may be right. But what's the use of it? I'm not trying to offend you, or to butt in where I don't belong. Your wife has left you; she's under my care; how can you blame me for wanting to make things easier for her? When she came to me she thought you wanted to marry another woman. . . ."

"If I did," Tarrant broke in, "it may have been because she had made my home . . . no longer what it should have been. . ."

Vance felt a new wave of discouragement. There they were, back again in the old verbal entanglements. "I wonder how many people—husbands or wives either —make their homes what they should have been? It doesn't seem as if they often pulled it off. But I don't

pretend it's my business to come here and talk to you
about your wife. . ."

"Ah, you admit that?" Tarrant sneered.

"Certainly. I'm here to talk to you about the
woman I want to take for a wife myself. There's a big
gap between the two. Whoever made the gap, or whatever made it, what does it matter now?" He paused a
moment to control his voice, and then added: "See
here, Tarrant, it's hell to see a woman suffering because you can't give her the place in your life that she
ought to have. . . That's what I came here to tell
you. . ."

Tarrant walked away again, and then came back to
the hearth. He raised his elbow against the mantelpiece.

"In my opinion she ought to suffer," he said.

"Why—because you do?" Tarrant was silent, and
Vance pressed on: "There's such a lot of suffering everywhere; what's the use of adding to it? For God's sake,
can't we both put aside the personal question and tackle
this as if it was just any ordinary human predicament?
The happiest people, somehow, aren't any too happy
. . . and I can't see that making them more miserable
ever made things pleasanter for the other party . . . at
least not beyond the minute when he's doing it."

Tarrant's face had whitened. He did not immediately reply; but at last he said, in a tone of elaborate po-
liteness: "I suppose I ought to be very much obliged to
you for your advice—though I didn't ask for it."

"Oh, all right. You can turn what I say into a ser-
mon, and try to laugh me out of it, if you choose. Only I
don't see the use of that either."

"Exactly," said Tarrant. "Neither do I see the use
of your forcing yourself in on me."

"But, my God, all the use in the world—if only I can
make you understand! Can't you see the misery it is not

to be able to give Halo the standing and the name she's got a right to? That woman tonight—that Mrs. Glaisher —insulted her. How can I stand by and see her treated as if she wasn't fit to be touched by the very people who used to grovel to get asked to her house?"

"*My* house," Tarrant interrupted ironically.

Vance's hopes sank. Up to that moment it had seemed to him that he might yet find a crack in the surface of the other's icy pride; now he had exhausted his last argument and knew that he had made no impression. "That's all you've got to say to me?"

Tarrant remained silent; Vance saw his lips twitch with the effort to control his temper. "I've never had anything to say to you," he replied.

Vance continued to lean against the door-jamb. The growing distress in Tarrant's face seemed to belie the bravado of his words. He knew all the accepted formulas; but as he recited them Vance saw that they no longer corresponded with what he was feeling—with the agony of envy, jealousy and resentment battling together in his soul. And Vance, who knew exactly what he himself wanted to say, did not know how to say it because he was ignorant of the language in which men of Tarrant's world have been schooled to disguise their thoughts. Here they stood, he reflected, two poor devils caught in the coil of human incomprehension; but the fact that he felt the pity of it, and that Tarrant did not, gave him an advantage over the other. From the moment when Vance understood this he became sure of himself, and unperturbed. "God," he thought, "when I go away and leave him how cold he'll feel inside of himself!"

He moved impulsively toward Tarrant. "See here, I daresay I don't know how to put things the right way . . . the way you're used to. . . But don't let that count against me. Don't think of you and me; think only of Halo. If there's anything I can do to persuade you to give her her freedom, tell me, and I'll try to do it. I suppose I haven't got what people in your crowd call pride; anyhow, the kind I have got don't count at a time like this. If there's anything I can say or do—short of giving her up—that would make you change your feelings about her, I'll do it now, this very minute. God, Tarrant—don't let me go away feeling I've done no good! Why should people go on hating each other because once in their lives their wants and wishes may have crossed? If you send me away now it isn't me you'll hate afterward—it's yourself."

Tarrant had moved to the farther end of the hearth. As if to give a motive to his withdrawal he took the packet of cigarettes from the mantel and lit another. "I really haven't anything more to say," he repeated.

"Except that you won't divorce."

"Certainly I won't divorce."

"Not on any condition?"

"Not on any condition."

Vance stood in the middle of the room and looked at him. "I can remember when I used to think he was a great fellow," he thought.

He turned away and picked up his drenched overcoat. It had left a dark pool of moisture on the light damask of the chair he had thrown it on, and the velvet pile of the carpet beneath. Tarrant looked gray and ghastly, standing alone between the illuminated wall-brackets of that frivolous room.

"Ah—you poor man," Vance thought, as he turned and left him.

ᕉ XV ᕉ

Halo, after Vance's return from Fontainebleau, felt the reaction that follows on a period of inward distress. When she recalled the desperate paths her imagination had travelled she shivered; but looking back at them from safety made the future seem more radiant.

How unworthy, she thought, for the lover and comrade of an artist to yield to such fears—and a comrade was what she most wanted to be. Women who cast in their lot with great men, with geniuses, even with the brilliant dreamers whose dreams never take shape, should be armed against emotional storms and terrors. Over and over again she told herself that her joys were worth the pain, that the pain was part of the rapture; but such theories shrivelled to nothing in the terror that had threatened her very life. If she were going to lose her lover—if she had already lost him—she could only tremble and suffer like other women. Everybody was reduced to the same abject level by the big primitive passions, love and jealousy and hunger; the delicate distinctions and differences with which security adorned them vanished in the storm of their approach.

Then Vance came back; and as soon as he appeared her fear was lifted. He had not been with another woman; he had gone off to think over his book. Her first look in his eyes convinced her that he had not deceived her; and instantly she swore to herself that never again, by word or glance, would she betray resentment or curiosity concerning his comings and goings. Whenever he wanted to get away she would accept his disappearance

without surprise. Her yoke should be so light, her nearness so pleasant, that when he came back it should never
be because he felt obliged to, but because he was happier with her than elsewhere. New strength and cun-
ning seemed to grow in her as she held him in her arms
that night.

The morning after Lorry's banquet Vance went
out early; he had already left the house when Halo
woke. She was not sorry to be alone; she had not yet finished typing the manuscript he had brought back from
Fontainebleau, and as soon as she had dressed, and given
the *bonne* the orders for the day, she returned to her
task. The hours passed in a flash, and she was still trying
to unravel the tangled manuscript when she heard his
latchkey.

"What—lunch already?" she exclaimed, without
lifting her head. He made no answer, and when she
stopped typing and looked up at him she was startled by
the change in his face.

"Why, Vance, how tired you look—aren't you
well?" she exclaimed. And instantly the little serpent of
jealousy reared its sharp head again in her breast.
Through her sleep, in the small hours, she had heard
Vance unlock the door, coming back from Lorry's feast,
as she supposed; but after all, how did she know? It was
nearly daylight when the sound of his latchkey had
waked her. What more likely than that one of the
women at Lorry's had taken him home with her after
the party? Would there never again be any peace for her
heart, Halo wondered?

Vance stood silently looking down on her. At
length he came up and laid his arm over her shoulder.
"Look here, Halo—" he said in a constrained voice.

"Yes?" she questioned, her own voice sounding to

her as odd and uncertain as his. *"Now—!"* she thought
with a tremor of apprehension. . .

Vance continued to look at her. "I know why you
sent me alone to Lorry's last night. It was because you
knew those New York women would be rude to you.
Wasn't that it?"

She returned his look in surprise; then the weight
slipped from her heart, and she almost laughed. "Why,
darling, how absurd! I've always hated big dinners
. . . and I'm so fed up with that crowd at Lorry's."

"Yes; so am I."

"Well, then, you can't blame me for not going."

"I blame you for not telling me why you wouldn't
go. Lorry told me. He said Mrs. Glaisher didn't want to
meet you because you've left your husband and are living with me."

Halo drew back from his arm to smile up at him.
"Why, you ridiculous boy! I daresay he's right. Mrs.
Glaisher cut me the other day when I met her at Lorry's
door. Oh, deliberately—it was such a funny sensation! It
amused me so much that I meant to tell you; but I forgot all about it."

"It doesn't amuse me," said Vance with lowering
forehead. "Do you suppose I want to associate with people who think you're not good enough for them? She
asked if she could come here to tea with some of her precious friends, and when I told her you were with me she
had the impudence to say she hadn't known, and of
course in that case she couldn't come. Before I left I told
Lorry what I thought about his asking me without you."

Halo was still laughing and looking up into his
eyes. "But, Vanny, it was I who urged Lorry to ask you,
because he said the Glaisher and Lady Pevensey were
dying to meet the author of 'The Puritan in Spain'; and

I thought if he got you to come it might induce Mrs. Glaisher to help him with his ballet."

"I don't care a damn about Lorry's ballet—"

"Well, I do; and I'm very sorry you didn't invite Mrs. Glaisher here. Think what fun for me to hide behind the curtains, and hear what fashionable ladies say to a rising novelist! I begin to think you've lost your sense of humour. . ."

But she saw that such pleasantries only perplexed him. For a long while he had not understood her sensitiveness about her position; but now that some one had taken advantage of it to slight her he was ablaze with resentment. She put her hand over his. "Vance—as if anything mattered but you and me!"

"Everything matters to me that's about you. I should think you'd see how I feel." He walked up and down the room with agitated steps. "I don't understand your being so offended about that old woman in Granada whom you'd never seen; and now, when your own brother, and people you used to know, behave as if it was a disgrace to meet you, you just sit and laugh."

Her eyes followed him tenderly. "But don't you see that it's simply because being with you has made everything else seem of no consequence?"

He came back and sat down by her, his brow still gloomy. "That's it . . . that's why it makes my blood boil to think that when people treat you like that I have to sit by and hold my tongue. I thought of course we should have been married by this time. And I want you to know I've done all I could."

Halo felt a tremor of joy rush through her. "But I know, darling . . . of course I know. . ."

"I went to see Tarrant last night—" Vance continued.

She interrupted him with an exclamation of astonishment. "Lewis? Do you mean to say Lewis is in Paris?"

"Yes. I thought perhaps you knew. That Glaisher woman told me. And she said he'd never let you have a divorce; he didn't approve of divorce, she said. I didn't believe her, because you'd always told me he wanted to get married himself, and I thought she just said it to spite me. But I was bound I'd get at the truth, and so I hunted him down at his hotel last night, and made him listen to me."

"Last night? You mean to say you were with Lewis last night?"

He nodded silently, and the unexpectedness of the announcement struck Halo silent also. She had not heard that Lewis Tarrant was in Paris, or indeed in Europe; and the shock of learning that he was in the same place as herself, and that only a few hours earlier, all unsuspected by her, her husband and her lover had been talking her over, silenced every other emotion. The vision of that scene—which, a moment ago, would have appeared too improbable to call up any definite picture —seized painfully on her imagination. It seemed to her that she was gazing at herself stripped and exposed, between these two men who were disputing for her possession.

"See here, Halo—you're not angry with me, are you? I couldn't help trying to see him," she heard Vance pleading; and dropping the hands she had raised to her face she turned to him.

"Vanny! Angry? How could I be? Only I don't see . . . what in the world made you think. . ."

"I don't believe I did think. I felt I had to see him." Her eyes filled, and he hurried on nervously: "Yes, but it was no good. I suppose I ought to have known it wouldn't be. He and I never could talk to each other long without one of us getting mad, or both."

She looked up in alarm. "You don't mean to say you had a quarrel?"

"Oh, no; that isn't his way. We just kept on getting politer and politer."

"Ah—" she breathed, and covered her eyes again. If only the pressure of her hands could blot out the vision he called up, the vision of Tarrant rigid and sneering, of Vance bewildered, passionate and helpless! She thought: "My darling—he's wrecked my last chance of freedom . . . and how I love him for it!"

But in a moment she recovered her self-control. "You must tell me just what happened, dear." She drew him down to the chair beside her, and quietly, her hand in his, listened to what he told her, weighing every phrase, every syllable, the meaning of which she knew he had only half-guessed, while to her it lay bare to the roots. She had seen at once that any influence she might still have had over Tarrant must have been forfeited by Vance's rash intervention. Tarrant would never believe that she had not known of it, and his disgust at a proceeding so tactless and indelicate would be aggravated by the idea that she had connived at it, perhaps even prompted it. She could hear him say, with the lift of the nostril that marked his strongest disapproval: "Things aren't done in that way between civilized people." It was his final form of condemnation.

She knew that Tarrant never forgave any one who wounded his vanity and tortured his nerves by forcing from him a definite statement on a question he was tacitly determined to ignore, and when Vance ended she sat silent, overcome by the probable consequences of his blunder. But she felt that he might misinterpret her silence, and she faltered out: "I suppose of course he thought I'd sent you."

"Well, he did at first; but I told him you didn't know anything about my coming."

She gave a nervous laugh. "Naturally he didn't believe that."

"Why shouldn't he believe it?"

Her impulse was to say: "Because he wanted a better reason for hating me—" but she suppressed the retort. "When he's angry he never listens to what any one says," she answered vaguely.

"But why is he so angry? He wouldn't answer me when I asked him that."

"You asked him—?"

"I reminded him that it was he who originally wanted you to divorce him."

"Ah—but there's nothing he hates so much as to be reminded of things he's finished with!"

Vance, who had stood looking down on her with gathering perplexity, turned away, and began to wander up and down the room. "I see you think I've made a colossal blunder," he said at length. She could not think of anything to say, and he went on: "I ought to have consulted you first, I suppose."

She took his hand. "If you had I certainly wouldn't have let you expose yourself to anything so painful."

"And so useless? I know what you're thinking. There might have been a chance of his coming round if I'd let things alone . . . and now there's none. That's it, isn't it?"

"I suppose so. For the present, at any rate. But what does it matter? Do you mind, dearest—our not being married?" she asked suddenly, laying her hands beseechingly on his shoulders.

"Yes; I hate it—I hate it every minute!" he burst

out. "At first I didn't see what it meant for you—it was enough for me that you and I were together. But now I wouldn't for the world have you go through again what you've had to endure this last year."

She drew back, wrinkling up her eyes in the way she knew he liked, and smiling up into his face. "How do you know, dearest, that all I've endured hasn't been a part of our happiness?"

"Not mine—not mine!" he exclaimed impatiently. "It's poisoned everything for me; and last night that woman made me wild. That's why I couldn't wait another minute. And now I see my doing what I did was all a monstrous mistake." He turned away and resumed his agitated pacing of the room. She wondered if he still had something on his mind, and what it could be; but after the shock of what he had told her she had no heart to question him further. After all, she knew the worst now, and must try to come to terms with that first. . .

Presently he came and sat down beside her. "Halo —there's one thing I've got to ask you. You'll hate it, maybe; but I want you to give me a straight answer. Tarrant says you've known all along about his having refused to get a divorce. Is that so?"

She made a sign of assent, and he went on: "Then —then; this is what I want you to tell me. Hasn't he refused because he's trying to get you back?"

She gave a start of surprise, and the blood rushed to her forehead. "Why, Vance, what an idea! You must be crazy. . ."

"Why not? I thought of it the minute I'd left him. The man was in agony; I could see that. He couldn't have hated me so if he hadn't still been in love with you."

"But, darling, I swear to you—"

He gave a shrug. "Oh, I daresay he hasn't said anything yet. He's feeling his way . . . trying to think of some dodge that'll save his face. . . But I'm sure of it, Halo, I'm sure of it!"

She smiled at his boyish violence. "Well—and what of it?"

"What of it? Nothing, of course. Unless— Look here, Halo, we've been together over a year now. When we went away I thought we'd be married in a few months; I wouldn't have dared to urge you to come if I hadn't been sure of it. And now there seems no hope of your being free; and I see what a bad turn I did you, persuading you to go off before things were settled. It's too late to mend that; the harm's done. But what I want to say is this—"

Halo sprang up, a new apprehension catching at her heart. "Yes . . . yes . . . you want to say . . . ?"

"I want to say that you're free . . . free as air. . ."

She gave him a long look, and then broke into a little laugh. "Free to go back to Lewis if he'll have me? Is that what you mean? I'm much obliged to you!"

His head drooped, and he looked away from her. "I mean, of course, free to do what you like."

There was a silence, during which neither looked at the other.

"If it comes to that, we're both free," Halo said at last, in a low voice. Vance was still silent, and she repeated insistently: "We're both free. Is that what you're trying to tell me? I've always understood it, I assure you!" The words were hardly spoken when she saw how they betrayed the dread she had determined to hide from him; but already she was being swept away on its current. "Ah, you make me too unhappy—too unhappy!" she burst out, and suddenly her hard anguish was loosened, and she fell with long sobs on his breast.

"Vanny, Vanny. . . I've never loved you as I do now!"
she heard herself crying; and felt far off, through the
streaming flood of her fears, his hand quietly pushing
back her hair.

BOOK III

ಕ XVI ಶಿ

FROM THE balcony of the little pink house Vance Weston looked out over a shabby garden and a barrier of palms to a bay between plum-blue headlands.

On this particular day the bay palpitated with glittering cubes of purple and azure that the waves tossed back and forth like mermaids playing with their jewels. To Vance these games of wind and water were a ceaseless joy. He was always leaving his work to watch the waves race in from the open sea, dodge past the guardian promontories, and fall crying on the beach below his balcony—those unquiet waves, perpetually escaping from something; cloud-shadows and sun-javelins, the silver bullets of the rain, the steady drive of the west wind's flails. There were other days, very different, when they were not in flight, but like immense grazing flocks moved backward and forward over their smooth pastures to a languid secret rhythm; when a luminous indistinctness falsified the distances, and the wild bay became a placid land-locked sheet of water. Divine days too; but not as inspiriting as those of flight and pursuit, or as exciting as those when the storm caught the frightened waves and turned their hollows livid as the olive trees along the shore.

Vance laid down his pen and went out on the balcony. Coming up the path of the adjoining Pension Britannique, between untrimmed tea-roses and tough-leaved yuccas, was the perpendicular form of the eldest Miss Plummet. Her hand, cased in a black glove worn blue at the seams, clutched a string bag, through the interstices of which were visible some books from the English Chapel library, a bottle from the chemist's, a handful of mandarins and a tiny bunch of faded anemones. Miss Plummet was almost as fascinating to Vance as the sea and the headlands. She represented, in all its angular purity, a vision as new and exotic: the English maiden lady whose life is spent in continental pensions kept by English landladies, and especially recommended by the local English chaplain. The type was familiar to Halo, so much of whose girlhood had been lived in continental pensions; but to Vance it was more novel and exciting than anything that Montparnasse could offer. "She's got an outline, an edge; she's representative. And what she represents is so colossal," he would explain to Halo, pressing her for further elucidations about the kind of life that Miss Plummet's family probably led at home, the kind of house she came out of, her background, her conception of the universe.

The passing of Miss Plummet always told Vance what time it was. Precisely at three every afternoon she returned from her shopping in the one narrow street of Oubli-sur-Mer, the little Mediterranean town curving its front of blotched pink-and-yellow houses along the harbour crammed with fishing-boats and guarded by a miniature jetty. Oubli-sur-Mer (Halo had explained, when she proposed to him that they should go there for the winter) was a queer survival: a pocket past which, since the war, fashion and money, jazz and cinemas, had swept eastward, leaving stranded in this dent of the coast, hemmed in by rusty pine-clad hills, the remnant of an old-fashioned English colony. The colonists were annually fewer, a dying race; but though the group had dwindled it held the more jealously to its habits and traditions, its English chaplain, English doctor, chemist, parish library, its sacred horror of "French ways", and inability to understand the humour of "what French people call funny".

But Vance never could give the proper amount of attention to Miss Plummet, for almost immediately after she had vanished into the interior of the Pension Britannique there always emerged from it Mrs. Dorman, the chaplain's wife. Mrs. Dorman was spreading where Miss Plummet was vertical, ambling where the other was brisk. She belonged to the generation which had known the south of France to possess a warm winter climate, and her large mild face looked forth astonished under a spreading straw hat wreathed with a discouraged dust-coloured feather, while she grasped a sun-umbrella in one hand and with the other tightened her fur tippet. Vance called her the regional divinity because her dual precautions against the weather so aptly symbolized the extremes of temperature experienced at Oubli-sur-Mer in passing from sun to shade.

"I'm afraid the winter climate of the Riviera is not what it used to be; in old times we never *dreamed* of covering up the Bougainvilleas," Mrs. Dorman would invariably proclaim to new arrivals at the pension, to the distress of her landlady, Madame Fleuret, who was the widow of a French Protestant *pasteur*, but herself unassailably English. "If only," Madame Fleuret privately complained, "she'd leave the new people alone till they've settled down, and made up their minds to have their letters sent here"—a view in which the Reverend Mr. Dorman heartily concurred. "But you know, dear Madame Fleuret, the Bishop *did* agree with me," Mrs. Dorman would gently protest, thereby recalling to Madame Fleuret's irritated memory the disastrous visit of the Bishop of Drearbury. His lordship, having been ordered south by his physicians for a rest, and having singled out the Pension Britannique after protracted correspondence with Lady Dayes-Dawes, had arrived on a *mistral* day, when the olive trees were turned inside out, the gale screaming down the chimneys, and the fire smoking furiously in what Madame Fleuret had lately been trained to call the "lounge"; and it was at that disastrous moment that Mrs. Dorman had put her stereotyped question: "We do so hope you're going to like the Riviera?" to which the Bishop, whom Mr. Dorman had just brought back from a good long walk in the teeth of the gale, had hissed out: "I'm afraid I don't like your foliage." ("If at least," Madame Fleuret said afterward confidentially to the other ladies, "Mrs. Dorman would give them time to get used to the olives! It took me *years*, I know; and there's no use trying to hurry people.")

Mrs. Dorman, Vance knew, was on her way to sit with Mrs. Churley, the wife of the retired Indian cavalry officer who lived up the hill. Colonel Churley, a long melancholy mahogany-coloured man with a drooping white moustache, and white rings under his pale blue eyes, walked past the pink house every morning to fetch his letters from the post office, and every afternoon to take a long tramp by himself along the shore or among the hills. He walked slowly, his arms clasped behind his back, his walking stick dragging through the dust, and looked neither to right nor left, but kept his stern eyes, under projecting shaggy brows, fixed steadily ahead of him, as if to avoid being accosted by acquaintances. Only when he met the Reverend Mr. Dorman, the short round chaplain, whose face was as rubicund as the other's was dark, did Colonel Churley stop for a few words before resuming his mournful tramp. Mrs. Churley, crippled with rheumatism and half blind, lay all day on her sofa at Les Mimosas, the dismal-looking house up the hill, and Mrs. Dorman and Miss Plummet took

turns to sit with her during her husband's solitary rambles. Halo had offered to share their task, but Mrs. Dorman had explained, with some embarrassment, that the
Churleys were very shy and unsociable, and perhaps it
would be best . . . though Mrs. Weston was so very
kind . . . and she would of course give the message
. . . but Mrs. Weston mustn't think it odd . . . even
dear Lady Dayes-Dawes had never been allowed to
call. . .

There was a Churley son, it appeared, a youth also
said to be invalidish and unsociable; Vance had not yet
seen him, but at times he was haunted by the thought
that a young fellow, perhaps younger than himself, lived
in that dreary house up the lane, in a place as lacking in
youthful life as Oubli-sur-Mer. Mrs. Dorman had told
Halo that young Churley was said to be "literary," and
the ladies of the Pension Britannique shook their heads
when he was mentioned, as if small good was to be
hoped of any one with such tendencies. The ladies had
been shy of Vance too when they learned he was an author; but Halo had had the happy thought of giving the
parish library a copy of "Instead", his romantic early
novel, and Miss Pamela Plummet, the invalid, who
ranked as the leading literary critic of Oubli-sur-Mer,
had pronounced it very pretty; after which, reassured,
the Pension Britannique had taken "Mr. and Mrs. Weston" to its bosom.

The pension had made the acquaintance of the
newcomers through the accident of their sudden arrival.
Halo and Vance, after the latter's encounter with Lewis
Tarrant, had both felt the desire to get away from Paris;
and Halo, with her usual promptness, had remembered
the obsolete charms of Oubli-sur-Mer, got hold of some
one who knew a house-agent there, and secured the little pink house after one glance at its fly-blown photo-

graph. A week later they had packed up and evacuated the Paris flat; but their arrival in the south had been too precipitate for Halo to engage servants in advance. The restaurants on the quay were too far off, and the nearness of the Pension Britannique prompted her to seek its hospitality. It was against Madame Fleuret's principles to receive boarders from outside; she was opposed to transients of any kind. Her established clients, she explained, did not like to be brought in contact with strangers, people you couldn't tell anything about, and who might turn out to be "foreigners", or even "peculiar". But Halo's persuasiveness, and the good looks and good humour of the young couple, had broken down her rule, and for a week Vance and Halo had been suffered to lunch and dine at the pension. It was then that Vance had laid in his store of impressions; had listened, fascinated, to the literary judgments of the invalid Miss Plummet on "The First Violin" and "Ships that Pass in the Night" (her favourite works of fiction); had gazed spell-bound on the mushroom hats and jet-beaded mantle of old Lady Dayes-Dawes, the baronet's widow, who knew more knitting and crochet stitches than any one else at Oubli, and whose first cousin was a Colonial Governor; had hung delighted on the conversation of the Honourable Ginevra Hipsley, who kept white mice on whose sensibilities she experimented by means of folk-songs accompanied by the accordion, and about whom she wrote emotional letters to "Nature" and the "Spectator"; had followed the Reverend Mr. Dorman's discreet attempts to ascertain if "Mr. and Mrs. Weston" belonged to the American branch of the Church of England (as their distinguished appearance made him hope) and would therefore be disposed to assist in the maintenance of the Bougainvillea-draped chapel in which he officiated, or whether they were members of one of the innumerable sects which so deplorably diversify the religious life of the States; and had gathered various items of information about the melancholy Churley family and the other British residents of Oubli-sur-Mer.

It was a little world seemingly given over to illness, poverty and middle-age; and the contrast between the faded faces and vanished hopes of its inhabitants and the boisterous setting of sun and gale that framed their declining days would have been depressing if Vance had not felt in them a deep-down solidarity of tastes and principles. It was enough that they all read the "Times", and did not like vegetables cooked in the French way; in the rootless drifting world into which Vance had been born he had never (even among Halo's friends and family) come across such a solid coral-isle of convictions. This little handful of people, elderly, disappointed and poor, forced by bad health or lack of means to live away from their country, drifting from pension to pension, or from one hired villa to another, with interests limited to the frugal and the trivial, yet managed by sheer community of sentiment to fit into the pattern of something big and immemorial. The sense of the past awakened in Vance by his first sight of the Willows, that queer old house on the Hudson which embodied a past so recent, now stirred in him more deeply at the sight of these detached and drifting fragments of so great a whole. It was odd, he thought, looking back: he hadn't felt Chartres, yet he felt Miss Plummet and Colonel Churley. Perhaps even Halo wouldn't have understood how it was that, seen from Euphoria, these human monuments seemed the more venerable.

Vance stood on the balcony and lit a cigarette. Behind him was his writing-table, scattered with the loose sheets of "Colossus"; before him, the joyous temptation of sun and sea. In the next room he heard the diligent click of Halo's Remington, re-copying the third version of Chapter VII. The work wasn't going as well as he had hoped; he thought enviously of the pace at which he had reeled off "The Puritan in Spain" the previous winter at Cadiz. What he was at now, of course, was a different matter; no glib tale, but a sort of compendium of all that life had given him—and received from him. He was attempting to transcribe the sum total of his experience, to do a human soul, his soul, in the round. At times, when his inspiration flagged, he told himself ironically that it looked as though he hadn't had enough experience to fill many pages. Yet there were days when a grain of mustard-seed, like an Indian conjuror's tree, would suddenly shoot up and scale the sky. He stood on the balcony, thinking restlessly of the sound of the wind in the pines along the shore, of the smell of lavender and sage on the hot slopes behind the town, and watching for the figure of Colonel Churley, gloomily silhouetted against the dazzling bay. If Miss Plummet were a moment late Vance could always put his watch right by Colonel Churley.

"Ready for the next!" Halo called.

"Yes. All right. . ." Ah, there the Colonel was, dragging his stick along behind him, punctual and desolate as a winter night. In another moment he would probably meet Mr. Dorman, and Vance would watch their two faces, one blankly melancholy, the other a-twitter with animation. But today Mr. Dorman was not visible, and Colonel Churley strode on, aiming for the hills. Vance shivered and turned indoors.

"All right. Only I'm afraid there's nothing more coming," he said.

As Halo looked up he saw a shade of disappointment cross her face and transform itself into a smile. "Another holiday?"

"Looks like it. I believe it's the sea," he said with a shrug.

"Well, you'd better go out and spend the rest of the day with it."

He stood in the doorway, irresolute. "Come along?"

"I don't believe I will. I want to go over the first chapters again."

"What a life for you!"

She laughed. "Do I look as if I minded?"

"No. That's what's so trying about you. . ."

They laughed together, and Vance swung joyously down the stairs.

The little house was full of a friendly shabby gaiety. Halo always managed to give that air to their improvised habitations. On the ground floor, where the kitchen and dining-room were, she had hidden the dingy papering of the hall under a gay striped cotton, and had herself repainted and cushioned the tumble-down chairs in the verandah. Vance's craving for order and harmony was always subtly gratified by this exercise of her skill. He recalled with a shudder the chronic disorder in which he had struggled through the weary years of his marriage, the untidy lair into which poor Laura Lou converted every room she lived in, the litter of unmended garments, half-empty medicine bottles and leaking hot-water bags that accumulated about her as lavender-scented linen, fresh window-curtains, flowers and books did about Halo—poor Laura Lou, who could never touch a fire without making it smoke, while Halo's clever hands could coax a flame from the sulkiest log.

Vance, thinking of all this, and of the golden freedom awaiting him outside, recalled another day as bright and beckoning, when he had fled from the squalid Westchester bungalow, and the monotony of Laura Lou's companionship, to wander in the woods and dream of a book he was never to write. He thought of the incredible change in his fortunes since then, of the love and understanding and success which had come to him together, and wondered why mercies of which he was so exquisitely aware had never yet stifled his old aching interrogation of life. He was glad to be at Oubli-sur-Mer, away from the incessant stimulus of Paris, in the country quiet which seemed a necessity to his creative mood. The queer little community, so self-contained and shut off from his own agitated world, gave him the sense of aloofness which his spirit needed; yet somehow—as so often before—the fulness of the opportunity seemed to oppress him, his work lagged under the very lack of obstacles.

He picked up his stick and cap, and was just emerging from the verandah when a young man who walked with a slight limp pushed open the garden gate. The visitor, a stranger to Vance, came toward him with an air of rather jaunty self-confidence. He had a narrow dusky face, with an unexpected crop of reddish hair streaked with amber tumbling over a broad forehead, and dark eyes with the look of piercing wistfulness that sometimes betrays spinal infirmity. A brilliant crimson tie, and a loudly patterned, but faded pull-over above a pair of baggy flannel trousers, completed his studied make-up.

"Mr. Weston? Would you give me an interview? I don't mean for a newspaper," the young man began abruptly, in a cultivated but slightly strident voice. "I've been asked to do an article for the 'Windmill', and

I'd be awfully glad if you'd let me talk with you for a few minutes."

Vance stood still in the path considering his visitor. He was not particularly interested in the idea of being interviewed or reviewed. From the outset of his literary career he had been unusually indifferent to the notoriety attained by personal intervention. He remembered the shock he had received, when he was reviewing for Lewis Tarrant on the "New Hour", on discovering the insatiable greed for publicity of such successful novelists as Gratz Blemer. It was not that Vance was indifferent to success, but because its achievement seemed to him so entirely independent of self-advertising. Halo abounded in this view, partly (he suspected) from disgust at what she had seen of the inner workings of the "New Hour", partly from an inborn disdain of any sort of cheap popularity. She wanted him to be the greatest novelist who had ever lived, and was still (Vance felt sure) gloriously certain of his eventually reaching that pinnacle; but she cared not a rush for the fame cooked up in editorial kitchens. As for Vance, though he had to the full the artist's quivering sensitiveness to praise, and anguished shrinking from adverse criticism, he felt neither praise or blame unless it implied recognition of what he had been striving for. Random approbation had never, even in the early days, perceptibly raised his pulse; and his first taste of popularity had only made him more fastidious.

But the young man in the faded pull-over interested him for other reasons. That eager dark face, with its strange shock of bright hair tossed back from a too prominent forehead, was full of intellectual excitement.

"I hate interviews—don't see any sense in them," Vance began, but in a tone so friendly that his visitor re-

joined with a laugh: "Oh, you're thinking of the heart-
to-heart kind, probably. With a snap-shot of yourself
looking at the first crocus in your garden; or smoking a
pipe, with your arm round a Great Dane."

"Well . . ." Vance acknowledged. "Transposed
into 'Windmill' terms. . ."

"Yes; I know. But that's not my line. Honest to
God, it isn't, as you say in the States." The young man
looked at Vance with a whimsical smile. "I wish it were
—for my bank-account. The human touch is worth its
weight in gold, and outlives all the fashions. But all I
care about is ideas; or else the world in which they are
completely non-existent. And I prefer the latter, only
it's too expensive for me." He paused, and then added:
"My name's Christopher Churley, by the way."

"Oh—you live up the hill, then?"

"Well, if you call it living. I say, can I have my talk
now? The 'Windmill' people are rather in a hurry. But
of course if it's not convenient—"

Vance was looking at him with compassionate interest. This was the sombre Colonel's son. The sombre-
ness was there—Vance perceived it instantly, under a
surface play of chaff and self-derision that was sadder
than the father's open gloom; but the youth's look of
flaming intelligence had no counterpart in the Colonel's
heavy stare.

"I was going for a tramp. But if you'd rather come
in now and have a talk—"

"Thanks a lot. You'll let me, then?" Chris Churley's eyes were illuminated. "But I don't mind walking,
you know; not if I can take it easy, on account of my
limp; and if you'll let me take the landscape for
granted."

"Oh, you can, can you? Take all this for granted?"
Vance interrupted.

"Yes. Rather a pity, I suppose. I daresay there are lots of poor devils looking at cats on a tin roof through a fog who'd expand in this Virgilian setting. But I can't. Give me the tin roof and the cats, if they're in a metropolis. Though what I really prefer is artifice and luxury. I revel in a beautiful landscape transformed by the very rich; not just the raw material, like this. . ." He waved a contemptuous hand toward the bright sea and fretted coast-line. "What I care about, you see, is the landscape of the mind; the intellectual Alps. Or else cocottes and oil kings round a baccarat table."

"Well, you've a wide range," said Vance, somewhat distressingly reminded of the stale paradoxes dear to Rebecca Stram's familiars and the satellites of Lorry's studio.

Young Churley flushed up, and Vance saw his eyes darken as if in physical pain. "I suppose this sort of talk bores you. I daresay you've had everything. . ."

"Oh, have I? Look here," said Vance good-naturedly, "come upstairs, and we'll talk shop as much as you like, since Oubli doesn't provide the other alternatives." He pulled out his cigarettes, and offered them to young Churley. Decidedly the sight of the Colonel had not prepared him for the Colonel's son.

❦ XVII ❧

ON THE threshold of the low-ceilinged study, with its rough yellow-washed walls, Chris Churley stopped to glance curiously about at the books and papers, the blossoming almond-branch in a big jar, the old brown Bokhara with the help of which Halo had contrived a divan piled with brown cushions. "I say—this is jolly!"

"Not much luxury," Vance grinned, always gratified at the admiration provoked by Halo's upholstery.

The other shrugged. I wish you could see Les Mimosas—no, I don't," he corrected himself hastily; and immediately drew from his pocket a letter which he handed to Vance. It was in a girl's hand, dated from London, under the letter-head: "Zélide Spring, Literary Agent and Adviser." It ran: "Darling Chris, the 'Windmill' people have just rung up to say they hear Vance Weston, who wrote 'The Puritan in Spain,' is at Oubli, and they'd like an article about him if you can get it done in time for the next number. Some one has failed them, and they want to shove this in at once. Of course that means doing it in a rush. Now, Chris, please, you simply *must*, or I'll never speak to you again—" and then: "P.S. You must see him, of course, and get him to talk to you about his books. How frightfully exciting for you! Get me an autograph, darling."

Vance laughed as he returned the letter. "This means, I suppose, that you don't like doing things in a rush."

"Do *you?*" said young Churley, looking enviously

at the divan. "The very word makes me want to go and stretch out over there."

"Well, do," said Vance, tossing a fresh packet of cigarettets in the direction of the divan.

"Honestly? You don't mind? Sprawling here while you're sitting in a chair makes me feel like a vamp in a talkie. But then that's the way I really like to feel— luxurious and vicious," Churley confessed, shaking up the cushions before he plunged his glowing head into them. "Match? Oh, thanks! Now, then—I suppose I ought to begin by asking you about 'The Puritan in Spain'."

"No, don't," said Vance, lighting a cigarette, and dropping into the chair by his writing-table. He was beginning to be interested and stirred by this vivid youth, who set his ideas tumbling about excitedly, as Savignac had in the early days in Paris. Sometimes he felt that he needed a sort of padded cell of isolation to work in, and then again, when a beam of understanding flashed through his shuttered solitude, a million sparks of stimulation rushed in with it.

"Oh, but I've got to! You said I might," Churley protested.

"I didn't say I'd answer. Not about 'The Puritan', anyhow."

Young Churley, with a glance of curiosity, raised himself on his elbow. "No? Why?"

"Because I hate it," said Vance carelessly.

"Oh, good! I mean—well, hang it, now I've seen you, I begin to wonder . . ."

"Why I did it? Yes. . . If I only knew—! What's that thing in Tennyson, about 'little flower in the crannied wall', if I knew what put you there, I'd know all there is to know; or something of that sort. Well, I was in Spain, and the subject caught me. What I call one of the siren-subjects. . . I never stir now without cotton in my ears."

Churley laughed. "Righto! Glad I don't have to ask you solemn questions about the book. I'm in rather a difficulty about you American novelists. Your opportunity's so immense, and . . . well, you always seem to write either about princesses in Tuscan villas, or about gaunt young men with a ten-word vocabulary who spend their lives sweating and hauling wood. Haven't you got any subject between the two? There's really nothing as limited as the primitive passions—except perhaps those of the princesses. I believe the novelist's richest stuff is in the middle class, because it lies where its name says, exactly in the middle, and reaches out so excitingly and unexpectedly in both directions. But I suppose you haven't a middle class in America, though you do sometimes have princesses—"

"I rather think we've got a middle class too. But no one wants to admit belonging to it, because we all do. It's not so picturesque—"

"Just so! There's its immense plastic advantage. Absolute safety from picturesqueness—you don't even have to be on your guard against it. Why don't you write a novel about the middle class, and call it 'Meridian'?" cried young Churley, with an inspired wave of his hand, which closed on the packet of cigarettes.

"Because I'm writing one about all mankind called: 'Colossus'."

"You're not? I say . . . where have those matches gone? Thanks. But that *is* a subject! Does it bore you to talk about your things while they're on the stocks?"

"N—no," said Vance, hesitatingly. All at once he felt the liberating thrill of the question. Of course it wouldn't bore him to talk about "Colossus" to anybody with those eager eyes and that lightning up-take. Here was a fellow with whom you could argue and theorize by the hour, and so develop the muscles of your ideas. It was queer he should ever have imagined he could grind out a big book in a smiling desert like Oubli-sur-Mer. But the desert animated by one responsive intelligence became exactly what his mood required. And he began to talk. . .

Churley listened avidly, his head thrown back, his eyes fixed, through the curl of incessant cigarettes, on the luminous glitter beyond the windows. As Vance talked on he was aware, in his listener, of a curious mental immaturity combined with flashes of precocious insight. Compared with his friend Savignac, in whose disciplined intelligence there were so few gaps and irregularities, this youth's impatient brain was as uncertain as the sea; but it had the sea's bright sallies and sudden irresistible onslaughts. Arguing with him about "Colossus" reminded Vance of the hour he had spent in the unknown church during a thunderstorm, when the obscurity was torn by flashes that never lasted long enough for him to do more than guess at what they lit up.

Chris Churley was probably not more than three or four years younger than himself; yet a world seemed to divide them. Churley still lived on the popular catchwords of which Vance had already wearied; yet he appeared to have discarded many of the ideas which were the very substance of Vance's mind.

They talked on and on, till the radiance faded into dusk and Halo came with a lamp and the suggestion of tea or cocktails. Churley, in her presence, was as easy and natural as with Vance. "I've come to make an article out of Mr. Weston for the Windmill'," he explained, smiling; "it's a tremendous chance for me," and Vance saw that Halo felt, as he had, the happy simplicity of the youth's manner. In the last few months he had grown more observant of Halo's changes of expression, and quicker in divining her response to the persons they were thrown with. She was going to like Chris Churley, Vance thought, listening to her friendly questions, and to their easy interchange of talk. The mere fact that the newcomer was going to write an article about Vance in a review of such standing as the "Windmill" was a sufficient recommendation to Halo; but, apart from that, Vance saw that she and Churley talked the same language, and would always be at ease with each other.

"I was wondering whether you were going to take to that chap or not," he said, when Churley, roused to the lateness of the hour, had sprung up exclaiming that he must hurry home and get to work. "I'll bring the article in a couple of days if I may," he called back from the threshold. "It's my chance, you know; if this thing suits them I hope they'll take me on regularly; and it's just conceivable that in time that might mean: London!" He pronounced the word with a mystical stress that lit up his whole face.

"Of course I take to him," Halo responded to Vance's question. "Poor boy! What life at Les Mimosas must be! I could see how he shied away from questions about his family. . . I suppose they're miserably poor, and gloomy and ill. We must have him here as much as possible; you must do all you can to help him with the article."

Young Churley reappeared punctually in two days; but he did not bring the article. It had taken, he explained, more thinking over than he had foreseen. And, if Weston didn't mind, there were just a few more questions he'd like to put.

This was the prelude to another long and exhilarating talk. The actual questions were not, as far as Vance could recall, ever put, either then or later; but the big psychological panorama which he was attempting in "Colossus" was the point of departure for an absorbing discussion of the novelist's opportunities and limitations. Young Churley seemed to have read everything, and thought about most things, without ever reaching any intellectual conclusions; the elasticity of his judgments was as startling to Vance as his uncanny quickness of apprehension. Good talk was doubtless a rare luxury to him, and he was evidently determined to make the most of his opportunity. Day after day he returned to the pink villa, at first apologetically, soon as a matter of course; and while he lolled on the brown divan, or lay outstretched on the sand of one of the rocky coves along the bay, every allusion that Vance made, every point on which he touched, started a new hare for young Churley's joyful pursuit. At one moment he seemed full of interest in Vance's idea of celebrating the splendour and misery of the average man, and produced a great Pascalian aphorism for his title-page; but the next he was declaring that the only two things in the world he really loathed were Oubli-sur-Mer and the Categorical Imperative, and urging Vance to write a novel about a wealthy, healthy and perfectly happy young man who murders his best friend simply to show he is above middle-class prejudices.

Halo, as her way was with Vance's friends, came and went about her daily occupations, sometimes joining the two on their picnics, sometimes finding a pretext for remaining at home. Young Churley continued to amuse and stimulate her, and she often urged him to come to dine, and sat late with the young men over the fire of olive-wood; but Vance noticed that she seemed increasingly anxious, as the months passed, to make him feel that he was free to come and go without consulting her, or seeking her company. Even where his work was concerned she had relaxed her jealous vigilance. She no longer asked how the book was getting on, or playfully clamoured for fresh copy; she waited till he brought her his manuscript, betraying neither impatience nor disappointment if the intervals of waiting were protracted. At times her exquisite detachment almost made it seem as if she were quietly preparing for a friendly parting; once or twice, with a start of fear, he wondered if, as he had once imagined, her husband were not trying to persuade her to come back; but whenever she and Vance were alone together she was so entirely her old self, so simply and naturally the friend and lover of always, that the possibility became inconceivable.

Meanwhile the days passed, and no more was said of Churley's article. Vance himself, in the rapid growth of his new friendship, had already lost sight of its first occasion; it was Halo who, a fortnight or so after the youth's first appearance, said one night, as he took leave: "Aren't we to be allowed to see the article, after all?"

"The article—the article?" Churley's brilliant eyes met hers in genuine perplexity. "Oh, that 'Windmill' thing? Glad you reminded me! It ought to have been done long ago, oughtn't it?" he added, in a tone of disarming confidence.

"Well, you told us it might be a chance—an opening; that if you could secure a regular job with the 'Windmill' you might be able to get away."

"Oh—if I could! If I only could! You're perfectly right; I *did* say so. I was all on fire to do the article. . ." He hesitated, wrinkling his brows, his eyes still wistfully on hers. "But the fact is—I wonder if you'll understand?—I'm in a frightful dilemma. I can't write here; and I can't make enough money to get away unless I do write. Can you suggest a way out, I wonder?"

Halo laughed. "The only one, I should say, is that

you should want to get away badly enough to force
yourself to write, whether you want to or not."

His eyes widened. "Oh, you really think one can
force one's self to write? That's interesting. Do you
think so too, Weston?" he asked, turning toward Vance
a smile of elfin malice.

Vance reddened. Halo's answer seemed to him in-
conceivably stupid. If only outsiders wouldn't give advice to fellows who were trying to do things! But probably you could never cure a woman of that. All his
sympathy, at the moment, was with Churley. . .

"That remark of Halo's was meant for me," he said,
laughing. "But I suppose if you were to shut yourself up
and set your teeth . . . that is, if you still feel you want
to do the article," he added, remembering that Churley
might affect inertia as a pretext for dropping a subject
he was tired of. The other seemed to guess his idea.

"Want to do it? I've got it all blazing away in my
head at this very minute! I never wanted to do a thing
more. But when I look out at this empty grimacing sea
. . . or think of Miss Pamela Plummet reading 'Ships
That Pass In The Night' for the hundredth time, or
Mrs. Dorman picking up knitting stitches for Lady
Dayes-Dawes—for heaven's sake, Weston, how can a fellow do anything in this place but lie on his back and
curse his God?" He looked from one to the other with
a comic plaintiveness. "But there; you think me a poor
thing, both of you. And so I am—pitiable. Only, hang it
all, even the worm can turn—can turn out an article!
And so can I. You'll see. Now that I think of it, I had a
desperate wire from Zélide this morning. The 'Windmill' people say they *must* have something about you,
and they offer to give me till the end of this week if I'll
produce it. When *is* the end of this week? I had an idea
today was already the beginning of next . . . but that's

just a dastardly pretext for not doing the article. . . By Jove, I'll go home and start tonight—and finish it too! Or at least, I'll do it this morning, because it's already morning. I say, Weston, can I drop in with it tomorrow after dinner?"

Churley did not drop in that evening, nor for the two days following. "He's really buckled down to it," Halo hopefully prophesied; but on the third day he reappeared, and said he had started writing the article and then torn up the beastly thing because it read so precisely like what every other literary critic had already said about every other novelist. "If only there was a new language perhaps we'd have new thoughts; if there was a new alphabet, even! When I try to harness together those poor broken-winded spavined twenty-six letters, and think of the millions and millions of ways they've already been combined into platitudes, my courage fails me, and I haven't the heart to thrash them onto their shaky old legs again. Why on earth don't you inventive fellows begin by inventing a new language?"

Vance shrugged. "I guess there'd be people turning out platitudes in it the very first week."

"Oh, I know what comes next. You're going to tell me that all the big geniuses have managed to express themselves in new ways with the old material. But, after all, history does show that every now and then culture has reached a dead level of stagnation, and then . . ."

"Well, go home now, and write that down!" Vance laughingly proposed; but Churley laughed too, and said he wasn't in the mood for writing, and if they were going on a picnic, as Mrs. Weston had suggested, was there any objection to his going with them?

Late that night Vance, as he often did at that hour, sat on his balcony looking out over the darkening waters. He liked these southern nights without a moon,

when the winter constellations ruled in a dark blue
heaven and rained their strong radiance on the sea. His
inspiration, which had begun to flag before Chris Churley's appearance, now flowed with a strong regular beat.
The poor boy's talk had done for Vance what Vance's
society had failed to do for him. Vance knew that his
creative faculty had grown strong enough to draw stimulus from contradiction instead of being disturbed by it.
To the purely analytical intelligence such questions as
their talks had raised might be unsettling and steriliz-
ing; but, as always in the full tide of invention, he felt
himself possessed by a brooding spirit of understanding,
some mystic reassurance which sea and sky and the life
of men transmitted from sources deeper than the reason.
He had never been able to formulate it, but he had
caught, in the pages of all the great creative writers,
hints of that mysterious subjection and communion, impossible to define, but clear to the initiated as the sign
exchanged between members of some secret brother-
hood. Ah, they were the happy people—the only happy
people, perhaps—these through whom the human turmoil swept not to ravage but to fertilize. He leaned on
the balcony, looking out at the sea, and pondered on his
task, and blessed it.

❦ XVIII ❧

A FEW DAYS later, after one of the unproductive mornings which often followed on his stretches of feverish work, Vance said to Halo: "When you said that the other day to Churley about a man's forcing himself to write, I suppose you were thinking of me, and the endless time I'm taking to do this book."

There had been a day when Halo would have protested, and he would have been sorry that he had spoken; but a new Halo, with steadier nerves and smoother temper, had replaced the pleasing anxious spirit of last year, and she only rejoined, with a glance of good-natured surprise: "Why, Vance, how absurd! With a book on the scale of this one you're bound to take a long time to get to the top of the hill."

That was sensible enough; but Vance was in the mood to feel that a sensible answer could only be a transparent attempt to humour him. "Oh, well—climbing's not bad exercise. But what you said has frightened away poor Churley. . ."

"Frightened him—why?"

"Writers don't much care to be told by outsiders to buckle down to their work. They generally get enough of that sort of advice in their own families."

"Oh, poor boy! I'm sorry! But how could he have minded? He's always joking about his own laziness."

"That's different," Vance retorted; and Halo, without appearing to notice his tone, suggested that he should go and hunt up his young friend. "Perhaps he may have stayed away because he's ill; he looks spectral at times. I'm sure it would please him if you looked him up."

Churley had never suggested his friend's coming to see him, and Vance thought he might interpret an unsought visit as an attempt to remind him of the article he perhaps no longer wished to write. To a youth so acutely self-conscious it would seem natural that an author should attach great importance to being reviewed by him. But the possibility that he might be lying ill in that dreary house made Vance decide to follow Halo's advice. As he mounted the hill, the house, rising above him in its neglected garden with windows shuttered against the sun, seemed to take the warmth out of the air, and he felt half inclined to turn back. While he stood there the blistered front door was jerked open and Colonel Churley came out. The Colonel looked at him with astonishment, and said: "Oh—" in a voice as sombre as his countenance, but somehow less forbidding; and on Vance's asking for his son, replied unexpectedly: "Ah—you're a friend of his, are you?"

Vance hesitated. "Well, a literary friend . . . yes. . . We both write, sir. . ."

The Colonel considered him thoughtfully. "Ah— you write? Indeed? I wish you'd persuade my son to do as much. But I've no idea where he is at present; none whatever. I seldom have any idea where he is," the Colonel concluded, in a voice more sorrowful than angered; and he lifted his hat with a gesture which implied that he expected Vance to precede him to the gate. If Chris were within his father evidently did not mean the visitor to know it. He did not even ask Vance's name. At the gate he turned with another bow, and strode away through the olives.

That evening Chris Churley reappeared. He looked drawn and colourless, and flinging himself down

on the divan plunged his hand into Vance's box of cigarettes. For a while they talked of a new book that Vance
had lent him (and which he had promised to return,
and hadn't) ; then, when Halo left the room for a moment, he said abruptly: "I suppose it was you who
looked me up this afternoon."

"Yes. I met your father at the door. He said he
didn't know where you were."

"And you told him you were a literary pal?" Churley laughed. "He didn't for a minute believe that. He
thought you were one of my waster friends come to
carry me off on a spree. My father and mother always
think that, when anybody they don't know comes to see
me."

"Wasters? I shouldn't think there were many in
this place," said Vance, smiling.

"*They* do. They think they're everywhere where I
am. My mother's convinced there's a private gambling
hell in one of the houses on the quay. I daresay there is
—and a filthy hole it must be. What my family can't understand is that riotous living, unless it's on the grand
scale, appeals to me no more than getting drunk on
cheap wine at a *bistro*. What I want to make me go ast-
ray is marble halls and millions; and Oubli is fairly safe
from both." He sat up and clutched his tossed red hair
in his brown hands. "Oh, God, Weston, if I could get
away! If only I could get away!"

Vance was moved at the cry. Well, why couldn't he
get away? And where would he go, and what would he
do, if he could?

"Go? Straight to London, by God!" Churley swung
around on the divan, his eyes dark with excitement under his flaming hair. "London, of course. If I could have
a month there, with nobody to nag me, or ask me when
I was going to get to work again (I know what my father

told you—I know) ; if I could have a fortnight, even, I could write that article about you, and a couple of others that have occurred to me during our talks; and with those articles I'd go to the 'Windmill', and from what Zélide says I'm practically certain they'd take me on permanently. But what am I to do, without a penny in my pocket? That's what my people can't be got to see. You must have found, haven't you, that there are places where a man can work, and places where he can't, though nobody but an artist can understand, and other people imagine you can say to a writer: 'Well, how is it you haven't turned out your thousand words this morning?' as they'd say to a child in the nursery: 'Now, then, down with that cod-liver oil, or I'll know why'."

The appeal reminded Vance of his own ineffectual efforts, the hours of agonizing inability to express what was in him, and the intervals when even the craving for expression failed because there was only emptiness within. Remembering his good fortune, the difficulties surmounted, the distinction achieved, the tenderness and understanding that had silently fostered his talent, he felt ashamed of the contrast between his fate and Churley's.

"Oh, see here; things may not be as bad as you think; we'll see what can be done . . ." he began, laying his hand on the other's shoulder; and at the terrible light in Churley's eyes Vance understood that he was already pledged to help the flight to London.

He had been rather afraid of Halo's disapproval when she learned what he had done. His earnings from "The Puritan in Spain" had not been large, for the book had been more fashionable than popular; and Halo's means were cramped by the necessity of helping her parents. Mr. and Mrs. Spear had always been a costly luxury, and Vance suspected that Lorry had taken advantage of his sister's being in Paris to extract from her a share of the spoils. But Halo was full of sympathy for poor Churley. "Of course you couldn't do anything else. I daresay he's right in saying he can do you better when he gets you in some sort of perspective." (This had been Churley's explanation to Halo, when she had returned to the study and found the two young men discussing Chris's departure.) "A 'close-up' must be horribly difficult, unless you're a Boswell; and I don't believe poor Chris will ever be anybody's Boswell but his own. Anyhow, I can see that his only chance is to get into another atmosphere. It's just like you, dear, to understand. . ."

The loan, they agreed, could not be less than twenty pounds; with the trip to London deducted that would barely leave him a carefree month. After he had gone Vance said to Halo: "I wish I'd told him straight off that I wanted to give him that money. There are times when it paralyzes a man to know that the money he's sweating to earn has got to be passed straight over to somebody else." He was thinking of his own early struggles, and of what it would have meant, at the moment of Laura Lou's illness, to have a friend guess his distress and help him out. Churley had already started—he had caught the first train the morning after his appeal to Vance; but Vance and Halo decided that as soon as he sent them his London address Vance should write that he wished the money to be regarded as a gift.

It was a surprise that the days passed without further news. After Chris's jubilant farewells Halo had expected a post-card from Toulon or Marseilles; but Vance, better acquainted with young men's ways, pointed out that Chris's chief difficulty seemed to be an inability to use his pen. "He'll send his address in time; but he may not even do that till he's finished the article. I think he felt rather uncomfortable at having talked so much about it, and then not having put a line on paper. Poor devil—I owe him more than he does me, for our talks seem to have given me a fresh start."

And so it proved. Churley had stirred up many ideas in the course of their long debates, and Vance's acceleration of energy rushed at once into the channels of his work. The weeks passed rapidly between ardent hours of writing and long loiterings on hill and shore. When Vance's brain was in full activity his hours of idleness acquired a new quality. It was as though he looked at everything through the powerful lens of his creative energy, so that the least detail of the landscape, the faintest fugitive play of cloud and sun, sufficed to enrich his dream.

With the end of January the southern spring began; clouds of translucent almond-bloom on rough red terraces, blue patches of borage in stony fields, the celandine shining in wet leafy hollows, blackthorn and tamarisk along the lanes; and a few weeks later, among the hills and above the sea, under the olives and through the vines, the miraculous snowfall of the daffodils.

Vance and Halo went off daily, staff in hand, prolonging their wanderings more and more, exploring secret valleys, mounting to granite mountain-crests or wading and scrambling along miles of red rock and amber sand, with a peacock sea glittering through the pine-trunks when they climbed or, when they dropped down to it, lapping their feet with silver. Sometimes, when they had planned a long excursion, Vance was up before sunrise, and got in two or three hours of writing before they started; and when they came back, at sunset or under a cool wintry moon, it was good to lie on the divan, fagged and happy, and dream of tomorrow's work.

The day came when Vance, looking back, understood that at that moment the Furies had slept, and life given him all it could. Even at the time he felt a singular peace and plenitude. His work was going well; his heart was quiet, and the sameness of his days seemed their most exquisite quality. One evening in particular when, looking up, he had seen Halo bending over to stir the fire, her dark head outlined against the flame, he had felt in his breast a new emotion, clear as that flame, as if out of their loving and quarrelling, the uneasy blazing and smouldering of their passion, something winged and immortal had sprung, and brooded over them.

He gave a chuckle of contentment, and Halo's smile questioned him. "What is it, dear?"

"Oh, I don't know. Perhaps the peace that passeth understanding. . . Poor Churley," he added, "I was just thinking of the way he has of using up things after one look at them. As if beauty weren't eternally different every morning."

"Perhaps it is to him, in London," Halo mused; then their talk, veering from Churley, wandered back to the day's excursion, and to their plans for the morrow.

Since they had left Paris neither Halo nor Vance had reverted to the subject of the latter's talk with Lewis Tarrant. Vance shrank from touching again on the question of the divorce, and if Halo had any news to impart she seemed reluctant to communicate it. The quiet weeks at Oubli had been a sort of truce of God, a magic interval of peace with neither ventured to disturb. But one day, not long after their happy evening by the fire, Halo, who sat going over the letters they had found on their return from a long tramp, uttered an exclamation of surprise.

"What's up?" Vance questioned; and she went over to his desk and laid before him a cutting from a New York paper. Vance read: "Prize-giving Millionairess

Announces Marriage to Gratz Blemer. Mrs. Pulsifer Privately Weds Novelist Who Won Her Ten Thousand Dollar Best-Novel Prize"; and beneath this headline· "Society and literary circles were electrified last night by the announcement that Mrs. Pulsifer, the wealthy New York fashion-leader and giver of numerous literary prizes, was privately married two months ago at Pinehurst, N.C., to Gratz Blemer, the novelist, famous as the author of 'This Globe', and whose last novel, 'The Rush Hour', was awarded a few months ago the new Pulsifer Best-Novel prize, recently founded by the bride. Mr. and Mrs. Blemer are spending their honeymoon on the bride's steam-yacht in the Mediterranean."

Halo and Vance looked at each other in silence; then Halo said with a faint smile: "That accounts for a great deal."

Vance nodded. He tried to smile too; but the brief paragraph had called up a vision of his midnight talk with Tarrant. He felt as if the world with its treacheries, shocks and torments had once again broken into the charmed circle of their lives; and looking up at Halo he saw the same distress in her eyes. "Well, we needn't bother; it's all outside of us, anyhow," he said defiantly; and she bent over to lay a kiss on his forehead.

XIX

THE NEXT day it rained. Vance, who had given himself a week's idleness, sat down before "Colossus", and Halo with equal heroism descended to the verandah to clean the oil lamps. She was deep in her task when Mrs. Dorman came up the path, sheltering her bedraggled straw hat under a dripping umbrella.

It was long since any one from the Pension Britannique had called at the pink house; Halo concluded that the chaplain's wife had come to ask for a contribution to the church bazaar, or a subscription to renew the matting in the porch, and hurriedly calculated what could be spared from their month's income, already somewhat depleted by the gift to Chris Churley.

Mrs. Dorman, when she had disposed of her umbrella, and been led indoors, did not immediately disclose the object of her visit. She hoped they were not in for a rainy spring, she said; but she had warned the new arrivals at Madame Fleuret's that, after the fine weather they'd had all winter, they must expect a change. "I saw dear Madame Fleuret making signs to me to stop," Mrs. Dorman continued complacently, "but Major Masterman, who was thinking of hiring a motor-cycle by the month, said he was thankful I'd warned him, and very likely if the bad weather continued he and Mrs. Masterman would dash over to the Balearics instead of staying on at the pension; and they telegraphed to some friends for whom they'd asked Madame Fleuret to reserve rooms that they'd better go elsewhere. So it was really a kindness to tell them, wasn't it? . . . But, dear Mrs.

Weston, what I've come for is to bring you a message
. . . a private message. . ." Mrs. Dorman continued,
her cheeks filling out and growing pink, as they did
when she had anything painful to impart. "It's just this:
you were kind enough, some weeks since, to offer to call
on Mrs. Churley. At the time she couldn't see any one;
but she's asked me to say that she'd be so glad if you'd
come up this afternoon . . . at once, if you could, as
the Colonel is rather opposed to her receiving visits, and
she'd like to be sure of his not getting back from his
walk while you're there. And she begs you, please, not to
mention that I've asked you. . ."

Mrs. Dorman's lowered voice and roseate flush gave
her words an ominous air; and Halo at once thought:
"Chris!" Her first impulse was to ask the reason of the
summons; but respect for Mrs. Churley's reserve, whatever it might conceal, made her answer: "Very well; I'll
wash the oil off and come."

As she and Mrs. Dorman climbed the hill, Mrs.
Dorman remarked that the mason had told her the roof
of Les Mimosas was certain to fall in the next time there
were heavy rains, and that when she had notified Colonel Churley he had said those fellows were always after a
job; but thereafter she relapsed into silence, as though
the first glimpse of that barricaded house-front had
checked even her loquacity.

In the vestibule the heavy smell of an unaired
house met the two women. A crumpled dishcloth trailed
on the stairs, and in a corner stood a broken-handled
basket full of rusty garden tools festooned with cobwebs.
It must have been years since they had been used, Halo
reflected, remembering the untended garden. Mrs. Dorman, who had tiptoed up ahead, leaned over and signed
to her to follow. A door opened, letting out a sickly waft
of ether, and Halo found herself pushed into a darkened

room, and heard Mrs. Dorman whisper: "There she is. Mind the footstool. I'll slip down and mount guard in case he should come back."

Halo paused, trying to make her way among the uncertain shapes of the furniture; then a shawled figure raised itself from a lounge, and a woman's voice exclaimed: "Mrs. Weston, what do you know of my son?"

Halo's eyes were growing used to the dimness and she saw a small muffled-up body, and a hollow-cheeked face with tossed white hair and burning eyes like Chris's. "She must have been very beautiful—oh, poor thing!" Halo thought; and the thin plaintive voice went on: "Do sit down. There's a chair there, isn't there? Please clear off anything that's on it. I'm nearly blind— and so unused to visitors. And the only thing I can think of is my boy."

"I'm so sorry. We've been wondering why there's no news of him," said Halo, taking the chair.

"Then you've heard nothing either?" Mrs. Churley, propped up among her cushions, gazed with a sort of spectral timidity at her visitor; as though, Halo thought, she were a ghost who feared to look at the living.

"No; nothing since he left for London."

"For London?" Mrs. Churley echoed, stressing the word. "Ah, he told you London too?"

Halo, surprised, said yes; and Mrs. Churley went on: "My poor boy . . . it was the only way to get his father to let him go." She lowered her voice to a whisper. "He told us he'd been offered a permanent position on a well-known review—the 'Windmill', I think they call it—and that the editor wanted him at once, and had sent him an advance of five pounds. It was a great opportunity—and of course his father had to let him go."

"Of course—" Halo murmured.

"And so I said nothing," the mother continued in her distressful whisper, "though I was sure editors don't often send advances to beginners; for I suspected that your husband had been generous enough . . . to . . . you understand. . ."

"Yes . . ."

"And I was so grateful, and so happy at my boy's having a job, because I hoped—my husband and I hoped—that it would make him settle down. You *do* think he has talent?"

"I think he's full of talent; we both do. Though as it happens we've never actually seen anything he's written. . ."

"Ah—" Mrs. Churley interjected in a stricken murmur, sinking back against the cushions.

"Only now, I'm sure—with such an opening, and the discipline of an editorial office. . . You'll see . . ." Halo went on reassuringly.

"Yes; that's what we thought. We felt so hopeful; I've never before seen my husband hopeful."

"Well, you must go on hoping. You'll hear from Chris as soon as he's settled."

Mrs. Churley again raised herself on her elbow, her face twisted with pain by the effort. "Mrs. Weston," she brought out, "my son hasn't gone to London." She paused, watching Halo with startled dilated eyes. "I've just heard, from a friend who saw him the other day, that he's at Nice!" The words fell into the silence of the muffled room as if every one rang out the knell of a hope. "At Nice, Mrs. Weston—*Nice!*"

It was an anti-climax, certainly; and Halo, after a first start of surprise, could not repress a smile.

"But are you sure? Was your friend sure, I mean? Did he actually speak to your son?"

"He didn't speak to him; but he saw him going into a night-club with a party of dreadfully fast-looking people." Mrs. Churley clasped her emaciated hands. "Mrs. Weston, I'm speaking in the deepest confidence. My husband would be very angry if he knew. He's convinced that Chris is in London, and if he were to find out that we've been deceived again I dread to think what would happen. My husband has never understood that people may be unable to resist temptation—he says: why should they let themselves be tempted? The artist's nature is incomprehensible to him. . ." She leaned forward, and caught Halo's wrist. "It was from me that my poor boy inherited that curse. I used to write poetry—but my husband thought it unsuitable in an officer's wife. . . Oh, if you knew how we'd struggled and fought to keep Chris out of temptation. . . When my husband was retired we came to Oubli, in the hope that here our boy would be safe. He has a real love of literature; he's always wanted to write. But something invariably seems to prevent him . . . the least little thing puts him off. We hoped he would choose a steadier profession; but when we saw that was useless we decided to come here, where there are so few distractions. . ."

"But don't you think that may be the reason?" Halo interposed. "Young men need distractions— they're part of the artist's training."

"Part of his training? Oh, Mrs. Weston! Forgive my asking: are those your husband's ideas?"

Halo smiled. "His idea is that the sooner Chris settles down to work the better."

"Ah, just so—just so! You're sure Mr. Weston didn't intend him to use the money to go to Nice?"

In spite of her pity for the unhappy mother Halo

felt a growing impatience. "If you wish to know the truth, we did give your son a—a small sum, but on the understanding that he was going to London to secure the job he had been promised."

"Oh, my poor Chris—my poor Chris! And now what is to become of him? For years I've been dreading lest he should get money and escape from us again. It happened once before." Mrs. Churley hid her face in her hands, and broke into stifled sobbing.

Halo knelt down by the lounge. "Mrs. Churley, please don't be so distressed. After all, we must all follow our bent . . . artists especially. . . It may be best in the end for Chris to work out his own salvation. . ."

"Salvation? Among those dreadful people? And weak as he is—and with no health? When I think it was I who laid on him the curse of the artist's nature! Oh, promise me that Mr. Weston will help to find him, and bring him back before his father knows."

"What is it his father's not to know?" came a tremulous bass voice, and Colonel Churley stepped into the room, with Mrs. Dorman wailing in the rear: "But, dear Colonel Churley, do wait! I assure you it may not be as bad as we fear!"

Halo discerned in the Colonel's frowning countenance the same quiver of distress as in his voice. "He minds it even more than she does," she thought, looking from the threatening jut of his white eyebrows to the troubled blue of his eyes. "This is an unexpected honour—my wife is able to see so few people." The Colonel bowed stiffly to Halo with a questioning sideglance at Mrs. Churley, whose eyes were anxiously fixed on him. "Mrs. Weston has been so kind. I wanted to thank her. . ." Her voice faded into silence.

"And knowing that visitors are too fatiguing for

you, you took advantage of my absence to do so," the Colonel interposed, lifting his lean brown forefinger in an attempt at playfulness.

"Oh, Colonel Churley, really . . . there's been no bad news as yet," Mrs. Dorman protested.

The Colonel turned with a frightened frown; his purplish lips trembled. "No bad news? Has there been any news? Has Mrs. Weston brought us news of my son?"

"No, no . . . it was only my idea that dear Mrs. Churley should ask her if she and Mr. Weston hadn't heard anything," Mrs. Dorman faltered, her round face red with fright.

The Colonel again bowed. "Most kind—most thoughtful. I'm extremely obliged to all our friends for their interest. Mrs. Weston may not know that Chris has gone to London to take up an editorial position; in the rush of his new duties he has delayed to write." He addressed himself to Halo with an apologetic smile. "My wife is an invalid; I'm afraid the time sometimes hangs heavily on her, in spite of the kindness you ladies show her—especially so when her son's away. She doesn't realize that young men are often bad correspondents; and knowing that you and Mr. Weston were kind enough to receive Chris, she fancied you might have heard from him."

"No," said Halo, "we've heard nothing."

"There, my dear," pursued the Colonel, "you see we've not been less favoured than others. The boy will write when he has time." Mrs. Churley's weeping had subsided into a little clucking murmur. The Colonel turned to Halo.

"I'm sorry you should have come when my wife is more than usually unequal to receiving company." He stood looking almost plaintively at Halo, who thought:

"What he hates most of all is my seeing this untidy neglected house, and that poor creature in her misery." She understood, and wishing Mrs. Churley goodbye turned toward the door. Colonel Churley opened it with a shaking hand, and Halo and Mrs. Dorman went from the room and down the stairs. Following them as they descended came the low clucking sound of Mrs. Churley's weeping.

XX

HALO HAD been so moved by the sight of the ailing woman and the angry ineffectual old man, left alone in that dismal house to heap each other with recriminations, that she communicated her emotion to Vance; and when he proposed going to look for Chris she welcomed the suggestion. "The boy haunts me. To do anything so dishonest he must be in a bad way; and I feel as if we ought to do what we can."

"Oh, he never meant to be dishonest. When he got to Toulon he probably saw a train starting for Nice, and was tempted by the idea of a night's fun."

"A night's fun! But it's a month since he went away, and it was only a day or two ago that Mrs. Churley's friend saw him."

"Well, it's pretty smart of him to have made the money last as long as that," Vance rejoined with a laugh; but in reality he too felt a vague pang at the thought of the irresponsible boy caught in that sordid whirlpool.

In the train his reflexions grew less emotional. It was obviously none of his business to find and reclaim Chris, even supposing the latter had deliberately deceived them, and used Vance's money to offer himself a few weeks' amusement; but there was something so droll in this act of defiance that Vance, in spite of his pity for the parents, was amused at the idea of being confronted with the son.

He was also acutely interested in the prospect of seeing for the first time the pleasure-seeking end of the

Riviera. The contrast between Oubli-sur-Mer and the succession of white cities reflected in azure waters emphasized the narrowness and monotony of the life he had been leading. Slipping past towering palace hotels, and villas girt with lawns and pergolas, he recalled the mouldy blistered fronts of the pink house and the Pension Britannique; when, at the stations, flower-girls thrust up great sheaves of freesias and carnations, he saw the handful of wizened anemones bargained for by Miss Plummet at the market, and brought home to her invalid sister; and the motors pouring along wide dustless roads to inviting distances evoked the lurching omnibus crowded with garlicky peasants which, through clouds of suffocating dust, carried Oubli-sur-Mer to Toulon or Marseilles. A few hours earlier the quiet of Oubli had seemed a spiritual necessity; but already the new scenes were working their old spell.

These alternations of mood, which he had once ascribed to instability of aim, no longer troubled him. He knew now that they were only the play of the world of images on his creative faculty, and that his fundamental self remained unchanged under such shifting impulses. By the time the train reached Nice he was so lost in the visionary architecture of his inner world that the other had become invisible. He gazed at the big station packed with gaily dressed people and busy flower-sellers without remembering that it was there he should have got out; and now the guard was crying "Monte Carlo", and above the station glittered the minarets and palms of the Casino.

"Well—why not?" Vance thought. Chris was as likely to be at Monte Carlo as at Nice; it was not probable that he would restrict his pleasure-seeking to one spot. Vance picked up his suit-case and jumped out. . .

Past sloping turf, palms imprisoned in bright blue

or glaring magenta cinerarias, borders of hyacinths and banks of glossy shrubs, he climbed gaily to the polychrome confusion of the Casino. Stretching up from it to a stern mountain-background were villas and restaurants, and café-terraces where brightly dressed people sipped cocktails under orange-and-white umbrellas. Nearer by were tall hotels with awninged and flowered balconies; rows of taxis and private motors between the lawns and flower-beds before the Casino; young men in tennis flannels and young women in brilliant sportssuits, and strollers lounging along the balustraded walks. Among half-tropical trees a band played a gipsy tune of de Falla's, and children with lovely flying hair raced ahead of nurses in long blue veils, who gossiped on the benches or languidly pursued their charges.

Halo would have called it a super-railway poster. She always spoke scornfully of the place, resenting such profanation of the gray mountain giants above it. In certain moods Vance might have agreed; but today the novelty and brightness struck his fancy, and the trimness of lawns, flowers, houses, satisfied his need of order and harmony. Everything wore the fairy glitter of a travelling circus to a small child in a country town, and the people who passed him looked as unreal, as privileged and condescending, as the spangled athletes of his infancy. He sat down on a bench and watched them.

The passing faces were not all young or beautiful; the greater number were elderly, many ugly, some painful or even repulsive; but almost all wore the same hard glaze of prosperity. Vance tried to conjecture what the inner lives of such people could be; he pictured them ordering rare delicacies in restaurants, buying costly cigars and jewels in glittering shops, stepping in and out of deeply-cushioned motors, ogling young women or painted youths, as sex and inclination prompted. "Chris's ideal," he murmured. He decided to take a look at the gambling-rooms; but it was luncheon-time, and people were coming out of the Casino, descending the steps to their motors or the near-by restaurants. As he stood there he suddenly caught sight of Lorry Spear; and at the same instant Lorry recognized him.

"Hullo, Vance—you? Halo here? I suppose she's a peg above all this. Sent you off on your own, has she? Very white of her. Not staying here, though? Of course not; nobody does. I'm over from Cannes with a party, to lunch on the Gratz Blemers' yacht—the biggest of her kind, I believe. You knew Blemer had carried off Jet Pulsifer under Tarrant's very nose? Sharp fellow, Blemer . . . they were secretly married to or three months ago. That accounts for Tarrant's turning down the divorce, I suppose," Lorry rattled on, his handsome uncertain eyes rambling from Vance's face to search the passing throng. "I say, though—why not come off to the yacht with us? When I say 'us,' I mean Mrs. Glaisher and Imp Pevensey, with whom I'm staying at Cannes. Mrs. Glaisher has taken a villa there, and we're working over the final arrangements for 'Factories'; at least I hope we are," Lorry added with a dubious grin. "With the super-rich you never can tell; at the last minute they're so darned scared of being done. But if Imp Pevensey can get Mrs. Blemer to take an interest she's sure that'll excite Mrs. Glaisher, and make her take the final step. Almost all their philanthropy's based on rivalry. . . Well, so much the better for us. . . See here, my boy, come along; they'll jump at the chance of seeing you. . . Ah, there's the very young woman I'm on the look out for!" he exclaimed, darting toward a motor which had stopped before an hotel facing the Casino.

It was wonderful how Lorry fitted into the scene. In Montparnasse he had been keen, restless, careless in dress and manner; here he wore the same glossy veneer as all the rest. The very cut of his hair and his clothes had been adapted to his setting, and as he slipped through the crowd about the hotel Vance was struck by his resemblance to the other young men strolling in and out of its portals.

He had been amused by Lorry's invitation. He had no intention of joining Mrs. Glaisher's party, but that Lorry should propose it after what had passed between them was too characteristic to surprise him. Lorry had obviously forgotten the Glaisher episode, though it had occurred under his own roof; on seeing Vance he had remembered only that the latter was a good fellow whose passing celebrity had once been useful to him, and might be again. As Vance waited on the curb he thought how jolly it would be to go and lunch at one of those little terrace-restaurants over the sea that he had marked down from the train. After that he would return to Nice, and devise a way of running down Chris.

"Look here, Vance; you will come?" Lorry, rejoining him, grasped his arm with a persuasive hand. "No? It's a pity—the yacht's a wonder. Not to speak of Blemer and Jet! As a novelist you oughtn't to miss them. . . Well, so long. . . Oh, by the way; won't you dine at Cannes tonight instead? At Mrs. Glaisher's—Villa Mirifique. I've just been arranging with that young woman over there to meet us here on our way back from the yacht. She's coming over to spend a day or two with Mrs. Glaisher, and I'm sure she'd be delighted to drive you to Cannes. Come along and I'll introduce you." Lorry, as he spoke, swept Vance across to the hotel door, where a young lady who stood with her back to them was giving an order to her chauffeur. The motor drove off, and she turned and faced them.

"Floss," Lorry cried, "here's a friend of mine, a celebrated novelist, who wants a lift to Mrs. Glaisher's this evening. Of course you've heard of Vance Weston—and read 'The Puritan in Spain'?"

The girl, who had been looking at Lorry, turned interrogatively to Vance. Her movements had a cool deliberateness which seemed to single her out from the empty agitation around her. She lifted her dusky eyelids, and for a few seconds she and Vance looked at each other without speaking; then: "Why, old Van!" she said, in a warm voice flattened by the Middle Western drawl.

Vance stood staring. As through a mist of wine he saw this woman, become a stranger to his eyes yet so familiar to his blood. She was very dark; yes, he remembered; a warm dusky pallor, like the sound of her voice; glints of red under her skin, and in the gloom of her hair. She rarely smiled—he remembered that too—when she did it was like a fruit opening to the sun. His veins kept the feeling of that sultriness. . .

"Hullo! Old friends, are you? First-rate! Monte Carlo's the place where nobody ever comes any more, yet where you meet everybody you know. All right—coming!" Lorry cried, gesticulating to a group on the other side of the square. "So long—Villa Mirifique; bring him along, Floss."

"Oh, I'll bring him," said the girl in her indifferent drawl; and Lorry vanished.

Vance continued to look at Floss Delaney. It was not till afterward that he noticed the quiet elegance of her dress, or remembered that he had seen her getting out of a private motor and giving an order to the chauffeur. He knew that late in life the shiftless Harrison Delaney of Euphoria had stumbled into wealth as accidentally, almost, as, years before, he had sunk into poverty. When Vance had gone home after Laura Lou's death Euphoria was still ringing with the adventure; Vance remembered the bitterness with which his father, the shrewd indefatigable little man who had failed to secure the fortune so often in his grasp, spoke of the idle Delaney's rise. "A loafer like that—it's enough to cure a man of ever wanting to do an honest day's work," Lorin Weston had growled. It all came back to Vance afterward; at the moment he was half-dazed by the encounter with this girl who had been the vehicle of his sharpest ecstasy and his blackest anguish. A vehicle; that was what she'd been; all she'd ever been. "The archway to the infinite"—who was it who had called woman that? It was true of a boy's first love. In the days when Floss Delaney had so enraptured and tortured him she had never had any real identity to his untaught heart and senses; she had been simply undifferentiated woman; now for the first time he saw her as an individual, and perceived her peculiar loveliness. He gave a little laugh.

"What are you laughing at?" she asked.

"I was thinking I'd nearly shot myself on your account once. Funny, isn't it?"

"Oh, 'nearly'—that's not much! If you do it again you must aim better," she said coolly; but he caught the glitter of pleasure in her eyes. "Old Van—only to think of coming across you here!" She slipped her hand through his arm, and they walked across the square and sat down on a bench under overhanging shrubs. "So you're a celebrity," she said, her full upper lip lifting in a smile.

"Well, so are you, aren't you?"

"Because father's made all that money?" She looked

at him doubtfully. "It's very pleasant," she said, with a defiant tilt of her chin.

"And what are you going to do with it all?"

"I don't know. Just go round, I suppose."

"Where's your father? Is he here with you?"

Yes, she told him; she was travelling with her father; they were staying at the hotel to which Vance had just seen her driving up. They had been going around Europe for over a year now: Rome, Paris, Egypt, St. Moritz—all the places they thought might amuse them. But her father wasn't easy to amuse. He was as lazy as ever; he didn't so much mind travelling, provided they went to places where he could have a game of cards; but he didn't care to go round with new people. She would have preferred to be at Cannes, where most of her friends were, and everything was ever so much smarter; but her father had found at Monte Carlo some old cronies whom he had met the winter before at Luxor, and he liked to be with them, or else to play baccarat at the Casino. That day he had gone over to Nice with some of his crowd; she didn't believe they'd be back till morning. He'd be so surprised to see Vance when he got back. "He's read your books," she added, almost ingratiatingly.

"That means you haven't?"

"Well—I will now." She glanced about her, and then down at the little jewelled watch on her wrist. "I'm on my own today. Can't you take me off somewhere to lunch?"

Vance sprang up joyfully. He felt ravenous for food, and as happy as a schoolboy on a holiday. He thought of the terrace-restaurants he had seen from the train, and wondered if they would be grand enough for her. "Let's go somewhere right over the sea," he suggested, trying to describe the kind of place he meant.

"Not swell, you know—not a crowd. Just a little terrace with a few tables." Yes, that was exactly what she wanted; away from the noise, and those awful bands— she knew the very place. It wasn't far off; a little way down the road toward Cap Martin; but she was too hungry to walk. They took a taxi.

The scene suited her indolent beauty. She was made for the sunlit luxury to which she affected such indifference. At Oubli she would have been a false note; here she seemed to justify the general futility by the way it became her. As he looked at her, the memory of the Floss Delaney of his boyhood came back to him, struggling through the ripened and polished exterior of the girl at his side. After all her face had not changed; it had the same midsummer afternoon look, as though her penthouse hair were the shade of a forest, her eyes its secret pools. A still windless face, suggesting the note of stock-doves, the hum of summer insects. Vance had always remembered it so. She hardly ever smiled; and when she laughed, her laugh was a faint throat note that did not affect the repose of her features. But her body had grown slenderer yet rounder. Before it had been slightly heavy, its movements slow and awkward; now it was as light as a feather. Halo had fine lines, but was too thin, the bones in her neck were too visible; this girl, who must have been about the same age, and had the same Diana-like curve from shoulder to hip, was more rounded, and her hands were smaller and plumper than Halo's, though not so subtle and expressive.

Vance was glad that he could take note of all this, could even calmly compare Floss Delaney's appearance with that of the woman he loved; it proved his emotional detachment, and made him feel safe and at his ease.

They sat under a gay awning, before a red-and-white table-cloth, and ate Provençal dishes, and drank a fresh native wine. Floss, wrinkling her brows against the sun, stole curious glances at him. "You've changed a lot; you've grown handsome," she said suddenly.

He laughed, and flushed to the roots of his hair; but she went on: "I heard you were married; are you?"

He wished she had not put the question; yet a moment later he was glad she had. It was best that everything should be clear between them.

"No; I'm not married—yet. But I expect to be. To Lorry Spear's sister."

"Oh," she murmured, with ironic eye-brows. "She's heard about Halo and me," he thought; and cursed Mrs. Glaisher.

"Well, I suppose I'll be married too some day," she went on, her attention wandering back to herself, as it always did after a moment; and he felt an abrupt shock of jealousy.

"I suppose you've got lots of fellows after you."

"Oh, I don't know. Anyhow, I'm not going to make up my mind yet; I like my freedom." She stressed the word voluptuously, bending her lips to her glass of pale yellow wine, and as he watched her he broke out, from some unconscious depth of himself: "God—how you made me suffer!"

She looked at him with a sort of amused curiosity. "You're thinking of Euphoria?" He nodded.

"Yes; I was a bad girl, I know—but you were a bad boy; and silly." Her eyes lingered on him. "I used to love to kiss you. Didn't you love it? But you didn't understand—"

"What?"

"A girl like me had to look out for herself. There was nobody to do it for me. But let's talk about what we are *now*; what's the use of going back? This is ever so much more fun. Don't you like being famous?" She leaned across and laid her brown hand on his. He looked at the polished red nails, and remembered her blunt dirty finger-tips, the day he had picked her up in the road after her bicycle accident. Even then, he thought, she used to spend every cent she could get on paint and perfume. He smiled at himself and her.

❧ XXI ❧

OVER THE coffee he proposed their going back to the Casino to gamble; but she refused. "Father gambles; that's enough for one family. I mean to keep what I've got," she said; and in her hardening eyes and narrowed lips he detected the reflection of the lean years at Crampton, and at Dakin, where she had gone (so his family had told him) as saleswoman in a dry-goods' shop. Those days had once been a tormenting mystery; but now he only pitied her for the background of dark memories overshadowing her brilliant present.

He had told her he would not go with her to Mrs. Glaisher's, and had been secretly gratified by her pout of disappointment. "I think you might."

"No; I don't like those people. And anyway, I've got to stop off at Nice tonight."

Her eyes grew curious. "I wonder what you've got to do at Nice?"

Half-laughing, he confessed his reason, telling her what he could of Chris Churley's story without betraying the secret of the boy's escapade. "His family are worried; they don't know where he is. The other day some friend of theirs said he'd seen him at Nice, in a night-club; so they asked me if I'd hunt him up."

"Well, that's funny—"

"I know; but they're poor, and sick—at least his mother's sick—and he's all they've got."

"I don't see how you can find him, rummaging round Nice without an address."

"Neither do I; but I'll have to try."

She sat with lowered lids, meditating. "Tell me again what his name is."

"Chris Churley."

"That's it. I heard Alders talking about him yesterday."

"Alders?"

"Mrs. Glaisher's secretary. He always knows about everybody."

"A little man who looks like a freckle?"

"Well—I guess so," she said hesitatingly, as if analogies were unfamiliar to her.

"Come to think of it, Alders is sure to be Mrs. Glaisher's secretary. It's absolutely predestined. You're certain you heard him mention Chris Churley?"

She still hesitated, and he recalled that she had never had a good memory for anything that did not directly concern herself, or hold out some possible advantage. "Well, it was something like Churley. But I hear so many names. Is he a newspaper man? There was some fellow I heard Alders talking about, who wanted to get introduced to Gratz Blemer, and write about him; Alders was going to fix it up." Vance laughed, and she added: "Do you think that's it?"

"Sounds like it," he said, picturing to himself the bewilderment of Blemer, who was used to "straight" interviewing, under the cross-fire of Chris's literary confidences.

They strolled back toward Monte Carlo. The distance was not great, and Miss Delaney had declared that she would like to walk; but she hailed the first taxi. "I guess I'm through with walking—as long as there's money enough left to go on wheels," she said; and Vance thought of her struggling four times a day on her bicycle through the frozen ruts or the bottomless mud between Euphoria and Crampton. He understood why the aspirations of the newly rich were so often what Halo would have called vulgar.

He was still resolved not to go to Mrs. Glaisher's, but he finally agreed to join Miss Delaney at her hotel, and motor with her as far as Nice; and she promised to telephone him if Alders knew where Chris Churley was to be found.

Vance went to the gambling rooms, risked a small sum, and carried away enough to pay for his outing. He was too much engrossed in the thought of Floss Delaney to lose his head over the game; but before leaving he made the round of the rooms, and assured himself that, for the moment, Chris was not in them.

When he came out he remembered that on arriving he had left his suit-case at the station. Oh, well, he thought, Floss was sure not to be on time; he could easily run down the hill and be back before she was ready to start. But when he returned to the hotel the hall porter, after an inspection of the lounge, and a consultation with the concierge, announced that Miss Delaney had gone.

Vance felt a moment of vexation. It was only half-past seven. Had she left no message? Not as far as the porter knew. Vance repeated the enquiry at the desk. He thought he detected a faint smile on the face of the gold-braided functionaries. How many times a day must that question be put to them! "Oh, well—." He was relieved to find that after all he didn't much care, though a twinge of vanity shot through his affected indifference.

On the threshold he was detained by a page-boy with a visiting-card. "The concierge thinks perhaps this is for you."

On the back of the card, in an untidily pencilled

scrawl, Vance read: "Tell him to come after us." He guessed this cryptic scribble to be Floss's way of ordering the concierge to send him in pursuit of her; but, as he had declined to go, the message had no particular point. He laughed, and absently turned the card over. On the back was engraved: *Duca di Spartivento*.

"Is it meant for you, sir?" the page asked; and Vance, with a shrug, pocketed the card and went out.

The Duke of Spartivento! What faint memory-waves did those sonorous syllables set rippling? Granada —Alders? But of course! This trumpet of a name was that of the young Italian cousin—or nephew?—of the old Marquesa to whose *tertulia* Vance had gone with Alders. He remembered that the latter, the day he had come to bid Halo and Vance goodbye, had spoken with his deprecating smirk of being about to join his Spanish friends for a shooting party in their cousin's honour, at the Marquesa's castle in Estremadura . . . it was then that the splendid name had shot before him up like a rocket. "Or like a line from the 'Song to David'," he remembered thinking.

Floss's having written her message on the back of that particular card seemed part of the fairy-tale enveloping him. Since his meeting with her, and their hour in the little restaurant, nothing that could happen seemed impossible, or even unlikely. Amusement conquered his vexation . . . it was all part of the fairy-tale. In the darkness already sparkling with lights, he stood wondering whether he should take the next train to Nice, or treat himself to a taxi out of his winnings. He decided on the taxi.

He was about to hail one when he felt another touch on his arm, and saw at his side a chauffeur in dark livery. "Are you the gentleman—?" Vance stared, and the chauffeur continued in fluent English: "Going to

Cannes with Miss Delaney, sir? That's right. Here's her car. She's gone on with the others; but she told me to wait and bring you." He had his hand on the shining panel of the motor from which Vance had seen Floss descend that morning; and Vance obediently got in. Let the fairy-tale go on as long as it would. When he got to Nice he'd tell the fellow to drop him at some quiet hotel. . .

He had no notion which way they were going. From the train he had seen the road only in uncertain glimpses, climbing between garden walls or dropping to the sea; and now darkness made the scene strange. They ascended between illuminated houses; then the streets ceased, and he found himself high up, flashing past dark wooded heights and looking across a sea of verdure to the other sea below, its shore thrust forth in black headlands or ravelled into long sinuous inlets. The moon had not risen, but the evening star hung in the sky like a lesser moon, and the early constellations pushed upward, deepening the night. But only for a moment; almost at once they paled and vanished in the spreading of artificial lights that festooned the coast, crested the headlands, flowed in golden streamers across bays and harbours, and flashed and revolved from unseen lighthouses, binding the prone landscape in a net of fire.

Overhead rose a continuous cliff, wooded and sombre; below a continuous city sparkled and twisted. Vance hung over the scene entranced. He had no thought of places or distances; as the motor climbed, descended and rose again, he felt like a bird floating above the earth, like an errant Perseus swooping down to free this dark Andromeda from her jewelled chains. Visions and images pressed on him. They mingled with the actual scene, so that what his eyes saw, and what his fancy made of it, flowed into one miracle of night and fire.

And now the motor had dropped to the shore again, and the sea, dim and unbound, swayed away into blackness. Vance longed to jump out and dash over the sands into that moving obscurity; but he felt that the incessant shifting of the scene was the very source of its magic, and leaned back satisfied.

Suddenly he was aware that the motor was ma-noeuvring at a sharp turn. They were out in the country again, or in a leafy suburb, with gate-ways and house-fronts seen through foliage. "See here—what about Nice?" he called to the chauffeur.

"Nice?" the latter echoed, busy with his backing; "this is the way up to Mrs. Glaisher's. Damned bad corner—"

"Oh, but it's all a mistake. I meant to get out at Nice. Can't you take me back there?"

"Back to Nice? You never said anything about Nice, sir." The chauffeur turned his head reproachfully. "What time do you suppose it is? Nearly half-past nine; and I haven't had no dinner yet. Have *you*?" His tone was respectful but aggrieved. "It's here Miss Delaney said I was to bring you. . ." The motor rolled between illuminated gate-posts and along a drive to a white-pillared portico. "This way," said a footman, who seemed to have been waiting for Vance from the beginning of time; and Vance followed his suit-case up a broad flight of marble steps. It was true—he had forgotten to tell the chauffeur that he wanted to get out at Nice.

In a hall paved with coloured marbles he saw, re-doubled in tall mirrors, a tired parched-looking self in faded flannel suit and shabby hat. Other footmen appeared, eyeing him expectantly yet uncertainly; had it depended on them, their look implied, he would never have been included in the party. Then a familiar falsetto exclaimed: "Here he is! D'you remember Alders? My dear fellow, how are you? Mrs. Glaisher's in the loggia with the others. Never mind about not being dressed. . ." It was the same old Alders, more brushed-up and sleek in his new evening clothes, but still timid yet familiar, putting Vance at his ease, gently steering him in the way he should go. Vance smilingly submitted.

The loggia was a sort of open-air dining-room. Arcaded bays of plate-glass looked out over a dim garden. In the diffused candle-glow Vance saw, at a long table, Mrs. Glaisher, Lady Pevensey, Lorry, and a dozen others: young women with shining shoulder-blades in soft-coloured dresses, men in evening clothes with bald or glossily-brushed heads. He recalled the evening parties to which the Tarrants used to take him, when he was planning a novel called "Loot", and absorbed in the faces and fashions of successful worldlings. But here the background supplied the element of poetry for lack of which the theme had ceased to interest him. The same trivial, over-dressed and over-fed people acquired a sort of Titianesque value from the sheer loveliness of their setting; grouped about the table with its fruit and flowers, framed in the pink marble shafts of the loggia, above gardens sloping away to the illuminated curve of the shore, they became as pictorial as their background, and Vance's first thought was: "If they only knew enough not to speak!"

But a plaintive lady in pearls was just declaring: "What I always say is: If you're going to buy a Rolls-Royce, buy *two* . . . it pays in the end"; and a flushed bald gentleman across the table affirmed emphatically: "We've run down a little place *at last* where you can really count on the caviar. . ."

Mrs. Glaisher, from the head of the table, shed an untroubled welcome on Vance. She too had clearly forgotten that anything had clouded their previous meeting. "Mr. Weston! This is too delightful." She held out a fat hand corseted with rings. "No, no, of course you mustn't dress. . . Sit down just as you are—this is potluck with a friend or two. . . Imp, where's Mr. Weston to sit? Floss, darling, can you make room for him?"

He sat down beside her, dizzy and excited. "I didn't know you when I first came in," he said. He had never before seen her in evening dress. For a moment she had been merged in the soft glitter of the other young women; but now they were all shadowy beside her, she alone seemed like some warm living substance in a swaying dream. "I never meant to come," he mumbled, half-laughing. His throat was dry with excitement; he emptied the glass of champagne beside his plate. "It was all your chauffeur's mistake."

"I'm sorry you think it was a mistake," she said, with a little lift of her chin; and he laughed back: "Oh, but I didn't say it was *mine!*"

Alders beamed over at them in his oblique and furtive way. Vance felt that Alders regarded him as his property, and the idea added to the humour of the situation. But in Floss Delaney's nearness nothing else seemed real or important, and while he ate and drank, and now and then touched her hand, or drew into his eyes the curve of her round throat as she tilted back her head, the chatter about them grew vague as the buzz of insects—as though the other guests had been great heavy bees gathering to loot the piled-up fruit and flowers.

Now and then a fragment of talk detached itself; Lorry haranguing about the future of the ballet, or Lady Pevensey shrilling out: "Duke, we won't let you carry off Miss Delaney on the Blemers' yacht unless you'll promise to land her in London next June. We've got to show her London, you know."

Vance did not know who the Duke was. The dark lean young man on Mrs. Glaisher's right (of whom Vance was just becoming faintly aware) gave a dry chuckle, and a large pale man opposite said, rather self-consciously: "What London wants is to be shown Miss Delaney." Vance concluded that this gentleman was the Duke, and wished he had looked more like one of the family portraits at the Marquesa's.

Miss Delaney seemed to think a faint laugh a sufficient answer to these comments. Her inarticulateness, which used to make her seem sullen, had acquired an aesthetic grace. It suited her small imperial head, the low brow, the heavily-modelled lids and mouth; and her silence suggested not lack of ease but such self-confidence that effort was unnecessary.

"It's funny—you're just the way you used to be, yet being so makes you so different," he said, with small hope of her understanding; but she replied with a murmur of amusement: "I don't believe anybody really changes."

"You might have waited for me this evening."

"You said nothing would induce you to come."

He laughed: "I guess you had me abducted, didn't you?" and she rejoined serenely: "No; I knew I didn't have to."

"Oh, look—" he exclaimed, laying his hand on her warm brown arm.

Slowly the full moon was lifting her silver round above the trees. With her rising a subtle alteration transformed the landscape. The lights along the shore waned and grew blurred, and the indistinct foreground of the garden began to detach itself in sculptural masses: wide-branching trees built up like heavy marble cande-

labra, alabaster turf edged with silver balustrades, a
jewelled setting of precious metals that framed the moving silver of the sea.

The talk about the table was struck silent as Mrs.
Glaisher's guests stared at the miracle; but presently
some one broke out: "By Jove, but tonight's the Fête of
the Fireworks at the Casino; who's going down to see
it?"

There was stir among the company, like the replete
diner's uneasy effort not to miss the culminating dish;
then Lorry Spear broke in with a laugh: "Going down
to the Casino to see fireworks? I should have thought
this terrace was the best proscenium we could find."

The others joined in the laugh, and the diners,
when wraps had been brought, wandered out onto the
terrace. The night was mild and windless; the younger
women, rejecting the suggestion of fur cloaks, stood
about in luminous groups of mother-of-pearl. Vance had
followed Floss Delaney, but two or three other men
joined her, and he drew back, content to watch her as
she leaned on the balustrade of the terrace, a gauze scarf
silvering her shoulders, her arms shining through it like
pale amber. The beauty of the night purged his mind
of the troubled thoughts his meeting with her had
stirred, and he felt her presence only as part of the general harmony.

A long "Oh-h" broke from the watchers. Far below
the villa sea and horizon became suddenly incandescent;
then a dawn-like radiance effaced the fires, and when
that vanished every corner of the night was arched
with streamers and rainbows of flashing colour.
Through them, as they shot up and crossed each other
in celestial trellisings, the moon looked down in wonder. Now she seemed a silver fish caught in a golden net,
now a great orange on a tree full of blossoms, or a bird

of Paradise in a cage of sapphires and rubies—yet so aloof, so serenely remote, that she seemed to smile down goddess-like at the tangle of earthly lights, as though she were saying: "Are those multi-coloured sparks really what the people on that little planet think the stars are like? Funny earth-children, amusing themselves down there with a toy-sky while up here we gods of the night are fulfilling our round unnoticed." Yet while she mused, he saw that she too changed colour with the change of lights, turning now blush-red, now gold, now pearl, like a goddess who reddens and pales because Actaeon has looked at her. . . Somehow that wondering moon, going her cool way alone, yet blushing and faltering in the tangle of earth-lights, suddenly reminded him of Halo.

"It's getting as cold as Greenland out here," one of the women exclaimed. "What's the matter with indoors and bridge?"

The guests trailed back, chattering and laughing, and through the windows Vance saw the footmen opening the card-tables and laying out the cards. He was about to follow when the thin dark young man who had sat at Mrs. Glaisher's right strolled up, holding out a cigar-case in a lean family-portrait-like hand. "Have one?" Vance's acceptance called to the other's narrow vertical face a smile lit up by perfect teeth: one would have supposed that in taking a cigar Vance had done him a quite exceptional favour. The smile persisted. "You make a good deal of money out of your books, I presume?" the young man continued, speaking English with a foreign accent to which a marked nasal twang was oddly super-added. The question jolted Vance out of his dream, and before he could answer the other continued earnestly: "Pardon *me* if I ask. Of course I know of your celebrity; your sales must be colossal—not? But very often you successful brilliant artists don't know how to invest your earnings. If that is your case I should be most happy to offer you expert advice. There are a number of opportunities on the market today for any one who's got the nerve to get in on the ground floor. . ."

"Duke—Duke! We're waiting for you to make up Mrs. Glaisher's table," Imp Pevensey's voice shrilled out across the terrace.

"Oh, hell—" remarked the dark young man, in an untroubled voice; adding, as he drew a card from his pocket: "If you require advice I guess we can fix you up as good as anybody. What my firm is after is to cater to the *élite,* social and artistic. So long!" He pressed the card in Vance's hand, and the latter read on it, wondering:

DUCA DI SPARTIVENTO

With
ROSENZWEIG AND BLEMP
Members New York Stock Exchange
New York and Paris

☙ XXII ☙

WHEN VANCE came down the next morning none of
Mrs. Glaisher's other guests were visible. Even Alders,
no doubt engrossed in secretarial business, did not show
himself; but the night before, when Vance had questioned him about Chris Churley, he had said instantly:
"Ah, you know Chris? So much the better. I was going
to ask if you wouldn't give him an interview—for an article in the 'Windmill', you know."

Vance laughed. "Yes, I do know; and I gave him
the interview a good many weeks ago."

Alders wrinkled his brows deprecatingly. "Ah—
there it is! No results, I suppose? A genius—certainly a
touch of genius, eh? But can't be pinned down. He
begged me to get him a chance to see Gratz Blemer, and
though Blemer's shy of publicity at present (or *she* is,
rather) I did persuade them that 'The Rush Hour'
ought to be written about in the 'Windmill', and Chris
spent an afternoon on the yacht—enjoying it immensely, by the way; but as for the article, nothing came of it.
Blemer keeps on asking me when he's to see the copy;
and what can I answer, when I can't even get hold of
Churley?"

"Ah—you can't get hold of him?"

"Vanished—like an absconding cashier. Some fellow saw him playing in the baccarat room at Monte
Carlo; but I've looked in two or three times without
finding him. And of course I don't know his address. I
daresay, though, he'll bob up when he hears you're
here."

227

Vance had good reasons for not thinking so; but there seemed nothing to do but to prosecute his search at Monte Carlo, since it was there that Chris had last been seen. A confidential enquiry at the police-station might possibly give some result; but in a big city like Nice the boy would be harder to trace.

Vance was still dizzy with the translation from Oubli-sur-Mer to the Villa Mirifique. Floss Delaney, unreal as the setting in which he had found her, seemed the crowning improbability of the adventure. But the villa, at any rate, was substantial. The morning sun, robbing it of its magic, merely turned it into an expensive-looking house from which splendour and poetry had fled. As he paced the terrace above the over-ornamented gardens Vance asked himself if he should have the same disillusionment when he saw Miss Delaney again. On the very spot where he now paused to light his cigarette he had stood beside her the night before while the moon turned her bare arms to amber. He had promised to meet her, with the rest of the party, that evening at Monte Carlo; they were to dine, he didn't remember where, with the fat pale man he had taken for the Duke of Spartivento, and who turned out to be somebody infinitely more important, an oil or railway king, Alders explained.

Vance had had only a short exchange of words with Alders when the party broke up, for the secretary had to hurry away to arrange for the morrow. Alders had undergone a curious transformation. In spite of all that the best tailoring could do he was as mothlike and furtive as ever; but under his apologetic manner Vance felt a new assurance, perhaps founded on financial security. Alders's literary earnings, he explained to Vance (who wondered by what they were produced), had become too precarious; in these uncertain times his publishers would give him no promise regarding the big book he had long been planning (Vance would remember?) on Ignatius Loyola . . . no, on El Greco; and his own small income having unfortunately diminished, he had accepted the post of secretary to Mrs. Glaisher rather than become a burden on his friends. He added that his wide range of acquaintances enabled him to be of some service to his employer, who, like the illustrious women of the Renaissance ("there's something of the Sforzas about her, I always think,") wanted to know every one eminent in rank or talent, and had shown herself very appreciative of his guidance. "Of course," Alders explained, in the same tone of timid fastidiousness in which Vance had heard him dilate on the Valencian primitives, or the capitals of Santo Domingo de Silos—"of course it's easy, even for women of Mrs. Glaisher's discernment, to be taken in by the flashy adventurers who are always trying to force their way into rich people's houses; and I do my best to protect her. As you see, the set she has about her would be distinguished anywhere. . . Sir Felix Oster (the stout pale man on her left at dinner; a Napoleonic head, I often say)—Sir Felix very seldom troubles himself to go to other people's houses. We're all dining with him tonight, at the new restaurant up at La Turbie; and as for my old friend, the Duke of Spartivento—he was tremendously excited at meeting you, my dear Weston—told me he'd heard all about your books; well, in the Duke's case," Alders summed up with his faint sketch of a smile, "I begin to think that in introducing him here I may have done him an even bigger service than I have his hostess." Alders laid his hands together with the devotional gesture Vance had seen him make in the presence of works of art. "An Italian Duke and a grandee of Spain . . . all I can say is, the prize is worthy of the effort."

At Alders's words a pang shot through Vance. What was the prize, and whose was to be the effort? Instantly he imagined that he had seen Alders's Duke watching Floss Delaney between his narrowed lids. And what was it that Lady Pevensey had said about the Duke's carrying Floss off for a cruise with the Gratz Blemers? A wave of jealousy buzzed in Vance's ears. Jealousy could outlive love, then, cling to it like a beast of prey to a carcase for which it no longer hungered? He had never loved Floss, in the sense in which he now understood loving; and he imagined that his fugitive passion had long since turned to loathing. Yet that night, while he tossed between the scented sheets of Mrs. Glaisher's guest-room, he could not shake off the torment. Floss Delaney—she was less than nothing to him! But the idea that other men coveted her made his flesh burn though his heart was cold. . . Why subject himself to further misery? What had he and she to do with each other? If he had not pledged himself to find Chris Churley he would have jumped into the first train for Oubli. Instead, when he had taken leave of Floss he had agreed to dine the next night with Alders's railway king in order to have another chance of meeting her. In the morning light, after coffee, and a stroll on Mrs. Glaisher's terrace, the situation seemed less lurid. He decided that if he spent the day hunting for Chris he had the right to an amusing evening, and that there was no reason why Floss's presence should prevent his taking it. She was only one pretty woman among the many at Mrs. Glaisher's; it was long since he had been among the flower-maidens, and now that the chance had come why should he fly from them?

He took the first train to Nice and went to the Préfecture de Police. Chris's name was unknown there, but Vance's description was noted down, and the sergeant said that they might have some information the next day. Vance continued his journey to Monte Carlo, where he made the same enquiries; then he decided that, the lunch hour being at hand, his best chance of finding Chris was to look for him in the fashionable restaurants. If he had carried away any winnings he was pretty sure to be spending them where caviar and new asparagus were to be had; if not, to be enjoying these delicacies at the expense of others. Vance went first to the restaurant which Floss had pointed out as the most sought after.

It was so full that the guests, overflowing onto the terrace, sat wedged under bright awnings and umbrellas; but Vance scanned the crowd in vain for a dark face with a mop of orange-coloured hair. He was about to seek out a more modest ordinary for himself when an elderly gentleman in smartly-cut homespun and a carefully assorted tie began to wave the *carte du jour* in his direction.

This gentleman, before whom head-waiter and *sommelier* were obsequiously drawn up, had a sallow complexion, weak handsome features and tremulous lids above eyes of the same gray as his thinnish hair and moustache. He might have been a long-since-retired American diplomatist, or the gentlemanly man in a bank who explains to flustered ladies why they mustn't draw a cheque when there's nothing to draw against. He looked either part to perfection, and Vance was wavering between the two when he heard himself hailed in a slow southern drawl. "Why, for the Lord's sake, if it isn't young Weston! Come right over here, my son, and let's open a bottle of wine to celebrate our escape from Crampton!"

It was Harrison Delaney, looking up at him with the same slow ironic twinkle that was like the reflection

of his voice. Vance saw him lounging in the dreary room
of the little house at Crampton, between his whisky-
bottle, his dog-eared copy of Pope, and the ledger which
lack of use had kept immaculate. As a real-estate agent
Delaney had been Euphoria's most famous failure.
Lorin Weston used to say that if there hadn't been any
other way for him to lose his money he'd have dug a
hole in the ground and buried it—that is, if he'd ever
had the guts to dig. By the time Vance was meeting
Floss down the lane her father had long since abandoned the struggle, and Euphoria remembered him
only when there was a distinguished stranger to be received or an oration to be delivered. Then, shaved,
pomaded and tall-hatted for the occasion, Delaney was
drawn from his obscurity by a community dimly conscious that, freely as it applied the title, he was in reality
its only gentleman. After all, a man who quoted Pope
and Horace the way Lorin Weston quoted prices on the
Stock Exchange did give his home town a sort of propri-
etary satisfaction; and when a fortune suddenly fell into
Delaney's lap the people who were not envious of him
said: "Well, he'll know how to spend it anyhow."

Apparently he did; at any rate in a way to impress
some of the most eminent head-waiters in Europe. In
the act of discussing the relative merits of *oeufs aux
truffes blanches* and *demoiselles de Caen* he paused and
waved Vance to the seat facing him. "Here, waiter—
where's that wine card? You choose for yourself, young
fellow. My palate's too burnt out by whisky to be much
good in selecting Bordeaux or Burgundies. But champagne, now—what, no champagne? Well, this fellow
here recommends a white Musigny—what'd you say the
year was, waiter?"

These details being settled in a leisurely and em-
phatic style, Mr. Delaney leaned back and scrutinized

Vance thoughtfully over his cocktail. The impression Vance received was of a man who had merely transposed the terms of his inactivity. He had leaned back in just the same way in his rocking-chair at Crampton, or among his cronies at the Elkington House or Mandel's grocery, the thumb of one long distinguished-looking hand thrust into the armhole of his waistcoat, and a cigar meditatively twirled in the other. The only difference was that the hands were now carefully manicured, that the waistcoat was cut by a master, the cigar heavily belted with gold. Mr. Delaney looked out on the world with the same ironic and disenchanted eye. He told Vance he was having a good time, but not as good a time as he'd expected. Now that they had plenty of money Floss would insist on dragging him around from one country to another, though he guessed she found all the places they'd been to were pretty much the same when you got there; he was sure he did. He guessed nowadays you could see all there was to see in the world if you just took a season ticket at the nearest movie-show. The only difference he could make out between all the places he'd seen was the way the barman mixed the cocktails— and the way some of 'em did it made you think they'd never tasted anything stronger than their mother's milk.

Florence (Mr. Delaney continued) seemed to think you ought to go round and see the real places. When she got to them he didn't believe she got much of a kick out of it; not unless there were a lot of fellows for her to dance with; but after the bad time she'd had when she was growing up he felt he owed it to her to let her have her way. As for him, when their tour was over he was going home to buy back one of the old Delaney farms near Richmond, and settle down there. The kind of life he wanted to lead was just what his father and grandfather had led before him: breed a few trotting-horses, and have a little shooting behind a couple of good dogs. He guessed that was as far as he'd ever got in the way of ambition. . .

Vance listened curiously. This man, who had been so familiar a part of his early memories, now detached himself as an alien being, never really identified with Euphoria, and nursing an indolent contempt for place and people even when these most righteously looked down on him. "Funny—I never could get any kick out of all that moral urge," he said with a reminiscent smile.

Vance laughed, and Delaney, his tongue loosened by the Burgundy he affected not to appreciate, went on more confidentially: "Fact is, I see now that I enjoy money as much as any of your model citizens; the only difference is that I never thought it worth sweating for. Floss, now—well, she wouldn't agree. She says money's her god, and I guess it is. . . She says it's the only thing that'll get her what she wants; and what she wants is the earth, or pretty near. Anything that stands out, that sticks up so that you can see it from way off—brains or titles or celebrity. I guess there's nothing on God's earth as undemocratic as a good-looking American girl." Mr. Delaney paused to go through the agreeable operation of cutting and lighting a fresh Corona. "Sometimes I feel like saying to all these grandees she's got round her: You think she's all impulse, do you? Got to get things the very minute she wants 'em? Well . . . you wait and see her stow away those impulses if they interfere with any of her plans. Sometimes, you know, Weston, I think the inside of my daughter is a combination of a ticker and a refrigerator. Of course I don't say this for her old friends . . . but when I see these Counts and Mar-

quises getting worked up about her, well, I have to lean
back and laugh."

He did lean back and laugh, fixing his watery eyes
on Vance. Floss, it appeared, the very day he'd made his
unexpected turn-over, had taken command of it—and of
him. Why, Vance wouldn't believe it maybe, but she'd
invested and re-invested that money so that the capital
had already doubled. And when she brought him the result of the first year's earnings she made him buy an an-
nuity for himself, and draw up a deed turning over all
the rest to her. Well, perhaps he'd been a little rash
. . . but, as Vance knew, a quiet life was all he'd ever
asked for. And Floss was a good daughter—a devoted
daughter—if only you let her have her way. She'd try to
break him of his bad habits—whisky and poker—and
when she found she couldn't she just read the riot act,
and before he knew it he'd signed the papers, and now
they were on the best of terms, and she was glad enough
to have him around with her. "Says it looks better—
besides, you know, damn it, the child's fond of me," Mr.
Delaney concluded emotionally.

Vance listened under a painful fascination. He
could not reconcile Mr. Delaney's picture—or, rather,
perhaps, he did not want to—with the capricious girl,
cynical yet passionate, who had set him aflame in a past
already so remote. But he reflected that Delaney's was
probably a one-sided version. Floss, aware of her father's
failings, had naturally wanted to put their suddenly acquired wealth out of his reach, and Delaney, for all his
affected indifference, doubtless resented her domina-
tion. But Vance could not talk of her with her father.
Too many memories stirred in him; and when he had
finished his coffee he got up and took his leave. His host
seemed surprised and disappointed. "Off already? Why,

what's your hurry?" he said plaintively. "I never know how to get through these blamed everlasting days. Nothing doing in the baccarat rooms before five." But happily two middle-aged gentlemen with expensive clothes and red innocent-looking faces came up and hailed him, and Mr. Delaney, explaining that they were two fellows from Buffalo that he'd made friends with in Egypt, moved on with them contentedly to the nearest bar.

Vance had promised Floss to be at her hotel at eight. She had told him she would stop there to pick him up on her way from Cannes to Sir Felix Oster's dinner at La Turbie. "Unless," she mocked, "you'd rather go with Mrs. Glaisher?"

"Well, I would, unless you'll promise to have nobody else with you." As he spoke, the blood rushed to his temples, and he thought: "You fool—what did you say that for?" But she returned, in her cool unsmiling way: "Come and see," and at the challenge his blood hummed. After all, if she didn't turn up, or if she had some of the other men with her, he would just turn on his heel and go off and dine by himself. This decision made him feel extraordinarily resolute and self-confident.

His self-confidence waned during the unavailing search for Chris. He had decided, in any case, to return to Oubli the next morning, leaving the quest to the police; and to fortify his resolve had telegraphed the hour of his arrival to Halo. But meanwhile the sense of depending on Floss Delaney's whim made the time weigh on him as heavily as it did on her father, and long before eight he was in the lounge of her hotel.

The hour came and passed; but twenty minutes later her motor drove up, and Vance saw that she was alone. He was astonished at his own excitement as he plunged down the steps to meet her. He saw her lean forward to wave to him, the porter opened the door, he was at her side, and they were driving away. "It won't last ten minutes," the pulses in his temples kept dinning into his brain. He had found out where La Turbie was, had looked up at the new restaurant from the Casino square. On its towering cliff it glittered close above them like a giant light-house—a few turns of the wheels, and the motor would be there. And the next morning he would be on his way back to Oubli—what a trifle to have made all this fuss about!

"Well—am I a good girl?" his companion said, touching his arm as the motor began to work its way through the crowd about the Casino.

"When you asked me to go with you I didn't know the place we're going to was just up that hill," he growled. "We'll be there before we can turn round."

"Well, I can't help that, can I?"

"If there'd been a longer way to go you'd have taken one of the other fellows. . . Why didn't you wait last night, and drive me to Mrs. Glaisher's, as you said you would?"

"Why, I wanted to—honest I did. But Spartivento said I'd promised to try out his new Bugatti racer with him."

"Promising don't cost you much—never did. You'd promised me."

"I'll promise now to go off with you tomorrow for the whole afternoon—just you and me: we'll go wherever you like. Will that satisfy you?"

He laughed impatiently. "It won't make any difference one way or the other. I've got to go home tomorrow morning."

"Oh,—*home*," she mimicked, with an undefinable accent in which irony seemed blent with a just perceptible resentment.

"Yes; home," he repeated with insistence.

She gave a low laugh. "Why, Van, your voice sounds just the way it did the days I was late, when we used to meet down by the river. But I guess you're so celebrated now you don't remember."

"So celebrated—!" He felt a lump in his throat. She ought not to have reminded him of those meetings—she ought not to. . .

"Well, you are celebrated, aren't you? Everybody's talking about you. I don't know why you should remember me; but I want you to." She leaned nearer, her hand on his. "Van, don't be cross. I was the first, wasn't I? Say you remember."

"I remember well enough the day I saw you down there with—somebody else," he said in a choking voice.

"Oh, Van—" She swung suddenly round on him. "All I remember is the days I was there with you. Those first days . . . how hot it was that summer . . . and there was a weed or grass that smelt so good. . . Van, say you remember!" Her bare arms were about him, her lips on his. The old glory flooded him, and everything was full of bells chiming, and stars dancing through wind-swayed trees. "Tomorrow," she said against his lips.

❦ XXIII ❧

THE ILLUMINATED room, the many faces, whirled about Vance. Ahead of him Floss Delaney's brown shoulders flashed like the dryad's in the Fontainebleau woods; he heard familiar voices, saw Mrs. Glaisher armoured in diamonds, Lady Pevensey's dry sparkle ("She looks like a cocktail," the novelist in him noted), and the dull enigma of Sir Felix Oster's full-moon countenance.

"We thought you two were lost," Mrs. Glaisher simpered; and Alders, fluttering up, whispered: "He's here, you know . . . such luck! I do hope you'll persuade him to do that Blemer article before they leave. . ."

And there was Chris.

Clearly he had not expected to meet Vance. He turned pale under his sallowness, then flushed to the roots of his orange-tawny hair. But his disturbance was only skin-deep; his eye remained cool, his smile undaunted. This was a new Chris, the man-of-the-world twin of the unhappy changeling of Oubli: evening clothes, sleeked hair, the lustre of his linen, transformed him into the ornamental frequenter of fashionable entertainments. "We always try to secure an author or two: Mr. Churley's one of the new literary critics, isn't he—on the 'Owl', or the 'Windmill', or something?" Lady Pevensey threw off, catching Vance's signal to Chris.

"Well—so you're here?" said Vance, laughing; and the other responded glibly: "Such luck! When I heard you were coming tonight I chucked another engagement. . ." ("Liar!" thought Vance, more amused than indignant). "Fact is, you're the very man I want to get hold of," Chris continued on a tidal rush of assurance. "You know Blemer, I suppose? Just as I was starting for London the 'Windmill' wired me that he was at Cannes, and told me to try to pick up an interview before I left the Riviera. Lucky job, getting the wire just as I was shaking the dust of Oubli from my feet," he grinned complacently. "But now that I've seen Blemer I—well, frankly, you might just as well ask a fellow to write an article about a fountain-pen. That's all Blemer appears to be: his own fountain-pen. Where's the man behind it? Haven't an idea! Have you? Alders says you know him, and it's a God-send my running across you, for I was just going to chuck the whole thing and start for London. If you'll let me go home with you tonight we might talk Blemer over, and I could get an inkling of what to say about him."

Vance was tempted to retort: "Have you got an inkling from Blemer of what to say about me?"—but the party was moving toward the lamp-hung loggia where the tables were set. "All right—come in tonight." He turned to follow his host, and Churley was absorbed in the group about another table.

Vance was with Lady Pevensey, and a pretty young woman on his right was soon deluging him with literary raptures. He had to listen again to all the old questions: were his novels inspired by things that had really happened, or did they just "come to him"? And his characters—would he mind telling her who the people really were? Of course she knew novelists always pretended they invented their characters—but wouldn't he be a darling, and just whisper to her some of the real names of the people in his books? And the love-scenes— she did so long to know how far the novelist had to *live* his love-scenes; in "The Puritan in Spain", for instance, there was that marvellous chapter in Valencia—oh, yes, she knew some people called it morbid, but she just adored it—where, after being with the dancer all night, the hero comes out into the street at daylight, just as the funeral of the woman who'd really loved him is passing . . . Had anything as tremendous as that actually happened in his own life? Because she'd heard people say that a novelist couldn't describe such things unless . . .

Across the lights and flowers Vance caught sight of Floss. She was at Sir Felix's table with Mrs. Glaisher. Next to her sat the Duke of Spartivento; her lids were lowered as he spoke to her. She wore a dress of some thin silver tissue, against which her arms and shoulders looked like sun-warmed marble. There was a bowl of silver-white gardenias in the middle of the table, and her neighbour reached over to it and drew out a cluster which she fastened on her breast. At another table Chris, flushed and handsome, was discoursing to Alders about the art of interviewing. As Sir Felix's Pommery circulated the spirits of the guests bubbled up with it, and talk and laughter drowned the pulsations of the harp and violin in the balcony. Outside, modelled by the rising moon, the couchant landscape stretched its Sphinx-like paws upon the sea.

Vance was seized by the longing to be alone with Floss—chatter silenced, lights extinguished, only he and she lifted above the world on a moon-washed height. But the dinner went on: more truffles, more champagne, more noise; and when it was over, and the party trailed out onto the terrace, as they had the night before at Mrs. Glaisher's, some one exclaimed: "Oh, but there are no fireworks tonight, are there? Don't let's stay out here in the cold for nothing. . ."

Floss was one of the first to re-enter the illuminated

room. Bridge-tables were being set out where the party
had feasted, and part of the floor had been cleared for
dancing. Two cabaret professionals were already weav-
ing their arabesques in the centre of the spectators, and
others awaited their turn in the background. Vance
went up to Floss, who stood watching the dancers.

"Don't you hate this? Aren't you fed up with it?
Why won't you come away with me now?"

She turned with slightly-lifted brows. "Why, aren't
we all going away presently? There's a cabaret down at
Monte, something fearfully exciting, with the new Bali
dancers. You must come along, of course. . ."

"That's not what I mean. Come off with me now,
up here on the mountain. It's heaven out there with the
moon—" Sir Felix was advancing toward them with a
dapper gentleman wearing a single eye-glass. "Miss Delaney, may I introduce the Marquis d'Apremont?"
"Well, give me one of those gardenias then," Vance persisted boyishly as she turned with a smile to the newcomer. She shrugged her brown shoulders, and he
walked away and wandered out alone onto the terrace.
What was he doing in that rubbishy crowd, and why
didn't he dash down the mountain and take the first
train to Oubli? What a fool he had been to imagine that
Floss would leave in the middle of a party to go out with
him alone into the wilderness! The night air was sharp
at that height, and he re-entered the restaurant, determined to leave as soon as he had had a final word with
Chris. But Chris was dancing with the pretty woman
who was interested in novelists, and Mrs. Glaisher exe-
cuting a slow fox-trot under the accomplished guidance
of the Duke of Spartivento. Vance leaned in the doorway and watched the revolving couples. Floss was not
dancing; she sat in a corner, a group of men about her;
from where Vance stood he noticed that she spoke little,
smiled even more rarely, but sat there, composed, al-

most indifferent, while the faces about her shone with curiosity and admiration. And he had been fatuous enough to think that she would exchange that homage for a moonlight ramble with an obscure scribbler!

When the party began to break up he roused himself to look for Chris. "You'll come down to my hotel now?" he suggested; but Chris gave a deprecating gesture. "Straight away? Awfully sorry; but Mrs. Glaisher's taking us on to the cabaret. You're not coming? I say, that's too bad. What's your hotel? Do you mind if I drop in on you tonight rather latish? If you're turned in I won't disturb you—"

"I shan't have turned in; come up, no matter how late it is," Vance insisted; and the other rejoined with his bright plausibility: "Thanks a lot! It'll be the greatest help; somehow or other I've got to grind out that article. . . There's Mrs. Glaisher wig-wagging at us. Who's driving you down? Miss Delaney?"

But Vance, plunging out through the swinging doors, strode away alone. At the stream of motors flowed by in the moonlight he recognized Floss Delaney's, and for a mad moment thought she had seen him and was signing to her chauffeur to stop; but she was only lifting her little mirror with one hand while with the other she retouched her lips. In the shadow he caught the gleam of a shirt-front, the outline of a man's head; then the motor swept on.

Vance waited in vain for Chris Churley. He left his door unlocked, and sat in the darkness smoking and listening; but Chris's was not among the footsteps passing down the hotel corridor in the small hours, and toward daylight Vance undressed and fell asleep.

He woke late and gloomily. The sun, pouring in at his unshuttered window, roused him to a violent contact with reality. What had he hoped and imagined the night before? A feverish escapade with this girl who had sent through him the same shock as when he had first known her? Only a few hours ago her lips had been on his, her arms about him, her whole body breathing promises; an hour or two later she had turned from him with a shrug, without even an allusion to her own proposal that they should spend the next afternoon together. She would never think of that promise again; she had not even told him where they were to meet, had seen him go without a word of reminder. Once she was back at the Villa Mirifique, and caught up in the old round of pleasure, he would pass out of her life as he had before.

But while reason argued thus, the thought that his real self was pursuing was simply: "Who was the man she drove back with her from La Turbie?" At one moment that question was gnawing him, at another he was saying to himself: "Well, what of it, and what business is it of mine? There's no novelty in finding out again what she is—I knew it well enough before. And supposing I'd been the man she went off with, should I have felt any differently about her?" The residue of it all was a sick disgust, a revolt from life such as he had felt when he had seen her down by the river with his grandfather. She seemed to distil a poison such as no other woman secreted; his veins were so heavy with it that he felt like a man recovering from a long illness. "Oh, well, I must get up and get home," he thought, and dragged himself unwillingly out of bed.

It was not till then that he remembered Chris— Chris, who had not come the night before, whose address, like a fool, he had forgotten to take, and who had doubtless given him the slip again. He dressed in a cold rage against himself, against the world and against Chris —and was just turning to leave his room when the culprit entered.

❧ XXIV ❧

HE WAS not the brilliant Chris of the previous night, but a down-cast being whose pale face and heavy eyes seemed to reflect Vance's own distress. He held out his hand in silence, and Vance asked if he had breakfasted.

Chris grimaced a refusal. "But a brandy-and-soda? Thanks. Shall I telephone the order?"

He did so without waiting for the answer; then he threw himself into the one armchair in the room, lit a cigarette, and looked absently about him, as though hardly conscious of Vance's presence. "Not a bad place you've got here." He puffed at his cigarette, and added suddenly: "Funny chap, that Duke of Spartivento. Who do you suppose he's out to marry?"

"I don't know—nor much care," Vance replied, with a quick twinge of apprehension.

"Well—Mrs. Glaisher! Didn't you see him dancing with her last night? I suppose he noticed I was rather chummy with Alders, and might be likely to know something about the lady's affairs; so he got me off into a corner to ask about her investments—of course on the pretext that he represents a stock-broking firm. Up-to-date fellow, the Duke. Naturally I told him I knew all about it; you ought to have seen his eyes as I piled up the millions! I wouldn't have missed it for a good deal." Chris's own eyes brightened with the appearance of the brandy-and-soda, and he reached out to pour himself a stiff draught.

Vance watched him impatiently. At the moment the boy inspired him only with contempt. "Well, suppose we get down to business now," he suggested, as Chris leaned back in silent enjoyment of his drink.

The word seemed to strike a tender nerve. The blood flooded up under Chris's sallow skin, as it had the night before when he caught sight of Vance. "Business—?"

"Didn't you tell me you wanted me to help you with your article on Blemer?"

"Oh—*that?*" Vance caught his look of relief. "Why, yes, of course . . . Blemer. . ." With pleasurable deliberation Chris helped himself to another brandy-and-soda. "I haven't written the first line of that article on Blemer."

"No?"

"Nor of the article on you—"

"No?"

"No—no—no! Damn it, Weston, I suppose you knew from the beginning that I never would." Chris jumped up and began to move uneasily about the room. He halted before Vance. "And it was all a yarn, you know, what I told you last night about the 'Windmill' having wired me to come here and interview Blemer. The purest kind of a lie. Much the 'Windmill' cares! They washed their hands of me long ago. I daresay you guessed that too. You knew I'd taken the money you lent me to go to London with, and come here to blow it in—didn't you?"

Vance was silent, and Chris rushed on with twitching lips: "I daresay you heard of my being here from Alders or somebody, and came to look me up and see how I'd invested your loan, eh?" He gave a laugh. "Well, the last penny of it went up the spout last night."

"It wasn't a loan," said Vance.

Chris broke off with a stare. "It wasn't—?"

"I hate loans—to myself or others. The day after you told me you wanted to go to London I looked you up to tell you so. You'd already gone, and I didn't know where to write; but the money was a present, so there's an end of it. It's your own look-out how you spent it; you don't even owe me an explanation."

Chris received this in silence. He had grown very pale, and his lower lip trembled. "I say, Weston—." He turned away and throwing himself down sideways in the armchair buried his face in his crossed arms. "Oh, God, oh, God!" It was such an explosion of misery as had burst from him when he had confessed to Vance his desperate desire to get away from Oubli. Vance's contempt gave way to pity; but he hardly knew how to put it into words without touching on a live nerve. Chris looked up again. "Well, I don't suppose you're much surprised, are you? I daresay you knew from the first that I wasn't serious about the 'Windmill'."

"No; I didn't. And I still believe you meant to go to London."

"You do?" The mockery in Chris's eyes vanished in a look of boyish compunction. "Well, you're right; I did. But just as I was getting my ticket there was a fellow next to me taking his for Nice. And the sun was shining . . . and I hate fog and cold . . . they shrivel me up . . .Oh, Weston, what am I to do? I can't write—I *can't*. I can only dream of it. I knew I'd never earn enough in London to pay back your twenty pounds, and that with any kind of luck I might give myself a month's holiday here and settle my debt besides. So I came . . . and I did make money enough, or nearly; only like a fool I blew in part of it the day before yesterday. And last night I went back to try and recoup, and come to you with the cash in my pocket; and I struck my first run of bad luck, and got cleaned out." He gave another of his shrill laughs, stood up and limped across to the mirror over the mantel. "Pretty sight I am. . . I look like an old print of 'The Gamester'. By God, I wish I was an old print—I might sell myself for a pound or two!" He turned toward Vance. "The fact is, I was meant to be a moment's ornament, and you all insist on my being a permanent institution," he said with a whimsical grin.

"Well, you've ornamented several moments by this time," said Vance. "The best thing you can do now is to pack up and come back with me."

"Back—to Oubli?"

"Of course. All that rot about not writing—why, nobody can write who doesn't set his teeth and dig himself in. Your mistake was ever imagining it was fun. Come along; you'll write fast enough when you have to."

Chris stood twirling a cigarette between his fingers. His hands shook like an old man's. "I say, Weston— you've been awfully decent. And I wonder if you won't understand—if you won't help me out this once. . . Not a big loan; just a few pounds. It'll be the last time . . . After that I'll go back."

"You'll come back now. Your mother's out of her senses worrying about you; it's not fair to keep her in suspense."

Chris dropped down into the chair again, limp and expressionless as a marionette with broken wires. "Look here," Vance began—but the other interrupted him. He knew all that Vance was going to say, he declared; hadn't he said it to himself a thousand times? But he was sick of pretending that he ought to buckle down to work, that he oughtn't to borrow money, that he ought to be kind to his parents, and not worry them out of their senses. What was the good of it all, when he didn't happen to be made that way? Talk of ineffectual angels —there were ineffectual devils too, and he was one of them. Didn't Vance suppose he knew what he was made for—to talk well, and make people laugh, and get asked out where there was jazz and fun and cards? Some millionaire's hanger-on—that was what he was meant to be; and yet he wasn't either, because he couldn't stand being ordered about, or pretend to be amused by stupid people, or dazzled by vulgar asses, or any of the things you were expected to do in return for your keep. In his heart of hearts he'd rather slave in an editor's office than nigger for rich morons as poor Alders did—an educated fellow, not half stupid, but who didn't know how else to earn his living. For his part, he'd rather give himself a hypo and be done with it. . .

"You might try slaving in an editor's office before you plump for the hypo," Vance answered. His compassion was cooling off. The perpetual spring of energy bubbling up in him made such weakness and self-pity almost incomprehensible. He could understand the rich morons getting themselves privately electrocuted, he said; after a day or two in their company he always wondered why they didn't. But to a man like Chris, with eyes and a brain, the mere everyday spectacle of life ought to. . .

"The wind on the heath?" Chris interpolated drily.

"Well, yes, damn it—the wind. . ." But the argument died on Vance's lips. Life wasn't like that to Chris's decomposing intelligence. His eyes and his brain seemed to drain the beauty out of daily things; there was the bitter core of the enigma.

Vance laid his hand on the boy's shoulder. "Listen, old man; your people are awfully unhappy. Come home; we'll see what can be done afterward."

Chris looked up with heavy eyes. "Now—today?"

"By the next train. I can't think why you're not fed up with this sort of thing. I am."

Chris sat staring down at his idle trembling hands. "You're a brick, Weston—"

"Oh, stow all that. Where's your hotel? Go along

and pack up, and I'll call for you in half an hour." But suddenly Vance reflected: "If I let him go, ten to one I'll never find him again.—Look here," he said, "just wait till I pitch my things into my bag and we'll go together. It won't take me ten minutes."

Chris sank more deeply into the armchair. A look of utter weariness stole over him. "Oh, all right—what's the odds?" His eyes followed Vance listlessly till the lids closed and he leaned back in a sort of doze. Vance, moving about noiselessly, collected his belongings and jammed them into his suit-case. He was consumed with the longing to get away—as much on his own account as on Chris's. The glare of the sun, the sparkle of flowers and foliage outside his window, the strains of Puccini coming up from the Casino Gardens, all the expensiveness and artificiality of the place, made him think longingly of Oubli, of the fishermen mending their nets on the beach, the shabby houses, the peasants ploughing and pruning. "Real people in a real place," he mused; and his heart warmed as he thought of Halo waiting at the station at Toulon, and their all jogging home in the old omnibus over the rough dusty roads. . .

As the porter came in to take the things down Chris roused himself. "Look here, Weston—I know what a worm I am. But I'm afraid there's something owing at my hotel. If you'd lend me enough to go on with, and I could stay another day, I might come out ahead after all."

"Come along. I'll settle with the hotel," Vance retorted, nervously wondering if his own funds would hold out. He slipped his arm through Chris's, and the latter let himself be led to the lift, and out of the hotel. As they emerged into the street a hotel porter came up to Vance with a letter. "Mr. Weston?"

Vance recognized the untidy scrawl in which Floss

Delaney had written her message on the back of the
Duke of Spartivento's card. "Wait a minute," he said
unsteadily. He turned back into the hotel and opened
the envelope. There was nothing inside but a bruised
discoloured gardenia. He stared at the livid flower; then
he pushed it into his pocket, and went out to rejoin
Chris. It meant goodbye, no doubt. . .

He paid Chris's bill, which was more moderate than
he had expected, helped the youth with his packing, and
led him firmly to a waiting taxi. "The station!" he ordered.

Chris sat passive. Vance tried to think of something
to say, but his own brain was in a whirl. . . That flower
—why the devil had she sent it? It must mean something, convey some kind of message. She was always lazy
about writing; hardly capable of turning more than a
bald phrase or two . . . shaky about her spelling too,
probably. But, after all, why should she have written?
She had made an engagement—a positive engagement—
with him for that afternoon: it had been made at her
own suggestion, she had sealed it with a kiss. What perversity of self-torture made him suppose that she would
forget it? She had even remembered his asking her for
the flower she was wearing—and here it was, to remind
him of her promise. The flower didn't mean "goodbye"
—if it meant anything it meant "remember". . .

But how could he keep the engagement? And did
he even want to now? The vision of Halo at the Toulon
station had quickened other impulses—at least until the
faded gardenia stifled them. Something within him whispered, half hypocritically, half cynically: "I must see
this thing through first."

At the station Chris again hung back. "Look here,
Weston . . . just till tomorrow. . ."

"Tomorrow and tomorrow! Come, get out, old

man. . ." In dragging Chris along the platform he seemed to be dragging himself too. The train rolled into the station. They followed the porter.

The train was crowded. Vance pushed Chris and his bag into a compartment; but there was no other vacant seat. "Never mind—I'll run along and jump in wherever I can." But as he spoke he felt another resolution forming in him. "If I can't find a place," he called out, his hand on Chris's door, "I'll take a later train. Let Halo know, will you? I'll taxi over from Toulon." He waved his hand and feigned a dash down the platform. But the train was moving; he was left behind. After all, he had done his duty in shipping Chris off.

He left his suit-case at the station and went back to the hotel where Floss had been staying with her father. From her having sent him the gardenia he inferred that her visit to Mrs. Glaisher was over and that she had returned to Monte Carlo and was awaiting an answer to her message.

The concierge told him she was expected back, but had not yet arrived. Vance's spirits rose. He wrote her name on an envelope, scribbled on a sheet of paper: "Where—and when?" and added the address of his own hotel. Then he went back there to lunch. But he was too much excited to eat, and leaving the restaurant he paced up and down the narrow lounge, smoking and watching the door. An answer was sure to come soon; she had not sent that flower for nothing. . .

The minutes and the half-hours passed. It was three o'clock now; then in a flash it was half-past. The hours of his precious afternoon were being blown by him like the petals of a flower dropping before it can be gathered. Unable to endure the suspense he hurried out and walked back to Floss's hotel. He saw her motor at the door. The interior was piled up with bags, and at first he thought she must have just arrived from Cannes; then he saw a man in shirt-sleeves lifting a motor-trunk into the trunk-carrier. He went up to the chauffeur. "Is Miss Delaney here?"

The chauffeur said he supposed so. She hadn't come down yet; but they were starting in a minute for the harbour.

"The harbour?"

"Yes, sir; for the yacht. I believe Miss Delaney's going on a cruise."

Vance did not wait to hear the end. He pushed past the porters, and as he re-entered the hotel the door of the lift opened and Floss stepped out. She carried a little bag of scarlet morocco with polished steel mountings and had a fur-collared coat hung over her arm. Behind her was a young woman carrying more wraps. Vance went toward the lift and Floss stopped and looked at him with lifted brows and a faint smile. "Why, Van—"

"Am I late?" he began quickly.

She continued to gaze at him, not embarrassed but merely in gentle surprise. "Late—for what?"

"For our engagement. I came before, but you weren't here. Are you coming with me now?"

Her lovely eyebrows still questioned him. "But, Van, I don't—"

He broke in with a bitter laugh. "Are you trying to tell me you've forgotten?"

"What I *had* forgotten was that this is the day I start for a cruise with the Blemers. I can never remember the day of the week. We're going to Sicily," she explained gently.

"No!" he burst out.

"*No?*"

"I say no. Last night you swore to me—"

She turned and threw her cloak over the maid's

arm. "Put that into the car. And my bag." The girl disappeared, and Floss laid her hand on Vance's arm. "Come." He followed her into the empty writing-room behind the lounge. Between two of the little mahogany writing-desks with green-shaded lamps she paused and stood smiling up at him. "Darling—it's such a stupid mistake."

"What's a mistake?"

"About the date. I'm sorry. I thought the Blemers weren't starting till tomorrow. Honestly I did."

"Well—can't you follow them tomorrow, if you're so bent on going with them? You owe me this one day."

She laughed. "Charter a yacht and give chase? That's an idea! But I'm afraid I couldn't find anything fast enough to catch up with them."

"Why need you go with them at all? You swore to me—"

Her lids drooped, and her lips also, dangerously. "Yes; I know. But please don't be a bore, Vance."

"A bore—?" He felt his heart stand still. Her face was as smooth as marble. "Why did you send me that flower, then?"

"That flower? Why—for goodbye. . ." She held out her hand with a smile. "Not for long, though. . . You'll be in London next summer? Father and I are going there in June.—Yes; *coming!*" she called out in a gay voice, signalling to some one in the door behind him.

Fierce impulses raged in him; he wanted to pinion her by the arms, to hold her fast. He caught at her wrist; but she laughed and shook herself free. "So long, dear. —Com*ing!*" she cried in the same gay voice as she swept past him into the hall.

BOOK IV

❧ XXV ❧

It HAD been raining steadily for the three days since Vance's return to Oubli. A soft regular rain; it came down on the roof of the Anglican chapel with a rapping like the rattle of palm-fronds in an African oasis. Why had that occurred to him? He had never been to Africa, never seen an oasis; but he had heard some one say: "In the dry season the rattle of palms in the wind sounds just like rain. God, it gets up a fellow's thirst!" Like drift on a swollen river, all sorts of unrelated thoughts and images jostled each other in his brain. He could not clear his mind of them, or fix it, for more than a moment or two, on the sombre words that Mr. Dorman, distant and surpliced, was speaking from the chancel.

"Thou makest his beauty to consume away, like as it were a moth fretting a garment. . .

"As soon as Thou scatterest them they are even as sheep. . . For when Thou art angry all our days are gone. . . O spare me a little that I may recover my strength, before I go hence and be no more seen. . ."

Ah, cruel implacable God of Israel, Who, among all the generations of men, sufferest so few to recover their strength before they go! What mockery to apply to this poor broken boy the stupendous words that shake the bones of the saints!

There he lay, under the pall and the wreaths, "turned to destruction", as Mr. Dorman told them— voluntarily turned to it, as Vance secretly believed. The shabby wreath of anemones and stocks was, of course, Miss Plummet's. Lady Dayes-Dawes had sent arums.

There was a hideous cushion of white immortelles with "Chris" on it in yellow—how he would have laughed at it! Halo had managed to find violets, heaps and heaps of them, though they were nearly over—with a spray of cherry-blossom, the first of the year. Ah, implacable God of Israel! But now—listen:

"It is sown in corruption; it is raised in incorruption; it is sown in dishonour; it is raised in glory. . ." What martial music the Prayer-book made out of the old cry of human mourning! This sorrow sown in dishonour, was it indeed to be raised in glory? A sob from one of the black-muffled figures in front seemed to ask the same question. Then silence again; the rattle of rain; and "Lead, Kindly Light" from the volunteer choir, with Miss Plummet, in tears, at the harmonium.

When they came out the rain had stopped. The coffin was lifted into the old weak-springed hearse, with its moth-eaten tufts of black feathers all bent one way. (How he would have laughed at the feathers too!) The procession straggled off. Oubli could not provide enough mourning coaches, and its two wheezy Fords closed the line, noisily resisting their drivers' attempts to keep them in step with the heavy black horses. In the English corner of the hard bare cemetery cypresses and laurestinus had been planted, green things trained over the graves. But to get there the mourners had to walk two by two (Mrs. Churley's weak swollen feet setting the uncertain pace) through arid rows of French graves with wreaths of wire and painted tin-foil, and china saints under glass bells. Vance remembered Chris's saying that French funeral wreaths always reminded him of the once-for-all thoughts that the living think of the dead: rigid indestructible opinions that there is never any need to renew.

"Inasmuch as it hath pleased Almighty God to take

out of this world the soul of our deceased brother—"
Mr. Dorman was saying across the yawning grave.

"Out of the world"; with all its laughing and crying and vain tumult. . . "The wind on the heath,
brother—" How Chris had shrugged away Vance's facile
admonitions! Wind on the heath, wind in the palms, all
the multiple murmurs of life—Chris Churley's ears
were forever closed to them.

Yes; he had been Vance's brother; and how had
Vance dealt with him? "What hast thou done with this
thy brother?" Why, deserted him at the last moment,
shoved him into the train and left him alone with his
self-derision, his bitter consciousness of futility and failure. Vance knew well enough what it felt like to be
alone in such a mood, without friends, without hope,
without future; he had been through it all in the early
days in New York. Yet he had not given it a thought
when he shoved Chris into the train and dashed away on
his own crazy errand. What had he done with his
brother?

"Ashes to ashes—dust to dust—" As Chris was today, so would he be in his turn, nailed up with his withered dreams. . .

The earth fell on the coffin; somebody piled the
wreaths on the mound. The sun came out, as if curious
to see what this little group of bowed-down people were
about; and in the dazzle of the indifferent day they
crawled back to the carriages.

In the taxi Halo burst into tears. Vance put his arm
about her. She seldom wept, and her grief moved him,
and made him feel ashamed of his own dry eyes. But
though his soul was heavy he could get no relief. Halo
wiped away her tears and looked up at him. "You still
think it wasn't an accident?"

"I'm sure it wasn't."

"But they said he didn't see the other train coming when he got out. The people in the other train said so."

"Yes."

"All the same, you think—?"

"Oh, what does it matter?" Vance groaned.

"I'm glad Mr. Dorman was convinced it was an accident. Otherwise there couldn't have been a proper funeral. . ."

"I know. . ."

"It would have killed Mrs. Churley if he'd refused."

"Sorrow don't kill people. It seems to give them a sort of kick. Look how she walked all the way to the grave and back."

Silence again; she pressed his hand tight. "Promise me, dearest, you won't go on thinking yourself to blame."

Vance laughed drearily. "People have got to think what they can. I ought to have come back with him. . ."

"What folly! You put him in the train."

"I ought to have come back," Vance repeated, as if to himself. The taxi stopped before the pink house and they got out.

At first Mrs. Churley had refused to see Vance; but two or three days after the funeral she deputed Mrs. Dorman to ask him to come up to the villa. Halo wanted to go instead; she seemed to dread the meeting between Vance and the Churleys. Vance, she argued, was still suffering from the shock of the dreadful news; he had told her what little there was to tell. Why not let Mrs. Dorman explain this to the Churleys, and suggest that Halo should go to them instead?

Mrs. Dorman pursed up her lips, and her cheeks

reddened, as they did when she saw a chance of impart-
ing unpleasant news. "It was Mr. Weston that Mrs.
Churley asked for."

"Of course I'll go," Vance roused himself to answer.

When he came back from the Churleys' he went
upstairs to the study and threw himself down on the old
divan where Chris had so often sprawled during the
long evenings full of laughter and discussion. Vance, on
his way back from Monte Carlo, had thought longingly
of that room; his old life seemed to hold out healing
arms to him. Then, on his threshold, he had heard the
stupefying news of Chris Churley's death—the accident
which had flung him under the wheels of an in-coming
express as he was getting out of his own train at Toulon;
and from that moment Oubli and everything about it
had become as hateful to Vance as the scenes from which
he had just fled.

He lay with his eyes shut, reliving the hours since
his return, and feeling as if he too had been flung out of
the security and peace of his life and crushed under the
sudden wheels of disaster. In the next room Halo was
moving about. She would not come in and torment him
with questions, as another woman might; she would
merely let him know by an occasional sound or
movement—the pushing back of a chair, the click of the
Remington—that she wanted him to be aware of her
nearness, and of the silent participation it implied.

The Remington. . . If only he could have got
back to work! In the first horror of seeing Floss Delaney
down by the river with his grandfather his anguish, he
remembered, had crystallized itself in words; the shock
had forced his first story out of him. And all through the
dark weeks before Laura Lou's death he had known the
same mysterious heightening of creative power: as if his

talent were an ogre, and lived on human suffering. But now he felt only an inner deadness; he seemed faced by a blank wall against which he might dash his brains out. Everything was stale and withered, without and within; he could almost taste the corruption—the same, no doubt, that Chris had tasted. . .

He got up and wandered into Halo's room. She turned as he entered, feigning surprise. "Back already? —Well?"

Vance stood beside her, drumming on the lid of the typewriter. "She knows—"

"Mrs. Churley? Knows what?"

"That it wasn't an accident."

"Vance! Did she tell you—?"

"No. He was there. But she didn't have to—"

Halo put out her hand and imprisoned his restless fingers. "Dear, aren't you just imagining—?"

"God! I don't have to imagine—"

"Tell me just what she said."

"She said she couldn't bear to have me there. It didn't last five minutes."

"Poor, poor woman!"

"I could see she hated the very sight of me. She thinks I killed him."

"But what folly—when it was you who gave him his best chance!"

"Did I? Perhaps they're right and we were wrong. Anyhow I ought to have come back with him."

"But surely you told them you couldn't find a place in the train?"

"Yes—I told them."

"Well, dear?" She lifted her grave eyes to his, and he thought: "If I told her the truth, would it make any difference?" For he knew well enough that what he was suffering from was not so much the shock of poor Chris's suicide as the dark turmoil in his own heart. It was his vanity that was aching, and his pride; in a sudden craving for self-abasement he longed to cry out his miserable secret.

"I wish you could get back to work," Halo said.

He made a derisive gesture. "Get back to work—that was what I used to tell Chris. I see now there wasn't much point in it." He turned away and threw himself again on the divan. What was the use of making some one else unhappy? His misery was his own; he had no right to ask any one to share it—least of all this woman who loved him.

The days dragged by. Vance, in spite of his curt retort to Halo, did try to take up his writing; but he could not. His imagination was dormant, his fingers seemed almost literally benumbed. The weather remained unsettled; day after day raw gales swept the sullen skies and rain burst from them with fitful violence. Every spring, the peasants told him, it stormed at Oubli in cherry-blossom time; and if the rain persisted it destroyed the fruit crop, and if it ceased the drought spoilt the early peas.

Vance resumed his long daily tramps. Halo had caught cold at the funeral, and in spite of her disregard for wind and weather he would not let her go with him. In truth he was glad to be alone. Some spring in him was broken; he felt like a man driving a motor with a disabled steering-gear. When he was with Halo he lived in dread of not being able to keep himself from some foolish burst of self-betrayal. When she said: "You mustn't let Chris's death make you so unhappy," he had to fight his impulse to burst out: "It's not Chris who's torturing me." He hardly knew the exact source of his pain. Since he had returned to Oubli, and slipped back

into the old familiar life with Halo, everything about
the interlude of Cannes and Monte Carlo had become as
unreal as the scenery of a stage-setting. He seemed to
have been moving in a world of flippant spectres; only
Floss Delaney kept her mordant reality. And the strange
thing was that, from the very moment of their meeting,
she had produced no illusions in him, excited no surprise. She had appeared, in that opulent environment,
neither rarer nor lovelier than when, as a raw boy, he
had worshipped and loathed her in the maple-grove at
Crampton. It was true that she had not changed; perhaps, as she had said, no one *does* change; and for that
very reason the common unimaginative girl who had
captivated the untried boy exercised the same spell over
the young man from whom a world of experience divided her. That was the dangerpoint. No alteration of
setting or of ideas—not even the profound shock of
Chris Churley's suicide—could shake him out of his unwilling subjection. It was because he saw her as she was,
and was still drawn to her, that his plight was hopeless.
Whenever he shut his eyes there was her bare arm, like
amber in the moonlight; the touch of it burned in him.
It was useless to tell himself that now that he knew the
world he could place her without difficulty, could class
her as the trivial beauty whom any intelligent man
would weary of in a week. Intelligence had nothing to
do with it. You might as well say that an intelligent man
would weary in a week of the scent of a certain flower,
when there are flower-scents that all through life work
the same magic. Vance knew there were selves under
selves in him, and that one of the undermost belonged
to Floss Delaney.

Again and again he was tempted to confess himself
to Halo; to do so might break the spell and tranquillize
him. And perhaps it would not be so difficult. When his

story, "One Day", had been discovered and published by Lewis Tarrant, and Vance, in an hour of expansion, had told Halo that he had written it to rid himself of his first sorrow, he had described Floss to her, and she had shuddered and sympathized. He would only have to say: "You remember that girl at Euphoria that I told you about?" to have her sympathy spring up. Ah—but would it? That other tale, when he had told it, already belonged to a distant past; neither he nor Halo could have dreamed that Floss Delaney would ever reappear in their lives. Now it was different. Intelligent though Halo was, could he hope to make her understand that a man may love one woman with all his soul while he is perishing for the nearness of another? Some day he might put that story in a novel; fitfully, even now, the idea came to him, he felt its richness and complexity— but only for a moment. The next he was back in the dark coil of his misery; and he knew that the impulse to confess himself was due not to any belief that confession would break the spell, but only to his monstrous craving to talk of Floss to any one, to every one, even to the woman he might wound to the heart in naming her. He thought: "I've hurt her so often without meaning to. At least I can keep myself from doing it with my eyes open."

Since Vance's visit no sign had come from the Churleys. He suspected that Halo resented their silence, resented the poor mother's harsh dismissal of Vance af- ter she had sent for him. It was cruel, certainly, for they knew that Vance had tried to befriend Chris, that Vance's comradeship had been the one brightness in the boy's last months. But perhaps that was what they re- sented, though Halo refused to admit it. "They can't be so wickedly unjust—." But that was precisely what great sorrow made of people—didn't Vance know? Perhaps it even comforted them, the poor creatures, to have some one against whom they could cherish a bitter resentment. Well, let them—!

One day, coming in from a solitary ramble, he found a letter awaiting him. He broke the seal and read: "Dear Mr. Weston, I have only just learned that my son's visit to Monte Carlo was brought about by your having lent him twenty pounds. Pray excuse my involuntary delay in sending you the enclosed cheque, which I beg you to accept with my thanks. Yours very truly, Augustine Churley."

Vance uttered an angry exclamation. Halo, who was sorting the papers on his desk, looked up. "Oh, Vance—it's Colonel Churley?" He tossed the letter over to her.

"It wasn't a loan—and Chris knew it!" Vance fumed. It seemed as though these people had divined how he hated himself for having left Chris, and were seizing on every pretext to increase his misery.

"But how did they know the amount? Chris must have told them—or have left a letter."

"Well, I won't take it," said Vance nervously. "They'll end by poisoning my memory of him. I daresay they think my giving him that money was the cause of his death."

Halo reflected. "No; you can't take it. Give it to me; I'll go and see Mrs. Churley."

"She won't see you."

"I think she will. Mrs. Dorman will arrange for me to go when her husband's out. She couldn't talk to you the other day because he was there. But you'll see—"

Vance drew a breath of relief. He was so used to Halo's smoothing out the asperities of life that he felt almost as certain as she did of her ability to cope with Mrs. Churley. And at least the question of the money would be effaced from his mind.

The next day he did not get back till late from his walk. As he mounted the stairs he caught Halo's voice: she was speaking excitedly, in a tone of irritation unusual to her. The study door was ajar, and he heard Mrs. Dorman replying, in the conciliatory voice in which she communicated anything likely to give pain: "I'm so sorry, Mrs.—Mrs.—. You must really tell me, you know, what I ought to call you," she interrupted herself with a faint cough.

Vance strode in. Halo was standing, her head high, her face pale; Mrs. Dorman confronted her with excited spots of red on her round innocent-looking cheeks. "You mustn't really take it so hard," she was protesting.

Halo turned to Vance. Her lips were as pale as her face, and her arm trembled slightly as she rested it on the desk; but her voice was quiet. "Mrs. Dorman tells me that Mrs. Churley would rather not see me."

Vance guessed instantly what had happened. Ireful words sprang to his lips; but Halo's glance checked him. How right she was—always! It would have been a pity to gratify Mrs. Dorman by any sign of discomfiture. "Since Mrs. Churley doesn't want to receive either of us," he rejoined, in a voice as quiet as Halo's, "I don't see that there's anything more to be said."

Mrs. Dorman looked undefinably disappointed. "But I didn't mean that, Mrs. Weston. On the contrary. Mrs. Churley's very sorry she was so overcome when you came the other day; she'd be glad to see you again. The message I brought was for Mrs. . . Mrs. . . ."

"My name's Weston," Vance interrupted.

"Exactly." Mrs. Dorman's face grew rounder and rosier. "And at first we all supposed . . . naturally . . ."

"Mrs. Dorman," Halo intervened, "has just told me that Mrs. Churley's reason for not wishing to see me is that she's heard we were not married."

"I told her I'd always understood that in the States you attach comparatively little importance to being married . . . that perhaps we oughtn't to judge you by our standards. But naturally that's not the general feeling in England; at least not among Church people—and Mrs. Churley was dreadfully upset. You know she always dreaded any . . . any demoralizing influence on that poor boy; and I'm afraid she's taken it into her head that his friendship with Mrs.—Mrs.—"

The red rushed to Vance's forehead. "This lady's name is Mrs. Tarrant; but it will be Weston soon. Please say to Mrs. Churley—"

Halo laid her hand on his arm. "No, dear; there's nothing more to say. Except that we both loved Chris, and that we feel for his mother with all our hearts."

Mrs. Dorman stared with the bewildered look of one who has lost her cue. "But you will come to see her, Mr. Weston?"

"There'd be no object in it. Mrs. Tarrant has told you all we have to say."

Mrs. Dorman uttered a baffled sigh. "It's so very sad," she murmured. She gathered up her boa, and Vance opened the door and silently saw her down the stairs.

"It all falls on you—always!" he broke out indignantly as he returned to Halo.

She surprised him by a gesture of appeal. "That poor mother—oh, Vance, don't be angry with her! If only there was anything we could do! I feel as if you and I were the real debtors—everybody's debtors; as if, to be as happy as we are, we must have stolen too many other people's happiness. Darling, do you suppose we have?" she burst out, her arms stretched to him.

❦ XXVI ❧

THE DAYS passed heavily. Vance and Halo held no further communication with the Pension Britannique. Vance returned the cheque to Colonel Churley, with a note saying that the twenty pounds had been a gift to Chris, and that Chris was aware of it; and the following week a copy of Mr. Dorman's parish bulletin was left at the pink villa, with an underscored paragraph announcing that Colonel Churley, in memory of his son, had given twenty pounds to the Church library (Purchasing Committee: the Chaplain, Lady Dayes-Dawes, Miss Plummet.) Vance was diverted at the thought of the works which would be acquired with this fund; he amused himself and Halo by drawing up a probable list, and they smiled over the brilliant additions that Chris would have made to it.

But Vance was still full of disquietude. Everything in his life seemed to have gone wrong, to have come to grief. He asked Halo, the day after Mrs. Dorman's visit, if she would not like to leave Oubli; but she said with a smile that she didn't see why they should alter their plans to suit the Pension Britannique. They had taken the villa for a year, and she wanted him to have a taste of the summer life, the boating and bathing, the long hot days on the sands. "There'll be nobody to be scandalized then—the Pension Britannique closes in summer. If you suppose I mind what those poor women say," she added carelessly; and he understood that nothing could be more distasteful to her than to seem aware that she was the subject of gossip and criticism.

Vance himself had no feelings of the sort. He resented furiously any slight to Halo, but saw no reason for appearing to ignore such slights. He supposed it was what he called the "Tarrant pride" in her; the attitude of all her clan; the same which had helped Tarrant to stiffen himself against the moral torture of his talk with Vance, and affect indifference when every nerve was writhing. It all seemed an obsolete superstition, as dead as duelling; yet there were moments when Vance admired the stoicism. He could think of girls—straight, loyal, decent girls—who, if they loved a man, and lived with him, would have gloried in the fact, and laughed at social slights and strictures. But Halo suffered acutely from every slight and stricture, yet bore herself with the gayest indifference. "All those old institutions—I suppose there was something in them, a sort of scaffolding, an armour," he thought. He felt how often his own undisciplined impulses needed the support of some principle that would not have to be thought out each time.

But if Halo did not want to leave Oubli, he did; and she was not long in divining it. There was no longer any question of his working; the manuscript lay untouched. If he were ever to finish "Colossus" he must get away—get away at once. When he had lectured Chris on the evils of idleness he had little imagined that within a few weeks he would be exemplifying them. "I told him he'd be able to work fast enough if he had to—such rot! Look at me now!" he said bitterly.

"But it's just because of Chris that you can't work. You're still suffering too much."

"A good many books have been made out of suffering."

"Perhaps; but not out of tattered nerves. You've got to get away." He was silent. "Why not go to London?" she suggested suddenly. "It's time you saw your publishers about 'Colossus'. Go now; it's just what you need. You could stay with Tolby, who's so often invited you."

Vance felt a rush of life in his veins. London— London! He remembered the look in Chris Churley's eyes when he had heard the magic suggestion. "I wonder if my eyes look like that to Halo," Vance thought with a twinge of compunction; but the twinge was fleeting. London, Madrid, Constantinople—it hardly mattered which. Freedom was what they all meant—change and freedom! And how good to see old Tolby again, and drop back into the current of their endless talks. Everything connected with the idea of departure seemed suddenly easy and inviting.

"You'd really rather stay here?" he faltered.

"I'd rather," she smiled.

In the train, on the boat, and now in Tolby's snug smoky quarters, Vance felt the same glow of liberation. With his first step on English soil had come the sense of being at home and at ease. The feeling of sureness and authority underlying the careless confidence with which life was conducted, soothed his nerves, and put him quietly yet not unironically in his place—a strangely small one, he perceived, yet roomy and comfortable as one of Tolby's armchairs.

Tolby lived off the King's Road, on top of a house divided into old-fashioned flats. Attached to his studio were two bedrooms, a kitchenette and a slit of a bathroom, with a geyser which had to be managed like a neurasthenic woman. "When you get to know her it'll be all right; she'll get tired of trying on her tricks. She's always a bit nervous at first," Tolby explained. No one else in the flat was nervous. From the kitchen, at stated intervals, a broad calm woman (who removed a black bonnet with strings when she entered the flat), appeared with crisp bacon, kippered herring, cold beef and large placid puddings. To Vance the diet was ambrosial. He delighted also in the tidiness of the studio, where everything was shabby and paintless, but neat and orderly, with a handful of spring flowers on the breakfast table, a pleasant fire in the grate, and a general seemliness that reminded him of Halo. "You must be glad to get back to this from Montparnasse," he said with a sigh of satisfaction.

"Yes; when I've had enough talk."

"Isn't there any talk in London?"

"Yes; but it's not a sport or a career. It's done in corners—furtively."

"At any rate," Vance thought, "I'm not likely to hear any of that drivel that poor Chris ran after."

Little by little the social immensities of London began to dawn on him, its groups within groups, each, in spite of all the broad-casting and modern fluidity, so walled in by silence and indifference, and he became more and more sure that there was no risk of any communication between Tolby's group and Sir Felix Oster's. Among the young painters and writers who came to the studio he found himself already known, but not what Floss Delaney would have called celebrated. These young people had read his books, and were interested in them but not overwhelmed. The discovery roused his slumbering energy, and he said to himself in a burst of creative enthusiasm: "They're dead right about what I've done so far; but wait till they see 'Colossus'—I'll show them!"

His first days were spent in wandering about the streets, alert yet dreaming, letting the panorama of churches, museums, galleries, stream through his attentive senses. Tolby, himself hard at work, seldom joined him till the evening, and then they either supped (since dining, in Tolby's group, was out of fashion) with other pleasant busy people, chiefly writers or painters, or went to hear old music or to see new dancing. But by the end of the first week the desire to write had once more mastered Vance, and he shut himself up at his desk for long hours of the day.

On Saturdays he and his host went off on their bicycles to some quiet leafy place where there was an inn with a garden full of lilacs and tulips, or else they stayed with friends of Tolby's in low-studded village cottages transformed into bungalows, with black cross-beams and windows latticed with roses. But as Vance grew more absorbed in his work even such outings became disturbing, and he asked to be left behind when Tolby went away for the next week-end.

Tolby took this as a matter of course (the blessed way they had in England of taking things like that!), and the following Saturday Vance, after his friend's departure, turned with a grin of joy to his work.

Toward evening the opening of the door broke in on a happy cadence. The placid woman who purveyed the kippered herrings pronounced: "Mr. Fane", and Vance's memory added: "Of the 'Amplifier'." It was in fact Derek Fane, the young critic whom Vance had met at Savignac's the previous autumn, and to whom he had given a verbal outline of "Colossus". The book had undergone such changes that Vance was glad to see Fane again, and allowed the talk to be led to his work with more affability than he usually showed to interviewers. He knew his publishers were anxious that the "Amplifier" should make the most of his visit to London, and a talk with a critic like Derek Fane would be very different from the "third degree" applied by newspaper reporters. Fane was one of the quietest men Vance had ever met, even in England. Everything about him was muffled and pianissimo; he did his interviewing by listening. Vance could hardly recall his having put a question; but his silence was not only benevolent but acute. After Vance's summing-up of the new "Colossus" he merely said: "It sounds as if you'd pulled it into shape"; but the remark carried such conviction that a glow of encouragement rushed through Vance.

The next morning the "Amplifier" had a brilliant survey of Vance's past work, and a discerning account of his projected book, inserted into a picturesque impression of the King's Road studio. Henceforth all literary and fashionable London, if it cared to know, would be aware of Vance's presence.

The first result was a shower of invitations; one from Lady Pevensey headed the list. She besought Vance to climb to her little flat on the roof of a new West End sky-scraper for the most informal of after-theatre suppers. He would find just the people he liked, and must of course bring his friend Mr. Tolby, whose pictures everybody was beginning to talk about. Tolby urged Vance to accept. "It's one of the penalties of your profession; you must go and film the animals in their native habitat. I can sit still and wait till they come to be painted—but it's your job to snap them at their games."

Vance hardly needed urging. It was not so much the novelty of the scene that attracted him as its atmosphere. Being in England felt like coming back to something known in a happier state, and, as the hymn said, "lost awhile". There was nothing like it in his conscious experience, yet it seemed nearer to him than his actual life. He discovered that the sense of security and solidarity emanating from the group of dowdy exiles at Oubli was the very air of England. Wherever he went it looked out of calm eyes and sounded in calm voices. Ah, those calm voices, their rich organ-tones, their still depths of sound! Vance never tired of them. Halo's way of speaking, and that of her group, was a thin reminder of those rich notes; but how staccato and metallic compared with the brooding English intonations! "It's the way your voices handle the words," Vance explained, struggling for a definition. "The way a collector touches gems or ivories, not fussily or mincingly, but surely and softly. Or the way a girl in a poultry-yard picks up downy chickens." Tolby laughed and said he liked the last analogy best.

The next day a voice with a different cadence broke in on his toil. "I'm Margot Crash," it shrilled, and Vance found himself confronting a slender young lady with a face adorned by movie-star teeth and eyelashes. Miss Crash's job, though brilliant, was probably less lucrative than if she had used her gifts on the screen: she represented in London the literary page of the Des Moines "Daily Ubiquity". Vance started up to protest at the intrusion; but the teeth and eyelashes mollified him, and in another moment their owner, snugly ensconced in Tolby's deepest armchair, was confessing that she was a beginner, and desperately in earnest about her job. "If I can get a good write-up off of you I'm made forever," she declared; "but I'm so scared I guess you'll have to do it for me. I'm too crazy about your novels to know how to talk about them to their author."

"Oh, well," said Vance, "the ones I've already written are still measurable by human instruments."

She lifted her long lashes with a vague laugh. "Well, what I want is to find out all about them—how you write them, I mean, and how you began writing anyhow. What made you think of it? Did you take a course?"

"A course—?"

"Why, I mean at college. Or did the idea just come to you? Did you educate yourself to be a writer? Did you begin by studying your contemporaries? That's the way they make you do in some courses."

"No; I believe I began with Mother Goose."

Her lovely stare widened; allusiveness was evidently as unintelligible to her as irony. "Oh, do you mean you started by writing children's books?" She drew out a little note-book in which Vance could almost see her inscribing: "Began by writing for children." "Like the Pollyannas, for instance?" she helped him out enthusiastically.

"Well—something."

She clapped it down. "But what I want to know is —how did you learn to write for adults? Did you pick one of your contemporaries and work out your style on his, or did you take one of the longer courses—the ones that go way back to the classics?"

"It depends on what you call the classics."

That puzzled her again, and provoked a lovely frown. "Well—Galsworthy, I suppose," she triumphed.

"Oh, no; not as far back as that." Her face fell, but she wrote on ardently till he signified to her, as humanely as possible, that there was really no more to tell, and that he must get back to his work.

"Oh—your *Work!*" she breathed, in awed acquiescence; and then, putting out her hand: "You see, I'm trying to write novels myself, and it just means everything to me to find out from somebody up at the top what you have to do to get there. But I don't believe I'll ever have time to go way back to those old classics," she sighed.

The next day the London edition of the Des Moines "Daily Ubiquity" brought out a heavily head-lined article on the celebrated young American novelist who was visiting London for the first time, and who had acquired mastery in his art by writing children's stories and taking a college course in adult fiction. Well, why not?

❧ XXVII ❧

To ANY one not chained by association to the old low-fronted London there was magic in looking down from Lady Pevensey's sky-terrace over the lawns of the Green Park and the distant architectural masses discerned through shadowy foliage. In the transparent summer night Vance leaned there, lost in the unreal beauty, and recalling another night-piece, under a white moon-washed sky, when the Mediterranean lay at his feet, and Floss Delaney's bare arm burned into his.

The momentary disappointment over, he had been glad that Floss was not among Lady Pevensey's guests. At first, among those white shoulders and small luminous heads, he had imagined he felt her presence; but he was mistaken. Tonight he was in another of Lady Pevensey's many sets, and apparently it had not occurred to his hostess that she might have given him pleasure by inviting Floss. Did she even remember that the two had met at Cannes? Vance was beginning to learn that in this rushing oblivious world one must jump onto the train in motion, and look about at the passengers afterward. As soon as he entered Lady Pevensey's drawing-room he found himself surrounded, as in old days at the Tarrants', by charming people who made much of him. Then he had imagined that they were throwing open the door of their lives to him; now he knew they were simply adding a new name to their lists. They marked him down as the entomologist does a rare butterfly, and he found the process not unpleasant, for he was experienced enough to enjoy watching them while they were observing him, and he liked the atmosphere of soft-voiced cordiality and disarming simplicity in which the chase went on. He recalled with a smile the days when he had supposed that people in society wanted to hear the answer to their questions, or to listen to the end of a sentence. He had learned that they were really indifferent to every one and everything outside of their own circle; but he did not care. They were a part of the new picture he was studying, and he wanted them to be as characteristic and self-sufficing as his conception of them, just as they wanted him to be the young genius with rumpled hair who says unexpected things and forgets to note down his engagements.

"But of course you know Octavius, don't you, Vance?" It was Lady Pevensey's voice, rousing him from his nocturnal vision to introduce a small quiet man with a bulging brow, who looked at him, through the bow-windows of immense horn-rimmed spectacles, with the expression of an anxious child.

Vance, lost in the tangle of Christian names which were the only sign-posts of Lady Pevensey's London, tried to make his smile speak for him. "By name at least—" Lady Pevensey added, throwing him a lifebelt as she drifted off to other rescues.

"It's the only way of knowing each other that we have time for nowadays—knowing each other's Christian names," said the little man rather sadly, aligning his elbows next to Vance's on the parapet. "I know you write books, though," he added benevolently. "Novels, are they—or popular expositions of the Atom? It's no use telling me, for I shouldn't remember. There's no time for that either—for remembering what other people write. Much less for reading their books. And if one does, it isn't always easy to tell if they're novels or bio-chemistry. So I stick to my own—my own writing. I'm buried in that up to the chin; buried alive, I trust. But even that one can't be sure of. It may be that already I'm just a rosy corpse preserved in a glacier." He glanced tentatively at Vance, as if hoping for a protest, but Vance was silenced by the impossibility of recalling any one named Octavius who had written a book. He hedged.

"Why should you call your books a glacier?" he said politely.

The other winced. "Not my *books;* my Book. One's enough, in all conscience. Even with the irreproachable life I lead, and only one slice of grilled meat three times a week—all the rest vegetarian—one is always at the mercy of accidents, culinary or other; and I need a clear stretch of twenty years ahead of me." Again he fixed Vance solemnly. "The day I'm assured of that I'll sit down and finish my book. Meanwhile I hope we shall meet again. Tell Imp to bring you to Charlie's—I'm nearly always there after midnight." He nodded and was lost in the throng.

A young lady with a small enamelled face and restless eyes came up to Vance. "Was Octavius *wonderful?* We're longing to know," she said breathlessly, indicating a group of young men and damsels in her wake. One of the latter interrupted: "He's never as good anywhere as he is at Charlie's," but the young lady said curtly: "Not to *you* perhaps, darling; but he's sure to have been wonderful to Mr. Weston—" at which her young followers looked properly awed.

Vance turned on them with a burst of candour. "How can I tell if he was wonderful, when I don't know who he is? It all depends on that, doesn't it?" The others looked their astonishment and incredulity, and the leading lady exclaimed indignantly: "But didn't that idiot tell you you were talking to Octavius?"

To confess that this meant nothing to him, Vance

perceived, would lower him irretrievably in the estimation of these ardent young people; and he was struggling for a subterfuge when the group was joined by a tall bronzed young man whose face was disturbingly familiar.

"Remember me, Mr. Weston? Spartivento. Yes: with Rosenzweig and Blemp. We met, I think, at Mrs. Glaisher's." The Duke turned his Theocritan eyes on the young lady who had challenged Vance. "See here, I guess you folks don't know that in the U.S. people call each other by all the names they've got. I presume Mr. Weston's heard of Octavius Alistair Brant—isn't it?" He shone softly on his interlocutor, and then turned back to Vance. "Mrs. Glaisher is demanding to see you; she asked me to remind you that she is one of your most admirative readers. She has taken Lanchester House for the season. You will call up, and give her the pleasure to dine? So long,—happy to meet you; I am going-gon with Lady Cynthia," said the Duke with his perfect smile, eclipsing himself before Vance could detain him.

The encounter woke such echoes that for the moment the identity of Octavius Alistair Brant became a minor matter, and it was not till the next day that Vance, reporting on the party to Tolby, found himself obliged to confess that he still failed to associate Mr. Brant's name with any achievement known to fame.

Tolby seemed amused. "Yes. How village-pump we all are, after all! Brant's a little god; but his reign is circumscribed. It extends from Bloomsbury to Chelsea. He's writing a big book about some thing or other—I can't remember what. But everybody agrees it's going to be cataclysmic—there'll be nothing left standing but Octavius. You know his Prime Minister, Charlie Tarlton? Oh, well, he's worth while—they both are. Get Lady Pevensey to take you to one of Charlie's evenings."

Vance was only half listening. Mrs. Glaisher had a house in London! She wanted him to call her up! If only he had had the courage to ask the Duke if Floss Delaney were with her. But he had not been able to bring himself to put the question. And even now, as he sat looking at Tolby's telephone, he could not make the decisive gesture. "If she's here we're sure to meet," he thought; and he got up and went back to his work. But it was one thing to seat himself at his desk, and another to battle against the stream of associations pouring in on him. Write? What did he care about writing? The sound of any name connected with Floss Delaney's set all his wires humming. He got up again uneasily and strolled back into the studio, where Tolby sat at his canvas, in happy unconsciousness of all else. Vance stood and watched him.

"How do you manage to shut out life when you want to work?" he questioned.

Tolby glanced up at him. "Life—work? Where's the antithesis?" He touched his canvas with the brush. "This *is* Life; the rest's simply hygienics," he said carelessly. Vance returned to his desk and continued to stare at the blank page. What a cursed tangle of impulses he was! Would he ever achieve the true artist's faculty of self-isolation? "Not until I learn to care less about everything," he thought despondently.

The next night, at the Honourable Charles Tarlton's little dove-gray house in Westminster, where everybody sat on the floor, and people came and went in a casual yet intimate way, without giving their large rosy host any particular attention, or receiving any from him, Vance had to acknowledge how good Octavius was.

His predominance over the rest of the company made itself felt in the quietest yet most unmistakeable way. He was the only person who did not sit on the floor. His legs were too short, he explained; when he got up it was mortifying to see that people expected him to go ever so much farther. He was provided with a horrible sculptured armchair, which had been known to his host's grandparents as "the Abbotsford", and from this throne Octavius poured out his wisdom on the disciples at his feet. Vance thought with a pang of Chris Churley. His talk, as it matured, would probably have been almost as good. And so, perhaps, would his unwritten book. The chief difference was that Octavius had known how to come to an agreement with life; also that he philosophized on barley-water, and had the minimum of material needs. Thus he had been able to adjust himself comfortably to failure, and make himself a warm nest in it, like a mouse in a cupboard.

But it was not as a failure that his disciples thought of him; nor even, in the first instance, as a brilliant talker. As Tolby had said, talk was not a career in England, and Octavius Brant had to be something besides, and preferably an author. The big book was his pretext and his justification, and the excuse of his audience for hanging on his words. Nobody seemed quite clear as to what it was to be, and Vance discovered that while there were those who resented being asked if it were a novel, others, perhaps the more sophisticated, retorted to his question: "Why, yes, a novel, of course! It's the only formula that's still malleable—" in which he recognized a dictum of Octavius's. In fact, according to Charlie Tarlton, if the book didn't at first seem like a novel, that would simply mean that Octavius had renewed the formula; that in future what *he* chose to call a novel would *be* a novel, whether you liked it or not. Charlie Tarlton did not speak often; in Octavius's presence he was just rosily silent, dispensing cocktails and cigarettes; but when the great man was late in arriving—and his hours were incalculable—Charlie, to keep the disciples in a good humour, would sometimes drop an oracle on the subject of his work.

"You've read it, then?" Vance one evening blundered into asking; and the elect looked grieved, and Mr. Tarlton slightly irritated. "Read it? Read it? What exactly does reading a book consist in? Reading the original manuscript—Octavius writes out every word with his own hand—or the typescript copy, or the proofs, or the published book? Every one of these versions is a different thing, has its own impact, produces its specific set of reactions. But what I've read is better than any of them—the author's brain. There's where you get the quintessential stuff. As Octavius says, it's the butterfly before the colours are brushed off." Mr. Tarlton leaned back satisfied, resting comfortable elbows on his cushiony knees.

"Well—exactly!" murmured a devout disciple, with a glance of reproof at Vance.

"Exactly what?" questioned Octavius, entering in his hat and overcoat, and removing his scarf with a leisurely hand. Charlie's rosy face became tomato-coloured and he scrambled uneasily to his feet.

"He was saying that the quintessence of your book is in your brain," exclaimed another imprudent devotee. Octavius's small face withered, and he looked more than ever like an anxious child. His glance swept over Charlie, searing him like flame. "Is that by way of apology for the book's not being finished?" he exclaimed, his voice rising to a high falsetto. "If so, I can only say that I prefer to do my own apologizing—when I find it necessary."

A pall of silence fell on the fervent group; Charlie stammered: "I didn't mean anything of the sort," and

Vance, squatting on a cushion at the great man's feet, ventured boldly: "You know you haven't yet told me exactly what it's about."

Octavius's countenance softened. There was nothing he liked better than toying with his theme before a newcomer. "Ah, rash youth," he murmured, dropping into his armchair, and leaning his little head back among the knobby heraldic ornaments. "Rash—rash!" His eyes glittered behind their sheltering panes, and his short-fingered hands caressed each other softly, as if his hearer's hand lay between them. But suddenly he shook his head. "No—no; I won't yield to the temptation. The lovely creature is there, swimming to and fro in the deepest deeps of my consciousness, shimmering like a chamaeleon, unfolding like a flower. How can you expect me to drag it up brutally into the air, to throw it at your feet, limp and discoloured, and say: 'This is my book!' when it wouldn't be, when I should be the first to disown it? My dear fellow—" he leaned forward, and laid his little hand on Vance's shoulder. "My dear fellow, *wait*. It's worth it."

Vance looked up at him with renewed interest. "In a way," he thought, "he's right. His book *is* written and I daresay it's as good as he thinks. It's the agony of exteriorizing that he dodges away from. And meanwhile his creation lives on inside of him, and is nourished by him and grows more and more beautiful." At the thought he felt the stealing temptation to dream his own books instead of writing them. What a row of masterpieces they would be! They die in the process of being written, he mused. And he thought what his life might have been if he could have drifted from one fancy to another, letting each scatter its dolphin-colours unseen as another replaced it. "If I'd called up Mrs. Glaisher the other day, for instance—" and suddenly he was seized with a terrible fear. Supposing Floss Delaney had already left England? Supposing she had been there, within reach of him, the night he had seen the Duke of Spartivento at Lady Pevensey's, and had now vanished again, heaven knew whither? But surely if she had been in London she would have heard of his being there, would have telephoned him, or written. His world turned ashen at the thought. What was he doing in this atmosphere of literary humbug, among the satellites of a poor fatuous dreamer? Life, real life, was a million miles away from these ephemeral word-spinners. . . The scene crumbled as if a sorcerer's wand had touched it. And then, just as he was getting to his feet, there was a stir on the landing outside, and the sound of a small high voice saying ingratiatingly to a parlour-maid who seemed doubtful of the speaker's credentials: "Mr. Alders—if you'll please simply say it's *Mr. Alders*—"

"Oh, Alders," murmured Charlie Tarlton, with an explanatory hand-wave to his guests. "Who was it he'd promised to bring, Octavius?" The question was answered by the parlour-maid's throwing open the door. On the threshold stood Alders, more dust-coloured and negative than ever, and behind him, like a beacon in the night, Floss Delaney. She moved forward with her light unhurried step and looked about her composedly, as if never doubting that it was she whom Mr. Tarlton's guests had assembled to behold.

"This is Floss Delaney," some one said, leading her up to Octavius. For a moment the little man's face took on the drowned look of the superseded; then pleasure lit it up, and holding out his hand he murmured: "Flos florum—I don't know how to say it in this week's American slang."

Miss Delaney scrutinized him with the cautious friendliness of a visitor at the Zoo caressing an unknown animal. She laid her hand on his arm, as if he and she were facing an expectant camera, and looked about at the assembled company. "Isn't he *gorgeous*?" she said in her deep drawl.

❦ XXVIII ❧

LADY GUY PLUNDER said that if you wanted to hear Octavius talk you went to Charlie's; but if you wanted to talk yourself you came, sooner or later, to her.

There was a good deal of truth in it. Her little house in Mayfair—even smaller than Charlie's, and mouse-coloured instead of dove—was packed to the doorstep for her cocktail suppers. Lady Guy (one of the rich Blessoms of Birmingham) had started her married career in a big house with tessellated floors and caryatid mantelpieces; but when taxes and overproduction had contracted the Blessom millions she had moved lightheartedly into the compactest habitation to be found, and Lord Guy had abandoned lawn-tennis championships for a job in the city.

Lady Guy, Vance had learned, headed one of the numerous groups within groups that made London such a labyrinthine adventure. Lady Pevensey commanded the big omnivorous throng of the rich, the idle and nomadic. Her name was known round the world to the echoes of palace-hotels, and was a sure key to sensational first-nights, theatrical or pugilistic. She was the woman who could always get you a seat for a coronation, a prize-fight, a murder trial or a show proscribed by the censorship; who juggled with movie-stars, millionaires and musicians, and to whom all were interchangeable values in the social market. Lady Guy said that Imp had a social ticker, and could quote prices in celebrities at any hour. That she could float them and boost them there was no denying; but could she also manufacture them?

No; it took Charlie and Lady Guy to do that, and at times the rivalry was hot between them. Lady Guy, a small woman with quick eyes and a tranquil manner, had, it was true, failed to capture Octavius, who was admittedly the biggest haul of post-war London. Charlie said it was because her atmosphere was too restless; she retorted that she wasn't going to be stagnant to oblige anybody. But the two remained on fairly good terms, Charlie because he needed Lady Guy's finds to entertain Octavius, and Lady Guy because she did not despair of luring Octavius away from him.

It was at Charlie's that she had discovered Vance, and immediately she had guessed his value. To the people in Imp Pevensey's set he was merely the clever new American novelist who had written "The Puritan in Spain", which was modern enough to make one feel in the movement, yet full of lovely scenery and rather sticky love-making. But that would not do for Lady Guy. She found out about "Colossus" from Derek Fane, and instantly, whenever Vance was mentioned, the Plunder set said: "Oh, 'The Puritan in Spain'? Y-yes—that belongs to his pretty-pretty period. But of course you know about 'Colossus'? Hasn't Gwen Plunder asked you for next Friday? He's promised to read us some fragments . . ." and Vance was immediately known as the author of "Colossus", that unfinished masterpiece of which the elect were already cognizant, and which was perhaps to surpass Octavius's gigantic creation, and probably to appear before it.

That this was clever of Gwen even her detractors had to admit. If she should succeed in deflating Octavius he might have to become one of her habitués, if only in order to be reinflated. And meanwhile there was Vance at her disposal, young, good-looking, fresh, a novelty to the London palate—while Octavius was already a staple

diet. Instantly Vance became the most sought-after figure in literary and artistic London, and certain disdainful personages who had affected indifference to Lady
Guy's previous celebrities now overwhelmed her with
attentions and invitations, all of which she smilingly accepted without committing herself with regard to the
Friday reading.

Lady Pevensey used her artists and writers as bait
for millionaires, and her millionaires (and especially
their females) as baits for Bohemia. If a budding society
novelist wanted to know what sort of gowns and jewels
were being worn at small dinners that year, or what
young Lord Easterbridge and the Duke of Branksome
really talked about when they were with their own little
crowd, Lady Pevensey instantly arranged a meeting between best-sellers and best-dressers. For her parties
women put on their emeralds, and the budding novelist
had to come in a white tie. Lady Guy's policy was the
reverse. The first inducement she offered you was that
you needn't dress; in fact she besought you not to.
There were few idlers at her parties, and people were
urged to drop in "just as they were". The men could
wear city clothes, or sweaters and plus-fours, the women
come straight from their studios, old-furniture shops,
manicuring establishments, dress-makers' *salons* or typ-
ists' desks. She had thus captured some of Bloomsbury's
wildest birds, and maddened the wearers of tiaras with
the unappeased longing to be invited.

Vance, as he took off his overcoat, and straightened
the dark brown tie which had been carefully chosen to
set off his gray striped flannel, examined his reflection
curiously in the glass at the foot of Lady Guy's stairs.
His selves, as he had long since discovered, were innumerable, and there were times when each in turn had
something interesting to say to him. But at the moment

only two were audible: the ironic spectator who stood aside and chuckled, and the hero of the evening, whose breast was bursting with triumph. Lady Guy had run over, carelessly, the names of some of the people who had asked to be asked; among them were a few for whose approbation and understanding Vance would have given every facile success he had ever enjoyed. And they were awaiting him now, they wanted to hear what he had to tell them, they believed in him and in his future. The ironic spectator shrank into the background as the laughing hero, besieged by smiles and invitations, sprang upstairs to greet his hostess.

With the unfolding of the manuscript both these light puppets were brushed aside, and Vance was the instrument to which the goddess laid her lips. He forgot where he was, who was listening, what judgment this or that oracle was preparing to pronounce on him, and remembered only that each syllable he spoke had been fed with his life, and was a part of him. At first he was aware of reading too fast, of slurring his words in the way that Halo reproved; then his voice freed itself and spread wings, and he seemed to hang above his creation, and to see that it was good.

For the most part he was listened to in silence, but he thought he felt a subtle current of understanding flowing between him and his audience, and now and then it escaped in a murmur of approbation that was like wind in his sails. Thus urged, he sped on. The pages seemed to take life, his figures arose and walked, and he felt that dizzy sense of power which eternally divides the creator from the rest of mankind.

As he laid his manuscript down Lady Guy's guests gathered around him. Every one had something to say, and at once he divined that for all of them the important thing was not what he had written but the epithets they had found to apply to it. The disenchantment was immediate. "It's the same everywhere," he thought, recalling the literary evenings at the Tarrants', where the flower of New York culture had praised him for the wrong reasons. He had learned then how short a way into an artist's motives the discernment of the cleverest ever penetrated. How his visions had dwindled 'under their touch—how he had hated them for admiring him for the wrong reasons, and despised himself for imagining that their admiration was worth having!

Now it was just the same. These brilliant sophisticated people, who had seemed so stimulating and discriminating when they talked of other people's books—how wide of the mark they went in dealing with his! He felt ashamed of his dissatisfaction, which resembled a voracious appetite for praise, though it was only a timid craving for such flashes of insight as Frenside and Tolby had once and again shed on his work. One or two men—not more; and not one woman. Not even Halo, he thought ungratefully. . .

Awkwardly he gathered up his pages. The cessation of the reading restored him to self-consciousness, and he wished he could have escaped at once, like an actor slipping behind the wings. But his audience was clustering about him, showering compliments, putting foolish questions, increasing his longing to be back among the inarticulate and the un-selfconscious. And suddenly, as he stood there, accepting invitations and stammering thanks, the door opened and Floss Delaney came in.

He had met her only once since their chance encounter at Charlie Tarlton's. She had urged him, then, to come and see her, and had named the day and hour; but when he presented himself at the hotel where she and her father were staying he found her absent-minded and indifferent, distracted by telephone-calls, by notes to be answered, and dress-makers to be interviewed, and abandoning him to the society of her father and Alders. He swore then that it should be the end, and assured himself that he was thankful to have had his lesson. But when Floss appeared in Lady Guy's drawing-room he felt a difference in her before which all his resolutions crumbled; for he knew at once that she had come for him, and him only.

She glanced about her in the cool critical way which always made it seem as if any entertainment at which she appeared had been planned in her honour; and to Lady Guy's expression of regret that she should have missed the reading, she replied lightly: "Oh, I'm glad it's over. I never was much on books."

Her hostess gave a slightly acid laugh. "That's why I hadn't meant to invite you, my dear."

"Oh, I know; but it's the reason why I wanted to come. I mean, your not wanting me," said Miss Delaney, with her grave explicitness. "I always like to see what's going on. Besides," she added, "I've known Vance a good while longer than any of you people, and it would have been no use pretending to him that I understood a word of what he was reading." She went toward him, and held out her hand. "You'll have to make the best of it, Vanny. I came to see you and not your book."

It was as if the crowded room had been magically emptied, and she and Vance were alone. He looked at her with enchanted eyes. Who else in the world would have known exactly what he longed to have said to him at that particular moment? Ah, this was what women were for—to feel the way to one's heart just when the Preacher's vanity weighed on it most heavily!

Lady Guy's guests were pouring down the stairs to the dining-room; as Floss turned to follow she threw a smile at Vance and caught his hand. "We'll go down together. I'm ravenous, aren't you? Get me something to eat as quick as you can, darling."

Vance had never seen her so radiant, so sure of herself. Her very quietness testified to her added sense of power. Her dark hair, parted in a new fashion, clasped her low forehead in dense folds which a thread of diamonds held in place, and she wore something light and shining, that seemed an accident of her own effulgence. In the crowded little dining-room the mere force of that inner shining—he didn't know how else to describe it— drew the men from the other women, who were so much quicker and cleverer, and knew so much what to say. Vance found himself speedily separated from her by eager competitors; but he had no feeling of unrest. For this one evening he knew she belonged to him, she was not going to forget him or desert him.

And when the party broke up he found himself again at her side, found that, as a matter of course, he had her cloak on his arm, and was following her out into the thin summer night. He got into the motor beside her, and the chauffeur looked back for orders.

"Oh, how hot it was in there! I'm suffocating, aren't you?" She lowered the front window. "We'll drive straight down to Brambles," she commanded, and the chauffeur nodded, apparently unsurprised. They sped away.

"Brambles? Where's that?" Vance asked, not in the least caring to know, but merely wanting to fit the new name into his dream.

"It's a little place father's hired for week-ends; somewhere under Hindhead, I think they call it. You go over the top of everything. Don't you think it would be lovely to see the sunrise from the top of a big hill? I believe we can make it; there's not much traffic at this hour. I'm dead sick of crowds, aren't you?" Her head sank back against the cushioned seat. "I wasn't going to have all those people think you and I'd never done anything together but talk high-brow!" she exclaimed, with her low unexpected laugh. She turned and kissed him, and then shook him off to light a cigarette. "Don't bother me—I just want to doze and dream."

❧ XXIX ❧

THEY FLEW on through empty streets, through lamplit suburbs and dark bosky lanes. They sped under park walls overhung with heavy midsummer foliage, past gates with guardian lodges just glimmering into sight, through villages asleep about their duck-ponds, their shaded commons and sturdy church-towers. The road wound and wound, then rose and breasted a wide stretch of open heath, soaring, soaring. Vance's heart rose with it, swinging upward to the light. He sat still, clasping her to him. She had fallen asleep, and her little head lay on his shoulder. As they reached the summit of the ridge the chauffeur lowered his speed, but without stopping, and slowly they glided along above shadowy sweeping distances, vales studded with scattered trees, villages and towns with a spire or tower starting up into the light from the gray crouching roofs.

"Oh, look, look!" Vance cried out, as far away to the east the day woke in fire through trails of Channel mist.

Floss opened her eyes reluctantly. "I'm cold." She shivered and drew her cloak about her. "We must be nearly there," she said contentedly, and her head fell back on Vance's shoulder. She had seen nothing, felt nothing, of the beauty and mystery of the dawn. There flashed through him the memory of another sunrise, seen from Thundertop at Halo's side, when he and she were girl and youth, and their hearts held the same ecstasy. All that was over—such ecstasies are seldom shared, and he had grown used to tasting his sunrises and his poetry alone. But he felt the beat of life in his arms, and

296

told himself that thus only can a man reach out of his solitude and be warm.

And now they were winding down again into the blue night of the lanes. The motor turned in at a gate and drew up before a low house among dewy flower-beds. There was a scent of old-fashioned roses; a lily-pool slept under a gray wall. Everything had the gliding smoothness and unreality of a dream.

"I wonder if there'll be anybody up to let us in? I telephoned; at least I think I did; but I don't believe they expected us before daylight. Oh, boy, aren't the roses just too heavenly? And what's that blue stuff that smells so sweet?" Floss, suddenly awake, sprang out of the motor and darted across the wet grass to a long pool edged with lavender. She knelt and plunged her bare arms among the sleeping water-lilies. "I want to wash off London, don't you? But I guess a hot bath would do it better." She jumped up again and caught him by the hand. "Come along; we'll come out again by and by, and pick millions and millions of roses. . ."

A rumpled but respectful housemaid stood at the door. Another was hurriedly lighting a fire in the chimney of the low-raftered hall; and Floss stood on the hearth, laughing and drying her wet arms.

"We didn't expect you, Miss, not till luncheon," the housemaid said; and Floss retorted gaily: "Oh, you'll have to get used to that. My watch never keeps the same time as other people's. I suppose we can have some coffee or something? And then I want to go to bed and sleep for hours—" She stretched her arms above her head with a happy yawn.

Coffee and toast, bacon and jam, invited them to a table near the fire, and they feasted there in the early sunshine streaming through low windows hung with roses.

Floss, it appeared, had meant to come off alone for two days. She was exhausted by London hours and the London rush, she wanted to get away by herself and think; she was like that sometimes, she explained. And then, seeing Vance again at Lady Guy's, she had said to herself how much jollier it would be to have him come with her—"and just for once pretend it's old times. Shall we, Vanny?" She leaned to him with one of her swift caressing touches, and he sprang up and bent over her, covering her neck and shoulders with impatient kisses. But she pushed him back. "Darling—I'm fagged out and simply dead with sleep. I'm going up to my room to bathe and go to bed. They'll give you a bed somewhere; and I daresay they can find some things of father's for you. Come down at one and we'll have lunch; and then there'll be the whole heavenly afternoon . . . the English afternoons are as long as whole days, aren't they?" She slipped through his arms, and ran singing up the stairs. The appearance of the housemaid on the upper landing prevented pursuit, and Vance, heavy with well-being, eager yet content, stood waiting before the fire. As she said, the English afternoons were as long as days—and it was hardly an hour after sunrise. He followed the housemaid sleepily to the room assigned to him.

Yes, that afternoon of late July was as long as a whole day; but to Vance it passed in a flash. She trailed down late for lunch, in a pale yellow cotton, a sun-hat on her arm, the heels of her red sandals clicking on the smooth oak stairs. They lunched in a thatched porch, its oak posts hung with clematis; and after coffee and cigarettes wandered out to explore the garden. It was full of bright midsummer flowers against dark hedges, of clumps and cones of shining holly. From an upper slope overhung by ancient Scotch firs they caught, between hills, a glimpse of the wide dappled country stretching southward. Then they came down again, and strolled along a lane to the village, with its low houses hunched about a duck-pond, and its square-towered church of slaty stone. The gardens before the houses were brimming with flowers, farm-horses waded in the pond, geese waddled in a regimental line across the common. All else slept in the peace of afternoon.

They came back and sat on a bench under an old mulberry tree, the long lily-pool before them. The air was full of the noise of midsummer insects. "Summer afternoon—summer afternoon," Vance murmured, the words humming in his ears like insect-music.

"Darling, you mustn't—they can see us perfectly from the windows," Floss exclaimed, slipping from his embrace.

"Let's go where they can't, then," he muttered, trying to draw her to her feet.

"No; not yet. It's so lovely here. Tonight—" she laid her hand on his arm. "By and by we'll go in and have tea in the porch. They have such lovely things for tea in England."

He looked at her without knowing what she said; now she wavered in the summer light like an apparition, now her nearness burned into his flesh.

She talked on ramblingly, in her level drawl, always about herself, telling him of her London experiences, her future plans, the difficulty she had in managing her father. "He's getting fidgety—he wants to go home. He says he's fed up with swell society. I guess he's told you about that old family place down south he wants to buy back. Sounds nice from here, don't it—an old family place! You'd think it was Windsor Castle. But I know what it would mean when he got there. A tumble-down house, and trotting-horses, and cards and racing, and everybody borrowing from him and swindling him, and the boys dropping in at all hours for drinks. And this is no time to sell out stocks, anyway. . . I'd have to go back and look after him."

She leaned her head against her crossed arms, and Vance's eyes followed the smooth amber of the underarms detaching themselves in an amphora-curve from her light sleeveless dress. "I'd rather get married at once than do that," she grumbled.

But when he asked her, with a forced laugh, whom she thought of marrying, she said she hadn't made up her mind yet which of the royal princes she'd settle on; but she'd be sure to let Vance know in time for him to choose a handsome wedding-present. "For you're certain to make a fortune out of your books after your London success, aren't you, Vanny? How much do you expect to make out of this new book? Forty thousand? They say Kipling gets fifty. Who looks after your money for you, darling?"

Tea was brought out to them under the mulberry, and she fell into ecstasies over the thick yellow cream, the buttered scones, the pyramid of late raspberries with a purple bloom on them. "Didn't I tell you it would be wicked to miss anything so heavenly?" She held one of the raspberries against her neck. "Wouldn't they make a lovely necklace—like dark coral?" She laughed at the crimson stain on her skin. But as Vance was bending over to kiss it away the parlour-maid advanced, a black-coated figure halting discreetly in her wake.

"The Vicar, please, Miss."

"The Vicar? Mercy, what's a Vicar?" Floss whispered hastily. "Oh, the minister of that church in the village, I suppose." She rose with sudden cordiality. "How lovely of you to call! Yes—I'm Miss Delaney. My father's taken this place for the summer. This is my cousin, Vance Weston—the famous American novelist. I guess you know him by name, anyhow. They're wild about his books in London." As she called Vance her cousin she slid a glance at him under her lashes.

The Vicar, an elderly man with a long purplish face and shy eyes, melted under her affability, and sat down on the edge of a garden chair. He looked timidly at Vance, and then away from him, as if famous novelists were too far out of his range to be communicated with. Then he remarked to Miss Delaney that the day was warm. She replied that he wouldn't think that if he'd been reared in Euphoria; and as this statement visibly deepened his perplexity she explained that it was the name of the town where she and her cousin had been brought up. She liked the English climate better, she added, because when you did get a hot day it stood right out from the others, and you felt it must have cost a lot of money to make.

The conversation rambled on slumberously till the Vicar, with some circumlocution, put in a modest plea for his parochial organizations. Would Miss Delaney perhaps take an interest in them? The tenants of Brambles had usually allowed him to hold the annual parish festival in the gardens. To Vance's surprise Floss listened with edifying attention, sitting in one of her quiet sculptural attitudes while the parochial plans were haltingly and laboriously set forth. It almost seemed to Vance that she was prolonging the conversation with the malicious intent of defrauding him of what was left of the day, and he got up and walked away, hoping the Vicar might take the hint and follow. But from the farther end of the orchard the intruder could be seen settling himself with deliberation before a dish of fresh scones, and another towering pile of raspberries, and

Vance, exasperated, wandered out of the gate and down the lane.

When he returned the garden was empty, and he went into the low-ceilinged hall, where the light was beginning to fade, though the day was still so bright outside. From the armchair in which she lolled Floss stretched out her hand.

"Darling, why did you run away? Didn't you think the Vicar was lovely? He told me all about School Treats and Mothers' Meetings." She drew Vance down and wound her arms around his neck. "I guess the girls are at supper now, and you can kiss me," she whispered, laughing.

He knelt beside her, pressing her fast, and throbbing with her heart-beats. With other women—even with his poor little wife—golden strands of emotion had veined the sombre glow; but to hold Floss Delaney was to plunge into a dark night, a hurrying river. It was as if her blood and his were the tide sweeping them away. Everything else was drowned in that wild current.

She freed herself and leaned back. "Why, Vanny, what a baby you are! It's like old times. Do you remember, down by the river? Do you like me better than any of those girls you've been going with up in London?"

"She's mine—I must keep her!" was his only thought. But suddenly the telephone shrilled through their absorption, and Floss started to her feet. Vance tightened his hold. "Don't go . . . don't go. . . What does it matter? Let the thing be damned, can't you?"

She shook him off. "No, don't stop me. I must see what it is." In an instant everything about her was changed: she looked alert and hard, her lips narrowed to a thin line. "I'm expecting a message," she threw back, hurrying across the hall to the passage where the telephone hung.

Vance sank into the chair she had left; his head felt the warmth where hers had rested. He smiled at her veering moods. At that moment nothing that she said or did could break the spell; and they still had the end of the long afternoon, and then the night, before them.

Through the door into the passage he caught snatches of question and ejaculation. "Yes—yes: Floss Delaney. Yes; I'm listening. . . . Oh . . . why, yes. . . . She did? She *is?* . . . Oh, gracious! . . . You're *sure?* . . . Yes . . . Yes. . . . I hear . . ." The door swung shut, and only the indistinct ups and downs of her voice came to him. He was not trying to listen; what she was saying did not interest him. His ears were full of their own music. "In a minute," he thought, "she'll be back . . ." His eyes closed on the vision.

"Well!" she exclaimed, suddenly standing before him. "Vance, are you asleep? Well, what on earth do you think—?" She dropped down on a stool before the hearth, and burst into a queer exultant laugh. Her eyes shone in the twilight like jewels. "Well, I know somebody who's down and out—and serve him right too!" Her laughter continued, in short irregular bursts, as if it were an exercise she was not used to. "Spartivento! Our darling Duke's got left! Why, yes . . . didn't you know he thought he was going to marry Mrs. Glaisher? I supposed Alders had told you. I thought everybody knew. He made a big enough fool of himself—going round asking everybody about her investments. I warned him she'd be sure to hear about it, but he only said: 'Well, what if she did?' Those Italians, even if they're the biggest swells in their own country, don't understand our ideas of delicacy. . . Well, and what do you suppose? Alders telephones that she's announced her engagement to the Grand Duke Basil! I had a bet with Spartivento— I told him I knew he wouldn't pull it off. I guess I'm a hundred dollars to the good on this; or would be, if he had the money to pay me—poor old Spart!"

She threw back her head, and in a leap of firelight Vance saw the laugh issuing from her throat like stamens from a ruby flower. He felt revolted and fascinated. She was like some one starting up out of a lethargy; he had never seen her so vivid, so passionate. What could this sordid story of Mrs. Glaisher and Spartivento matter to her? He sprang up and pulled her to her feet. "What do I care about those rubbishy people? Are you trying to tell me you're in love with the man yourself, and that you thought you'd lost him?" he burst out, pressing her wrists angrily. He knew his anger was ridiculous, yet he could not master it.

"Vance—let me go, Vance! You hurt—let me go!" She twisted furiously in his hold. "Me in love with Sparti? Well, you think of good ones! Much obliged!" He dropped her hands, and instantly she came up and laid her head on his breast. "You're a nice boy, you are, when a girl's carried you off with her like this, to accuse her of being in love with another fellow. Have I acted as if I was?" She lifted her heavy lids and gave him a long look. He put his arms about her, trembling with joy. "Then, darling—come."

"Yes—yes." She leaned on him a moment; then she drew back softly. "We can't behave exactly as if there was nobody but us in the house, can we? They'll be bringing in dinner soon, and I want to go to my room first, and have a rest. I'm beginning to feel that we started our elopement somewhere about three A.M.— aren't you?" She rested her warm sleepy gaze on his. "He was cross with me, was he, because he thought I wanted mother Glaisher's leavings? Looks that way, don't it? Why, I guess I could have bought her Grand Duke for myself easily enough if I'd wanted to! What I *do* want, the worst way, is a hot bath, and a good sleep before dinner." She slipped out of his arms, and paused half way up the stairs to wave back at him. "So long, darling!"

Well—if she chose to play her old game, let her. Vance smiled with the security of the happy lover. Even her childish excitement over the Glaisher-Spartivento episode amused him. It was a mind in which everything was exactly on the same level of importance. Hadn't he discovered that long ago? One didn't ask for intelligence or sensibility in women of her sort. He felt light, detached, pleased with his own objectivity. What danger was there in wasting a few hours over her when his judgment remained so unaffected?

He strolled out into the garden. The lengthening shadows seemed to have brought out new scents in the still air. He looked back and saw a curtain sway out from an upper window—hers no doubt. His heart stirred; the warmth of her beauty seemed to envelop him.

He went out of the gate, and roamed through a network of hushed lanes. The softness of the air entered into his veins. He met a farm-wagon driving homeward with its load; the hot flanks of the big slow-footed horses brushed him as they passed. Farther on, he heard the soft padding of a flock of sheep, and scrambled up in the bracken to let them pass. Mounting upward he reached a stretch of open moor, where the clear daylight hung as if perpetually suspended, and threw himself down in the rough heather.

As he lay there his mind wandered back over the day. From that height it seemed to lie spread out before him, clear yet distant, as if its incidents had befallen some one else. Queer that the girl's power over him could co-exist with such lucidity! An hour or two ago everything had been blurred in his brain; now each fantastic episode detached itself, standing out in beauty or absurdity. The absurdity, of course, was provided by Floss's excitement at the report of Mrs. Glaisher's betrothal. Humiliating as the admission was, Vance had to own that the news had instantly put him out of her mind. And why, unless, as he had jokingly suggested, it gave her the hope of capturing Spartivento? He had joked at the moment; but as the scene came back to him he winced. Yet why was he suddenly measuring poor Floss by standards he had never before thought of applying to her? He had always known that money, flattery and excitement were all she cared for; to make her forget them for a moment was probably the most he could hope. Luckily, he reflected, he was still clear-sighted enough not to sentimentalize the situation.

He sprang up with a laugh. "Well, it's up to me now. If I can't get her away from the other fellow I'm no good!" He began to scramble down the hillside in the gathering darkness as if he had been racing his rival back to Floss's feet.

When he got down into the shade of the lanes, he was bewildered by the sign-posts with names of unknown villages, and taking a wrong turning, wasted half an hour in getting back to the point he had missed. Under the thick branches the velvet dusk was beginning to gather, altering the look of things; but as soon as he was on the right trail again he began to run, and before long he saw the first roofs of the village, and beyond them the trees of Brambles. He pushed open the white gate. The low windows still stood open; their welcome streamed out across the lawn. Vance ran toward them like a breathless schoolboy. She might belong to Spartivento tomorrow, but tonight she was his. He gave a happy laugh.

At the door he met the parlour-maid who had received them that morning. With her black dress and afternoon cap she seemed to have regained her professional superiority, and he fancied she looked at him coldly.

"Oh, it's you, sir?" She seemed surprised. "Miss Delaney thought you'd taken the train back."

Vance returned her look blankly. "The train—?"

"But she said, if not," the parlour-maid continued with manifest disapproval, "we was to serve dinner for you just as if she'd been here."

Vance continued to stare at her. At first her words conveyed no meaning to him; then his heart gave a dizzy drop. "What's the matter? Isn't she coming down? Is she—I suppose she's too tired?"

The parlour-maid stared in her turn. She did so with an icy respectfulness: "Down to dinner, sir? Miss Delaney left for London an hour ago."

Vance stood motionless. The dizziness seemed to have got into his throat: it was so dry that he could hardly speak. He repeated: "London?"

The parlour-maid pursed up her lips and drew aside to let him enter. "You'll dine here, then, sir?"

"Left—but why did she leave? What's happened?"

"I couldn't say, sir. I was to give you this if you came back." She took a note from the table, and Vance carried it to the light and tore it open.

"Don't be cross, Vanny. I've had a hurry call back to London and couldn't wait for you to come in. Didn't we have a lovely day? The girl will tell you about the trains. Love and goodbye. Floss.

"*P.S.* No use trying to see me. I'm not going to be in town for some days."

He read the note over slowly. Then he crumpled it up and stood looking straight ahead of him. He thought: "Well, I must go and pack up my things"; then he remembered that he had come down only that morning, and had brought nothing with him. That gave him a fugitive sense of relief.

"Which way is the station?"

The maid explained that it was about a mile beyond the village, and that you took the first turn to the left. "But there's no train now till eleven."

He had already turned away and was walking down the drive. He swung along, the gravel crunching under his feet in the silence. Now he had passed the pool, then skirted the deep shadows of the holly-garden; now the gate glimmered white before him. He went out of it and turned toward the village. It was nearly a mile away, and the dusky lane that led to it was deserted. A little owl called wistfully in the twilight. He walked on to the village, across the common, past the duck-pond and out onto the road that led to the station. That road too was deserted.

Vance walked along at a good pace until he reached the last turn before the station; then he sat down under the hedgerow and began to cry.

❦ XXX ❧

HALO TARRANT was at work in the garden of the pink house. The seeds she had sown in the spring—phlox, zinnia, larkspur, poppy—contended in a bonfire of bloom. As she knelt over it, weeding, snipping and staking, her shoulder-blades ached and the afternoon sun burnt through her broad hat-brim and lay like burning lead on the nape of her neck.

She liked the muscular fatigue and the slight dizziness caused by the sun; liked, at the end of each long silent day, to stagger back into the empty house so stupefied by heat and labour that she hardly knew where she was, and sleep came down on her like a fit of drunkenness. In that way the days and the weeks passed, and the calendar had almost ceased to exist—except when she started up at the postman's ring. She supposed she would never be able to cure herself of that start, or of knowing instinctively when letters were due, though she was so careful to leave her wrist-watch in her drawer upstairs.

She had heard from Vance only twice since he had left—a telegram on arriving ("Everything fine quartered with Tolby"), and about a week later a short word, in which he apologized for haste and brevity, explaining that his head was surging with new ideas, that he had settled down at Tolby's to a long spell of work, and that she mustn't mind if he didn't write often. She didn't mind at all—at first. She was too thankful to know that he had got back into the creative mood; there could be no better proof that he was rid of morbid memories of Chris Churley. But gradually, as the days passed, and the silence closed in on her, she felt herself too cruelly shut out from his adventures and experiences. Not a word of how the work was going, no acknowledgement of her letters and telegrams (all so studiously cheerful and comrade-like) , no hint of regret at her not being with him, no briefest allusion to Oubli— or to herself! He had shed all that, had entered on another phase. Was it just the intoxication of the return to creative activity, of contact with new people, tapping fresh sources of admiration (there were times when he liked that more than he was willing to acknowledge) , or was it—was it a new woman?

She remembered her agony of jealousy in Paris, when he had vanished so unaccountably for three or four days, and had then reappeared with a stack of manuscript. She was not going to let herself suffer such torture again. It had been unwarranted then, and would probably prove to be so now. From time to time he needed a change of place and people to set the creative engine going: was she still narrow-minded enough to grudge it him?

No; only the days were so long, and in his place she would have found it so easy to write a short letter now and then. . . Well, men were different. She couldn't help jumping each time she heard the postman's step; but she had forced herself not to count the days since the one letter had come, and really, thanks to hard work and stupefying sun, she now no longer remembered whether it was days or weeks since she had heard from him.

She paused in her work, and looked attentively at one of the flowers. How exquisitely imagined, how subtly wrought! What patient and elaborate artifice had gone to the inventing of its transient loveliness! Not so long ago she had scattered seed in little boxes, and later, dibble in hand, had moved each tiny plant to its own place. Other seeds she had sown in the beds, in even furrows, and watched the plants sprout through the light soil. Between them now, under their spreading foliage, the brown leaves of the spring bulbs were decaying and turning into mould. Season followed season in blossom and decline; the fresh leaf drooped and fell, the young face of the flower withered and grew old, the endless function unrolled its cruel symbolism unheeded by those it might have warned.

"If only it wasn't for the caterpillars!" Halo groaned, lifting a riddled leaf against the light. She knew well enough what the caterpillars symbolized too: the mean cares, the gnawing anxieties, that crawl over the fair face of life. She stood up and stamped vindictively on a writhing green body. And then there were the seeds that failed—and the young shoots the slugs devoured. . . To the general rhythm of rise and fall the heart might have adapted itself; but the accidental ravages, snail-tracks, caterpillar slime, the disenchantment and failure. . . "I suppose I've been too long alone," she mused, suddenly sick of her work and her thoughts.

Her solitude was self-imposed; for though the Pension Britannique and the little cluster of villas belonging to the pre-war colony were, as usual, closed for the summer, life was active on the farther side of the town, where the long sand beach, once so lonely, had begun to be fringed with tin-roofed "dancings", cheap restaurants and mushroom bungalows. Halo could once have found plenty of entertainment among the literary and artistic Bohemians who were already populating this new settlement. If Vance had been there it would have amused her to swim and drink cocktails, to sun-bathe and discuss

life and the arts with these boisterous friendly people
who flashed by her in rattling Citroëns or strowed the
sands with naked silhouettes. But by herself it was
different. Paris had cured her of artistic Bohemia, and as
soon as she was alone she felt how deeply rooted in her
were the old instincts of order and continuity. In Vance
too they existed—had they not first drawn him to her
out of the sordid confusion of his life with Laura Lou?
But he was young (she had long since discarded the
epithet in thinking of herself), he was impressionable
and inexperienced, above all he had the artist's inexhaustible appetite for "material". What more natural
than that he should still crave what for her had lost its
savour? "If you wanted to do the same thing every day
at the same hour for the rest of your life," she told herself, "you ought to have married a teller in a bank, or a
statistician who had to live within a five minutes' walk
of the British Museum, and not a live-wire novelist."
But the argument, from frequent reiteration, had lost
its force. "We are what we are," she thought, "and that's
the end of it. At least I suppose this time it's the
end. . ."

She heard a step in the path, and her heart gave a
jump. It was not the postman's hour; she needed no
watch to tell her that. But it might be a telegram, or a
registered letter—if he had something extra-important
to tell her—or it might even . . .

She turned quickly, and the garden-scissors dropped
from her hand. It was over two years since she had seen
that short thick figure, always in a dark "business suit"
of the same citified cut, and the blunt Socratic face with
its shrewd sceptical eyes guarded by old-fashioned American *pince-nez*. Over two years? A life-time! George
Frenside came to her out of a dead world.

"Frenny—oh, Frenny!" She ran to him with outstretched arms. The sense of her loneliness rushed over her; the words choked in her throat. Her work-roughened hands sank into her friend's, and they stood and looked at each other.

"Well, it looks to me like the same old Halo," said Frenside with his short laugh; and she slipped her hand through his arm and drew him up the path to the house.

She was too surprised and excited to ask him whence or how he had come. It was only afterward that she remembered, vaguely, his alluding to an unexpected holiday in Europe, and to his having been unable to notify her in advance because his plans depended on those of a friend with whom he was making a dash to the Mediterranean. "So I just jumped over from Marseilles on the chance of finding you," she remembered his ending. She did not ask his friend's name; her mind could not fix itself on what he was telling her. She felt only the comforting warmth of his nearness, the nearness of an old friend whose memories were so interwoven with hers that his voice and smile and turns of phrase started up countless fragments of experience, scenes of her nursery days, of her girlhood with its fervours and impatiences, and the cold gray years of marriage. Through all those phases his shrewd eyes had followed her; he was the one being who had understood her revolts and her submissions, her vain sacrifices and her final clutch at happiness. To see him sitting there in the half-darkened room, his head slanted back against the shabby arm-chair, his short legs stretched out before him, his ever-lasting cigar between his lips, was to become again the Halo of Eaglewood and New York, and to measure the distance between that eager ghost and her new self. "I wonder which is the ghostliest," she thought, as she bent over to mix a lemon-squash for her friend.

He was waiting for her to speak, to give an account

of herself; but how could she? She had not put her
spiritual house in order, she hardly knew what she was
feeling or whither she was drifting. Solitude had woven
its magic passes about her, pouring a blessed numbness
into her veins. And now, at this sudden contact with the
past, every nerve awoke.

"So you've liked it pretty well down here?" Frenside asked, looking up at her as he took the glass.

She rallied her scattered wits. "Oh, immensely. You
see, I was here in old times with father and mother, and
always wanted to come back. And we had the luck to
find this darling little house—don't you think it's a darling? Did you notice the big mulberry at the door, and
the flagging around it? That was the old threshingfloor.
They used to make oil here too. Wouldn't you like to
come down and see the old oil-press in the cellar?" She
chattered on, smothering him in trivialities, yet knowing all the while that he would presently emerge from
them as alert as ever, and as determined to have her tell
him whatever he wanted to know.

"Thanks. But I'm too well off here. I don't think
I'll go down and see the oil-press. I really came to see
you."

"Oh, *me?*" She laughed. "There's not much novelty
about me."

"I didn't come to see a new Halo. I came to find
out if the old one survived."

"Survived what?" she said captiously.

"Why, the storm and stress."

She gave a little laugh. "Dear Frenny, you're incor-
rigibly romantic! Being happy is much simpler than
people think."

"Well, most of us have to take it on hearsay, so it's
excusable if we're misinformed. You might give a poor
devil some lights on the subject."

She laughed again, but found no answer. Under the

banter she felt his thoughts searching hers, and she was frightened, and for the first time in her life wanted to shut him out, and could not. To break the silence she said: "But at least you'll stay till tomorrow, won't you? I can make you very comfortable in Vance's room."

"I wish I could, my dear; but I've got to get back to Marseilles. We're off tomorrow."

There was another silence. Then he went on: "You said: 'Vance's room'. He's away, then?"

Suddenly she became fluent. "Oh, yes; I forgot to tell you; he's in London. I packed him off to see his publishers and talk to people about his new book. He's got a big thing under way; you'll like it better than 'The Puritan in Spain'. I know without asking that you didn't care much about that. It had a good deal of success . . . but that's no reason. . . This new book is going to be—well, rather immense in its way: a sort of primitive torso. A fragment of experience dug up out of the sub-conscious. . ." She felt that she was talking into the void, and stopped. "But it's no use telling you, when you have to take it all on faith."

"But you believe in it yourself?"

"Of course I do!" she cried with angry fervour.

Frenside seemed not to notice the energy of her reply. The worst thing about talking with him was that he never did notice the screens you hung up in front of things.

"Has he been away long?"

"Oh, no; only a few weeks. I can't remember just how long. . . It's too hot here to remember dates. . . He'll be so sorry when he hears he's missed you."

"And you haven't felt lonely down here all by yourself?"

She paused a moment; then she said quietly: "I stopped being lonely two years ago."

"I see." It was the first time he had taken any notice

of her answers. For a while he was silent, busy with the relighting of his cigar. After a while he said: "Why didn't you go to London with him? You could have helped him to find his way about."

"He doesn't need to have any one find his way about for him. And I hate that sort of life."

"Seeing intelligent people, and breathing in ideas? You didn't use to." He threw his cigar impatiently onto the hearth. He was visibly embarrassed and irresolute. "Look here, child; you and I used to say things straight out, no matter how unpalatable they were, and this fencing's a waste of time. I wish to God you and Weston were married; that's what I came to tell you."

The blood rushed to her forehead; she hoped that in the shaded light he would not notice it. "It's so dear of you, Frenny. But you know as well as anybody why we're not."

"I know Tarrant has blundered. Weston went to see him; and I'm afraid that didn't help."

She lifted her head quickly. "It ought to have!"

"Certainly, in an ideal world. It was a fine gesture. But you must take into account men's passions and weaknesses."

She was silent for a moment; then she said wearily: "If you knew how little it all seems to matter now."

"It ought to matter, child. At least if I understand the case. You ought to be Weston's wife."

"Oh, Frenny, don't go on!" She started to her feet, the need of avowal overmastering her. The frozen depths were broken up; she must lay her troubled heart in a friend's hands. "You see—it's not as simple as I said. Being happy, I mean. That was bluff." She gave a faint laugh. "I used to think marrying him would be the solution. I used to think: if only Lewis would set me free! But now I don't know—I don't seem to care. I suppose it's too late; or perhaps it never would have made any difference. Perhaps I wasn't meant for storm and stress, though I was so sure they were my element!" She sat down on the arm of his chair and hid her face, while her old friend's arm embraced her.

"I'll tell you the only thing that's too late in this business," Frenside began abruptly. "It's your marriage. We most of us need a frame-work, a support—the maddest lovers do. Marriage may be too tight a fit—may dislocate and deform. But it shapes life too; prevents growing lopsided, or drifting. I know you've both felt that, I know it's not your fault if you're still at loose ends. I've done my best—"

She bent down and pressed her lips on his frowning forehead. "Frenny, my darling friend—don't go on."

"How can I help it? I know it hurts; but let's have the bandage off—do!"

She sprang up. "If you mean talking of ways and means, planning to coax Lewis—I forbid you! I forbid you to say a word to any one!"

Frenside took off his glasses, rubbed them, put them on again, and examined her anxiously. "Take care, Halo! Don't defy opportunity. She's a resentful jade."

"What opportunity?"

"The fact of Tarrant's realizing he's been in the wrong, and wanting to make amends—as soon as possible."

Halo gave a short laugh. This was so like life that she somehow felt she had always been expecting it. "I suppose you're his ambassador?"

"Well, I suppose so—with the proviso of being disavowed if I don't succeed."

She threw back her head and closed her eyes as the possibilities he suggested went rushing through her.

Then she looked at him through eyes screwed up with amusement. "How you must have hated the job!"

"Not for you."

"Good old Frenny! Isn't it enough that I'm endlessly grateful?"

"No, it's not."

"Well, then—" She paused. "Fren, you remember that old story we used to like, of Firdusi and the gifts from the Sultan? They were magnificent when they finally came; but he was dead."

Frenside nodded. He took off his glasses, and wiped them again. "Yes; but it's not really a good allegory, because we never *do* know when we're dead. I thought I was, years ago; and here I am aching all over again with your aches."

"Oh, my aches are not bad enough for that. Only, it's no use your pleading my cause with Lewis now."

"I'm not here for that. I'm here to plead Tarrant's cause with you. He regrets his attitude; he's honestly sorry to have created such a situation for you. That's what I'm here to say."

She threw herself down on the divan, and sat for a while with her face hidden. She no longer wanted to conceal anything from Frenside, but she did not quite know how to put her feeling into words. "Even if he were to give me my freedom tomorrow I shouldn't tell Vance," she murmured.

"Not tell him—for God's sake, why?"

"Because the only thing I care for is *his* freedom. I want him to feel as free as air."

"H'm—free as air. The untrammelled artist. Well, I don't believe it's the ideal state for the artist, any more than it is for the retail grocer. We all of us seem to need chains—and wings."

She laughed. "All right—only in Vance's case I'd rather be the wing-giver."

"How do you know you're not chaining him up all the tighter? The defenceless woman, and all that. If you were his wife, you and he'd be on a level."

"The defenceless woman? Bless you, he never thinks of me as that! He thinks only of his work—and his genius."

"Well, you wanted him to, didn't you?"

"Of course I did. And I want it still—with all my soul!"

"Then settle your own situation first. Let me tell Tarrant you'll bring proceedings at once. I can almost promise he won't make any difficulty."

She mused again, something deep down in her still resisting this belated charity from either husband or lover. "It would be such a mockery. . ."

"What would be?"

"The whole business. If I had my divorce my people would expect me to marry Vance. And I can't—I can't. If there were a divorce I couldn't prevent his hearing of it, and if he did he'd feel he ought to marry me—and that might ruin his life, and ruin mine too." She forced a faint smile. "If being happy is simple, being happy with an artist isn't. It's been a beautiful adventure, but, to adopt your bold metaphor, I want it to end before the wings turn into chains."

She stood up, and Frenside also got to his feet. They stood and looked at each other like people signalling out of hearing across a hurrying river. At length Frenside spoke. "There's one thing more. You say Weston doesn't worry about your situation—doesn't think of it at all. Yet he did his best to get Tarrant to yield about the divorce."

She returned to the present with a start. Was it possible, she thought, that Vance had done that? It sent a flush of triumph through her—yet how far away and improbable it all seemed!

"Oh, yes. He did it because some one had spoken to him rudely about me. But he forgot all about it when I pretended I didn't care."

"Ah—you pretended?"

She shrugged. "What's loving but pretending?"

Frenside stood looking at her with angry compassionate eyes. "My poor girl—if it's come to that, why not crown the affair by the biggest pretense of all? Let Weston think you want to be free. He won't make any difficulty, will he?"

Halo stood silent, her head sunk, her eyes fixed on the ground. This cruel surgeon of a Frenside—how straight he had probed to the central pain!

"Let him think I want to leave him?"

"It's the logical conclusion, isn't it? The one towering generosity that will justify the rest?"

She stood before him motionless. He was speaking to her with her own inward voice, but she could not bear the words when another spoke them. "He may be back now—any day," she brought out.

"And then you'll begin the patching-up business all over again?"

"I suppose so."

Frenside was silent. The travelling-clock on Vance's desk ticked with sudden sonority, and she thought: "For how many weeks now have I wound it up for him every Saturday?"

Frenside seemed to hear it also. He pulled out his watch. "By Jove, I've got to be off. My taxi's waiting down by the hotel. I've just got time to make my train."

She stood rooted to the ground, feeling that with

the least word or movement her great loneliness would break in tears. He held out his hand. "I hate to leave you here, child."

"Thank you, Fren. But I've got to stay."

He turned away, and she listened to his short steps rapping their way down the stairs and along the path to the gate.

❦ XXXI ❧

WHEN FRENSIDE had left her Halo tried to collect her thoughts; but his visit had shaken her too deeply. He had roused her out of her self-imposed torpor into a state of hyper-acute sensibility, and detaching her from the plight in which she was entangled had compelled her to view it objectively. What was her present relation to Vance—what was their future together likely to be? They had never quarrelled since the day at Granada when she had reproached him for having gone to the party from which the old Marquesa had excluded her. A mere honeymoon flurry; and since then there had been unbroken outward harmony between them. Yet how far they were from each other—much farther than the couples who quarrelled and kissed again once a week, and to whom quarrelling and kissing were all in the day's work. It was her fault, no doubt. She had wanted the absolute—and life had handed her one of its usual shabby compromises, and she had not known what to do with it.

She shivered at the recollection of Frenside's advice. Perhaps, as he said, true magnanimity would consist in leaving Vance; but she had not strength for it, and the only alternative was the patching-up business, as he called it. The patching-up would have to begin all over again, and this time with little faith, on her part, in the durability of the repairs. Was it not unfair to Vance, and deteriorating to herself, to cling to a relation that had grown less real than the emptiest marriage? Ah, marriage—she understood now! The maddest of us need

322

a frame-work; perhaps the maddest most of all. . .
Well, what of it? Vance would marry her as soon as she
was free; and an hour ago she had received Tarrant's
offer to release her!

At the thought all her doubts and scruples seemed
like so much morbid hair-splitting. Why should she and
Vance not marry and take their chance with other ordinary people? They might have a child, and then there
would be something about which to build the frame-
work. They would become a nucleus, their contradic-
tory cravings would meet in a common purpose, their
being together and belonging to each other would
acquire a natural meaning. Her heart swelled with the
emotion she had suppressed during her talk with
Frenside—the healing tears ran over.

She sat down and wrote out a telegram to Vance.
Then she tore it up, and wrote another: this time to
Tolby. Vance had not answered any of her previous letters and telegrams, he might not answer this one; it was
safer to apply to his friend. "Fear have lost a letter from
Vance. If no longer with you please send me his present
address." She winced at the pretense of the lost letter;
but what did it matter? Her one object was to have
news.

She carried her telegram to the post office, and as
she walked along the glaring sea-front, past the sun-
bathers sprawling on the sand, and the light boats skim-
ming before the breeze that always sprang up toward
sunset, the familiar scene grew suddenly gay and inviting. How natural that these young people should be enjoying it all! She felt young again herself, her heart beat
in tune with theirs. As long as one was alert and sound,
and could show a fresh face to one's glass, the world was
a holiday place after all. Tomorrow she was sure to hear
from Vance. . .

The morrow, however, brought only a note from Frenside, despatched from the station at Marseilles. Apparently, during his visit, he had told her all his plans, though she had remembered nothing of the first part of their talk except that he had given her good news of her parents, and had said something about a trip to Corsica or Sicily—she didn't know which. What an unnatural monster she must have become, to have ears and memory only for her own concerns! She had been brooding over them too long alone.

Frenside gave an address at Palermo, and added that he would be returning in a month to Paris, where, if she wished to write, she could do so in care of his bankers. She hastily noted both addresses, and wondered sadly if she would ever see him again. Suddenly it occurred to her that he was probably travelling with Tarrant, and that the latter might have been at Marseilles awaiting her answer, or even—who knows?—at the hotel at Oubli. She flushed up at the thought; but it was soon crowded out by anxious speculations as to Tolby's reply. That evening seemed the longest and loneliest she had spent since Vance had gone. . .

The next morning Tolby's telegram came. It read: "Vance left England a fortnight ago. Gave me no address. Sorry." She sat and puzzled over it till her eyes ached, as if it had been a cipher of which she had forgotten the key. "Left England—left England: no address." He had vanished into space again, and this time for how long? Had it never occurred to him that in his absence something might happen to her: that she might fall ill, or be suddenly called home by illness in her family, or, for one reason or another, need his presence—or at least require to communicate with him?

Idle questions! The truth was that he had simply forgotten her. But it is almost unbearable to be forgotten. The victim invents a thousand pretexts rather than admit that one fact. Halo smiled at her own credulity. The night Vance had gone off to Fontainebleau without telling her that he was leaving she had imagined that he might have had an accident, had thought of applying to the police to have him traced. Luckily common-sense had prevailed on that occasion, and she meant that it should on this. She would simply wait and see. But meanwhile Frenside's counsel returned to her. This man whom she could no longer make happy, who needed her so little that he could disappear for weeks without giving her a sign—how much longer was she going to burden him with her unwanted devotion? Had they not reached the hour for a magnanimous farewell?

She turned the problem over and over, too agitated to examine it, too possessed by it to think of anything else. She tried to rehearse the farewell scene (or the farewell letter—since there was no knowing when he would come back); she tried to visualize her solitary return to America, her meeting with her parents, the painful effort of adapting herself to the new lonely life before her: a woman without a lover, without a husband, without a child. But her imagination shrank from the picture, and she lay all day on the divan in Vance's study, her mind a formless darkness.

Toward evening came the postman's ring, and she dashed out before the *bonne* could extricate herself from her saucepans. Letters? Yes, there were letters. Several for Vance, as usual: from publishers, from news agencies, from his tailor, his dentist. But none for her from Vance. She took the letters up to the study and added them to the pile already awaiting him. He had asked her to forward only his personal correspondence and that was small: most of the letters were obviously concerned with his work, and these lay in orderly stacks on his desk. Many of the envelopes bore the names of newspaper-cutting agencies. Vance subscribed to none, but for that very reason they bombarded him with appeals and tempted him with specimen paragraphs. She could never bear to be long idle, and it occurred to her to go through these envelopes, and select any cuttings that might interest him, though she knew he would probably pitch them all in the scrap-basket without a glance.

She went through them one by one, and gradually they built up a picture of his London life: a much more worldly one than she had imagined. While she had thought of him as chained to "Colossus" he had been ranging from Mayfair to Bloomsbury, spending his week-ends at fashionable country-houses, and even condescending to let himself be interviewed. She smiled at the change in him. The Vance she thought she knew would have loathed such publicity. . .

She was more familiar than he with the intricate pattern of social London, and it began to amuse her to trace his ascent from the small chafing-dish parties with Tolby's painters and art-critics to Lady Pevensey's gilded promiscuities, the gathering of the elect at Charlie Tarlton's, and the final apotheosis of the reading at Lady Guy Plunder's. Halo knew all about Lady Guy Plunder and her rivalry with Charlie Tarlton. She thought how happy Vance's publishers would be at the battle the two were waging over the new celebrity. How funny to think of Vance as a fashionable novelist! He had read fragments of "Colossus" at Lady Guy's; the party had apparently been given for that purpose. Halo found an account of it in one of the "society" papers, ran over the list of names, all well-known, many distinguished, and lit on the closing paragraph: "Among Mr. Weston's most enthusiastic hearers on this very exclusive and privileged occasion was his lovely compatriot Miss Floss Delaney, whose father, Colonel Harrison Delaney of Virginia, has lately bought back the old Delaney estate, 'Court Pride', on the James River. Miss Delaney, who was a childhood friend of the brilliant novelist's, had the luck to carry him off after the party to Brambles, the enchanting little place in Surrey which Colonel Delaney, who is said to lavish millions on his only child, has hired for her for the summer. Many were the rival hostesses who envied her for capturing the author of 'Colossus' for a week-end.''

She laid the paper down. Suddenly, among the other names, familiar but indifferent, this one glared out at her. Floss Delaney—? Halo blinked and tried to see the syllables more clearly. Her mind ran back over the rambling distances of Vance's early recollections. He had poured them out so profusely during the first days of their friendship in New York, when talking with her was his one refuge from loneliness, that she did not immediately connect any definite association with this particular name. Then, abruptly, a memory woke. Floss Delaney: it was the name of the girl he had been infatuated with as a boy, the girl he had surprised one day with his disreputable old grandfather, at the spot where his own trysts with her had been held. This girl . . . this vile creature who had given him his first bitter insight into life. . . How his voice had choked as he stammered out the shabby tale! Yes; it must be the same. It was difficult to account for her sudden transformation into a fashionable London figure; but Halo remembered that the girl's father was said to have come of a good southern family, and she also recalled that Vance, returning from Euphoria just before he and she had left for Europe, had brought back the fairy-tale of the Delaneys' sudden rise to wealth. Halo had been too much absorbed in her own happiness to pay much heed at the time; but gradually the story came back to her, even to Lorin Weston's resentful comment on it: "And now the Delaneys have gone to Europe to blow it all in. Gay Paree!"

Yes; it all fitted into the pattern. Floss Delaney—Vance's "childhood friend"! The idea was revolting. While Halo was wearing out her soul for him he was spending his days in such company! She felt as if she were puzzling over the actions of a stranger. The Vance she loved would have recoiled with disgust from such an encounter. It was bitter to think that these were the companions he had chosen, the people who had been sharing his pleasures, listening to his talk, perhaps receiving his confidences and laughing at his inflammable enthusiasms, while she, who had given him her life, sat alone, forgotten, as utterly cut off from him as if she had never had any share in his existence.

The crowning pretense! Yes: Frenside was right; it was time to make it. She got up, and went into her own room. She would pack her things and go—it was so easy; perhaps easier than she had imagined. Why not begin at once? She would wind up everything decently: pay off the servant, put the house in order, leave the key with the agent—the old instinct of order reasserted itself even at such a moment—and then pile her bags into a taxi, and drive to the station. It was all perfectly easy. . .

She stood looking about, wondering how to begin. Her mind was too tired—she couldn't think. After all it might be simpler to write. She would certainly have to leave a letter; she would not appear to retaliate by walking off without a word. And it might be less difficult to take the final step after she had put her reasons on paper. . .

She went back to Vance's desk and sat with her pen suspended over a sheet of paper. Tell Vance that she was leaving him? It was unthinkable! It would be easier to go away than to explain her going. She would pack, and take the train to Paris, and just before sailing she would leave a letter at his bank. She must get away before her courage failed her. . . She crossed the room to the bookshelves where Vance's few works were ranged, and drew out the volume of short stories containing the tale he had written after the discovery of Floss Delaney's betrayal. "One Day"—Halo remembered the evening when Tarrant had brought it home, and she had read it in a rush, her heart beating at the thought that Lewis had discovered a new genius. Now the crudeness and awkwardness of the story struck her; but she was mastered again by the power of the presentation. Yes—it must have happened exactly in that way. And how he must have suffered! There were phrases like the cries of a trapped animal. . . She shut her eyes, unable to read on. He had suffered thus agonizingly—as she was suffering now—but by pouring his suffering into a story he had been able to cleanse his soul of it. Ah, happy artists! No wonder they were careless of other people's wounds, when they were born with the power to heal their own so easily. . .

She must have fallen asleep. The room was dark when she awoke, roused by a sound in the still house. The book fell to the floor and she sat upright, brushing back the hair from her forehead.

A ray of light was advancing up the stairway; behind it she heard the *bonne* clumping up, lamp in hand.

"Monsieur wants to know if Madame will have dinner out-of-doors—there's a moon. . ."

"Monsieur?" Halo stared confusedly at the woman, whose coarse good-natured features were grotesquely

foreshortened by the upward slant of the light. To Halo
the goblin figure seemed a part of her dream. What was
it saying to her? Monsieur—?

"Monsieur got back an hour ago. When I told him
that Madame seemed very tired and had fallen asleep he
said not to disturb her, and he'd go first for a swim. But
he'll be back now, hungry for his dinner, so I had to
wake Madame. . . There's not much in the house, but
I think I can manage a *soufflé*. Shall I carry the table out
into the garden—yes?"

She put the lamp on the desk and clumped down
again to her kitchen. Halo continued to sit on the edge
of the divan, only half wakened out of her exhausting
sleep. She got to her feet at last, looking about her
vaguely. Then she lifted the lamp and carried it into her
bedroom. She put it down on a corner of her dressing-
table, and peered at her reflection in the glass. Her face
was almost as grotesquely illuminated as the servant's;
her eyes looked swollen with sleep, her cheeks drawn
and sallow. "I'm an old woman," she thought. "How
can he ever care for me again?"

She heard a familiar call from the garden. "Halo—
Ha*lo!*" and jumped up, quivering, one happy heart-beat
from head to foot.

"Oh, Vanny! Coming!"

℘ XXXII ℘

VANCE STOOD in the little study and looked about him. He had been gone only a few weeks, yet he felt like a grown man revisiting the house he has lived in as a child, and finding that the rooms he thought he had remembered so vividly are unfamiliar, and different from his recollection. He looked at Halo, and she too seemed strange. Had she always been so pale, with such shadows in the hollows of her lids? At the corners of her mouth there were little lines he had never before noticed.

"You haven't been ill, have you?" he asked with sudden anxiety.

"Ill? No. Do I look so? I suppose the heat's been rather wearing. . . But I loved it," she added, as though to quiet his fears.

"But Sidonie said you'd been lying down all day, and that you don't eat anything."

"What nonsense! She's bored because you haven't been here to devour her *bouillabaisse* and sea-urchins."

Vance continued to scrutinize her. "I oughtn't to have left you so long alone," he said, as if he were speaking to himself.

"Why, Van, how absurd! You needed the change— and I wanted to stay. Now tell me all about 'Colossus'."

It was curious, how strange their voices sounded; his own no less then hers. He seemed to be moving in a mist of strangeness, through which he barely discerned her, remote and ghostly, though his arm was about her and her shoulder against his. "This closeness," he thought desperately, "I suppose it's the only real distance. . ."

331

She drew him toward the stairs. "Come, darling, let's go down. Sidonie has put the table outside, under the old mulberry."

"Under the mulberry?" At the word he was again in the garden at Brambles, assailed by the rush of images against which he had been battling for three desperate weeks. He felt tired, bruised, inarticulate. Would he ever again learn to fit into this forgotten life?

"Yes, come; it'll be terribly jolly," he agreed, his arm in hers.

She leaned close, her face lifted, wrinkling her eyes in the way he liked. "Oh, Van, you *are* glad to be back?"

"Glad? You old darling!" They went down into the garden together.

During his miserable wanderings since he had left England he had imagined that the healing springs would flow as soon as he got back to the pink house. There were days when the longing to be there, when the blind animal craving for Halo's nearness, was so strong that only a vague sense of shame and unworthiness kept him away. He had wanted, in some dim way, to suffer more before he brought his sufferings to be comforted. And now he and she were sitting together under the mulberry in the moonlight, the lights of the little house blinking out at them, the old whisper of the sea in their ears, and he was not really there, and the woman opposite to him was as strange and far away as the scene.

The mere fact that she was so patient with him, didn't nag, didn't question, didn't taunt, somehow added to the sense of her remoteness. Did that curious tolerance make her less woman, less warm to the touch? He had been bracing himself for a struggle, holding himself on the defensive, dreaming of reproaches that should end in tears and kisses; and her quiet unquestioning tenderness was like a barrier. "I shall be better when I get back to work," he thought.

After dinner they sat on in the garden, under the great warm moon, and fragments of talk floated between them on a dividing sea of silence. At length she asked him if he wasn't tired, and he said he was, and got up to help her carry the table in under the glazed porch. Sidonie had gone to bed, and Halo stayed below to clear away the dishes while Vance went up to the study. When he re-entered it alone the room seemed more familiar, the sense of constraint and strangeness fell away. How orderly and welcoming it all looked—the flowers in the brown jar, the quiet circle of lamplight on the letters and papers neatly sorted for his inspection, his old armchair, and the divan where Chris Churley used to sprawl. . .

Vance began to turn over his correspondence. He was not in the mood for letters, but his glance lingered on a bunch of newspaper-cuttings held together by a clip. Evidently Halo had sorted them, and kept those that she thought might interest him. This proof of her care gave him a soothing sense of warmth and ease. He didn't give a fig for newspaper cuttings, but he liked the thought that she had prepared them for him.

He detached the clip and his eyes ran over the articles. He was still looking at them when she came upstairs, and bent above his shoulder. He looked up at her. "You picked these out for me?"

"Yes. I know you don't care for them as a rule, but I thought these few might amuse you."

He continued to look at her. "They were about the only news you had of me, weren't they? I ought to have written oftener—I meant to."

"What does it matter, now you're back?"

"Yes. That's the great thing, isn't it?" He laughed, and pressed her hand against his cheek.

"Don't sit up too late, Van. You look awfully tired."

"No. I'll just go through the rest." Her hand slipped from his shoulder, and he heard her cross the floor and go into her own room. The sound of her moving about there, as she prepared for the night, was pleasant to him, like the purr of a fire on the hearth, the blink of a light through a familiar window. He turned back to the articles, and read on, unwilling to admit that they interested him more than he had suspected. Formerly, when life and his work were in harmony, he had been indifferent to this kind of publicity, contemptuous of it; but now it helped to restore his shaken self-confidence. After all, when people talk about a fellow as these papers did he's not exactly a nonentity, is he?

He read on to the last cutting. It was the account of his evening at Lady Guy Plunder's. The report was cleverly done, and it amused and excited him to reconstitute the scene. Halo had read the notice too, he reflected, and no doubt her pride in him had been flattered. He glowed secretly with the reflection of that pride. And then he came to the last paragraph, that which recounted his departure for Brambles. Who could have given that information, he wondered? Why, Alders, of course—it was Alders who had telephoned to Floss.

The blood rushed to Vance's temples. He concluded instantly that Halo must have read this article, must have seen his name coupled with that of the girl of whom he had spoken with such scorn and self-loathing . . . He felt mortified at what her judgment of him must be, and resentful, almost, that she should have exposed him to divining it. Had she put that particular cutting

there on purpose? No doubt it was to attract his notice
that she had filed it under the others, let them lead him
up to it unsuspectingly. He felt a rush of anger at the
idea that she knew his weaknesses and was concealing
her real thoughts about him. He wasn't going to be
pitied by anybody, least of all by her. . .

Hitherto he had never found either consolation or
excitement in drink. He had seen too much drunkenness all his life to be shocked, or even actively disgusted,
by the sight of it in others; but he felt a cold contempt
for the fools who could blur their minds and besot their
bodies when life was so short, and every minute of it so
packed with marvels. The sheer waste of drunkenness was
what revolted him. But now he felt a sudden longing to
blot out at a stroke all the tormenting memories of the
last weeks, and the exasperating sense of his own weakness. "It's all a failure—everything I touch is a failure,"
he thought. He went to the cupboard in which Halo
kept the bottles of spirits, and cocktail ingredients, and
poured himself out a stiff measure of gin-and-soda. He
drank it down, and felt better. He filled another glass,
and drank that too; then he threw himself onto the
divan, heavy with fatigue and sleep. But in another moment he was sitting up again, his brain tingling with excitement. Halo had ceased to move about in her room;
the house had become intensely silent, and the silence
frightened him. He felt the same awful loneliness as
when, after Laura Lou's death, he had sat in the tumble-
down bungalow while she lay on the other side of the
closed door. He began to tremble at the memory. If
Halo were dead! If he were to open that door and go in,
and find her on the bed white and waxen, like Laura
Lou. He started up, and went to her door and opened it.
She was in bed; over the chair beside her hung her old
red silk dressing-gown, the one she had thrown over her

when she had met him on the night of his return from Fontainebleau. The hair lay loose on her forehead, as it had then, and she sat propped against her pillows, a candle faintly lighting her pale face.

"Not asleep?" he said in a sheepish voice, sitting down by her and furtively stroking the folds of the dressing gown.

"No; it's too hot." She looked at him. "Aren't you going to bed?"

He got up restlessly, and wandered to the window. "This light'll bring in mosquitoes."

She blew out the candle and he came back and knelt down beside her. "Halo, I'm a damned fool—a damned worthless fool." He hid his face against the sheet, and felt her hand in his hair. He melted at the reassurance of her touch, the feeling that it was drawing him out of himself and back into the old warm shelter of habit.

"I'd have come back sooner—only I wasn't fit to," he muttered.

"Silly Van!"

"But now I want to get back; take up our old life. It's not too late, is it? Some time I'll tell you—don't ask me to now, will you? Just say if it's possible still—if you're not done with me. . . If you are, tell me that too —straight out. I can't sleep till I know if it's really you here, or only a ghost of you, who's sorry for me. I don't want that either. . . I'd rather get out now, and go on. . ." He hardly knew what he was saying; the words tumbled out as they could.

He felt her lean over and lay her arm on his neck. She did not attempt to draw him to her; her arm trembled a little as it touched him. "I'm here," she said, so low that he hardly heard. He buried his head against her, and was still.

The days that followed passed quietly. Halo was nervously conscious of every word and look of Vance's, yet determined that he should not see she was watching him. After his outburst of remorse and tenderness on the night of his return he seemed to have slipped back into his usual attitude toward her, except that she was aware of something shy and dependent in him, something that besought her compassion yet would have resented her showing it. The thing to do, she told herself again and again, was just to be natural, to behave as if nothing were changed; and gradually she felt that he was becoming used to her, and to the life out of which some mysterious influence had abruptly wrenched him.

She refrained from questioning him about his weeks in England, and he never spoke of them except, now and then, to allude to an encounter with some critic or writer whom she knew he had wished to meet. To the social side of the adventure he never referred; nor did he mention the interval which had elapsed between his taking leave of Tolby and his reappearance at Oubli.

Tolby thought he had left England—or said so. But did he know? Perhaps Vance had simply vanished from Tolby's ken without revealing his plans. Why should he have been so secretive about them unless he had wished to conceal his whereabouts, and what motive for concealment could he have had except that he had gone away with some woman? The riddle continued to revolve in Halo's brain, but she tried to ignore it; and as the days slipped by, and she saw Vance gradually settling down into his old habits of work, the whole matter seemed less important. Whatever had happened, it was probably over; he had passed through a phase, and come back to her—and that was all that mattered.

The summer was coming to an end; the tumultuous sun-bathers were vanishing from bungalows and restaurants, scattering with their wireless sets and shrieking motors to all the points of the compass, and leaving Oubli to the quietness of autumn. Already the great arched avenues of planes had turned into golden tunnels, the kindled vineyards were flushing to flame and embers, the figs purpling through their fanlike foliage. The pink house was almost the only one that had not barred its shutters for the dead interval between the seasons. When Halo and Vance went down to bathe they had the bay almost to themselves; in their rambles through the olive terraces and among the pine-woods they met no more "hikers", and the cry of Ford and Citroën grew remoter through the sylvan hush.

Vance was more silent than of old; but though he had no explosions of enthusiasm he seemed as sensitive as ever to the beauty about him. To Halo he was like some one recovering from a long illness, and yielding gradually to the returning spell of life; there were moments when she could hardly help lowering her voice and treading as if in a sick-room—yet she knew nothing would irritate him more than any sign of exaggerated sympathy. "Be natural, be natural," she kept repeating to herself, wondering if there were any lesson in the world as hard to learn.

Sooner than she could have hoped he returned to his work; there were days when he threw himself into it with such sombre ardour that she feared for his health and urged him not to write for too many hours at a stretch. But he received the suggestion irritably, and she saw that she must adapt herself to these days and nights of furious labour, which alternated with others of heavy lassitude. After a while she noticed that he had begun to drink to make up for the exhaustion following on his long bouts of writing. The discovery was a shock, and half-jokingly she tried to hint her surprise. In former times, she knew, Vance would have been humiliated by any allusion to such a weakness; but he received her hints with a sort of bantering indifference. "I know— you women think God created the universe on lemonade and lettuce sandwiches. Well, maybe He did; but I can't. Don't be frightened—you haven't acquired an habitual drunkard. But I've got to get this book off my chest somehow, and I can't do it without being bucked up now and then. I wish you'd tell Sidonie to make me a good thermos-ful of black coffee every night, will you? She can leave it on my desk when she goes to bed."

Hitherto he had not spoken of the progress of his book; but Halo was used to that now. Since the old days at the Willows he had never really taken her into his confidence while his work was in hand. Even when he was writing "The Puritan in Spain", in the solitude of their long *tête-à-tête* at Cadiz, he had used her as an ear to listen, not as an intelligence to criticize. And since he had been in England he had taken to doing his own typing, so that even her services on the Remington were no longer required, and his book was a secret garden into which he shut himself away from her as he might have done into a clandestine love-affair. But one afternoon, as they lay under the olives on the hillside, he turned to her with a half-shy half-whimsical smile. "See here; I'm beginning to wonder whether you're going to take to 'Colossus'."

She smiled back at him. "So am I!"

"Well, I suppose it's about time we tried it out. I want to know how it strikes you."

She tried to repress her eagerness, to look friendly yet not too flattered. "I want to know too, dear— whenever you feel like it." As they scrambled down the hill through the golden twilight she seemed to be carried on wings. "He's come back to me—he's come back to me!" she exulted, as if this need of her intellectual help were a surer token of his return to her than any revival of passion.

The book had advanced much farther than she had expected. In spite of the social distractions of London, Vance had got on with his writing more rapidly there than during the quiet months at Oubli, and as Halo looked at the heaped-up pages she asked herself whether a change of scene—figurative as well as actual—might not be increasingly necessary to him, and at more frequent intervals. On the night of his return he had confessed to her that he had been a fool, that he would have come back sooner if he had not been ashamed of his folly; but perhaps the experience he had in mind, whatever it was, had roused his intellectual activity and fed the creative fires. It was all mysterious and unintelligible to Halo, whose own happiness was so dependent on stability and understanding; but her intelligence could divine what perplexed her heart. At any rate, she thought with secret triumph, he hasn't found any one to replace me as a listener.

That very evening he began to read the book aloud. They had meant to take the chapters in instalments; Halo had stipulated for time to reflect, and to get the work into its proper perspective. But when Vance was in the mood for reading aloud the excitement of getting a new view of what he had written always swept him on from page to page, and the joy of listening, and the sense that for the first time since the writing of "Instead" he needed her not only as audience but as critic, kept Halo from interrupting him. By the time he had finished they were both exhausted, Vance almost voiceless, and Halo in a state of nervous agitation that made it difficult for her to speak, though she knew he was impatient for what she had to say. He waited a moment; then he gave an uneasy laugh. "Well—?"

"Van—" she began; but she broke off, embarrassed.

He was gathering the pages together with affected indifference. "No reaction—that about it?"

"No; oh, no! Only—you remember that time I took you to Chartres?" She smiled, but there was no answering light in his face. He was looking down sullenly at the manuscript.

"I remember I was as dead as a mummy. Couldn't see or feel anything. I suppose you're in the same state now?" he suggested ironically.

"Nonsense; you weren't dead, you were stunned, bewildered. And so am I—just at first. I want more time—I want to re-read it quietly."

"Oh, the critic who asks for a reprieve has already formed his opinion." He laughed again. "Come—out with it! What's wrong with the book? I don't know why you take me for such a thin-skinned idiot that I can't bear to be told."

She saw that his lips were twitching, and suddenly suspected that he himself was not wholly satisfied with what he had written, and had feared in advance that she might share his dissatisfaction.

"I wish you'd let me sleep over it," she urged good-humouredly. "I really don't know yet what I think."

"You mean you don't know how to sugar-coat it," he interrupted. "Well, don't try! Just say straight out how the book strikes you. Remember that an artist is never much affected by amateur judgments, anyway."

She flushed up at the sneer. "In that case, mine can surely wait."

"Oh, it doesn't have to! I know already what you think. You don't understand what I'm after, and so you assume that I've muddled it. That's about it, isn't it?"

The taunt was too great a strain on her patience. If he had to be praised at all costs she felt that he was lost; he must be shaken out of this lethargy of self-appreciation. "Isn't it rather too easy to conclude that if your critics are not altogether pleased it's because they're incapable of understanding you?"

He swung round with an ironic smile. "Which simply means that you're not al-to-gether pleased yourself?" he mimicked her.

"No; I'm not. But I don't think the reason you suggest is the right one."

"Naturally!" He caught himself up, and went on more quietly: "Well, then, what *is* the reason?"

Halo's heart was beating apprehensively. Why was she thus deliberately risking their newly-recovered understanding? Was it worth while to put his literary achievement above her private happiness—and perhaps his? She was not sure; but she had to speak as her mind moved her. "I'll tell you as well as I can. I'm a little bewildered still; but I have an idea you haven't found yourself—expressed your real self, I mean—in this book as you did in the others. You're not . . . not quite as free from other influences . . . echoes . . ." As the words formed themselves she knew they were the most fatal to the artist's self-love, the hardest for wounded vanity to recover from. But if she spoke at all she must speak as truth dictated; she could not tamper with her intellectual integrity, or with his.

Vance had dropped back into his chair. "Echoes!" he said with a curt laugh. "That's all you see—all you hear, rather? What sort of echoes?"

"Of books you've been reading, I suppose; or the ideas of the people you've been talking to. I can't speak more definitely, because I've been with you so little lately, and it's so long since you've talked to me of your work. But I feel that you may have let yourself be too much guided, directed—drawn away from your own immediate vision."

"In other words, if I'd submitted the book to you page by page I should have been more likely to preserve what you call my immediate vision? Is that it?"

The outbreak was so childish that it restored her balance, and she smiled. "I can't tell about that, of course; but if you think such a consideration would really affect my opinion, I wonder at your ever caring to hear it."

Vance gave a shrug. "My dear child—shall I give you the cold truth, as you've given it to me? It's simply this: that the artist asks other people's opinions to please *them* and not to help himself. There's only one critic who can help us—that's life! As for the rest, it's all bunk . . ." He pushed the pages into their folder, and got up, stretching his arms above his head. "You're right, anyhow, about our both being too dog-tired to keep up the discussion now. It was brutal of me to put you through the third degree at two in the morning. . ."

Halo's heart sank. She did not resent his tone; she knew he was overwrought, and was talking with his nerves and not with his intelligence; but again she was frightened by the idea that her over-scrupulous sincerity might check his impulse to turn to her for advice and sympathy. "And after all," she reflected, "it's only sympathy that matters. He's right, in a sense, when he says it's about the only thing an artist requires of his friends. As for the work itself, self-criticism is all that counts." She looked at him gaily.

"It's not two in the morning yet; but I *am* tired, and so are you. I wish you hadn't made me feel that I can't help you. If only by listening, by giving you my whole mind, I believe I can; but you'll be able to tell better tomorrow. At any rate, you must give me the chance to explain a little more clearly what I feel."

He looked embarrassed, and half-ashamed of his outburst. "Of course, child. We'll talk it all over when our heads are a little clearer. Now I believe I'll go to bed." He went up to the cupboard and poured himself out a glass of whisky. As he emptied it he turned to her with a laugh and a toss of his head above the tilted glass. "Here's to my next book—a best-seller, to be written under your guidance." He tapped her on the shoulder and turned her face toward his for a kiss.

ONE DAY he said to her: "Well, the book's finished." He spoke in a low apprehensive voice, as if he had been putting off the announcement as long as possible, and now that it was made, did not know what to say next.

Since the night, weeks before, when Halo had ventured her criticism he had never again proposed to show her what he was doing, never even asked her to take his dictation or to copy out his manuscript; he had definitely excluded the subject of "Colossus" from their talks. The intellectual divorce between them was increasingly bitter to Halo. That the veil of passion must wear through was life's unescapable lesson; but if no deeper understanding underlay it, what was left? Had not Frenside's advice been the only answer? In the joy of Vance's return, and the peaceful communion of their first days, when the mere fact of being together seemed to settle every doubt and lay every ghost, it had been easy to smile at her old friend's suggestion, and to reflect how little any one could know of lovers' hearts except the lovers. But now she understood on what unstable ground she had rebuilt her happiness, and trembled.

Vance stood in the window looking out over the bay. The palms were wrestling in dishevelled fury with the first autumn gale; rain striped the panes, and beyond the headlands a welter of green waters stretched away to the low pall of clouds. Halo saw him give a discouraged shrug. "Good Lord—Miss Plummet!"

The Pension Britannique had reopened its shutters the previous week, and after a prelude of carpet-shaking

345

and tile-scrubbing Madame Fleuret's lodgers were taking possession of their old quarters. The Anglican chapel was to resume its offices on the following Sunday; already Halo had encountered Mrs. Dorman, cordial though embarrassed, and eager to tell her that after the first rains a bad leak had shown itself in Lady Dayes-Dawes's room, and that the mason was afraid they would have to rebuild the chimney of the lounge.

Halo stood by Vance watching Miss Plummet swept homeward by the south-easterly blast, her umbrella bellying like a black sail. After she had passed there was an interval during which the promenade remained empty, like a stage-setting before the leading actor's entrance; then, punctually as of old, Colonel Churley stalked into view, his mackintosh flapping, his stick dragging in the mud, his head thrust out angrily to meet the gale. Vance followed his struggling figure with fascinated eyes. "I suppose they all think they're alive!" he groaned.

Halo laid her arm on his shoulder. She knew what thoughts the sight of Colonel Churley had stirred in him. "Why should we stay here any longer?" she said.

Vance drummed on the pane without answering. His eyes still followed the bent figure lessening between the palm-trunks.

"Now that your book's finished—"

"Oh, my book! I don't believe it is a book—just a big dump of words. And not mine, anyhow; you've made that clear enough!" He gave an irritated laugh.

"I have? But you only let me hear a few chapters."

"Exactly. And on those you gave me your judgment of the finished book. Without a moment's hesitation. Look here, child," he added abruptly, "don't think I was surprised, or that I minded. Not in the least. It's the sign of the amateur critic that he must always conclude, never leave an opinion in solution."

Halo's arm dropped from his shoulder. "Then it can't much matter to the author what the conclusion is."

Vance stood uneasily shifting from one foot to the other, his eyes bent to the ground. "If only it didn't matter! The devil of it is that when a book's growing the merest stupidest hint may deflect its growth, deform it. . . The artist loses confidence, ceases to visualize. . . Oh, what's the use of trying to explain?"

"Don't try, dear. You're too tired, for one thing."

"Tired—tired? When a man's at the end of his tether a woman always thinks he's tired. Why don't you suggest a bottle of tonic?"

"If you're at the end of your tether it would be more to the point to suggest new pastures. Why shouldn't we try some other place?"

He moved away and began his restless pacing; then he came back and paused before her. "It's the landscape of the soul I'm fed up with," he broke out.

She stood silent. The landscape of the soul! But that must mean his nearest surroundings—must mean herself, she supposed. She tried to steady the smile on her trembling lips. "I wish you'd let me help you as I used to," she began. "But if I'm of no use to you in your work, and only in the way at other times, perhaps . . ." She felt a blur in her eyes, and hurried on. "Perhaps the real change you need—" and now she achieved a little laugh—"is not a new place but a new woman."

The words dropped into a profound silence. Was he never going to speak, to deny, to protest at the monstrousness of her suggestion? He stood in the window, looking out into the rain, for a time that seemed to her interminable; and when he turned back his face was expressionless, closed. She felt as if a door had been shut against her. She essayed her little laugh again. "Is that it? Don't be afraid to tell me!"

"That?" He looked at her vaguely. "Oh—another woman?" He stopped, and then began, in a hard embarrassed voice: "I suppose you put that newspaper cutting on my desk on purpose the night I came back? You wanted me to understand that you knew?"

She returned his look in genuine bewilderment. The weeks since his return had been crowded with so many emotions and agitations that for the moment she had forgotten the paragraph in which Floss Delaney figured. Suddenly the memory rushed back on her, and she stood speechless. It was that, then—her first instinct had been right, had led her straight to his secret! She stiffened herself, trying to thrust back the intolerable truth. "What cutting? You mean—about that girl?"

"Yes; that girl."

"Oh, Vance . . . you don't . . . you don't mean that it's for her . . . ?" There was another silence. "You mean that when you left London it was to go away with her?"

He gave an angry laugh. "It was to go away *from* her—as far as I could go! Now do you understand?"

Halo's eyes clung to his labouring face. Did she understand—dared she? She spoke very low. "To get away from her . . . because you realized . . . ? Because it was all over—like a bad dream? Is that it?"

"A bad dream, yes; but not over. I'd rather you knew everything now. . . I didn't run away from her. . ."

"Then—?"

"She kicked me out. Can't you see? Do I have to put everything in words of one syllable?"

Halo looked away from him. "No; you don't have to." Suddenly her contracted heart seemed to expand a very little. "Then those weeks after you left London—when Tolby said he didn't know what had become of you—she wasn't with you all that time?"

"Merciful heaven—she? No!"

"Then where were you, Vance?"

"Somewhere in hell. I believe they call it Belgium."

"All alone there, all that time?" she cried pityingly. He mistook her intonation.

"Do you suppose that as fast as one woman throws me over I hook on to another—like a sort of limpet?"

"I wasn't thinking of another woman. I hoped you'd had one of your friends with you."

"A man's got no friends when he's going through a thing like that . . ." He stopped, and then a rush of words broke from him. "You don't know—how should you? She threw me out; and I trailed back after her to London; and she threw me out again. That time I had my lesson."

He dropped into his armchair and leaned back, looking up at the ceiling. She thought how young his face looked in spite of its drawn misery, and said to herself: "He'll get over it and I shan't. He'll use it up in a story, and it will go on living in me and feeding on me." Aloud she said: "I'm very sorry for you, Vance. I shouldn't have thought—"

"No! I understand. You'd have thought it would be any other woman—only not that one. Well, it's the other way round. I'm pitiably constant." He continued to lean back, his arms crossed behind his head. He no longer looked at her, seemed hardly to know she was there; yet every word he spoke cut like a blade sharpened to wound her. She leaned against the desk, her arms stretched behind her for support. She felt a kind of inner rigidity that almost seemed like strength. While it lasted, she thought, she must speak. "If you feel like that you must marry her. You're free, dear—you know that."

He started up with a choking sound in his throat. "Marry her? She's going to marry somebody else." He buried his face in his hands and sat a long while without speaking. He was not weeping; his shoulders did not stir; he just sat there in dark communion with his grief. Halo did not move either till she felt a stiffness in the muscles of her arms; then she turned from the desk and stood looking out of the window at the storm-darkened world. As she stood there Colonel Churley went by, driven back by the storm from his solitary tramp. How she had pitied him last winter, when she and Vance, from the safe shelter of their love, had looked out on his lonely figure!

Night was falling; soon the lamp-lighter would come along and the gas-lamps along the promenade flicker into life. They said the streets would be lit by electricity next year. Their landlord had even spoken of putting in an electric cooker. . . That reminded Halo that if they meant to leave Oubli she ought to write at once and give notice. You sent your landlord a registered letter, and then he couldn't say that he hadn't been notified, because there was his signature.

She turned back into the room, which was already dark, groped for matches, and lit the two candles in the brass candlesticks on the chimney. The fibres of her heart were wound about every object in that homely friendly room. How many evenings she and Vance had sat there, between fire and candles, joking and planning! One flesh—they had been one flesh. And now they were to be divided. She felt like some one facing a surgical operation: the kind of which the surgeons say to the family: "There *have* been cases in which it has proved successful; and if it's not done we refuse to answer for the consequences."

She tried to picture what her future would be—what she herself would be—if the operation were to be successful. Perhaps in the end she would marry some-body else, have children, live on as a totally different being, preoccupied about ordering another man's din-ner and bringing up his family, though the same face continued to look back at her from her mirror. How odd if in years to come she should meet Vance somewhere—in the street, in a train—and they should not recognize each other, and some one, perhaps her husband, should say afterward: "You didn't know? Why, that's the man who wrote 'Colossus'. I thought you used to know him. That handsome common-looking woman was his wife."

Vance stood up, shook himself and passed his hand over his forehead. "I think I'll go out."

Halo moved toward him. She must make use of her factitious energy before it flickered out. "Vance—just a minute. I want to tell you . . ."

He stopped unwillingly. "Yes?"

"You're free as air. You understand that, don't you?"

He lifted his eyes and looked at her heavily. "You mean—you want to make an end?"

Her voice was hardly audible, even to her own ears. "Hadn't we better?"

He still looked at her in a wounded suffering way. "All right, then; I understand."

"Vance—it's better, isn't it?"

"It's all I'm worth."

She went closer to him. "Oh, not that—don't say that! I only want you to feel that if there's any hope . . . any happiness for you . . . elsewhere . . . I want you . . ." Her voice grew suddenly louder, and then broke into a sob. The tide of her tears rushed over her. She dropped down on the divan and wept as if she were weeping away all the accumulated agony of the last weeks. How brief a way her strength had carried her! She fought back her tears, straightened herself, and lifted her face to his. "This is nothing—just nervousness. I suppose I've been alone too long . . ."

He knelt down at her side, and she felt his arms about her. Their treacherous warmth melted her resistance away. "Oh, Van . . . my Van . . ." while he held her thus, could any other woman come between them?

BOOK V

❧ XXXIV ❧

From the window of every English bookshop in Paris "Colossus" stared at Halo. The book had appeared a few weeks after its last pages were written, the chapters having been set up as they were finished, in order to hasten publication. Otherwise the winter sales would be missed, and "Colossus" was obviously not a work for the summer holidays. Halo suspected that the publishers, while proud to associate their name with it, were not sanguine as to pecuniary results. "Colossus" had most of the faults disquieting to the book-seller; it was much too long, nothing particular happened in it, and few people even pretended to know what it was about.

No reviews had as yet appeared when Halo saw the first copies in the rue de Rivoli windows, where they must have flowered over night. She stood hesitatingly outside the shop; there had come to be something slow and hesitating in her slightest decisions, in her movements even. She found it more and more difficult to make up her mind even about trifles—more so about trifles than about the big decisive acts. The spring of enthusiasm that used to give a momentary importance to the least event seemed to have run dry in her.

She went in and asked for a magazine. While it was being brought she glanced at the copies of "Colossus" conspicuously aligned on the New Book counter, and asked the clerk how it was going.

"We've sold a good many already. Anything by the author of 'The Puritan in Spain', you understand. . . Can I do up a copy for you?"

It was the answer she had expected. The book would benefit for a while by its predecessor's popularity; but when that flagged—what? She paid for the magazine she had asked for, and went out.

It was a cold day of early winter, and Paris, once like home to her, seemed empty and unfriendly. She had seen no one since her arrival. Lorry, she had learned at his studio, was away. Both Mrs. Glaisher and Mrs. Blemer had failed in the end to regard "Factories" as a profitable venture, and he was negotiating for its production with a Berlin impresario. Halo had not the heart to look up Savignac—again her stealing inertia held her back; and Tolby, whom she would have been glad to see, was still in London. Paris had been a feverish desert to her before; now it was a freezing one.

She walked back through the Tuileries gardens, and across the Seine to the quiet hotel on the left bank where she was staying. She had lingered on alone in Paris for a week or ten days—ever since she had come there to see Vance off, when he had hurriedly sailed for New York—and she had a queer feeling that there was no use in trying to make any further plans, that any change, any new decision, must be imposed on her from the outside. It was as though her central spring were broken . . . yet, in a way, she knew that her future had already been settled for her.

At her hotel she asked the porter if there were any letters. She was sure he would say no; of course there would be none; and when, after a hunt through the pigeon-holes behind his desk, he handed her an envelope, she felt suddenly dizzy, and had to sit down on the nearest chair and leave the letter unopened. How strange, how incredible, to see herself addressed as "Mrs. Tarrant" in her husband's writing! It reminded her that in spite of all that had happened she was still Mrs. Tarrant, still his wife—and it was by his own choice that it was so. That was the strangest part of it, the part she could not yet understand.

She had learned of Tarrant's presence in Paris by seeing his name among the hotel arrivals in a daily paper. That was two days ago; and after twenty-four hours of incoherent thinking she had abruptly decided to move to another hotel, and register there under her real name—her husband's. That night she had written to him. That night; and here, the very next morning, was his answer! One might almost have supposed that he had been waiting for some sign from her. . . She sat with her cold hands folded over the letter till her strength returned; when she could trust herself to her feet she rose and went up to her room.

The variableness of Tarrant's moods had made her fear that he might reply harshly, or perhaps not at all. Even now she thought it likely that, if he should agree to see her, he would propose their meeting at his lawyer's; and that would paralyze her, deprive her of all power to plead her cause. Over three months had passed since he had sent Frenside to her on that unsuccessful mission; and as she looked back on her own attitude at the time it seemed hard and ungrateful. In her self-absorption she had forgotten to send Tarrant a word of thanks, a conciliatory message; and she knew the importance he attached to such observances. For her sake he had humbled his pride, and she had seemed unaware of it. With his sensitiveness to rebuffs, and the uncertainty of his impulses, what chance was there of finding him in the same frame of mind as when he had made his advance and she had rejected it? He had a horror of reopening any discussion which he regarded as closed; might he not justly say that the message she had sent through Frenside had been final? She looked at the unopened envelope and wondered at her courage—or her folly—in writing to him.

At length she opened the letter, and read the few words within. In the extremity of her relief she felt weak again, and had to sit down and cover her face. There was no mention of lawyers; there was nothing curt or vindictive in the tone of the letter. Tarrant simply said that he would be glad to see her that afternoon at his hotel. The sheet trembled in her hand, and she found herself suddenly weeping.

The porter said that Mr. Tarrant was expecting her, and the lift carried her up to a velvet-carpeted corridor. It was the hotel where he and she had stayed whenever they were in Paris together; the narrow white-panelled corridor was exactly like the one leading to the rooms they usually had. At its end she was shown into a stiffly furnished white and gray sitting-room, and Tarrant stood up from the table at which he had been pretending to write. He was extremely pale, and catching her own reflection in the mirror behind him, she thought: "We look like two ghosts meeting . . ."

She said: "Lewis," and held her hand out shyly. He touched it with his cold fingers, and stammered: "You'll have tea?" as though he had meant to say something more suitable, and had forgotten what it was.

She shook her head, and he pushed an armchair forward. "Sit down." She sat down, and for a few moments he stood irresolutely before her; then he pulled up a chair for himself and reached out for the cigarettes on the table. "You don't mind?" She shook her head again.

Suddenly it came over her that this was perhaps the very room in which, on that unhappy night, Vance had so imprudently pleaded for her release; and the thought deepened her discouragement. But she must conquer these tremors and find herself again.

"Thank you for letting me come," she said at length. "I ought to have thanked you before."

He raised his eyebrows with the ironic movement habitual to him when he wanted to ward off emotional appeals. "Oh, why—?"

"Because you sent Frenny to me with that offer. And I didn't thank you properly."

The blood rose under his sensitive skin. "Oh, that, really. . . I understood that you . . . that at the time you were undecided about your own future. . ."

"Yes; I was. But I want to tell you that I was very grateful, though I may not have seemed so; and that now—now I accept."

Tarrant was silent. He had regained control of his features, but Halo could measure the intensity of the effort, and the inward perturbation it denoted. After all, he and she had the same emotional reactions, though his range was so much more limited; in moments of stress she could read his mind and his heart as she had never been able to read Vance's. The thought cast back a derisive light on her youthful illusions.

After the first months of burning intimacy with Vance, and the harrowing extremes of their subsequent life, Tarrant had become a mere shadow to her, and she had not foreseen that his presence would rouse such searching memories. But she was one of the women on whom successive experiences stamp themselves without effacing each other; and suddenly, in all her veins and nerves, she felt that this cold embarrassed man, having once been a part of her life, could never quite cease to be so. No wonder she had never been able to adapt herself to the amorous code of Lorry's group! She sat waiting, her heart weighed down with memories, while Tarrant considered her last words.

"You accept—?" he repeated at length.

"I—yes. The divorce, I mean. . . I understand that you . . ."

"You've decided that you want a divorce?" She nodded.

He sat with bent head, his unlit cigarette between his fingers. "You're quite certain . . . now . . . that this is really what you wish?"

"I—oh, yes, yes," she stammered.

Tarrant continued in contemplation of her words, and she began to fear that, after all, he might have let her come only for the bitter pleasure of refusing what she asked. She had nearly cried out, appealed to him to shorten her suspense; but she controlled herself and waited. He got up, and stood before her.

"I ask the question because—if Frenside gave me a correct account of your talk—you took the opposite view at that time: you didn't want to take proceedings because you thought that if you did so Weston might feel obliged to marry you." He brought out the words with difficulty; she felt sorry for the effort it was costing him to get through this scene, which she might have spared him if she had accepted Frenside's intervention. "Are you positively sure now?" he insisted.

"Yes."

"You wish to divorce me in order to marry your lover?"

"Lewis—!"

He smiled faintly. "You object to the word?"

"No; but it seems so useless to go into all this again."

He took no notice, but pursued, in the same level

voice: "You and Weston have come together again, and wish to marry? Is that it?"

She lowered her eyes, and paused a moment before answering. "I am not sure—that we shall ever marry. I want my freedom."

"Freedom? Freedom to live without a name, or any one to look after you? What sort of a life do you propose to lead if you don't marry him? Have you thought of that?"

She hesitated again. She might have resented his questioning; but his tone, though cold, was not unkind. And she knew him so well that she could detect the latent sympathy behind those measured phrases.

"I haven't thought of the future yet. I only know it seems best that I should take back my own name."

"If you're not to take his—is that what you mean?"

"I'm not sure . . . about anything. But I want to be free."

He went and leaned against the mantelshelf, looking down on her with dubious eyes. "The situation, then, is much the same as when you saw Frenside; it's only your own attitude that has changed?"

"Well . . . yes . . . I suppose so. . ."

There was a silence which she measured by the nervous knocking of her heart. At that moment her knowledge of her husband seemed of no avail. She could not guess what his secret motive was; but she felt dimly that something deep within him had been renewed and transformed, and that it was an unknown Tarrant who confronted her. He twisted the cigarette incessantly between his fingers. "I heard you'd been unhappy—" he began abruptly.

She flushed and lifted her head. "No!"

He smiled again. "You wouldn't admit it, I suppose. At any rate, you're alone—at present. Don't you think that—in the circumstances—my name is at least a sort of protection?"

The question surprised her so much that she could find no words to reply; and he hurried on, as if anxious to take advantage of her silence: "I've no doubt my attitude, all along, has been misrepresented to you. Perhaps it was partly my own fault. I'm not good at explaining—especially things that touch me closely. But for a long time now I've felt that some day you might be glad to have kept my name. . . It was my chief reason for not agreeing to a divorce. . ." He spoke in the low indifferent tone which always concealed his moments of deepest perturbation. "You never thought of that, I suppose?" he ended, as if reproachfully.

"No—I hadn't."

"H'm," he muttered with a dry laugh. "Well, it doesn't matter. My pride sometimes gets in my way . . . particularly when I think I haven't been fairly treated. But that's all over. I want to help you. . ."

"Oh, Lewis, thank you."

"No matter about that. The thing is—look here, can't we talk together openly?"

She felt her colour rise again; and again her knowledge of him gave her no clue to what might be coming. "Certainly—it will be much better."

"Well, then—." He broke off, as if the attempt were more difficult than he had foreseen. Suddenly he resumed: "If you and Weston have parted, as I understand you have . . ." In the interval that followed she felt that he was waiting for her to confirm or deny the assertion.

"He went to America ten days ago—to his own people. He felt that he ought to go and see them. Beyond that we've made no plans. . ."

"You mean that there's no understanding between

you as to his coming back—or as to your future relations?"

"I don't wish that there should be! He's free—perfectly free. That's our only understanding," she exclaimed hastily.

"Well—that's what I wanted to be sure of. If it's that way, I'm ready to wipe out the past . . . let it be as if nothing had happened. It's nobody's business but yours and mine, anyhow. . . You understand? I'm ready to take you back."

She sat looking up at him without finding any words; but the weight in her breast lifted a little—she felt less lonely. "Thank you, Lewis . . . thank you . . ." she managed to say.

His lips narrowed; evidently it was not the response he had expected. But he went on: "Of course, at first . . . I can understand. . . You might feel that you couldn't come back at once, take up our life where it broke off—at any rate not in the old surroundings. I've thought of that; I shouldn't ask it. I should be ready to travel, if you preferred. For a year—for longer even. The world's pretty big. We could go to India . . . or to East Africa. As far as you like. Explore things. . . I don't care what. By the time we got back people would have forgotten." He straightened himself, as though the last words had slipped out of a furtive fold of his thoughts. "Not that that matters. If *I* choose, nobody else has a word to say. And nobody will! I—I've missed you, Halo. I ask you to come back."

She stood silent, oppressed. On Tarrant's lips, she knew, such an appeal meant complete surrender. If he owned that he had missed her—*how* he must have missed her! Under all her cares and perplexities she felt a little quiver of feminine triumph, and it trembled in her voice as she answered. "Thank you, Lewis . . . for saying that . . . I wish things could have been different. Please believe that I do."

She caught the gleam of hope in his eyes. "Well, then—let it be as if they had been different. Won't you?"

The talk had led them so far from the real object of her visit that she began to fear for the result. If Tarrant, in refusing to divorce her, had really had in mind the hope of her return, what chance was there now of his yielding? It had never been in his nature to give without taking. She felt bewildered and at a loss.

"Can things ever be as if they'd never been? Life would be too easy!" she said timidly.

His face darkened and the nervous frown gathered between his eyes. "Is that your answer?"

"I suppose it must be."

"Must be? Not unless you still expect to marry Weston. Is that it? You owe the truth to me."

She saw instantly that if she said yes her doing so might provoke a refusal to divorce her; and that if she said no he would go on insisting, and her final rejection of his offer would be all the more mortifying to him. She reflected wearily that the Tarrant she knew was already coming to the surface.

"I've told you the truth; I don't know any more than you do what my future will be. I'm bound to no one. . . But if I agreed to what you suggest, how could we avoid unhappiness? You would always remember . . . and the differences in our characters probably haven't grown less. . ." She went toward him with outstretched hands. "Lewis—please! Let me have my freedom, and let us say goodbye as friends."

Without noticing her gesture he continued to look at her somberly. "How easily you settle my future for me! Your character at any rate hasn't changed. Here I've waited for you—waited and waited for this hour; for I was sure from the first that your crazy experiment wouldn't last. And now you tell me it's over, and that your future's not pledged to anybody else—which means that you're alone in the world, a woman deserted by her lover (you know as well as I do that that's what people will say). And yet you continue to let your pride stand between us . . . or if it isn't pride, what is it? Some idea that things can't be as they were before? Well, perhaps they can't—entirely. Perhaps we can neither of us forget. . . But if I assure you of my friendship . . . my devotion. . . God, Halo, what I'm proposing shows how I feel . . . there's no use talking . . ."

She caught the cry under his pondered syllables, and saw that he was struggling with emotions deeper than he had ever known. The sight woke her pity, and she thought: "Am I worth anything better than this? Shall I ever be wanted in this way again?"

"Lewis, if you knew how sorry I am! I *am* grateful —I do feel your generosity. It's true that I'm alone, and that the future's rather blank. But all that can't be helped; nothing can change it now. You must give me my freedom."

"What I feel is nothing to you, then?"

"No. It's a great deal." She looked at him gravely. "It's because I might end by being tempted that I mustn't listen to you; that you must let me go."

"Let you go—when you've confessed that you're tempted? Listen, Halo. You see now how right I was to refuse to divorce you; to wait; to believe that you'd come back. Now that you're here, how can you ask me to give you up?"

She stood motionless, her heart trembling with the weight of his pleading. His words piled themselves up on her like lead. "How can you, Halo?" he repeated.

"Because I'm going to have a child," she said.

"Oh—" he exclaimed. He drew back, and lifted his hands to his face. Then he turned from her and walked up to the mantelpiece. He must have caught sight of his own disordered features in the mirror, for he moved away, and stood in the middle of the room, livid and silent.

Halo could think of nothing to say. He forced a little laugh. "I see. And you want a divorce at once, because now you think he'll have to marry you?"

"I have never thought anything of the sort. I don't want him to marry me—I don't want him to know what I've told you . . . I want to be free and to shift for myself . . . that's all."

He looked down with knotted brows. "Then this divorce business—what's your object? If what you tell me is true, I don't see what you want—or why you should care about a divorce, one way or the other."

She flushed. "I've no right to give your name to another man's child. Isn't that reason enough? Can't you understand that a woman should want to be free, and alone with her child?" she burst out passionately.

She saw the reflection of her flush in his face. When the blood rose under his fair skin it burned him to the temples, and then ebbed at once, leaving him ashcoloured. He moved about the room vaguely, and then came back to her.

"I had no idea—"

"No; of course. But now you must see . . ."

He lifted his eyes to hers. "There are women who wouldn't have been so honest—"

"Are there? I don't know. Please think of what I've asked you, Lewis."

She saw that he was no longer listening to what she

said. All his faculties were manifestly concentrated on some sudden purpose that was struggling to impose itself on his will. He spoke again. "Some women, if only for their child's sake—"

"Would lie? Is that what you mean?"

"Well—isn't it perhaps your duty? I mean, to think first of your child's future? Consider what I've said from that point of view if you can . . ."

She returned his gaze with a frightened stare. What was he hinting at, trying to offer her? Her heart shrank from the possibility, and then suddenly melted. Lewis— poor Lewis! What were these depths she had never guessed in him? Had she after all known him so little? Her eyes filled, and she stood silent.

"Halo—you see, don't you? I . . . I want you to realize . . . to think of it in that way. You'll need help more than ever now. Halo, why don't you answer? I'd be good to the child," he said brokenly.

She went up to him and took his hand. It was cold and shook in her touch. "Thank you for that—most of all. It can't be as you wish; but I'll never forget. Words are stupid—I don't know what to say."

"To say—to say? There's nothing to say. The child . . . the child would be mine, you understand."

She shook her head. "I understand. And I shall always feel that you're my best friend. But I can't go back to you and be your wife. You'd be the first to regret it if I did. Don't think me hard or ungrateful. Only let me go my way."

He turned and rested his elbows on the mantelpiece, and his head on his clasped hands. She saw that he was struggling to recover his composure before he spoke again. "Ah, your pride—your pride!" he broke out bitterly. She was silent, and he turned back to her with a burst of vehemence. "I suppose, though you won't acknowledge it even to yourself, you really hope Weston will come back and marry you when he hears of this?"

"If he hears of it he will certainly offer to marry me. But for that very reason I don't want him to know —not at present. I don't want him to feel under any sort of obligation. . ."

"Has he made you as unhappy as that?"

"Don't we all make each other unhappy, sooner or later—often without knowing it? I sometimes think I've got beyond happiness or unhappiness—I don't feel as if I were made for them any more. I have nothing to complain of—or to regret. But I want to be alone; to go my own way, without depending on anybody. I want to be Halo Spear again—that's all."

Tarrant listened with bent head. She saw that he was bewildered at the depth of his own failure. He had been prepared—perhaps—to regret his offer; but not to have it refused. It had never occurred to him that such an extreme of magnanimity could defeat itself. "Is that really all—all you've got to say?"

"Since I can't say what you wish, Lewis—what else is there?"

His white lips twitched. "No; you're right. I suppose there's nothing." He had grown guarded and noncommittal again; she saw that to press her point at that moment was impossible. She held out her hand.

"It's goodbye, then. But as friends—as true friends, Lewis?"

"Oh, as friends," he echoed rigidly.

He did not seem to notice her extended hand. She saw that he hardly knew where he was, or what he was doing; but some old instinct of conformity made him precede her to the door, open it for her, walk silently at her side down the passage to the lift.

"I'd rather walk downstairs," she said; but he insisted gravely: "It's four flights. You'd better wait. In a moment; it will be here in a moment."

They stood by each other in silence, miles of distance already between them, while they waited for the preliminary rattle and rumble from below; then the mirror-lined box shot up, opened its door, and took her in.

THE EUPHORIA "Free Speaker" had expended its biggest head-lines on the illustrious novelist's return, and Vance, the morning after his arrival, woke to find himself besieged by reporters, autograph-collectors, photographers, prominent citizens and organizers of lecture-tours.

He had forgotten how blinding and deafening America's greeting to the successful can be, and his first impulse was to fly or to lie concealed; but he saw that his parents not only took the besieging of the house for granted, but would have felt there was something lacking in their son's achievement had it not called forth this tribute. Even Grandma Scrimser—now rooted to her armchair by some paralyzing form of rheumatism—shone on him tenderly and murmured "The college'll have to give him an honorary degree now," as he jumped up to receive the fiftieth interviewer, or to answer the hundredth telephone call.

"You remember, darling, that summer way back, when we sat one day on the porch at Crampton, and you told me you'd had a revelation of God—a God of your own was the way you put it? A sort of something in you that stretched out and out, and upward and upward, and took in all time and all space? I remember it so well, although my words are not as beautiful as yours. At the time I was sure it meant you had a call to the ministry. But now, sitting here and reading in the papers what all the big folks say about your books, I've begun to wonder if it wasn't your Genius speaking in you,

and maybe spreading its wings to carry you up by another way to the One God—who is Jesus?" Her great
blue eyes, paler but still so beautiful, filled with the easy
tears of the old as she drew Vance down to her. And after that she advised him earnestly not to refuse to address his fellow-citizens from the platform of the new
Auditorium Theatre. "They've got a right to see you
and hear you, Vanny; they expect it. It's something you
privileged people owe to the rest of the world. And besides, it's good business; nothing'll make your books sell
better than folks being able to see what you look like,
and go home and say: 'Vance Weston? Why, sure I know
him. I heard him lecture the other day out at Euphoria.
Of course I'm going to buy his new book'. It's the human touch you see, darling."

The human touch, artfully combined with a regard
for the main chance, still ruled in Mrs. Scrimser's world,
and her fading blue eyes shone with the same blend of
other-worldliness and business astuteness as when she
had started on her own successful career as preacher and
reformer. All the family had been brought up in the
same school, without even suspecting that there might
be another; and they ascribed Vance's reluctance to be
made a show of to ill-health and private anxieties.

"It's all that woman's doing. He's worn to a bone,
and I can hardly get him to touch his food," Mrs. Weston grumbled to her mother; and Vance, chancing to
overhear her, knew that the woman in question was
Halo. He understood that his life with Halo was something to be accounted for and explained away, and that
the pride the family had felt in his prospective marriage
("a Park Avenue affair", as Mrs. Weston had boasted)
increased the mortification of having to own that it had
not taken place. "Some fuss about a divorce—don't they
have divorce in the Eastern States, anyhow?" she en-

quired sardonically, as if no lack of initiative would surprise her in the original Thirteen. The explanation was
certainly unsatisfactory; and sooner than have it supposed that Vance might have been thrown over, she let
slip that he and the young woman were living together
—"society queen and all the rest of it. Of course she
won't let him go. . ." That had not been quite satisfac-
tory either. It had arrayed against him the weightiest
section of Mapledale Avenue, and excited in the other,
and more youthful, half, an unwholesome curiosity as
to his private affairs, stimulated by the conviction that
the family were "keeping back" something discredit-
able, and perhaps unmentionable; since it was obvious
that two people who wanted to live together had only to
legalize their caprice by a trip to Reno.

All this Vance had learned from his sister Mae during a midnight talk the day after his arrival. His eldest
sister, Pearl, who was small and plain, and had inherited
her mother's sturdy common-sense, had married well
and gone to live at Dakin; but Mae, who was half-pretty
and half-artistic and half-educated, and had thought
herself half engaged to two or three young men who had
not shared her view, had remained at home and grown
disillusioned and censorious. She did not understand
Vance any better than the rest of the family, and he
knew it; but the spirit of opposition caused her to ad-
mire in him whatever the others disapproved of, and for
want of an intelligent ear he had to turn to a merely
sympathetic one.

"The Auditorium's sold out already for your reading; and I know they're crazy to invite you to the Saturday night dinner-dance at the new Country Club. But
some of the old cats want to know what this is about
your living abroad with a married woman—that Mrs.
Dayton Alsop, who was divorced twice before she caught

old Alsop, is one of the worst ones, I guess." Vance
laughed, and said he didn't give a damn for dinner-
dances at the Country Club, and Mae, with sudden bitterness, rejoined: "I suppose there's nothing out here
you do give a damn for, as far as society goes. But of
course if you don't go they'll say it's because they
wouldn't ask you. . ."

The next day his grandmother seized the opportunity of Mrs. Weston's morning marketing to ask Vance
to come to her room for a talk; and after the exchange
of reminiscences, always so dear to the old, she put a
gentle question about his marriage. He told her that he
didn't believe he was going to get married, and seeing
the pain in those eyes he could never look at with indifference, he added: "It's all my fault; but you mustn't
let it fret you, because Halo, who's awfully generous,
understands perfectly, and agrees that the experiment
has probably lasted long enough. So that's all there is to
it."

"All?" She returned his look anxiously. "It seems to
me just a beginning. A bad beginning, if you like; but
so many are. That don't mean much. I understood the
trouble was she couldn't get her divorce—the husband
wouldn't let her. Is that so?"

"Yes. But I suppose she'd have ended by going out
to Reno, though the crowd she was brought up in hate
that kind of thing worse than poison."

"Hate it—why?" Mrs. Scrimser looked surprised.
"Isn't it better than going against God's command-
ments?"

"Well, maybe. But they think out there in New
York—Halo's kind do—that when one of the parties has
put himself or herself in the wrong, they've got no right
to lie about it in court, and Halo would have loathed
getting a divorce on the pretext that her husband had

deserted her, when the truth was she'd left him because she wanted to come and live with me."

This visibly increased Mrs. Scrimser's perplexity, but Vance saw that her native sense of fairness made her wish to understand his side of the case.

"Well, I always say it's a pity the young people don't bear with each other a little longer. I don't think they ought to rush out and get a divorce the way you'd buy a package of salts of lemon. It ain't such a universal cure either. . . But as long as you and she had decided you couldn't get along without each other—"

"But now we see we can, so it don't matter," Vance interrupted. His grandmother gave an incredulous laugh.

"Nonsense, child—how can you tell, when you haven't been married? All the rest's child-play, jokes; the only test is getting married. It's the daily wear and tear, and the knowing-it's-got-to-be-made-to-do, that keeps people together; not making eyes at each other by the moonlight. And when there's a child to be worried over, and looked after, and sat up nights with, and money put by for it—oh, then. . ." Mrs. Scrimser leaned back with closed eyes and a reminiscent smile. "I'd almost say it's the worries that make married folks sacred to each other—and what do you two know of all that?"

Vance's eyes filled. He had a vision of the day when Laura Lou's mother had entreated him to set her daughter free, when release had shone before him like a sunrise, and he had turned from it—why? Perhaps because, as Mrs. Scrimser said, worries made married folks sacred to each other. He hadn't known then—he didn't now. He merely felt that, in Laura Lou's case, the irritating friction of familiarity had made separation unthinkable, while in regard to himself and Halo, their perpetual mutual insistence on not being a burden to each other, on scrupulously respecting each other's freedom, had somehow worn the tie thin instead of strengthening it. This was certainly the case as far as he was concerned, and Halo appeared to share his view. Splendid and generous as she had been when he had come to her with his unhappy confession, their last weeks at Oubli seemed to have made it as clear to her as to him that their experiment had reached its term. It was she who had insisted on his going to America to see his family and his publishers; she who had expressly stipulated that they should separate as old friends, but without any project of reunion. But it was useless to try to explain this to his grandmother, whose experience had been drawn from conditions so much more primitive that Halo's fine shades of sentiment would have been unintelligible to her.

Suddenly Mrs. Scrimser laid her hand on his. "Honour bright, Van—is it another woman?"

He flushed under her gaze. "It's a whole complex of things—it's me as the Lord made me, I suppose: a bunch of ill-assorted odds and ends. I couldn't make any woman happy—so what's the use of worrying about it?"

Mrs. Scrimser put her old withered hands on his shoulders and pushed him back far enough to scrutinize his face. "You young fool, you—as if being happy was the whole story! It's only the preface: any woman worth her salt'll tell you that."

He bent over and kissed her. "The trouble is, Gran, I'm not worth any woman's salt."

She shook her head impatiently. "Don't you go running yourself down, either. It's the quickest short-cut to losing your self-respect. And all your fine writing won't help you if you haven't got that." She stretched out her hand for her spectacles, and took up the last number of "Zion's Spotlight". "I guess there'll be an article about you in here next week. They're sure to send somebody over to hear your talk at the Auditorium," she called after him proudly as he left the room.

Vance walked slowly down Mapledale Avenue, and through the centre of the town to the Elkington House. The aspect of Euphoria had changed almost as much as his father's boasts has led him to expect. The fabulous development of the Shunts motor industry, and the consequent growth of the manufacturing suburb at Crampton, had revived real estate speculation, and the creation of the new Country Club on the heights across the river was rapidly turning the surrounding district into a millionaire suburb. The fashionable, headed by the Shuntses, were already selling their Mapledale Avenue houses to buy land on the heights; and a corresponding spread of luxury showed itself in the development of the shopping district, the erection of the new Auditorium Theatre, and the cosmopolitan look of cinemas, garages, and florists' and jewellers' windows. Even the mouldy old Elkington House had responded by turning part of its ground floor into a plate-glass-fronted lobby with theatre agency, tobacconist and newspaper stall. Vance paused to study the renovated façade of the hotel; then he walked up the steps and passed through the revolving doors. On the threshold a sudden recoil checked him. Memory had evoked the night when, hurriedly summoned from the office of the "Free Speaker", he had found Grandpa Scrimser collapsed under the glaring electrolier of the old bar, his legs dangling like a marionette's, his conquering curls flat on his damp forehead. Vance heard the rattle of the ambulance down the street, and saw the men carrying Grandpa's limp body across the lobby to the door—and it was hateful to him that, at this moment, the scene should return with such cruel precision. It was as if, all those years, Grandpa had kept that shaft up his ghostly sleeve.

Vance turned to the reception clerk. "Miss Delaney?" he asked, his voice sounding thick in his throat.

The clerk took the proper time to consider. He was showy but callow, and a newcomer since Vance's last visit to Euphoria. "I guess you're Mr. Weston, the novelist?" he queried, his excitement overcoming his professional dignity. "Why, yes, Miss Delaney said she was expecting you. Will you step right into the reception room? You won't be disturbed there. But perhaps first you'll do me a great favour—? Fact is, I'm a member of the Mapledale Avenue Autograph Club, and your signature in this little book. . ."

Vance's hand shook so that he could hardly form the letters of his name. He followed the grateful clerk, who insisted on conducting him in person to a heavily-gilded reception room with three layers of window curtains and a sultry smell of hot radiators. "Why, this is where the old bar was!" Vance exclaimed involuntarily. The reception clerk raised his eyebrows in surprise. "That must have been a good while ago," he said disdainfully, as if the new Elkington did not care to be reminded of the old; and Vance echoed: "Yes—a good while."

He stood absently contemplating the richly-bound volumes of hotel and railway advertisements on the alabaster centre-table, the blood so loud in his ears that he did not hear a step behind him. "Why, Van!" Floss Delaney's voice sounded, and he turned with a start. "Is it really you?" he stammered, looking at her like a man in a trance.

"Of course it's me. Do I look like somebody else?"

"No . . . I only meant. . . I didn't ever expect to see y u again." He paused, and she stood listening with her faint smile while his eyes felt their way slowly over her face.

"But didn't you get my note?" she asked.

"Yes. I got it. I only landed last week. I meant to stay in New York and see about my new book—the one that's just out. And then I saw in the New York papers that you were out here; and so I came."

She took this halting avowal as if it were her due, but remained silent, not averted or inattentive but simply waiting, as her way was, to see what he would say next. He paused too, finding no words to utter what was struggling in him. "The paper I saw said you'd come out on business."

Her face took on the eager look it had worn at Brambles when Alders had called her to the telephone. "Yes, I have. There's a big deal going on in that new Country Club district; I guess you've heard about it from your father. I got wind of it last summer—just after that time you were down in the country with me, it must have been—and I cabled right home, and bought up all the land I could. And now I've had two or three big offers, and I thought I'd better come and look over the ground myself. I've got the Shunts interests against me; they're trying to buy all the land that's left, and I stand to make a good thing out of it if I keep my nerve," she ended, a lovely smile animating her tranquil lips.

Vance looked at her perplexedly. When he had lit on that paragraph the day after landing, the idea of seeing her again swept away every other consideration, and he had thrown over his New York engagements and hurried out to Euphoria lest he should get there too late to find her. But on his arrival a note reassured him; she

had gone to Dakin for two or three days with her lawyer, on some real-estate business, but would soon be
back at the Elkington, where she asked him to call. And
there she stood in her calm beauty, actually smiling
about that day at Brambles, as if to her it were a mere
happy midsummer memory, and she assumed it to be no
more to him! Probably the assumption was genuine; she
had forgotten the end of that day, forgotten his desperate attempts to see her and plead with her in London—
as she had no doubt forgotten the remoter and crueller
memories roused by seeing her again at Euphoria. It was
perhaps the contrast between her statue-like calm and
his own inward turmoil that drew him back to her.
There was something exasperating and yet mysteriously
stimulating in the thought that she recalled the day
when she had deserted him at Brambles only because it
was that on which she had first heard of a promising real-
estate deal.

"Do you know what this room is?" he exclaimed
with sudden bitterness. "It's the old bar of the hotel."

She lifted her delicately curved eyebrows. "Oh, is
it—? What of it?" her look seemed to add.

"Yes; and the last time I was here it was in the middle of the night, when they rang me up at the 'Free
Speaker' to say that my grandfather'd had a stroke.
There's where the sofa stood where I saw him lying." He
pointed to a divan of stamped velvet under an ornate
wall-clock.

Her glance followed his. "I don't believe it's the
same sofa—they seem to have done the whole place up,"
she said indifferently; and Vance saw from her cloudy
brow that she was annoyed with him for bringing up
such memories. "I hate to hear about people dying," she
confessed with a slight laugh; "let's talk about you, shall
we?" But he knew it was herself and her own affairs that

she wanted to discourse upon; and merely to hear her voice again, and watch the faint curve of her lips as she spoke, was so necessary to him that he stammered: "No —tell me first what you've been doing. That's what I want to know."

She gave a little murmur of pleasure and dropped down on the divan under the clock. Probably she had already forgotten that it was there that Vance had seen his grandfather lying, as she had also forgotten, long since, that for her anything painful was associated with the old man's name. A soft glow of excitement suffused her. "Well, I have got heaps to tell you—oceans! Why do you stand off there? Here; come and sit by me. . . So much seems to have happened lately, don't it? So you've got a new book coming out?" She made way for him on the divan, and shrinking a little at his own thoughts he sat down at her side, her arm brushing his. "And if I can get ahead of the Shuntses, and pull this off. . . See here, Van," she interrupted herself, with a glance at the jewelled dial at her wrist, "I'm afraid I can't let you stay much longer now; young Honoré Shunts, the son of the one who's trying to buy up the heights, has asked me to run out with him to the Country Club presently, and of course it's very important for me to be on good terms with that crowd just now. You see that, don't you?"

The dizzy drop of his disappointment left Vance silent. "Now, at once? You're sacking me already?"

"Only for a little while, dear. Everything depends on this deal. If I can get young Shunts so I can do what I want with him. . ." She smiled down mystically on her folded hands.

"Get him to think you're going to marry him, you mean? I thought you were engaged to Spartivento when I saw you in London?"

She gathered her brows in the effort to explore

those remote recesses of the past. "Was I, darling? Being engaged don't count much, anyhow—does it? What I've got to do first is to get this deal through. Then we'll see. But I'm not going to think about marrying anybody till then." She looked at her watch again. "There's somebody coming round from the bank too, with some papers for me to sign. . . But couldn't we dine together somewhere, darling? Isn't there some place where there's a cabaret, and we could have a good long talk afterward? I'm off to New York tomorrow."

"Tomorrow? And of course every minute's filled up with business till then—" he interrupted bitterly.

"Well, business is what I came for. Anyhow, why can't we dine together tonight?"

"Because it's just the one night I can't. I'm engaged to give a lecture at the Auditorium, with readings from my book." Black gloom filled him as he spoke; but her eyes brightened with interest. "You are? Why, Van, how splendid! Why didn't you tell me so before? I've never been inside the Auditorium, have you? They say it seats two thousand people. Do you think you'll be able to fill it? But of course you will! Look at the way the smart set rushed after you in London. And they told me over there that this new book was going to be a bigger seller than anything you've done yet. Oh, Van, don't it feel *great* to come back here and have everybody crowding round because you're so famous? Do you suppose there's a seat left—do you think you can get one for me, darling? Let's go out and ask the ticket-agent right off—" She was on her feet, alive and radiant as when they had driven up to Brambles and she had sprung out to plunge her arms into the lily-pool.

"Oh, I can get you a ticket all right. I'll get you a box if you like. But you hate readings—why on earth should you want to come? Besides, what does all that matter? If you're going away tomorrow, how can I see you again—and when?"

He remembered her talent for eluding her engagements, and was fiercely resolved to hold her fast to this one. He had something to say to her—something that he now felt must be said at any cost, and without delay. After that—. "You must tell me now, before I go, how I can see you," he insisted.

She drooped her lids a little, and smiled up under them. "Why, I guess we can manage somehow. Can't you bring me back after the reading? That would be lovely. . . I'll wait for you in the lobby at the Auditorium. I've got my own sitting-room here, and I think I can fix it up with the reception clerk to have some supper sent up. He was fearfully excited when I told him who you were." She looked at him gaily, putting her hands on his shoulders. "I guess I owe you that after Brambles—don't I, Van?"

❧ XXXVI ❧

WHEN HE got back to the house, his brain reeling with joy, Mae pounced out at him with a large silver-gray envelope crested with gold.

"There! You say you won't fill the Auditorium! And I told you myself that Mrs. Dayton Alsop was dead against you on account of—well, the things we talked about the other night. And here's what it is to be a celebrity! She's invited you to a supper-party after the reading—she's invited us all. Mother says she won't go; she's got no clothes, to begin with. And I guess father won't, if she don't. But I've got my black lace with paillettes. You won't be ashamed to be seen with me in that, will you, Van? I never thought I'd see the inside of the Alsop house—did you?" Her sallow worried face was rejuvenated by excitement and coquetry.

Vance stood gloomily examining the envelope. "Supper—tonight?" He thrust the invitation back into her hand. "Sorry—I can't go. I've got another engagement. You'll have to coax father to take you."

Mae grew haggard again. "Vance! Another engagement—tonight? You can't have! Why, the supper's given for you; don't you understand? Mrs. Dayton Alsop—"

"Oh, damn Mrs. Dayton Alsop!"

His sister's eyes filled. "I think you're crazy, perfectly crazy . . . the supper's *given for you*," she repeated plaintively.

"I've told you I'm sorry. I was never told anything about this supper. . . I've got another engagement."

Mae looked at him with searching insistence. "You can't have an engagement with anybody that matters as much as Mrs. Dayton Alsop. Everybody'll say—"

He burst into an irritated laugh. "Let 'em say what they like! My engagement happens to matter to me more than a thousand Mrs. Alsops."

"You say that just to show how you despise us all!" his sister reproached him.

"Put it on any ground you please. The plain fact is that an engagement's an engagement. Write and tell her so, will you? Tell her I'm awfully sorry, but her invitation came too late."

"But she explains that in her letter. She got the party up at the last minute because she wasn't sure if she could get the right band. She wanted to make sure of the Dakin Blackbirds. She always wants the best of everything at her parties. . . You'll have to write to her yourself, Vance."

"Oh, very well." He flung away and went up to his room. He knew that to refuse this invitation would be not only a discourtesy to Euphoria's ruling hostess but a bitter blow to the family pride. How could he account to them for his mysterious midnight engagement? An evasion which would have passed unnoticed in a big city would be set all Euphoria buzzing. Everybody in the place would know that no other party was being given that evening; it would be assumed at once that he was going off on a drinking bout with some low associates, and the slight to his hostess and his family would be all the greater. But at that moment he could not conceive of any inducement or obligation that could have kept him from meeting Floss after the reading, and going back to the hotel with her. It was not only his irresistible longing for her that impelled him. He wanted something decisive, final, to come out of this encounter. He had reached a point in his bewildered course when the need to take a definite step, to see his future shape itself before him in whatever sense, was almost as strong as his craving for her nearness. A phrase of his grandmother's: "Nothing counts but marriage" returned unexpectedly to his mind, and he thought: "It ought to have been Halo—but that's not to be. And anyhow I'm not fit for her." With Floss Delaney it would be different. Certain obscure fibres in both their natures seemed inextricably entangled. There was a dumb subterranean power in her that corresponded with his own sense of the forces by which his inventive faculty was fed. He did not think this out clearly; he merely felt that something final, irrevocable, must come out of their meeting that night. He took up his pen, and began: "My dear Mrs. Alsop—"

Three days later, in the New York train, Vance sat trying to piece together the fragments of his adventure. Everything about it was still so confused and out of focus that he could only put his recollections together in broken bits, brooding over each, and waiting for the missing ones to fit themselves in little by little, and make a picture.

The theatre: gigantic, opening before him light and glaring as the Mouth of Hell in a mediæval fresco he and Halo had seen in a church somewhere. . . Rows and rows of faces, all suddenly individual and familiar, centered on him in their intense avidity, as if his name were written in huge letters over each of them. . . Then, as he settled his papers on the little table in front of him—in the hush following the endless rounds of applause which pulled his head forward at rhythmic intervals, like an invisible wire jerking a marionette—the sudden stir in a stage box, Mrs. Alsop's box (that heavy over-blown figure was hers, he supposed, and at her side, slim and amber-warm, Floss standing up, looking calmly about the house while her dusky furs slipped from her. . .)

Yes, it was God's own luck, he saw it now, that before he could get that cursed letter to Mrs. Alsop written Floss had summoned him to the telephone (ah, Mae's face as she brought the message!) to announce peremptorily that she couldn't meet him in the lobby after the theatre because Mrs. Alsop had invited her to the party, and she was to go to the theatre in Mrs. Alsop's box, and young Honoré Shunts was going with them . . . and oh, *please,* Vance wasn't to make a fuss, and the party wouldn't last all night, would it, and afterward what was to prevent—? And wouldn't he be very very sweet, and give her just one look—the very last—before he began his lecture? . . . Well, no, the party wouldn't last all night, he supposed. . .

And now he was speaking: "Ladies and gentlemen, if anybody had told me in the old days—" God! What a flat beginning! He didn't pretend to be a professional speaker. . . But at last the preliminaries were over, and he found himself in the middle of "Colossus." First he read them the fragment about the buried torso in the desert—the episode which symbolized all that was to follow. . . How attentive they were, how hushed! As usual, the wings of his imagination lifted him above mortal contingencies, and his voice soared over the outspread silence. But gradually he began to be conscious of the dense nonconductive quality of that silence, of the fact that not a word he said traversed its impenetrable medium. The men were fidgeting in their seats like children in church; the women were openly consulting their pocket-mirrors. A programme dropped from the gallery, and every head was turned to see it fall. Vance could hear his voice flagging and groping as he hurried on from fragment to fragment. . . Which was it now? Ah: the descent to the Mothers, the crux, the centre of the book. He had put the whole of himself into that scene—and his self had come out of Euphoria, been conceived and fashioned there, made of the summer heat on endless wheat-fields, the frozen winter skies, the bell of the Roman Catholic church ringing through the stillness, on nights when he couldn't sleep, after the last trolley-rattle had died out; the plants budding along the ditches on the way to Crampton, the fiery shade of the elm-grove down by the river . . . he had been made out of all this, had come out of all this, and there, in rows before him, sat his native protoplasm, and wriggled in its seats, and twitched at its collar-buttons, and didn't understand him. . . And at last it was over, and the theatre rang and rang with the grateful applause of the released. . .

And at Mrs. Alsop's, with champagne sparkling and the right band banging, and flowers and pretty women and white shirt-fronts, how quickly the boredom was forgotten, the flagging ardour rekindled, how proud they all were of their home-made genius, how they admired him and were going to swagger about him—how the President of the College hinted playfully at an Honorary Degree, and the pretty women palpitated, and the members of the Culture Club joked about the bewilderment of the Philistines: "You've given them something to take home and think about this time!" And after that everything melted again into a golden blur of heat and wine and crowding, out of which Floss Delaney detached herself, firm and vivid, and while Mrs. Alsop's guests scattered in a sudden snow-fall, and the Dakin Blackbirds scuttled away with raised coat-collars under the leafless elms, Vance had found himself in a motor at her side, twisting down the new road from the heights, crossing the bridge, gliding through the snow-white streets to the hotel, and descending there at a mysterious side-door. ("I gave the reception clerk my ticket for the lecture—and here's his private key," she said with a little laugh.)

He had meant to stay at Euphoria for a week or two longer. He knew the bitter disappointment that his hurried departure was causing his family, and especially his grandmother and Mae, one of whom had dreamed of further ovations for the genius, the other of opportunities to be invited to the new houses on the heights. But he could not put off seeing Floss again, could not leave the tormenting ecstasy of their last hours together without a sequel. Everything drew him on to a dark future shot with wild lightnings of hope.

Floss had not realized till then what a public figure he was. The way people had crowded around him at Mrs. Alsop's seemed to have struck her even more than his popularity in London. She admitted it herself. "It does feel funny, don't it, Van—you and I being in the spotlight out here at Euphoria? In Europe it's different —don't you suppose I know that not one of the big people over there care a hoot where we come from as long as we amuse them? If we'd served a term they wouldn't care. . . But out here in Euphoria, where they know us inside out, and yet have got to kotow to us, and get up parties for us, and everybody fighting to be introduced, and people who've only been here since the boom pretending they played with us when we were children . . . Yes, I guess that 'dough-face', as you call him, who was following me round everywhere, *was* young Shunts. Looks as if I'd got him running, don't it? But he's not

half as crazy about me as the President of the College—
did you notice? Oh, Van, I'd love to make them all feel
that way in New York, wouldn't you? And I guess it
would be a lot easier than at Euphoria."

Yes; New York was what she wanted now. And she
was sure of it if only she could pull off her deal, and
force the Shuntses to buy her out at a big figure. If she
could get round that young Shunts, who knew what
might happen? At daylight, when they parted, she made
Vance promise with her last kiss to come to New York as
soon as he could. She said she didn't dare try her luck
there without an old friend to back her up; and in a
flash of joy and irony he understood that she was already
calculating on the social value of his young celebrity, on
the fact that he could probably "place" her in New
York, get her more quickly into the inaccessible houses
that were the only ones she cared about. "You will, darling, darling?" . . . And now he was on his way to keep
his promise.

He remembered thinking, before the reading, that
when he met Floss again that night, something final, irrevocable, must come of it. He meant to make her understand that this was no mere lovers' tryst without a
morrow, but a turning-point in his life, a meeting on
which his whole future depended. It was as if he could
justify his break with Halo only by creating for himself
a new tie, more binding, more unescapable. He would
have felt ashamed to admit that anything but the need
to stabilize his life, to be in harmony again with himself
and his work, could have forced him to such a step.
Halo had seen that, he was sure; she had understood it.
If he was to follow his calling he must be protected from
the sterile agitation of these last years. Marriage and a
home; normal conditions; that was what he craved and

needed. And Floss Delaney seemed to personify the strong emotional stimulant on which his intellectual life must feed. Intellectual comradeship between lovers was unattainable; that was not the service women could render to men. But the old mysterious bond of blood which seemed to exist between certain human beings, which youth sought for blindly, and maturity continued restlessly to crave—that must be the secret soil in which alone the artist's faculty could ripen. He saw it all now, looked on it with the wide-open eyes of passion and disillusionment. A few years ago he would have plunged into the adventure blindly, craving only the repetition of its dark raptures. But now it seemed to him that while his senses flamed his intelligence remained cool. He knew that Floss would always be what she was—he could no more influence or shape her than he could bend or shape a marble statue. But he needed her, and perhaps she needed him, though for reasons so different; and out of that double need there might come a union so deep-rooted and instinctive that neither, having once known it, could do without it. Perhaps that was what his grandmother had in mind when she said marriage made people sacred to each other. If, after a life-time with Grandpa Scrimser, she could still believe in the sanctifying influence of wedlock, then the real unbreakable tie between bodies and soul must have its origin in depths of which the average man and woman were hardly conscious, but which the poet groped for and fed on with all his hungry tentacles.

All this he had meant to make Floss understand— not in the poet's speech, which would mean nothing to her, but in the plain words of his passion. He must make her see that they belonged to each other, that they were necessary to each other, that their future meetings could not be left to depend on chance or whim. He meant to plead with her, reason with her, dominate her with the full strength of his will. . . And all that had come of it was that, as her arms slipped from his shoulders, and her last kiss from his lips, he had promised to follow her to New York.

☙ XXXVII ❧

DURING THE two months since Vance's return to New York "Colossus" had taken the high seas of publicity, and was now off full sail on its adventurous voyage. Where would the great craft land? It had been reviewed from one end of the continent to the other, and from across the seas other reviews were pouring in. The first notices, as usual in such cases, were made largely out of left-over impressions of "The Puritan in Spain"; but a few, in the literary supplements of the big papers, and in the high-brow reviews, were serious though somewhat bewildered attempts to analyze the new book and relate it to the author's previous work, and in two or three of these articles Vance caught a hint of the doubt which had so wounded him on Halo's lips. Was this novel, the critics asked—in spite of the many striking and admirable qualities they recognized in it—really as original, as personal as, in their smaller way, its two predecessors had been? "Instead" and "The Puritan in Spain", those delicate studies of a vanished society, had an individual note that the more ambitious "Colossus" lacked. . . And the author's two striking short stories—"One Day" and "Unclaimed"—showed that his touch could be vigorous as well as tender, that his rendering of the present was as acute and realistic as his evocations of the past were suffused with poetry. . . Of this rare combination of qualities what use had he made in "Colossus"? On this query the critics hung their reserves and their regrets. The author's notable beginnings had led them to hope that at last a born novelist had arisen among the self-conscious little essayists who were trying to substitute the cold processes of the laboratory for the lightning art of creation. (The turn of this made Vance wonder if Frenside had not come back to fiction reviewing.)

It was a pity, they said, that so original a writer had been influenced by the fashion of the hour (had he then, he wondered, flushing?) at the very moment when the public, not only the big uncritical public but the acute and cultivated minority, were rebelling against these laborious substitutes for the art of fiction, and turning with recovered appetite to the exquisite freshness and spontaneity of such books as David Dorr's "Heavenly Archer", the undoubted triumph of the year. (David Dorr? A new name to Vance. He sent out instantly for "Heavenly Archer", rushed through it, and flung it from him with a groan.)

Some books fail slowly, imperceptibly, as though an insidious disease had undermined them; others plunge from the heights with a crash, and thus it was with "Colossus". Halo had been right—slowly he was beginning to see it. "Colossus" was not his own book, brain of his brain, flesh of his flesh, as it had seemed while he was at work on it, but a kind of hybrid monster made out of the crossing of his own imaginings with those imposed on him by the literary fashions and influences of the day. He could have borne the bitterness of this discovery, borne the adverse criticisms and the uncomfortable evidence of sales steadily diminishing, as the book, instead of gathering momentum, flagged and wallowed in the general incomprehension. All that would have meant nothing but for two facts; first that in his secret self he had to admit the justice of the more enlightened strictures, to recognize that his masterpiece, in the making, had turned into a heavy lifeless production, had literally died on his hands; and secondly that its failure must inevitably affect his relations with Floss Delaney. He had always known that she would measure his achievement only by the material and social advantages it brought her, and that she wanted only the successful about her. And he was discovering how soon the green mould of failure spreads over the bright surface of popularity, how eagerly the public turns from an idol to which it has to look up to one exactly on its level. (" 'Heavenly Archer'—oh, God!" he groaned, and kicked the pitiful thing across the floor.)

Had he gone back to his old New York world—to Rebecca Stram's studio and the cheap restaurants where the young and rebellious gathered—he might have had a different idea of the impression produced by his book. These young men, though they had enjoyed his early ardours and curiosities, had received his first novels with a shrug; but "Colossus" appealed to them by its very defects. Like most artistic coteries they preferred a poor work executed according to their own formula to a good one achieved without it; and they would probably have championed Vance and his book against the world if he had shown himself among them. But there was no hope of meeting Floss Delaney at Rebecca Stram's or the Cocoanut Tree, and Vance cared only to be where she was, and among the people she frequented. His return to the New York he had known when he was on "The Hour" was less of a personal triumph than he had hoped. In certain houses where he knew that Floss particularly wanted to be invited he was less known as the brilliant author of "The Puritan in Spain" than as the obscure young man with whom Halo Tarrant had run away, to the scandal of her set; and in groups of more recent growth, where scandals counted little, celebrity was a shifting attribute, and his sceptre had already passed to David Dorr.

David Dorr was a charming young man with smooth fair hair and gentle manners. He told Vance with becoming modesty what an inspiration the latter's lovely story "Instead" had been to him, and asked if he mightn't say that he hoped Vance would some day return to that earlier vein; and none of the strictures on "Colossus" made Vance half as miserable as this condescending tribute. "If any of my books are the kind of stuff that fellow admires—" he groaned inwardly, while he watched Dorr surrounded by enraptured ladies, and imagined him saying in his offensively gentle voice: "Oh, but you know you're not fair to Weston—really not. That first book of his—what was it called?—really did have something in it. . ."

But there were moments when the mere fact of being in the same room with Floss, of watching her enjoyment and the admiration she excited, was enough to satisfy him. Mrs. Glaisher had reappeared in New York as a Russian Grand Duchess, with Spartivento and the assiduous Alders in her train, and Floss, under the grandducal wing, was beginning to climb the glittering heights of the New York world, though certain old-fashioned doors were still closed to her. "I told you it'd be harder to get on here than in London. They always begin by wanting to know who you are," she complained one day to Vance. "I guess I'm as good as any of them; but the only way to make them believe it is to have something, or to be somebody, that they've got a use for. And I mean to pull that off too; but it takes time." She had these flashes of dry philosophy, which reminded Vance of her father's definition of her character. Mr. Delaney was not in New York with his daughter. He had been prudently shipped off to Virginia to negotiate for the re-purchase of one of the Delaney farms. "It'll keep him busy," Floss explained—"and out of the way," her tone implied, though she did not say it. But she added reflectively: "I've told him I'll buy the place for him if he can get it for a reasonable price. He'll want somewhere to go when I'm married."

Vance forced a laugh. "When are we going to be married?" he wanted to ask; but he had just enough sense left to know that the moment for putting that question had not come. "Have you decided on the man?" he asked, his heart giving a thump.

She frowned, and shook her head. "Business first. Do you suppose I'm going to risk having to hang round some day and whine for alimony? Not me. I've told you already I'll never marry till I'm independent of everybody. Then I'll begin to think about it." She looked at him meditatively. "I wish your new novel wasn't so dreadfully long," she began. "I've tried to read it but I can't. The Grand Duchess told me people thought it was such a pity you hadn't done something more like your first books—why didn't you? As long as you'd found out what people wanted, what was the use of switching off on something different? You needn't think it's only because I'm not literary. . . Gratz Blemer said the other night he couldn't think what had struck you. He says you could have been a best-seller as easy as not if you'd only kept on doing things like 'The Puritan in Spain'. He doesn't think that Dorr boy's book is in it with your earlier things."

"Oh, doesn't he? That's something to be thankful for," Vance retorted mockingly.

The renewal of his acquaintance with Gratz Blemer had also been a disappointment. Vance had always respected Blemer's robust and patient realism, and his gift of animating and differentiating the characters of his densely populated works; Vance recalled the shock he had received when he had first met the novelist at the Tarrants', and heard him speak of his books as if they were mere business enterprises. Now, Vance thought, his greater literary experience might enable him to learn more from the older man, and to make allowances for his frank materialism. No one could do work of that quality without some secret standard of excellence; perhaps Blemer was so sick of undiscriminating gush that he talked as he did to protect himself from silly women and sillier disciples, and it would be interesting to break through his banter and get a glimpse of his real convictions.

Vance had seen Blemer one night at the Opera, at the back of his wife's box, and had been struck by the change in his appearance. He had always been thick-set, but now he was fat and almost flabby; he hated music (Vance remembered), and sat with his head against the wall of the box, his eyes closed, his heavy mouth half open. They met a few nights afterward in a house where the host was old-fashioned enough to take the men into a smoking-room after dinner; and here Blemer, of his own accord, came and sat down by Vance. "Well," he said heavily, "so you've got a book out."

Vance reddened. "I'm afraid it's no good," he began nervously.

"Why—isn't it selling?" Blemer asked. Without waiting for an answer he continued in a querulous tone: "I wish to God I'd brought my own cigars. I ought to have remembered the kind of thing they give you in this house." He waved a fat contemptuous hand toward the gold-belted rows in their shining inlaid cabinet. "The main thing is to get square with the reviewers first," he continued wearily. "And generally by the time a fellow's enough authority to do that, he doesn't give a damn what they say."

"I don't think I've ever cared," Vance flashed out.

Belmer drew his thick lids together. "You don't think they affect sales, one way or the other? Well, that's one view—"

"I didn't mean that. I only care for what I myself think of my work." As he spoke, Vance believed this to be true. But Blemer's attention had already wandered back to himself. "I wish I could get away somewhere. I hate this New York business—dinners and dinners—a season that lasts five months! I'd like to go up the Nile—clear away to Abyssinia. Or winter sports—ever tried 'em? Of course the Engadine's the only place. . . Write better there?" he interrupted himself, replying to a question of Vance's. He gave a little grumbling laugh. "Why, I can't write anywhere any more. Not a page or a line. That's the trouble with me." He laughed again. "Not that it matters much, as far as the shekels go. I guess my old age is provided for. . . Only—God, the days are long! Well, I suppose they're waiting for us to begin bridge." He got up with a nod to Vance. "I wish I was young enough to read your book—but I hear it's eight hundred pages," he said as he lumbered back to the drawing-room.

As the weeks passed Vance became aware that he was no nearer the object for which he had come to New York. He continued to meet Floss Delaney frequently, and in public she seemed as glad as ever to see him. But on the rare occasions when he contrived to be alone with her she was often absent-minded, and sometimes impatient of his attempts at tenderness. After all, she explained, he was the only old friend she had in New York, and it did seem hard if she couldn't be natural with him, and not bother about how she looked or what she said. This gave him a momentary sense of advantage, and made him try to be calm and reasonable; but he knew he was only one in the throng of young men about her, and not even among the most favoured. At first she had made great play of the fact that he and she came from the same place, and had romped together as children (a vision of their early intimacy that he was himself beginning to believe); but she presumably found this boast less effective than she had hoped, for though she continued to treat him with sisterly freedom he saw that she was on the verge of being bored by his importunities, and in his dread of a rebuff he joined in her laugh against himself.

For a time she talked incessantly about the Euphoria deal, and boasted of her determination to outwit the Shuntses and make them buy her out at her own price. Though Vance had grown up in an atmosphere of real-estate deals the terminology of business was always confusing to him, but he saw that she was trying to gain her end by captivating young Shunts; they were even reported to be engaged, though the fact was kept secret owing to the opposition of the young man's family. But Vance bore with this too, knowing that, even if the rumour were true, she was not likely to regard a secret engagement as binding, and trying to believe that in the long run he was sure to cut out so poor a creature as young Shunts. Of late she had ceased to speak about Euphoria, and had even (judging from the youth's love-lorn countenance) lost interest in Shunts; and this strengthened Vance's hope. She had said she would never marry till she had secured her independence; but once that was done, why should she not marry him sooner than one of the other men who were hanging about her?

He had always instinctively avoided the street in which the Tarrants used to live. He did not know if Tarrant still occupied the same flat, or even if he were in New York. He seemed to have vanished from the worldly circles which Vance frequented, and the latter had not even heard his name mentioned. "The Hour", he knew, had changed hands, and under a more efficient management had kept just a touch of "highbrow", skilfully combined with a popular appeal to cinema and sartorial interests. All this part of Vance's life had fallen in ruins, and he wished he had not been so haunted by the fear of stumbling upon them; but his visual associations were so acute that he had to go out of his way to avoid the sight of that tall façade with the swinging glass doors and panelled stone vestibule that used to be the way to bliss. One night, however, returning from a dinner where Floss had promised to meet him, and had failed to come, he was driven along on such a tide of resentment and bitterness that, without knowing where he was, he turned a corner and found himself before the Tarrant door. He was on the farther side of the street, and looking up he saw a light in the high window of the library. It gave him a sharp twist, and he was standing motionless, without strength to turn away, when the doors swung open and George Frenside's short clumsy figure issued from between the plate-glass valves. Frenside paused, as if looking for a taxi; then he crossed to Vance's side of the street, and the two men suddenly faced each other under a lamp. Vance noticed Frenside's start of surprise, and the backward jerk of his lame body; but a moment later he held out his hand. "Ah, Weston—I heard you were in New York."

Vance looked at him hesitatingly. "I'm going home soon—to my own home, at Euphoria," he explained. "I've got to be alone and write," he added, without knowing why.

He saw the ironic lift of Frenside's shaggy brows.

"Already? You've brought out a magnum opus just lately, haven't you?"

"Yes. But it's not what I wanted it to be."

"No," said Frenside bluntly. "I didn't suppose it was."

"So he's read it!" Vance thought, with a sudden flush of excitement; but Frenside's tone did not encourage further discussion. Both men stood silent, as if oppressed by each other's presence; but just as Frenside was turning away with a gesture of farewell, Vance brought out precipitately: "I suppose you see Halo's people. Can you tell me how she is?"

Frenside's face seemed to grow harsher and more guarded. "Quite well, I believe."

"She. . . I haven't heard lately. . . She's not here . . . is she?"

"In New York? Not that I'm aware of." Frenside hesitated and then said hurriedly: "If there's any message—"

Vance felt the blood rush to his forehead and then ebb. His heart shook against his breast. "Thank you . . . yes . . . I'll ask you. . ."

The two men nodded to each other and separated.

Vance walked away with his thoughts in a turmoil The meeting with Frenside had stirred up deep layers of sleeping associations. It was only three months since he had said goodbye to Halo in Paris, but the violent emotional life he had plunged into after their parting made those days seem infinitely distant. Gradually, almost unconsciously, his memories of Halo had taken on the mournful serenity of death; they lay in the depths of his consciousness, with closed lips and folded hands, as though to say that they would never trouble him again.

But his few words with Frenside, and the mere speaking of Halo's name to some one who had perhaps been with her or heard from her lately, disturbed the calm of these memories, and brought Halo back to him as a living suffering creature. Yes—suffering, he knew; and by his fault. For months he had been trying to shut his eyes and ears to that fact, as sometimes, in camp as a boy, when he heard a trapped animal crying at night far off in the woods, he would bury his head under the blankets and try to think the wail had ceased because he had closed his ears against it. . . Ah, well, no use going back to all that now. It was over and done, and he must hide his head again, and try to make himself believe the sound had ceased because he did not want to hear it. . .

Why had Floss not come to the dinner? His hostess, visibly annoyed, said she had called up at the last moment, excusing herself on the plea of a cold; but Vance suspected her of having found something more amusing to do—where, and with whom? The serpent-doubts reared their heads again, hissing in his ears; even if he had tried to listen for that other faint cry they would have drowned it. A cold? He didn't believe it for a minute. . . But it would be a pretext for calling at her hotel to ask. The hour was not late, and he would go straight to her sitting-room, without sending his name up first. Very likely she would not be there; almost certainly not. But he would leave a note for her and then go away. . . It seemed to him that even if she were out (as he was certain she would be) it would quiet him to sit in her room for a little while, among the things that belonged to her and had her scent.

The lift shot him up, and in answer to his knock he was surprised to hear her voice call out: "Come in." She lay curled up on a lounge, in a soft velvet wrapper, her hair tossed back, her feet, in gossamer stockings and heelless sandals, peeping out under a Spanish shawl. The room looked untidy yet unlived in: her fur cloak, a withered cluster of orchids pinned to it, had been flung across the piano beside an unwatered and half-dead azalea from which the donor's card still dangled; and on a gilt table stood an open box of biscuits, some dried-up sandwiches and an empty cup. Perhaps it was the fact that he had been thinking of Halo that made the scene seem so squalid in its luxury. Floss had none of Halo Tarrant's gift for making a room seem a part of herself —unless indeed this cold disorder did reflect something akin to itself in her own character.

She smiled up at Vance through rings of smoke; but she seemed too lost in her musings to be either surprised, or otherwise affected, by his appearance. "Hullo, Van," she greeted him in a happy purr.

"All that smoke's not the best thing for your throat, is it?" he said, bending over her; and she answered: "Throat? What's the matter with my throat?"

"Mrs. Stratton said you'd telephoned you couldn't dine with her because you had a cold—"

"Oh, to be sure—it was the Stratton dinner to-night." She gave a little laugh. "How was it? Who was there? Did I miss anything?"

"What were you doing instead?" he retorted; and she pointed toward an armchair at her elbow. "Oh, boy—sit down and I'll tell you." She tossed away her cigarette, and crossing her arms behind her, sank her head into the nest they made, and lay brooding, a faint tremor on lips and eyelids. Vance looked at her as if he were looking for the first time; there was a veiled radiance in her face which he had seen in it only once or twice, in moments of passionate surrender. "Van," she said slowly, as though the words were so sweet that she could hardly part with them, "Van, I've pulled it off. The cheque's locked up in my bank. The Shuntses have bought me out at my own price—I knew they would. I didn't knock off a single dollar." She laughed again and waited, as if for the approval which was her due.

Vance stood looking at her, his heart in a tumult. If she were free, if she were independent, as she called it, perhaps his moment had come! He moved forward to snatch her to him, to entreat, reason, smother her replies against his heart—but something checked him, warned him it was not yet the moment. She wanted to go on talking about herself and her triumph, and if he thwarted her with his clumsy declaration his last chance might be lost.

He dropped back into the armchair. "Tell me all about it."

The smile lingered softly on her lips. "Oh, darling, what a fight it's been! I'm half dead with it. That poor boy's only just left. I did feel sorry for him—I couldn't help it."

"What poor boy?" Van echoed, his tongue feeling dry in his throat. But he knew the answer before she made it.

"Why, Honoré Shunts, of course. That's why I had to throw over the Stratton dinner. I had to go out and dine with him—and then he came back here. He wouldn't listen to reason; but he had to. I never saw anybody cry so. I told him I couldn't stand it—it was unmanly of him, don't you think it was? And I couldn't keep his letters, could I, when the family were so set on getting them away from me? I thought I'd never make him understand. . . But now I guess I can take a holiday." She sank more deeply into her cushions, her lids drooping, her lips slightly parted, as though with the first breathings of sleep. "I'm dead tired, dead. . ."

Vance sat with his eyes fixed on her. Every word she spoke burned itself slowly into his consciousness. He wanted to cry out, to question her—to fling his indignation and horror into her face. It was all as clear as day. She had held the socially ambitious Shuntses through the boy's letters; she had forced them to buy up her land at her own price through their dread lest the heir to their millions should marry her. By this simple expedient she had attained fortune and liberty at a stroke—there had been nothing difficult about it but the boy's crying. She had thought that unmanly; an obvious warning to Vance not to repeat the same mistake. Floss always liked the people about her to be cheerful; he knew that. And after all perhaps she was right. Was a poor half-wit like young Shunts worth wasting a pang over? Yes; but the boy had cried—that was the worst of it. Vance seemed to feel those tears in his own throat; it was so thick with them that he could hardly bring out his next question. "Didn't you hate the job—seeing that poor devil all broken up, I mean?"

"Of course I hated it. I've told you I did. It was horrid of him, not being willing to see how I was placed. But he's just a spoilt baby, and I told him so."

"Ah—you told him so." He stood looking down on her, remarking for the first time that her cheek-bones were a little too high, that they gave her a drawn and grimacing look he had never before noticed. He thought: "This is the way she talked about me to the fellow who kept her at Dakin." For he no longer believed in the legend of her having gone to Dakin to get a job in a dry-goods store. He felt his strength go from him, and Honoré Shunts's tears under his lids. She was not really like that—he couldn't endure the thought that she was like that. She must instantly say something, do something to disprove it, to drag him up out of the black nightmare of his contempt for her.

He flung himself down beside the lounge. "Floss, you're joking, aren't you, about those letters?"

"What do you call joking? As long as the family wanted them back, what was I to do with them?"

"Oh, God—not that. Not that! You must see. . . I suppose I haven't understood. . . You can't mean you've used his letters that way . . . not that?"

She lay looking up at him, half-amused, half-ironic; but as she saw the change in his face her own grew suddenly blank and cold. "I don't know what you mean by using them. It wasn't my fault if he wrote them; you wouldn't have had me keep them, would you, when his people wanted them so badly? I did my duty, that's all. It isn't always a pleasant job—and you men don't generally make it easier for us."

He hardly distinguished the words; her voice poured over him like an icy flood. It seemed as if he and she were drowning in it together. "Dearest, you're not like that, you're not like that, say you're not like that," he besought her blindly.

She gave a slight laugh and drew back from his imploring arms. "I'm dead tired; I've told you so before. I like people who can take a hint; don't you, darling?" She sat up and stretched out her hand for a cigarette. "Look here—you needn't look so cross," she said. "I'm not throwing you out for good. You can come back tomorrow, if you'll try to treat me a little more politely. But I'm rather fed up with scenes just now, and I'm going to tumble straight into bed. So long, dear."

She reached for her cigarette-lighter and he heard its dry snap as he got to his feet and turned away from her.

❧ XXXVIII ❧

ON THE table in his room, when he re-entered it that night, he saw a telegram; but he left it lying. Whoever it was from, whatever it contained, could hardly matter at that moment. He dropped into a chair and sat staring ahead of him down a long tunnel of darkness. Nothing mattered—nothing would ever again matter. He felt like a man who has tried to hang himself because life was too hideous to be faced, and has been cut down by benevolent hands—and left to face it. He thought of the day when he had staggered into his parents' room at Euphoria to find his father's revolver and make an end—and the revolver had not been there, and he had been thrown back on life as he was thrown back on it now. He felt again the weakness of his legs, the blur in his sick brain, as he staggered down the passage from one room to the other, groped about among the familiar furniture like a thief in a strange house, found the drawer empty, and crawled back again to his own room. It was dreadful, the way old memories of pain fed their parasitic growth on new ones, and dead agonies woke and grew rosy when the Furies called. . .

The winter daylight came in at the window before he thought of the telegram again. Then something struck him about the way it lay there, alone, insistent, in the smoky dawn, and he reached out and tore it open. The message was from his sister Mae and read: "Grandma has pneumonia wants you badly come as soon as you can."

In the train that was hurrying him homeward it

occurred to him for the first time that the telegram
might have been from Halo. He wondered why that possibility had never presented itself to his mind before;
but in the moral wreckage of the last hours he had not
seen her struggling and sinking. She seemed to be hidden away in some safe shelter, like the Homeric people
when a cloud hides them from mortal peril. But now
the thought of her stole back, he felt her presence in his
distracted soul. He seemed to lie watching her between
closed lids, as a man on a sick bed watches the gliding
movements of his nurse, and weaves them into the play
of light on the ceiling. . .

At the door of the Mapledale Avenue house, where
Mae and his father met him, some one said: "She's conscious . . she'll know you . . ." and some one added:
"You'd better come into the dining-room and have some
coffee first—or did you get it on the train?"

On the landing upstairs he met his mother. Mrs.
Weston was a desiccated frightened figure. They were
not used to death at the Westons', it did not seem to
belong to the general plan of life at Euphoria, it had no
language, no ritual, no softening conventions to envelop
it. Mrs. Weston's grief was dry and stammering. "The
minister's been with her, but he's gone away. She says
she won't see anybody now but you," she whispered.

Mrs. Scrimser's room was full of crisp winter sunlight and its brightness lay across her bed. She sat up
against her smooth pillows, small but sublime. All her
great billowing expanse of flesh seemed to have contracted and solidified, as though everything about her
that had roamed and reached out was gathered close for
the narrow passage. She was probably the only person in
the house who knew anything about death, and Vance
felt that she had already come to an understanding with
it. He knelt down and pressed his face against the bed.

"Van," she said, "my little boy. . ." Her fingers wandered feebly through his hair. He remembered that only two nights before he had been kneeling in the same way, his arms stretched out to snatch at another life that was slipping from him, not into death but into something darker and more final; and that other scene lost its tragic significance, became merely pitiful and trivial. He put away the memory, pressing his lips to the wise old hands, trying to exclude from his mind everything but what his grandmother had been, and still was to him. For a long time they held each other in silence; then she spoke softly. "I've been with you so often lately. At Crampton, on the porch. . ."

Yes; to him too those hours were still living. In some ways she had been nearer to him than any one else, though he knew it only as their souls met for goodbye. He buried his face in those tender searching hands, feeling the warm current of old memories pass from her body to his, as if it were she who, in some mystical blood-transfusion, was calling him back to life. A door opened, and some one looked in and stole away. The clock ticked quietly. She lay still. "Van," she said after a while, in a weaker voice. He lifted his head. "There's something I wanted to say to you. Stoop over, darling." He stood up and bent down so that his ear was close to her lips. "Maybe we haven't made enough of pain— been too afraid of it. Don't be afraid of it," she whispered.

Apparently it was her final message, for after that she lay back, quiet and smiling, and though he knew she was conscious of his presence the only sign she gave him was, now and then, the hardly audible murmur of his name. Gradually he became aware that even he was growing remote to her. She began to move in the bed uneasily, with the automatic agitation of the dying, and he rose to call his mother. He noticed then that his aunt Sadie Toler had crept in, and was sitting, a dishevelled stricken figure, in a corner waiting. She came to her mother.

When Vance returned to his grandmother's room, twilight had fallen and the room was quieter than ever. But now a short convulsive breathing seemed struggling to keep time with the tick of the clock. Some one whispered: "Oxygen"; some one else stole out and came back with a heavy bag. The doctor came, and Vance wandered out of the room again. He joined his father, and the two men sat, aimless and vacant-minded, in Mrs. Weston's bedroom across the passage. Mr. Weston said with a nervous laugh: "That was a big turnover those Delaneys made the other day—" but Vance was silent. His father drummed on the table, stealthily drew a cigar from his pocket, fixed on it a look of longing, and put it back. "You'd better go and lie down on the bed and try and have a nap," he suggested to his son. To cut short the talk Vance obeyed, and almost immediately fell into a black pit of sleep. He seemed to have lain plunged in it for hours when he was roused by steps in the room and the flash of electric light in his eyes. Mae stood before him. "Do you want to see her?"

"See her? Has she asked for me—?" But before the phrase was ended he understood, and as he stumbled to his feet he remembered the agony it had been to go into Laura Lou's room after she was dead, and look down on the smooth empty shell which some clever craftsman seemed to have made and put there in her place. "No, no!" he cried, and threw himself back on the bed.

Vance sat in the Mapledale Avenue dining-room the day after his grandmother's funeral. For a while he had been separated from her by the long-drawn horror of the burial service, with its throng of mourners gathered from every field of her beneficence, the white-haired orators pressing on the *vox humana*, the bright eye-glassed women stressing uplift and service, and the wrong it would do their leader's memory to think of her as dead and not passed over, the readings from Isaiah and James Whitcomb Riley, intermingled by a practised hand.

Now the house was silent and deserted, and she could come to him again. The strange people who assemble at the call of death had vanished, the neighbours had called and gone away, the women were upstairs, busy with their mourning, and Lorin Weston had gone back to the office. He had wanted Vance to go with him, had suggested their running over in the Ford to see the land the Shuntses had just bought from Floss Delaney; he had evidently been a little hurt at his son's declining to accompany him.

After Mr. Weston had left the house Vance sat alone and stared into his future. He could not stay another day at Euphoria; too many memories, bitter or sorrowful, started up from every corner of that featureless place. But where should he go, how deal with the days to come? All thought of returning to New York had vanished. Those hours in his grandmother's room seemed to have washed his soul of its evil accretions. He felt no heroic inspiration to take up life again, but only a boundless need to deal with himself, cut a way through the jungle of his conflicting purposes, work out some sort of plan from the dark muddle of things. "Pain —perhaps we haven't made enough of it." Those last words of his grandmother's might turn out to be the clue to his labyrinth. He didn't want to expiate—didn't as yet much believe in the possibility or the usefulness of it; he wanted first of all to measure himself with his pain, to wrestle alone with the dark angel and see how he came out of that conflict.

It was Mae who came to his rescue. He told her he wanted to get away from everything and everybody, and try to do some work—though at the moment he didn't believe he would ever write another line. Mae was impressed, as he intended she should be, by the urgent call of his genius, and immediately exclaimed: "That Camp of Hope up at Lake Belair always has somebody to look after it in winter. I guess they'd take you in up there."

The solitude of the northern woods in winter! A wild longing to be there at once possessed him. But he wanted to make sure that there were no hotels near by, no winter sports, nothing but stark woods and frozen waters. Mae knew the man who lived there, and could reassure him. He was a poor fellow who, having developed tuberculosis, had had to give up his career as a school-teacher and accept this care-taker's job for the sake of the air and the out-door life. He had been cured, and might have gone back to his work; but he had turned into a sort of hermit, and would only take a summer class in natural history at the camp, returning to his frozen solitude in winter. Mae proposed to telegraph to find out if he would receive Vance as a boarder, or make some other arrangement for him, and Vance accepted.

Two days later he was on his way to Lake Belair. After a day's journey the train left him at dusk at a wayside station, and as he got out the icy air caught him by the throat and then suddenly swung him up on wings. He heard sleigh-bells approaching in the dark, and a few minutes later the cutter was gliding off with him into the unknown.

❦ XXXIX ❦

THE EX-SCHOOLMASTER, Aaron Brail, a thin slow man of
halting speech, seemed neither surprised nor unduly
interested by Vance's coming. He explained that he
sometimes took a boarder in winter to replenish his
scanty funds, and said he hoped Vance wouldn't be dis-
satisfied with the food, which was supplied by the wife
of one of the lumbermen from the near-by camp. Vance
was given a small bare room with a window looking out
on vastnesses of snow and hemlock forest, and Brail and
he seldom met except at meals, and when they smoked
their pipes after supper about the living-room stove.
There was a rough book-self against the wall, with a row
of third-rate books on various subjects, chiefly religion
and natural history. Brail was a half-educated naturalist,
and spent his evenings making laborious excerpts from
the books he was reading. He was too shortsighted to be
a good field-observer, and his memory was so uncertain
that when he was not mislaying the notes he had made
the night before he was hunting for the spectacles without which he could not re-read them. But though he was
not interesting the solitude of his life in that austere setting of hills and forests had given him a kind of primitive dignity, and his company was not uncongenial.

Every morning early Vance started off on a tramp
of exploration with one of the lumbermen, but he soon
dispensed with his guide, and spent the white-and-gold
hours in long lonely rambles. Sometimes he would pick
up a meal in a lumberman's house, but oftener he carried his provisions with him and ate them on a warm

ledge in the sun. The hours flowed by with the steady beat of the sea—there were days when he almost imagined himself lying again on the winter sands and watching the shoreward march of the waves, as he had done during his honeymoon with Laura Lou. His mind travelled back to his first adventures and discoveries, which already seemed so remote; he felt like a very old man whose memory, blurring the intervening years, illuminates the smallest incidents of youth. Sometimes he came home so drunk with sunlight and cold that sleep struck him down in the doorway, and he would throw himself on his hard bed and not wake till Brail called him to supper.

At first he paid for these bouts of sleep by lying awake all night, his brain whirling and buzzing like a gigantic loom. It was as though he were watching some obscure creative process, the whirl and buzz of the cosmic wheels. The fatigue was maddening, and when sleep finally came there was no rest in his brief unconsciousness. Two women peopled these agitated vigils; the one that his soul rejected and his body yearned for, the other who had once seemed the answer to all he asked of life, but had now faded to a reproach and a torment. The whole question of woman was the age-long obstacle to peace of spirit and fruitfulness of mind; to get altogether away from it, contrive a sane and productive life without it, became the obsession of his sleepless midnights. All he wanted was to be himself, solely and totally himself, not tangled up in the old deadly nets of passion and emotion.

But solitude and hard exercise gradually worked their spell. His phases of excited insomnia gave place to a quiet wakefulness, and he would lie and watch the night skies wheel past his unshuttered window, and recover again his old sense of the rhythmic beat of the

universe. The feeling brought a kind of wintry quietude, a laying on of heavenly hands, and he would fall
asleep like a child who knows that his nurse is near.

On stormy days he lingered in the lumbermen's
huts, talking with them and their families, and he felt
refreshed by the contact with their simple monotonous
lives. But they lived unconsciously in those cosmic
hands in which he felt himself cradled, and as vigour of
mind and body returned he began to crave for a conscious intelligence, an intelligence not complicated or
sophisticated but moulded on the large quiet lines of
the landscape. He tried to think that Brail might satisfy
this need; but Brail was not so much uncommunicative
as lacking in anything to communicate. He was not hostile to Vance, he seemed even, as the weeks passed, to
find a mild pleasure in their evening talks. But he had a
small slack mind, to which his rudimentary studies as a
naturalist had given no precision; and Vance suspected
that his flight to the woods had been not toward something but away from something. It was the same with
Vance himself: but as his nerves grew steadier he understood that he would never be able to rest long in evasion or refusal, that something precise and productive
must come out of each step in his life. He began to think
of himself less as a small unsatisfied individual than as
an instrument in some mighty hand; and one day he was
seized by the desire to put this rush of returning energy
into words. On starting for the woods he had snatched
up a few old books left at Euphoria since his college days
—an Odyssey and a Greek grammar among them—and
during his sleepless nights he had laboured over the
grammar and refreshed his spirit with glimpses of the
sunlit Homeric world, which was spacious and simple
like the scenes about him. But with the revival of the
desire to write his studies slackened, and the books lay

untouched, with two others which Mae had taken from the shelf by his grandmother's bed, and handed to him as he was leaving. These he had not even looked into—the mood for books had passed. He must write, write, write. But to his dismay he found he had brought no paper with him. This would have been a small misfortune at a season when the general store was open and the mails came regularly; but a succession of snowstorms had interrupted the postal service from the nearest point on the railway, and nobody at the camp had any paper. Even Brail could produce only a few sheets of letter-paper, and this absurd obstacle aggravated Vance's fury to begin. At length he coaxed some torn sheets of packing paper from one of the lumbermen's wives, and set himself to work. The fact of having only these coarse crumpled pages at his disposal seemed to stimulate his imagination, and in those first days he felt nearer than ever before to the hidden sources of inspiration.

The return to work steadied his nerves, and his tramps over the frozen hills carried him back into that world of ecstasy from which he had been so long shut out. He had written "Colossus" in a fever, but his new book was shaping itself in a mood of deep spiritual ardour such as his restless intelligence had never before attained, and these weeks outside of time gave him his first understanding of the magic power of continuity.

Now that his energies were all engaged he could let his thoughts return to his grandmother's death. At first that misery, so meaningless in its suddenness, had been unendurable; but now he could think about her calmly, recognizing that her course was run and that she would not have wished to outlive herself. In her way she had been happy, in spite of ups and downs of fortune, in spite of Grandpa Scrimser, and of blows (not infrequent, he suspected) to her pride as an orator and evangelist. She was too intelligent not to be aware of her own ignorance, too impulsive to remember it for long; but he felt that all these contradictions were somehow merged in a deep central peace. Vance had always ascribed this to the optimism he found so irritating in her; but her last word had been a warning against optimism. "Maybe we haven't made enough of pain—" that had been her final discovery, and it completed his image of her.

One evening, as he brooded over these memories, feeling the warmth of her soul in his, he remembered the two books that Mae had brought him as he was leaving Euphoria. They stood on his table with the others, and he took them up and glanced at them. One was a thumbed anthology of "Daily Pearls", collected by the editor of "Zion's Spotlight"; the kind of book from which pressed pansies and scraps of pious verse drop in a shower when they are opened. The other volume had obviously been less often consulted. Vance opened it and slowly turned the pages. In a few minutes they had possession of him, and he read on deep into the night, read till his oil-lamp had sputtered out and his candle followed it; and when sunrise came he was sitting up in bed in his old leather coat, still reading. "The Confessions of Saint Augustine"—though the title was familiar the book had never come his way, and he had only a vague idea of its date and origin. But before he had read a dozen pages he saw that it was one of the timeless books with which chronology is unconcerned. Who was this man who reached out across the centuries to speak to him as never man had spoken before? He felt his whole life summed up in each of these piercing phrases.

"Come, Lord, and work: arouse us and incite; kindle us, sweep us onward; teach us to love and to run. . .

"I said: 'Give me chastity and self-control—*but not just yet.* . .' I was shaken with a gust of indignation because I could not enter into Thy Will, yet all my bones were crying out that this was the way, and no ship is needed for that way, nor chariot, no, nor feet; for it is not as far from me as from the house to the spot where we are seated. . .

"And Thou didst beat back my weak sight, dazzling me with Thy splendour, and I perceived that I was far from Thee, in the land of unlikeness, and I heard Thy voice crying to me: 'I am the Food of the full-grown. Become a man and thou shalt feed on Me'."

The food of the full-grown—of the full-grown! That was the key to his grandmother's last words. "Become a man and thou shalt feed on Me" was the message of experience to the soul; and what was youth but the Land of Unlikeness?

Night after night he returned to those inexhaustible pages, again and again after that first passionate encounter he re-read them slowly, broodingly, weighing them phrase by phrase in the light of his brief experience, feeling his soul expand to receive them, and carrying away each day some fragment of concentrated spiritual food to nourish him in his lonely rambles.

The thaw came early, with rainy winds and intervals of frost; and on one of his excursions Vance was caught in a storm of sleet, lost his way when night fell, and got back to camp exhausted and shivering. That night he flamed in fever and shook with coughing, and the doctor who came over from the nearest town muttered in a corner with Brail, who looked frightened and bewildered. Vance was aware that he must be seriously ill, and that Brail would have liked him to be taken away; but it was evidently thought unadvisable to move him, and he felt weakly thankful when he understood that he was to be left where he was. Brail and the lumberman's wife nursed him to the best of their ability, but the woman was ignorant and clumsy, and Brail in a state of chronic bewilderment, always mislaying his spectacles, and totally unable to remember any instructions the doctor had neglected to write down. In spite of all this Vance gradually worked his way back to health, and the weeks wore on slowly but not unhappily till a day came when he got to his feet again and shambled a little way along the wet path in the mild spring sun.

After that the time passed pleasantly enough. The subdued ecstasy of convalescence was in his veins, and he looked out with eyes cleansed by solitude on a new world in which everything was beautiful and important, and seemed to have been created for his special use. His physical suffering and helplessness seemed to have matured his mind, and detached it from the things of the past like a ripe fruit from the tree. Saint Augustine's words came back to him: "Become a man and thou shalt feed on Me"; and he felt that at last he was ready to taste of the food of the full-grown, however bitter to the lips it might be.

He had thought vaguely of staying on at Belair till the Camp of Hope reopened, and then of hiring a bungalow higher up in the hills and settling down to his new book. He had not yet worked out any plan beyond that, though a plan there must be if he were to regain a hold on himself. He wanted first to secure a few months of quiet for his book, and to watch the advance of spring, and the sudden blazing up of summer, in that powerful untamed landscape; but he saw that to recover his bodily strength he must get away to better care and more food. It was queer how even a touch of pneumonia did you in—his legs still rambled away from him like a baby's when he attempted his daily walk. . .

His family did not know of his illness; he had sworn Brail to secrecy on the first day, and the timid creature had obeyed, no doubt privately relieved at not having to provide for other visitors. Vance had been touched by Brail's awkward devotion during his illness. He had found out that Brail had tramped twenty miles through the snow to get the doctor, and that his reluctance to keep Vance at the camp was due merely to the fear of not being able to give him proper care. The men had grown to feel more at ease with each other, and one day Brail, in a burst of confidence, confessed to Vance that his great desire had been to enter the ministry, but that he had been discouraged by the difficulties of theological study. He had been unable, after repeated attempts, to pass his examination, and his failure had been a lasting mortification. "I never could seem to take to any other profession, not even zoology," he said mournfully, wiping the mist from his spectacles.

"Was that what made you decide to stay up here?" Vance questioned idly; and to his surprise he saw the blood rise under the other's sallow skin.

"Oh, no," said Brail hastily, turning away to fumble for his spectacle-case.

Vance lay back in his chair and looked up at the low smoke-blackened ceiling. There was a long silence, and his mind had wandered away to other matters when he became aware that Brail was still standing before him, his hands in his pockets, his narrow forehead anxiously wrinkled, "I've been wanting to tell you for some time," said Brail, through a cough of embarrassment.

"Tell me what?"

Brail bowed his head and spoke low. "It was a woman," he said. "I met her when I was observing animals at a circus. She was a lion-tamer," he added with another cough.

Vance stared up at him, convulsed with sudden laughter; but he saw the other's tortured face, and mastered his muscles in time. "Well—isn't that what they all are?" he said.

Brail stared back, blinking down through his spectacles. "Er—lion-tamers? Ah, yes—I see!" he exclaimed, his cautious wrinkled smile suddenly responding to the pleasantry. "But I meant it literally," he jerked out, and turned in haste from the room. Vance, lying back, saw him pass in front of the window and walk away with mournful strides through the mud. "The food of the full-grown," he murmured to himself as Brail disappeared among the hemlocks.

Yes, it was time to eat of that food; time to grow up; time to fly from his shielded solitude and go down again among the lion-tamers. He was glad that his possessions were already packed, and that he was to leave the next morning; but when the cutter stood at the door, and his bags were stowed under the seat, he turned to Brail with a final pang of reluctance. "Well, goodbye. You may see me back yet."

Brail blinked and shook his head. "You'll think so, maybe; but you won't come," he answered, and stood watching Vance drive away.

The first night in Chicago nearly made Brail's prophecy come true. Vance had gone there straight from the camp. Now that his grandmother was dead he could not face the idea of returning to Euphoria; and he meant to stay a few days in Chicago and try to think out some plan for the next months. But the sudden transition from the winter silence of the hills to the tumult of the streets was more than his shaken nerves could bear. These millions of little people rushing about their business and pleasure in an endless uproar of their own making were like strange insects driven by unintelligible instincts; and he was too tired to be interested in observing them. Ah, how tired he was—how unutterably tired! All the factitious energy accumulated during his last days at Belair had been lost in the descent to the heavy atmosphere of the city. He felt will-less and adrift, and the food of the full-grown seemed too strong a fare for him.

The next morning he got as far as the telegraph office in the lobby of the hotel. He inscribed Brail's name on a telegraph blank, and was about to write under it: "Can I come back?" when he was checked by a vision of the poor man shambling off alone down the muddy path to the camp, spectrally followed by the limping figure of Chris Churley. There went the two deniers, the two fugitives—poor Chris, poor Brail! No—that was not the solution to Vance's difficulty; it lay somewhere ahead of him, in the crowd and the struggle. At present he couldn't see just where; but a weak longing overcame him to be again among familiar faces and in scenes associated with his past. It occurred to him that he might have gone back to Laura Lou's mother if she had still lived at Paul's Landing, in the tumble-down house above the Hudson where he had been so happy and so miserable; but doubtless she was still in California with her son, who had gone out there to work as a nurseryman. Vance went up to his room and lay down on the bed. He felt too weary to think, or to want anything, or to make any fresh resolves, since he knew they would be broken. . . The next morning he took a ticket for Paul's Landing.

❦ XL ❧

WHEN THE train left him at Paul's Landing Vance knew that what had taken him there was not the wish to see the cottage where he had lived with Laura Lou. That past was buried under the dead leaves of too many seasons. What he craved for, with a sort of tremulous convalescent hunger, was a sight of the Willows, the old house where his real life had begun.

It was less than three years since he had come to Paul's Landing to implore Halo Tarrant to go away with him, instead of waiting to obtain her divorce; but on that feverish day he had not given the Willows a thought, and his last sight of the fantastic old house and the abandoned garden, though not remote in years, seemed to belong to his embryonic stage.

The day was soft, the air full of spring scents and the shimmer of sun through wrinkled leaves. Vance got into the tram which passed by the lane leading to the Willows. The mean outskirts of the town were meaner than ever; new cottages had been built, but the old ones had not been repainted. The suburb, evidently uncertain of its future, awaited in slatternly unconcern the coming of the land-speculator or of the municipal park-designer. But in the lane that climbed to the Willows Vance felt his boy's heart wake in him. From the ruts underfoot too the elm boughs overhead, nothing around him was changed; and when he reached the gate and gazed across the lawn to the house, its inconsequent turrets and gables showed uncertainly through the same veil of weeping willows.

So completely was he drawn back into the past that he felt in his pocket for the key he used to take from his mother-in-law's drawer when he stole up the lane to meet Halo Spear—and later to meet Halo Tarrant. The key was not there, but as he leaned on the gate in the attitude of the sentimental wanderer he felt it yield to his pressure, and walked in.

Every fibre of his past was interwoven with that scene. Long before he had flown there to his first meetings with Halo, he and Laura Lou and her brother had ranged through the decaying garden and waked the echoes of Miss Emily Lorburn's strange old dwelling. In the arbour at the back of the house Vance had put a first kiss on Laura Lou's fluttering eyelids; on the doorstep he had sat and waited through a long afternoon for Halo Spear, who had promised to meet him and forgotten her promise; among the musty book-shelves of the library, and under the sad painted gaze of Miss Emily Lorburn, he had first travelled in the realms of gold, with Halo guiding him.

In that setting she came suddenly back to him, poised for flight as he had first known her; then, after her marriage, under a shadow of disquietude torn by laughter and irony, but never dispelled till he took her in his arms on the night of their flight. Thus detached from the uncertainties and irritations of their life together, her renovated image leaned to him from that enchanted world where they had first met. The memory caught him about the heart, and if she had come to him across the lawn at that moment all his scruples and resolves might have been swept away in a flood of tenderness. But he was determined not to abandon himself to such dreams. His future, wherever it led, was to be ruled by realities, not illusions. He had thought he loved her, and he had failed her; she had accepted the fact, and faced it with her usual ironic courage; and the one service his unstable heart could do her now was to leave her in peace and go his way.

He stood for a long time on the lawn, remembering how, when he had first come there, fresh from the mediocrity and uniformity of Euphoria, the house had seemed as vast as a Roman villa and as venerable as a feudal castle. Through its modest doorway he had entered into a legendary past; its shingled tower was Sister Anne's outlook, its bracketed balconies overhung the perilous foam on which his imagination had voyaged ever since. The old house had been his fairy godmother, and it was only now, as he looked at it again, that he understood.

He went up to the door, studying the shuttered windows, looking for signs of change, catching at each stray tendril of association. Of change he saw little; the family had always kept the house in decent repair, and its be-gabled front and bracketed balconies looked hardly more blistered and weather-streaked than when he had first seen them. Last year's dead geraniums still dangled from the fluted iron vases flanking the door; and from the fretwork of the porch a honeysuckle hung.

On the other side of the house, where the library looked out over a sloping lawn, the verandah was still clutched and enveloped in the huge twining arms of the ancient wistaria. It was already heavy with budding clusters, and Vance closed his eyes and called up the June day when from roof to cellar it had poured in a cataract of silvery lilac. He noticed that the library windows were open, as they used to be on cleaning days; and his heart beat fast as he mounted the verandah steps and looked in. But the room was empty, the books stood undisturbed. He remarked only one change: a sheet had been hung over Miss Lorburn's portrait, and her sad eyes no longer looked down on him. The covering of the picture suggested that there might be cleaners or painters at work; but all the other windows were barred, and he heard no sounds within, and saw no one about.

He turned and looked across the lawn at the broken-down arbour where he and Laura Lou had sat. His thoughts went out to it in an act of piety, as though its broken trellis were arched above her grave. But he no longer recognized himself in the boy who had sat there on that June morning and caressed her frightened eyelids. His real life had long been elsewhere, and the thought of her stirred only a shadowy tenderness. He went a little way down the lawn and then turned back.

The house, at that distance, looked more than ever like the steel engraving in the old book on landscape-gardening which he and Halo had once laughed over— but oddly shrunken and small, as though from a full-page picture it had dwindled to the ornamental tail-piece of a chapter. And that, after all, was what it was, he mused; though he was still in the twenties the picture of the Willows seemed to close the chapter of his youth. . . He walked back to the gate, and went out.

In the lane a man was repairing the palings. He looked at Vance, and the latter asked him if any one was living at the Willows. The man said there was generally a caretaker there, but he believed the place had just been sold, and the new people were moving in. A pang went through Vance; he remembered how often he and Halo, in their European wanderings, had talked of coming back some day to live at the Willows. An idle fancy then; but now it had the poignancy of an unfulfilled dream. Where were the people from? he asked. The man said he was new to the place, and didn't know; but he'd heard they were from New York, and the carpenter who employed him had been told to start work that week. He guessed the old place needed a good deal done to it to make folks comfortable there.

Vance walked slowly back to the town. He had meant to take an afternoon train to New York; but he felt weak and tired, and the idea of big cities frightened him—perhaps also the possibility that in that particular one he might run across Floss Delaney. When he left Belair he had felt equipped to meet not only old memories but the people who embodied them; now a singular lassitude possessed him, and he thought enviously of Brail's figure retreating alone into the depths of the hemlock forest. He left his luggage at the dingy hotel opposite the station, and went out again.

He wandered through the town in the direction of the road that led up to Eaglewood, the old house above the Hudson where Halo Spear had lived before her marriage. A myriad arms seemed to draw him along that steep ascent; but half way up he turned, and began to walk resolutely back to the town. It came over him that he was seeking the solace of these old memories as a frightened child runs to hide its face in its nurse's lap; and in a rush of self-contempt he strode down the hill to the station. What he wanted was to regain his strength and then face life afresh, not to go whining back to a past from which he had cut himself off by his own choice.

❦ XLI ❧

Halo Tarrant sat on the verandah at Eaglewood, pencil and note-block in hand. She murmured over: "Six enamelled pails, eight ditto hot-water jugs, a set of aluminium saucepans, ten coal-scuttles. . . I suppose some day I may be able to afford central heating. . . Oh, Frenny, if you knew how those coal-scuttles bore me!"

She dropped the note-block to the floor, and leaned back, her eyes fixed on the great sweep of the river shining far below through the woodlands. "If I hadn't had cousin Emily's linen-closet I should never have the courage to begin. . ." The words sounded slightly plaintive, but a smile interrupted them. "Isn't it providential, Frenny, that the poor lady's disappointed love affair should have provided me with those dozens and dozens of unused napery? I'm sure napery was what she called it, aren't you?"

Frenside, who had come up to Eaglewood to be with Halo for the week-end, gave an ironic grunt, and murmured: "Your sentiments are as inhuman as they are natural. But how do you know she had a love affair?"

Halo lifted her eyebrows in surprise. "Why, Vance" —she began, and then broke off, not because she was reluctant to pronounce his name, but because she realized that in her thoughts the romance he had woven about Emily Lorburn had gradually substituted itself for the reality. "Vance always said she had," she declared, still smiling. She had made it a rule from the first

428

to speak of him, simply and naturally, when the occasion required; at first it had cost her an effort, but now she could name him without pain, almost with a melancholy pleasure—as if he were dead, she sometimes mused. In truth there was a sense in which all her past had died, leaving in her the seed of a new vitality—the life of her child. During the long slow months since she had parted from Vance in Paris this detachment and reassurance had grown in her with the child's growth; a kind of calm animal beatitude of which she was at first ashamed and then glad, as she understood that this was the season allotted to her by nature for rest and renewal.

Her inward tranquillity had not come to her suddenly. The first weeks after Vance had gone to America had been a dark blur of pain. She had played her part valiantly, affected to accept their separation as natural, and perhaps only temporary, yet rejected any definite suggestion of a future reunion. The future was to take care of itself; for the moment they both needed a change. . . She got through the parting on this note; and then blackness closed in on her.

After her visit to Tarrant her existence for a time had no distinguishable features. She thought the dead in their graves must be as she was. But out of that annihilation slowly a new life had emerged, her own interwoven with her child's. The numbness gradually became quietude, the quietude a kind of sober joy, till she could now look back on that first phase of anguish as mystics do on the dark passages of their spiritual initiation. When she decided to return to America and establish herself at the Willows she had reached a degree of composure which made it almost easy to speak of the past, and even to let her mind dwell on it.

The decision to live at the Willows had been her

final step toward recovery. The thought of the old place drew her back with a thousand threads of association; and the mere fact that the house was her own, the only place on earth that she could dispose of as she chose, made her wish that her child should be born there. But for a long time after her return she had postponed her decision. At first she wondered whether she could face life alone in that mournful old house; then whether her presence there might not be an actual embarrassment to her parents. She had been prepared for her family's opposition to the plan, but hardly for their dismay at her return to America. To be reunited to their darling after such a long separation was a joy indeed; but it was really incredible that Halo should not have understood how much simpler it would have been to . . . to get through the unfortunate business that lay ahead of her before returning to New York. . . Her mother would of course have gone to Europe to join her. . .

"But I want my child to be born at the Willows," Halo quietly interposed.

"But at the Willows you can't keep it a secret, you can't possibly keep people from talking—"

She gave a little laugh, and bent to kiss Mrs. Spear's anguished forehead. "But I *want* people to talk about my baby; the people I'm fond of, I mean. And what do I care for the others? He's going to be the most wonderful baby in the world—you don't suppose I'm going to make a mystery of him, do you?"

Slowly her parents understood that nothing could alter her attitude, and they accepted the situation, Mrs. Spear secretly excited at the idea that the defiance she had always longed to fling at society was actually being flung by her own daughter, Mr. Spear incurably depressed, but silenced by the fact that here at last was a grievance he could not ventilate in the newspapers.

Gradually Halo's quiet ascendancy asserted itself over both, and before she had been at home for many weeks they had fitted into their lives the new fact that she meant to follow her own way, neither defiantly nor apologetically, but as if it were of more concern to herself than it could possibly be to others. Still, she understood that her parents would be happier if she went to Eaglewood as soon as possible, and after staying with them for a short time in New York she had opened the house and settled herself there with two servants; and with the approach of summer the desire to be installed at the Willows before her child was born overcame her hesitation, and she began to confer with painters and contractors, and to draw up her housekeeping lists. The renewed contact with practical questions seemed to dispel her last uncertainties, to make her feel that she had a plan of life again, and was in the salutary hold of habit; and the days which had dragged by so heavily began to move at a more normal pace. It was curious, she thought, how far pots and pans could go toward filling an empty heart; and she remembered how she had vaguely resented Vance's faculty for escaping from anxiety and unhappiness by plunging into his work. Housemaking and housekeeping were her escape, she supposed: she must build up a home for her son. . .

Two or three times her mother had come to spend a day with her, and now and then Frenside turned up for a week-end; but at other times she remained by herself, increasingly busy with her child's affairs and her own, letting her mind wander among the crowding memories of her own childhood, and watching the slow changes of the familiar landscape from spring to summer. There were moments when she wondered if, after her baby was born, she would lapse from her state of ruminating calm, and become again the passionate anxious Halo of old; but it was idle to think of that now, and she put the question quietly from her.

Frenside had not immediately taken up her allusion to Vance; she noticed that it still embarrassed him to speak to her on the subject. But after a moment he said: "I've been wanting for some time to tell you—"

Her heart gave a start at the preamble. "Yes?"

"Speaking of Weston—I don't believe I ever mentioned that I ran across him in New York three or four months ago, did I?"

It was the first time that any one had spoken to her of having seen Vance since he and she had said goodbye in Paris, and the careful structure of her composure trembled on its base and gave way. "No; you didn't." . . Her voice failed her.

"Well, there wasn't much point in it—I mean in telling you. He wanted to know how you were; he said he might ask me to take you a message—but he never has. So I waited."

Halo's heart dilated and then sank back to its usual frozen quiet. "He never has." She wondered why Frenside had told her, then?

"Only," Frenside pursued, "I've been wondering, now that your divorce proceedings are well under way, and everything's clear on that score, whether I oughtn't—"

Halo reflected for a moment. "Do you know where he is?"

"Not a notion; I've never laid eyes on him since; but I suppose a letter to his publisher would be forwarded."

She made no answer to this, and he went on: "The fact is, I said nothing at the time because the rumour was that he was in pursuit of that meteoric young woman—what's her name? The girl who was married the other day to the Duke of Spartivento. People seemed to think Weston meant to marry her."

"Yes; I know." She drew a deep breath. "And now that she's married, you think—?"

"I think Weston ought to know how things stand with you."

There was another silence; Halo could not bring any order into her agitation. But at last she said slowly: "What does it matter? I've thought all that out. If it's not Floss Delaney it will be some other woman. . ."

"*Dichterliebe,* eh? Well, you're probably right. Most artists are incurably polygamous. When they're not it's because they die young—and their books generally do too. But I don't know that their loving so lavishly matters as much in itself as in what it makes of them; what sort of stuff they turn it into. I don't pretend to know yet what Weston's going to turn into. After all, you can't squeeze the whole of any human being into an epigram. But Weston went to see Tarrant, and said some things to him that came out of his very soul; and it's not easy to say things that come out of the soul to Tarrant."

The blood rose to Halo's face, and she bent to pick up her papers and pencil. She had disciplined herself to hear Vance blamed and disparaged, but to hear him spoken of with sympathy and understanding sent a sudden anguish through her. She tried to answer but could not, and sat fluttering her list between her fingers, and murmuring over to herself: "A set of aluminium saucepans—ten coal-scuttles—"

Frenside stood up from his chair; the sun had veered round, leaving the verandah in shade, and the evening air was chilly. "My dear, you're very young to cut your life in two like this. Won't you let me try to see him?"

She shook her head. "Don't think I'm ungrateful. But don't ask me again, please; it's useless."

Frenside shrugged, and turned away. "Let's go in, then; it's getting cold."

She made no answer, and he left her sitting there and walked into the drawing-room, where a wood-fire was smouldering. She meant to follow him in a moment, but first she must let the troubled waves subside. It was too soon, after all, to talk of Vance even with so old a friend. . .

Presently she felt quieter, and got up to follow Frenside. But first she opened the French window into the hall, in order to hang her cloak on its usual peg under the stairs. As she crossed the hall she noticed that the front door was open. She went forward to shut it; but when she approached she saw that a man was standing on the steps, his back to the door. He must have heard her footfall on the oak floor, for he turned abruptly, and in the failing light she recognized Vance. She gave a little cry, and they stood and looked at each other. "Halo—" he began in a dazed voice.

"Oh, Van! Where did you come from? How tired you look! But you've been ill—you must have been very ill! What's been the matter?" She swept forward on a great rush of pity, but he drew back, passing a slow bewildered hand over his forehead. "No—I'm all right. . . I'm all right again. . ."

The change in his appearance frightened her, almost made her feel as if she were speaking to a stranger. He had grown so thin that he seemed taller, and his face was changed too. All its boyishness was gone; it was drawn and stern, like that of a man who has been through some inward ordeal which makes everything else remote. She felt that she was a part of that remoteness, and the feeling made her speak to him almost shyly. "Van—why do you stand there? Don't you mean to come in?"

"Yes; I'll come in." His voice was low and automatic; he spoke as if he were reciting a lesson. "I didn't intend to come here now," he added, as if it were an afterthought.

"Not now?"

He shook his head, and took a few steps into the hall. "No. I really came back just to look at the Willows. And then they told me down at the station that you were here."

"At the Willows? You've been there now?"

"Yes. I had to. . . They said you'd sold it, and the contractors were going to begin work; I came just in time. I suppose some instinct told me."

"Sold it? I'm going to live there myself!" she exclaimed, her voice trembling with the announcement.

He looked at her with a kind of slow surprise. "You—at the Willows? I hadn't thought of that. . ."

"We used to think of it—don't you remember?"

He gave an uneasy laugh. "I can't always separate what we've talked of from what I've imagined."

"That's because you've been ill, Van—"

"Yes; I've been ill." He stood looking about the hall with timid unfamilar eyes. "Is there any place where I can talk to you alone?"

Halo opened the door of her father's study, and led him in, closing the door after her. Vance still looked about him with that odd estranged look which frightened her more than his thinness and his pallour. She felt almost as if he did not see her. But after a moment his eyes turned back to hers. "You see, I wanted to tell you why I'm not coming back—"

Her heart gave a frightened plunge. "Not—you're not coming back?"

He shook his head. "No; not now. Not for a long time, perhaps. You see, it's this way; I swore to myself when I was up in the woods that I must pull myself together first, make something out of myself, be worth something. . . You understand, don't you?"

Halo stood looking at him with troubled eyes. "Up in the woods, dear? Where were you?"

"Oh, up at Belair. It's in Wisconsin. I went there after my grandmother died. She died last winter—you didn't know? After that there were things I had to fight out alone. I was getting hold of myself, I really was— and then I was knocked out, and had pneumonia, or something. . ."

"Vance, I knew you'd been terribly ill!"

"I'm all right now—I'm as right as ever. Only I've got no will and no purpose. That's what I wanted you to understand. I wanted to come back some day, though I didn't know whether you'd ever have me. But I didn't mean to come till afterward, not till I was fit to know my own mind, and stick to my purpose, and be of some use to you. And all that's gone . . . blown away like ashes. . . I'm burnt out; I'm just cinders. . ."

As he spoke, Halo's scruples were borne down by a fresh wave of solicitude. To see him so powerless and broken made her feel strong, confident, sure of herself. Whatever might come later, for the moment the way was clear. "But the very time to come back, dear, was when you needed me. We can let afterward take care on itself."

Vance shook his head, his anxious eyes still fixed on her. "No. It's not the time; I've got to make good first. Maybe it's my pride—I don't know. Anyway, I wanted to explain to you and then go off again. You understand?"

Her hopes sank under a return of perplexity. Did

she understand—would she ever? She returned his look with a faint smile. "Did you really come all the way to Paul's Landing just to tell me that you were going away again?"

He flushed feverishly under his drawn pallour. "No; I came because I couldn't help myself. I've been down in hell, and I wanted to see the stars again. That's all."

"All?" She tried to keep the smile on her twitching lips. "One glimpse is enough, you mean?"

"No; it's not enough. But it's more than I've got a right to." He straightened his shoulders abruptly. "Till I'm sure of myself, anyhow."

Halo hesitated. The unseen barrier between them seemed as impenetrable as ever; she felt that she might wound her hands, and waste her strength against it, in vain. There might be subterfuges, tricks—appeals to his emotion by the display of hers. But that had never been her way; her pride met his with an equal shock. If that was his view of their relation, he had a right to it. But she was resolved first to make sure that the reason he gave was the true one.

"Van," she said, "when you say you're not sure of yourself, are you thinking of Floss Delaney? I've got a right to ask you that, you know."

A painful contraction passed over his face, and she wondered if she had not committed a folly in touching on the wound. But she was not good at subterfuges, and it seemed more loyal to repay his frankness by her own. "Floss Delaney . . . ?" He repeated the name slowly and half-wonderingly, as if asking himself what it signified to him at that moment.

"If there'd been any likelihood of your marrying her," Halo hurried on, "I should have been the first to stand aside—you know it was on that account that I suggested our parting. . . But now that she's married. . ."

She saw Vance turn pale, and stretch out his hand to the back of the armchair against which he was leaning. "Ah, she's married—? Up in the woods I hardly ever saw the papers. . . I didn't know. . ." He stood looking down at the floor for a moment or two; then he raised his head with a nervous laugh. "She's put through that deal too, has she? Spartivento, I suppose. . . Well, it's nothing to me. . . I'd said goodbye to her long before."

A great weight was lifted from Halo's heart; but in another moment it descended on her again, this time with a more intolerable oppression. She looked into his face, and said to herself that there are farewells which are powerless to separate. "A real goodbye, Vance? Are you sure?"

"God, yes. All that's ashes. . . Only, you see, she took something with her; my belief in things, my old reasons for living and working. It's as if my mainspring was broken. I've got to get it mended first." Suddenly he moved toward her with a gesture of passionate entreaty. "Don't you see, Halo—*can't* you see? I can't come back to you just because I'm at the end of everything. To any other woman—not to you. But I wasn't strong enough to go away without telling you; the only strength left to me is the strength not to pretend, or to invent lying reasons. And that's not much."

She continued to look at him with something of his own timidity. "It might be enough—" she began, as if a voice within her had spoken without her will.

He shook his head, but she hurried on: "If you say no, it must be because I'm less to you than any other woman, and not more."

He said slowly: "It's not being more or less; you're

different. I read something up there in the woods about God . . . or experience . . . it's the same thing . . . being the food of the full-grown. That seemed to explain a lot to me. I'm not fit for you yet, Halo; I'm only just learning how to walk. . ."

She leaned against the mantelpiece, fighting down the old tremors in her breast; at length she gave a little laugh. "But then I shall have two children to take care of instead of one!"

He raised his eyes to her, and she moved across the room and stood before him. With a kind of tranquil gravity she lifted up her arms in the ancient attitude of prayer.

For a moment his brow kept its deep furrows of bewilderment; then he gave a start and went up to her with illuminated eyes.

"You see we belong to each other after all," she said; but as her arms sank about his neck he bent his head and put his lips to a fold of her loose dress.

THE END

❧ AFTERWORD ❧

The Gods Arrive is a sequel to *Hudson River Bracketed*. It can be read on its own, but it is more resonant when read after its predecessor. It continues the story of Vance Weston, a boy from the raw American Midwest of the turn of the century, who enters adulthood with vague, uninformed religious inclinations and a vague sense that he wants to write; and his relation with Halo Spear Tarrant, the cultivated woman who first introduces him to literature, art, and a sense of the past.

Edith Wharton was almost seventy in 1932 when she finished *The Gods Arrive*, which she included, along with *Hudson River Bracketed, The Custom of the Country, Summer*, and *The Children*, as her favourites among her novels. Critical opinion has not agreed, but then Wharton, like other women authors, has been critically underrated for decades; only now is her work being re-evaluated. Most critics find *The Gods Arrive* weak, insufficiently focused, didactic, and too derivative of her earlier work (as in the character of Floss Delaney, an echo of Undine Spragg of *The Custom of the Country*). They intimate that the failure of these late works may be attributable to Wharton's age and the conditions of her life in her late years. She considerably depleted her financial resources and exhausted herself during the First World War, assisting orphaned and sick children, poor women, and the homeless; afterwards, she had to work unremittingly to earn enough money to provide for the many people for whom she took responsibility—domestic retainers and her sister-in-law. She suffered many emotional blows: Walter Berry, her dearest and oldest friend, to whom *The Gods Arrive* is dedicated, died in 1927; Wharton herself was extremely sick and nearly died in 1929 of influenza; and friends, relatives, and familiars were dying all around her in the last decade of her life. She herself lived until 1937.

It is hard not to join in the critical consensus about some elements of *The Gods Arrive*. Wharton intended *Hudson River*

Bracketed and *The Gods Arrive* to be the portrait of an American artist as a young man, to treat the development of a writer of genius who is raised and semi-educated in the crude Midwestern United States of the early decades of this century—a place inhospitable to any form of art, a place from which artists fled. Insofar as this is the theme of the novel, it must be judged a failure: the character of Vance Weston does not reflect genius, does not display a strong artistic sensibility or a talent for literature. His experience, especially as described in this novel, does not seem to arise from a developing central vision of life or language sufficient to motivate him to endure the particular difficulties of an artist's life. The passages describing artistic creation are less vivid here than in *Hudson River Bracketed*, contain less felt life; they seem inorganic, inadequately rooted in Vance's character. Wharton's portrayal of American society and modern literary society is shallowly, unthinkingly—almost bitterly—satiric. Indeed, the literary society of New York (described in *Hudson River Bracketed*), London, and Paris (in *The Gods Arrive*) is shown to be so thin and superficial, so concerned with status and fame, and so ignorant and uninterested in artistic values, that it is impossible to imagine *any* significant literature could emerge from it—yet even as we read, we cannot forget that among the pieces of shoddy modern literature Wharton mocks, indeed the one she singles out with most distate, is *Ulysses*. Finally, we are told that Vance has wonderful conversations with a few people, brilliant, nourishing talk. But such conversations are only referred to, and never realized in the novel; since we cannot hear them, we cannot experience the texture of Vance's mind or world.

Yet despite all this, *The Gods Arrive* is compelling. Not only do the main characters draw the reader's sympathy, so that one cares about what happens to them; but beneath the story of Vance's search for himself as a writer, there is another drama that grips us, and whose resolution feels enormously significant. This is the story of the relationship between Vance and Halo.

Wharton's treatment of this relationship has something large about it, suggesting that it is not simply a personal drama but a universal confrontation between male and female. I think of Scott Fitzgerald's *Tender is the Night* (published two years after

Wharton's novel), which also treats a male/female sexual and domestic relationship and attempts to confer upon it a more than personal significance; but which, for me at least, does not succeed in that. *The Gods Arrive* does: it seems to reflect Wharton's deepest vision of male/female relations, seen with considerable objectivity.

The very structure of *The Gods Arrive* reflects its dual focus—the point of view alternates between Halo and Vance throughout the novel. This is not to say they are given "equal time": Vance's point of view appears almost twice as often as Halo's; and just as important, Halo's thoughts are almost completely centred on Vance, whereas he rarely gives Halo serious attention. This disparity essentially constitutes the plot, which concerns Halo's love for Vance and her desire to help him become the great writer she feels he can be, and Vance's floundering, emotionally and artistically. Halo is rooted in Vance; Vance is rootless.

From the first, they have unequal power. Because Vance cried out to her in need, Halo Tarrant has joined her beloved without waiting for divorce. Her husband, Lewis Tarrant, wants a divorce because of a lack of sympathy between him and Halo, and also because he wishes to marry a powerful and wealthy woman, benefactor of the famous literary award, the Pulsifer; but divorce takes a long time. Sexual morals have changed so that divorce itself is not sufficient to ruin Halo's reputation and make her an outcast in society, as it would have twenty years earlier; but joining a lover before divorce *is*. In flying to Vance as she has, Halo has forfeited her place in society, a small price, she feels, for helping and inspiring the man she adores.

As always in Wharton, society is a force like nature; its decrees and manners affect everyone, whether or not they subscribe to its rules; and its judgements insidiously affect people's self-respect. This is an area about which Wharton is more honest and profound than most of her male counterparts, partly because men are not as oppressed by societal rules as women, and partly because the tradition of Western literature—in fiction, philosophy, and social thought—endows masculinity with an immunity not found in actual life.

The couple goes to Spain, to Cordova. Halo has a modest inheritance, enough to support the two of them. But that she is the one who provides their economic support is of almost no consequence in the novel. Halo has no legitimacy except under the protection of a man. Although it is Halo who makes all practical arrangements for their life, although she is the caretaker of the erratic, irresponsible Vance, Vance tells Lewis during a confrontation between the two men, that Halo is "under my care". Later, Lewis urges Halo to remain in their marriage, reminding her that in her circumstances, his "name is at least a sort of protection". Halo is cut by wealthy society women like Mrs Glaisher, and by the impoverished middle-class Mrs Churley: she is excluded even by Alders, the penny-ante hanger-on of an impoverished noble family. Once people realize the man she lives with is not her legal husband, they turn their faces away from her utterly. She is unwelcome in any "respectable" society. And this judgement isolates her, for there is no possibility of her finding companionship outside of respectable society.

She *is* accepted in the bohemian studios of Paris, but the women who frequent those studios are not her sort, and, it is suggested, there is something unsavoury about them. Jane Meggs, for example, sells censored books from the back room of her bookstore, and the aura Wharton hangs around Jane and her colleagues is tinged by the sordidness of back rooms. (Yet among the banned books being sold around that period in Paris were the works of James Joyce and Henry Miller; and among those who supported such work were brilliant and perceptive avant garde patrons—and bookstore owners—like Sylvia Beach and Adrienne Monnier.) Wharton's figure, Jane Meggs, is a fool and a lightweight; she is unmarried yet involved with Halo's brother Lorry, who has re-named her because her real name was too pretty, and who, Halo believes, "despised Jane, and laughed at her".

Exiled from the company of women, abandoned emotionally—and sometimes physically—by Vance, Halo is utterly alone, and she envies the consolation men possess—work. She asks her brother to help her find work, but he dismisses the idea out of hand and urges her to marry Vance as soon as it is possible. Her old friend and mentor, George Frenside, offers her the same advice. For a woman like Halo in the early decades of this century, marriage was the only possible career. Unmarried middle-class women who work—in Wharton as in Woolf—are inevitably condemned to dingy and rather lonely lives, sometimes (as with Jane Meggs and her friends) tainted by suggestions of a sordid sexuality.

Halo's only career is her man. Still it is a shock to find the brilliant and beautiful Halo of *Hudson River Bracketed* thinking, early in this novel: "If she were not Vance Weston's for always the future was already a handful of splinters." The one vital point for her is "Would he weary of her, or would she be able to hold him?" The function of a woman for a man is to serve: "she wondered what happiness could equal that of a woman permitted to serve the genius while she adored the man"; nothing matters to her "except that she should go on serving and inspiring this child of genius with whom a whim of the gods had entrusted her". She wants to be the "air ... [he] breathes", but finds herself simply "a peg to hang a book on". For her Vance is "a burning core of passion"; she admonishes herself to "adapt": "I must learn to keep step." Yet no matter what she does, Vance eludes her, and despite her desire to use all her talents to "serve the man she loved ... it was to be her privilege to give him what he had always lacked," she finds herself "dropped to the level of any nagging woman".

It is just as startling to find Vance, who in *Hudson River Bracketed* looks up to Halo, adores her as mentor and muse, critic and object of desire, so changed in this book. He recalls "starving for Halo":

What he needed was not her critical aid but her nearness. His apprentice days were over; he knew what he was trying to do better than any one could tell him, even Halo; what he craved was the one medium in which his imagination could expand, and that was Halo herself.

But within months of their being together, he can no longer feel

her imagination flaming through him as it had when they used to meet at the Willows ... She listened intelligently, but she no longer collaborated; and now that the book was done he knew she did not care for it. Perhaps that was the real source of his dissatisfaction; he told himself irritably that he was still too subject to her judgements.

Soon he feels he no longer needs her presence or advice; he looks back sadly to the time when "communion with Halo had ... been the completion of his dreams"; she has become an obstacle.

He begins to patronize her, to adopt an attitude of male superiority. He assumes her lack of interest in his talks with a friend: "Of course," he says to Halo, "general ideas always bore women to death." And later: "See here, Halo, I didn't mean to bother you again with this kind of talk. Nobody but a writer can understand." He resents her comments when she tries to discuss his work with him, and bridles at any criticism. Eventually, he stops talking to her about his work at all, informing her with disdain that artists are never much affected by amateur (he is referring to Halo's) judgements. Yet he blames her for not warning him that his new book was not first-rate, and towards the end of the novel, he ruminates over his professional loneliness, recognizing that there is no one to talk to about his work: "One or two men— not more; and not one woman. Not even Halo, he thought ungratefully."

The egocentricity and lack of consideration that mark the relations of Vance with his first wife, Laura Lou, in *Hudson River Bracketed* become more pronounced in this novel. He ignores Halo's advice and her needs and makes major decisions without consulting her:

> The next morning Vance announced that he meant to spend at least a month at Cordova. He said "*I* mean," as naturally as if the decision concerned only himself and he would not for the world have restricted his companion's liberty ... It was not that he was forgetful of her, but that, now they were together, his heart was satisfied, while the hunger of his mind was perpetual and insatiable.

He announces innocently, "I just want to please Vance Weston", and expects her to acquiesce in this desire. As she does: "She would prove to him that her only happiness was in knowing that he was happy. Already she marvelled that anything else had seemed of the least moment."

But Vance's lack of attention to Halo grows more serious. He is invited to a party at the home of a Marquesa—expressly without Halo. She later discovers that her exclusion was based on her social situation, and is perturbed at the humiliation. Vance, however, is unconscious of it. He questions her: did she not choose her situation? She responds,

"When I did, I imagined you would know how to spare me its disadvantages!"

But he does not understand. "I thought you didn't care a straw about that sort of thing."

"I shouldn't if I felt you knew how to protect me."

… "What is there to protect you from?"

Eventually, Vance does come to see the anguish implicit in Halo's social position, and exclaims "It all falls on you— always!" But that is much later—after he has insisted that they move to Paris even though he knows she is reluctant to live there, fearful of meeting people she knows and being cut by them; and after he has twice abandoned her: once he disappears without telling her he is going away, and simply telegraphs her that he will be absent, offering no explanation; the second time he goes to London and remains for months without writing, then again disappears. When it occurs to him that his behaviour might upset Halo, he thinks "Halo understood there are times when a man needs his liberty." He takes for granted Halo's "smoothing out the asperities of life"—whether problems with people or the problems inherent in each of their many moves—finding a place to live, finding servants or doing the work herself, creating a home. He assumes he need not give practical difficulties a second thought—he has "more important" work to do, something Wharton points out subtly:

> The next day it rained. Vance, who had given himself a week's idleness, sat down before "Colossus" [his new novel], and Halo with equal heroism descended to the verandah to clean the oil lamps.

Vance's refusal to consider anyone but himself extends beyond Halo. In *Hudson River Bracketed*, he ignores a loving letter from his grandmother, offering help; in *The Gods Arrive*, he ignores, for a time, a telegram from home—even though he knows his grandmother is near death. He befriends Chris Churley, a young aspiring writer, with whom he holds "brilliant" conversations. When Chris disappears, Vance goes, with Halo's blessing, to seek him on the Riviera. He finds the young man in despair, "without friends and hope," and insists on taking him home—yet he abandons the young man on the train back, with tragic results.

Vance and Halo are complements, however: he thinks only of himself and she thinks only of him, believing her entire fulfilment must come through a man. The novel suggests that Vance's nature is forgivable because he is a genius, an artist.

"He ... seemed to regard his genius as a beautiful capricious animal, to be fed and exercised when it chose, and by him alone." During a solitary walk in the woods, he sees a sleeping girl; later he tells himself the girl "had been put there" for him "to make his first chapter out of". He compares himself to deity, reproaching Halo when she shows distress about his increased drinking: "I know—you women think God created the universe on lemonade and lettuce sandwiches. Well, maybe He did; but I can't."

It is important to recognize that Vance's view of himself as entitled to privilege is shared not only by Halo but by the world around the pair. Artists, it is assumed, are totally self-centred, sexually promiscuous, and concerned only with their work. When Vance asks his friend Tolby, a painter, how he manages to shut life out when he wants to work, Tolby replies,

"Life—work? Where's the antithesis? ... This *is* life [painting]; the rest's simply hygienics."

But the prerogatives of the Artist are merely the prerogatives of the male writ large. Halo's attitude towards Vance's abuses is not unique—it pervades fiction about male/female relations throughout the nineteenth and early twentieth century. The good woman, the good wife, sacrifices her emotions and bows to her husband's will in the novels of George Sand (*Indiana*, or *Francois le Champi*, for instance) and Henry James (*Portrait of a Lady*); Hemingway and Fitzgerald imply that only a bitch fights back. The necessity of keeping silent, of not saying what one thinks and feels, and of not opposing one's husband is a major theme in Wharton's work, and Halo is a prime example of its consequences. Hesitant to offer Vance criticism of his work which he might resent, she finds herself "so much afraid of laying clumsy hands on his capricious impulses that she felt herself sinking into the character of the blindly admiring wife". When she feels it important to tell him his new novel is not good, she asks herself if it is "worth while to put his literary achievement above her private happiness—and perhaps his".

Although it is a severe blow to her, Halo keeps from Vance the news that her husband has decided not to give her a divorce. She finds that discussing things with Vance "was like arguing with someone who did not use the same speech," and she learns not to argue. Even when he reproaches her she keeps silent: "A year ago she would have complained. She was too wise for that now." When he is away in London, silent, she writes him regularly letters "all so studiously cheerful and comrade-like," with "no hint of regret at her not being with him, no briefest allusion to Oubli—or to herself!" And when Vance praises Halo for being able to disguise her dislike of an acquaintance, she informs him "It's the first principle of every woman's job."

But Vance does grow and change in the course of the novel. He comes to see Halo's social position for what it is, and decides they must marry as soon as possible—not knowing it is not possible. Returning home after his sudden absence, he thinks Halo is out and wonders what she is doing. "It was the first time since they had been together that he had pictured her as having a life of her own, a personality of her own, plans, arrangements, perhaps interests and sympathies unknown to him." Like a child moving into adulthood who suddenly becomes aware his mother is a person with a life apart from him, Vance suddenly sees Halo as a person and grows "more observant of [her] changes of expression, and quicker in divining her response to the persons they were thrown with".

But Halo does not change in response to Vance's change. She tries for a kind of sainthood or martyrdom (although this is not how she thinks about it), imagining that she can completely conceal her anxieties and the anger she must feel—but is unaware of. But this is not possible, and Vance feels it. Expecting a fight when he returns home after his first unexplained absence, he is relieved that she accepts his return easily, without reproach. But a moment later he feels that "at the very heart of their intimacy the old problem lurked, and that never, even in their moments of closest union, would they really understand each other". He catches sight of her expression in sleep—her face is worn and guarded. And thinks:

"This is the real Halo ... If only I could remember beforehand not to make her unhappy."

But he does not remember beforehand; nor does she educate him to do so. She avoids saying or doing anything that might make him angry, in the process detaching herself from her feelings and from him: "At times her exquisite detachment almost made it seem as if she were quietly preparing for a friendly parting", Vance thinks, imagining she is planning to return to her husband. He cannot even ask her what is happening with Lewis: "if Halo had any news to impart she seemed reluctant to communicate it". Later, this sense of distance recurs:

> The mere fact that she was so patient with him, didn't nag, didn't question, didn't taunt, somehow added to the sense of her remoteness. Did that curious tolerance make her less woman, less warm to the touch?

He had been prepared for a fight and "her quiet unquestioning tenderness was like a barrier".

Even Halo becomes aware of the destructiveness of her reticence: she considers that since a dispute many months earlier,

> there had been unbroken outward harmony between them. Yet how far they were from each other—much farther than the couples who quarrelled and kissed again once a week, and to whom quarrelling and kissing were all in the day's work. It was her fault, no doubt. She had wanted the absolute—and life had handed her one of its usual shabby compromises.

The closest to an authorial comment on this situation is offered by George Frenside. He comes to see Halo at Oubli and tells her Lewis is now prepared to give her the divorce she has wanted. Halo says, "Even if he were to give me my freedom tomorrow, I shouldn't tell Vance ... the only thing I care for is *his* freedom." She tells her old friend that she has pretended she didn't care that society was cutting her. Frenside is incredulous:

> "You pretended?"
> "What's loving but pretending?"

And Frenside, with "angry compassionate eyes," laments "My poor girl—if it's come to that ... "

The Gods Arrive cannot be called a feminist novel. Yet the situation it depicts is set firmly in a context that can only be called sexist. Halo's behaviour is inexplicable unless one perceives the position of women generally in the society of her period. Misogynistic remarks are sprinkled through this novel (as they are through *Hudson River Bracketed*). Such remarks are not common in Wharton's work; they are not part of her attitudes (as they are of some women authors, alas!); they are part of the context she is emphasizing in this novel.

Women are referred to slightingly: a brilliant young acquaintance thinks "a man of Weston's quality" ought not to be "doing novels like ladies' fancy-work, or an expensive perfume"; the shower in Tolby's bathroom "had to be managed like a neurasthenic woman"; Vance himself tells Halo that "you women think God created the universe on lemonade and lettuce sandwiches"; and Vance and Alders share the belief that women are not capable of abstract thought—this despite the fact that Halo was Vance's first true mentor in literature and the arts. When Vance becomes infatuated with Floss Delaney, he thinks of her power over him as "a poison"; and Halo thinks about Jane Meggs, "the power of such women was ... insidious".

The tasks performed by women are taken for granted and minimized in importance. Moral deviance—like living with a man to whom she is not married—ruins a woman, but not the man, who is as acceptable in society as if he were single. And all the personae of the novel share this view of women. Women exist for the sake of men. Vance, returning home uncertainly after his sudden, unannounced absence, expects Halo to be angry. Instead, she has made herself lovely on the mere expectation of his return; and has prepared a small exquisite supper for them before the fire. Vance thinks, "How she knew how to take a man, to ease off difficult moments, what to take for granted, what to leave unsaid."

When Floss Delaney appropriates him at a literary salon, Vance melts and thinks "This was what women were for—to feel the way to one's heart just when the Preacher's vanity weighed on it most heavily!" He is willing to discard Halo for Floss because "intellectual comradeship between lovers was unattainable; that was not the service women could render to men". Floss offers

Vance the "strong emotional stimulant on which his intellectual life must feed". Women are men's food.

Halo's thoughts about herself and her situation universalize it, make it every woman's situation. She realizes that all people, whatever their class, suffer the human condition, are "reduced to the same abject level by the big primitive passions, love and jealousy and hunger; the delicate distinctions and differences with which security adorned them vanished in the storm of their approach". But concealment is "the first principle of every *woman's* job": not just "ladies", women of gentility, but *all* women must learn to adapt, to keep step.

When Vance goes off without warning, Halo imagines herself abandoned, and it occurs to her that "everything she had done for the last year—from choosing her hats to replenishing the fire, getting the right lamp shades, the right *menu* for dinner, the right flowers for the brown jar on Vance's table—everything had been done not for herself but for Vance". And she understands suddenly her kinship with other women, understands "how a young woman full of the pride of self-adornment might turn into a slattern if her lover left her". (Wharton adds an ironic thrust to this meditation, as Halo thinks she should suggest that to Vance for a story.)

Halo attempts to avoid giving Vance any pain, as one would avoid giving a child pain. But in the process, she places no responsibility on Vance—she accepts whatever he does. There is an implicit suggestion that if men are to become adult, women must educate them—an idea many women hold even today.

I said earlier that this novel is really about a relationship—and so it is; but the relationship is traced as it is in order to show what is necessary for a young man to become adult. It is in that sense a *Bildungsroman*, a tracing of the development of a male from self-centred ignorance of emotion, art and society to a degree of knowledge, of sensitivity, and awareness. The pain of the relationship with Halo (for in the end she cannot spare him that); his remorse over his treatment of Chris Churley; his unhappiness about the poor quality of his work; and anguish about her rejection of his overwhelming passion for Floss combine to desolate Vance. He suffers a moral collapse; he goes away to the wilderness; in a return to a theme mentioned early in *Hudson River Bracketed*, he considers suicide. He falls sick and nearly dies. But he finds religion again, at least, he finds St. Augustine:

I perceived that I was far from Thee, in the land of unlikeness, and I heard Thy voice crying to me: "I am the food of the full-grown. Become a man and thou shalt feed on me."

He recalls the last words to him of his Christian evangelist grandmother, the one person in his family who has loved him: "Maybe we haven't made enough of pain—been too afraid of it. Don't be afraid of it."

These words, uttered by Grandmother Scrimser, serve to universalize Vance's experience, for in a sense she incarnates America, its energy and ambition, its conflation of the spiritual with the material, its naive optimism. Vance is Wharton's "American", a very different but somehow more recognizable one than James's. Like America, he is adolescent, self-involved, brusque, inconsiderate, childish, using people as means instead of ends and seeking above all not to suffer.

The conclusion of the novel suggests that Vance has truly found adulthood, that he has realized the state predicted in the Emersonian title—"When half gods go/The gods arrive." Some of us may demur, however. For Vance returns to Halo less as husband than as son; and she has become mother incarnate, pregnant with a foetus she continually refers to as male. Vance says he fears returning to her because he is not yet full-grown: "I'm not fit for you yet, Halo; I'm only just learning how to walk." She replies, "But then I shall have two children to take care of instead of one", informing him for the first time that she is pregnant. And Vance, sitting, embraces the standing Halo, bending his head and kissing her womb—or as Wharton describes it, "a fold of her loose dress".

For some of us, living fifty years after this novel was written, a relation of mother/son is an unsatisfying solution to the problems that beset male/female relations. We might complain that those problems are not caused by nature, but by nurture—that male self-centredness and immaturity can be modified by a changed set of social standards allowing women to maintain themselves independently, both financially and socially, and to find a centre outside themselves in work. Nevertheless, the problems Wharton described still exist: what she saw is still what we see. Despite some social changes, her analysis of the problems between the sexes remain very much the same, and her careful depiction of those problems remains vital.

Marilyn French, New York, 1986

VIRAGO MODERN CLASSICS

The first Virago Modern Classic, *Frost in May* by Antonia White, was published in 1978. It launched a list dedicated to the celebration of women writers and to the rediscovery and reprinting of their works. Its aim was, and is, to demonstrate the existence of a female tradition in fiction which is both enriching and enjoyable. The Leavisite notion of the 'Great Tradition', and the narrow, academic definition of a 'classic', has meant the neglect of a large number of interesting secondary works of fiction. In calling the series 'Modern Classics' we do not necessarily mean 'great' — although this is often the case. Published with new critical and biographical introductions, books are chosen for many reasons: sometimes for their importance in literary history; sometimes because they illuminate particular aspects of womens' lives, both personal and public. They may be classics of comedy or storytelling; their interest can be historical, feminist, political or literary.

Initially the Virago Modern Classics concentrated on English novels and short stories published in the early decades of this century. As the series has grown it has broadened to include works of fiction from different centuries, different countries, cultures and literary traditions. In 1984 the Victorian Classics were launched; there are separate lists of Irish, Scottish, European, American, Australian and other English speaking countries; there are books written by Black women, by Catholic and Jewish women, and a few relevant novels by men. There is, too, a companion series of Non-Fiction Classics constituting biography, autobiography, travel, journalism, essays, poetry, letters and diaries.

By the end of 1986 over 250 titles will have been published in these two series, many of which have been suggested by our readers.